SEA STAR

SEA STAR

THE PRIVATE LIFE OF *ANNE BONNY,* PIRATE QUEEN

By PAMELA JEKEL

HARMONY BOOKS : NEW YORK
1983

for

MY HUSBAND, BILL—

who put a roof over my head,

freedom at my fingertips,

and joy in my heart.

Published by Harmony Books, a division of Crown Publishers, Inc., One Park Avenue, New York, New York 10016, and simultaneously in Canada by General Publishing Company Limited

HARMONY BOOKS *and colophon are trademarks of Crown Publishers, Inc.*

Manufactured in the United States of America

LIBRARY OF CONGRESS CATALOGING IN PUBLICATION DATA

Jekel, P.L.
Sea star.

1. Bonny, Anne, b. 1700—Fiction. I. Title.
PS3560.E46S3 1983   813'.54   82-21232

ISBN: 0-517-55108-X
ISBN: 0-517-54946-8   (paper)

Cartography by Wendy Cohen
10 9 8 7 6 5 4 3 2 1
FIRST EDITION

Contents

~~~

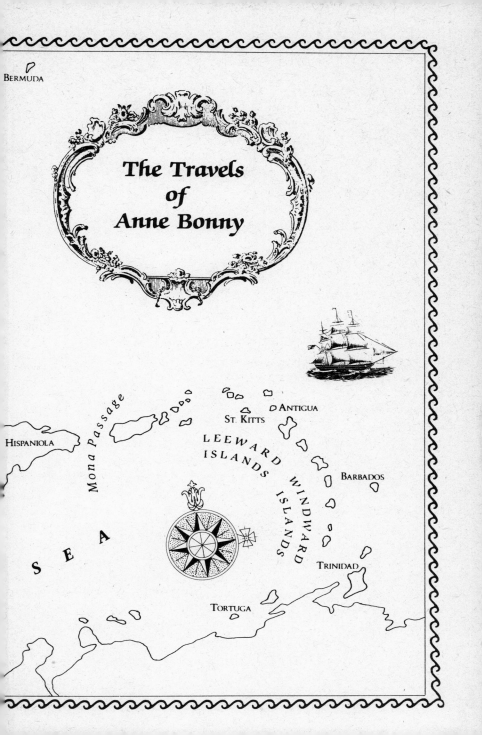

PART ONE

Cork, Ireland, 1700

Drain, drain the bowl, each fearless soul,
Let the world wag as it will,
Let the heavens growl, the devil howl,
Drain, drain the bowl and fill!

Old Pirate Song,
Attributed to ANNE BONNY

M ARGARET MARY BRENNAN lay in a sweating, unsparing labor for torturous hours. Her once flat and maiden belly was swollen and blotched with the impending birth. Her auburn hair spilled over the coarse linen, and she keened hoarsely to herself between pains.

"Bellow forth all ye want, my girl," the midwife chided. "There's none to hear but me." Her leather hands deftly pressed and alternately tugged at Mary's trembling limbs, dancing an ancient rhythm over her stretched skin. The light from a smoky farthing-dip flickered over the rough stone of the cottage wall. Mary heard the wind from the harbor in the thatched roof; through her waves of pain she imagined she felt the swell and the surge of the sea beyond.

"The wind is high tonight from the bay," she gasped. Anything, anything to lead her mind from this tearing agony that knotted her belly like angry fists wrenching wet bed sheets.

"Ay. 'Tis a black March wind, a-blowin' in yer wane like a lion." The midwife glanced from Mary's arching body to the candle, now half-gone in the dim light.

"Ye must push with all yer strength now. Push to burstin', for yer water's broke near a day ago, an' the babe must be born tonight or die."

Suddenly the midwife leaned forward, wrenched the moaning young woman up by the shoulders, and forced her swollen breasts against the heavy mound of her belly. Mary gasped and writhed. Her eyes flew open in shocked rage. The pain of the sudden jolt forced her to scream out in terror, but she had no wind left to curse. Her dark eyes squeezed tightly shut again, and her white skin mottled red with the effort to breathe.

It was her first and only loud cry, torn from her in spite of her fierce determination to be silent through this birth, her strong desire to keep this babe from the pickthank eyes of the town. Her scream throttled into an animal grunt of wheezing labor.

"I see a head, a head of hair! Push! Ye must push once more!" The midwife reached for her legs again.

With one exhaustive effort, Mary slapped her hands away and pulled her own knees closer to her belly, piercing through her howling pain to sudden deliverance. She felt the bony edges of the child jar through her then slide as if pulled by a heavy tide. Her trembling legs parted, and she heaved one final time. Mary fell back on the sodden linen, freed of this bloody mewling infant, a burden she had carried in defiance for nine long months.

Through the gray gauze of oblivion that veiled her mind, Mary heard the midwife chant her litany.

" 'Tis a fine girl-child with red hair, a fair colleen perfect as a new day."

The baby waved bloody fists and squalled loud in the fetid room. Mary opened her eyes with deep weariness. She began to pull her violated body back together from within and turned her face from the child.

"A girl-child. When I promised him a strong son to spit in her eye." She closed her eyes to the infant. "Fetch a wet nurse to quiet her bawlin'. Then send her father to me."

Mary's hands fluttered. feebly up in an effort to smooth her matted hair and wipe her brow. She set her lips firmly and dozed, waiting for William.

WILLIAM CORMAC'S ESTATE stood back from the harbor of Cork, well up a hill but still within sight of the bristling black masts of the huge ships that had helped to build the large brick house. In this year of 1700 Cork was a teeming port, the last western land between Europe and the Atlantic and a sister city to Bristol across the Channel. Her lowland bay refuged two- and three-masted vessels from Dublin, Bristol, London, the south coast of France, Spain, Lisbon, Tangiers, and even the southern colonies of the New World.

William Cormac's father had been in the early sea swell of Protestant merchants who invaded Ireland after Cromwell's scourge. He built his grand English manor on the ruins of the defeated Catholic landholders with monies squeezed by the tightened reins of the Royal Shipping Acts—acts that all but strangled the Irish colony and her trade.

When William came of age, he was sent to England to study law and returned, expecting to use the tiny island kingdom as his own. He was English—as his father reminded him frequently— and had therefore won first prize in the lottery of life. Like his father, a true colonist, he came to perceive the Irish as little more than willing hands for the English consumer, and Ireland as only a convenient warehouse for his lands and holdings.

Now, as he stood at the dark window, watching the March wind rip at the trees down the road, he waited for word of his love and future heir. There was a slow knock at the door and his man Thomas entered, carrying a bright taper.

"What news?" Cormac turned to him urgently, sensing that the birth was over.

" 'Tis a well birth, milord." Cormac felt his hesitation. He grabbed at his arm in irritation, causing the candle to flicker.

"Well, be quick, man! And the maid?" Thomas had come from England with Cormac's father, knew William well, knew precisely how to use his silence as censure. He turned slowly to place the taper on the table with cold dignity. When he faced Cormac, his face was bland.

"Mary is well, milord. She has borne you a girl-child." Cormac heard, somewhere back in his mind, that Thomas used his woman's Christian name, a sign of disrespect—but his attention was riveted completely by the more important news.

At the surprise in his master's face, the old servant's heart was softened. He remembered William's impetuousness as a child—a rollicking, defiant young boy who cared little for the priorities of his elders.

"I'm sorry, milord. But perhaps next year the Lady Elizabeth can give you a son."

The expression on William Cormac's face changed rapidly from surprise to aversion. He shrugged off Thomas's consolations.

"Blast you, man. I'd rather a single worthless girl-child from Mary's loins than a whole passel of sons from Elizabeth Sweeney's fat and barren belly. But you say she's well? Does she ask to see me?"

Without waiting for the frozen reply, he grabbed his heavy cloak from the chair. "I'll go to her now."

As he rode out of Cork to the nearby village where Mary lay, he remembered the ripe and wanton lass that chance had placed in his bedchamber. She was buxom and pliant even before she began to blossom with his child. He'd been lonely—not for his wife, Elizabeth—but certainly for a woman. He recalled the first time he saw Mary. Her dark hair was pinned beneath her cap, but long curled tendrils inched down her neck. Her deep green eyes met his with never a flinch and returned his gaze steadily. Her breasts heaved against her tight bodice as she struggled with Elizabeth's heavy trunks. Elizabeth was so eager to be off to her mother's house that she never noticed the way William's eyes followed the servant she left behind.

At first, he admitted wryly to himself, Mary had been nothing more than good and convenient sport. Margaret Mary Brennan had seemed the antithesis to his frumpish complaining wife. Slender and tall with alert dark eyes and translucent skin, her delicate features reminded Cormac of a seabird—pure of line and sleek. He was, after all, not a man to be left without feminine solace for long. He was in his early thirties, large-boned and vital, and few of his appetites were satiated by the heady profits he took from the ships in the bay. He often felt a tension, a recklessness that hummed through him like dockside rum.

Away from the prying eyes of Cork and the rest of the Sweeneys, Mary had come to his bed willingly. She was no virgin, yet she had enough maiden modesty to make his seduction a challenge—he grinned to himself—or at least she was wise enough to make it seem so.

William did not know at which point he ceased to see Mary as sport and began to think of her as his woman. Perhaps when he realized that he cared if she found pleasure with him. He began to notice her quiet dignity. She was taller than most women, with long legs and full hips that gave her skirts a grace and swirl he found most seductive. Though she had little education, she was surprisingly articulate, alert, and even intelligent. She could read and write a bit, which was unusual for a woman of her station.

But now Mary's station had changed. He'd seen to that. He had allowed her to leave the manor house for her birthing time only because she had insisted. Like a vixen seeking a private den, she'd looked for a dark, secret spot to bear this child. Already, he could deny her little. William spurred his horse faster over the last mile to the little cottage, part of the string of shareleases he owned in the village.

He remembered how she had returned his passion and growing love, embrace for embrace, with a fierce determination and an eager joy. Soon, there were times she stayed all night in his bed, yet they never felt lust . . . only clinging desire. Even now, in this cold March wind, he could feel her open mouth, and he wanted her. Elizabeth seemed a spinster in comparison. Mary had life in her. Pregnancy had made her more erotic than ever. And now she had borne him a child. A girl-child. No matter. He knew that he could not give her up—neither her nor their child.

Mary heard the clatter of the hoofs over the wind and knew that William had come. She had not slept, would not hold the child, until he was with her. She raised up on one elbow off the bed and was bewildered at the weakness she felt. Glancing at the midwife in the corner and to the child in her lap, she whispered, "Bring the babe to me and leave us. Master Cormac will pay you for my care."

The midwife rose and brought the baby swathed in clean linen with only a frizz of red hair showing at the top of the cloth. Mary thought of asking her to say nothing of the birth in the village but knew instinctively that such a request was futile. This babe would soon be the gossip of the entire county. And she was not certain she was sorry.

William burst into the room breathlessly as the midwife slipped out. He was heedless of anyone or anything else in the cottage save his Mary. He sank to his knees at her head. Wordlessly, he took both her hands and pulled her hair back across the pillow, spreading it out fan-shaped on the linen, smoothing its tangles.

"My pegeen. Thank God, you're well."

At the touch of his lips on her face, Mary felt a strength rise in her from some unknown well. She gazed up at his swarthy skin and black hair, blacker than any Englishman's had a right to be. Only his piercing blue eyes and finely arrogant features bespoke his heritage. Then she took his head in both her hands and pulled it to her breast.

"See what we have made, my William, with our passion. A wee lass with hair as red as the sun." She showed no apology in her face or in her voice but watched his face carefully for the signs of disappointment that she felt would be inevitable—yet none appeared.

Instead, he silently gathered both woman and child to his chest in his great arms and gently squeezed them together as if molding them into one unit. Pressed against his shoulder, Mary smiled quietly, and the tumult in her ceased.

They talked into the night while the child slept in the crook of her father's arm.

"Mistress Sweeney knows of the birth, does she not?" Mary could never bring herself to refer to her former mistress by her Christian name.

"Ay, my love. You can be sure she knows of the babe by now." He laughed wryly. "No doubt she is sorely grieved to hear it's a girl-child."

"Are you?" Mary did not watch him so closely this time, for she already knew the answer.

"My dear, I care not a tinker's damn. Where is it written that only a male can inherit the world? This lady may be another Elizabeth, another queen of the empire in her own right." He stroked the infant's cheek with his thumb, and her tiny mewling mouth turned to his finger blindly, reaching with her lips for the source of such pleasure. "Whatever she is, she is ours. And the county be damned."

"Ay. Well, Mary Brennan has a lovely daughter, but such shall not admit her to the grand house on the hill." She reached for the infant and put her to her breast. "And we both must eat, milord. Do you think the bitch will be back?"

Cormac grinned as he always did at Mary's rare vulgarity. "No. Elizabeth has made it clear she's done with me. She's gone home to the cursed Sweeneys for good."

Mary smoothed the down on the infant's head and kept her eyes lowered, not wanting to see the pain her next question would bring. "But what of your own mother, William? Has she not softened to ye yet?"

Cormac turned from the sight of the infant at the full breast; his face went blank for a moment as if remembering an ancient memory, then he shrugged. "The old woman's determined to punish me for my transgressions." He grinned determinedly in the face of Mary's frown. "Let her leave every last farthing to Elizabeth and her fat sweating palms. It's all she'll have of mine, to be sure."

Mary laughed softly as the baby's mouth reached again for her slippery engorged nipple. She sucked a few more times and then fell asleep.

"Never fear, pegeen. We can get on without her blood money. The profits should be fine this season, and the taxes are all paid. The price of Irish woolens is so dear that only the gentry can afford them, and I've a warehouse full of that and good linen besides. When the *Caroline* arrives from Bristol, she'll carry a fortune for us both. You'll not starve, nor will the babe."

He reached out and plucked the sleeping infant from her breast. The child opened her small eyes, as blue as the sky. Her cheeks were pink, and her eyelids were so transparent that the network of tiny veins showed each pulse of her new life. She opened a red mouth and yawned, clenched searching fists, and jerked them towards the light.

"And what shall we name this little baggage? Would you call her Catherine or Isobel after one of the benighted saints of the parish?"

"Never after a saint. See how she yawns? She's fair bored with us both already." Mary smiled up into his face. "We'll call her after a queen, as you said. But not a queen of the past. One of the future. . . . She shall be called Anne."

*T*HE OPEN CHALLENGE of Cormac's bastard child rocked the tight Cork community. The Catholics were not surprised by anything that a godless Protestant merchant might do, but even the Protestants of the village clustered together in a union of censorship. Clandestine liaisons between master and servant were common, as were the illegitimate issues of such dalliances. But for a master—and a well-set one at that—to prefer a serving wench and her offspring to his own legitimate wife and future heirs was not romantic. It was an insult and a threat to the fabric of the entire social system.

The Sweeneys blustered about legal action, but Elizabeth would have none of it. She remained at her father's house and frostily refused to have any further contact with William Cormac. Deep down she was almost relieved, for she'd found marriage and its shared linen not at all to her liking. Cormac's own mother, humiliated and grieved by the county's ostracism, fell ill and finally died. As she had threatened, in a last gesture of placation, she left all of her estate to Elizabeth Sweeney and any future heirs, hoping to lure William back to his lawful wife.

Elizabeth sent word through the Sweeney clan that she would settle a yearly allowance on William from his mother's estate if he would live apart from "his private whore." Cormac reluctantly agreed. He had little choice. The profits from his ventures had not been as high as he'd hoped, and the call for his legal skills had fallen off considerably in the face of the scandal.

For seven long years he dwelt apart from Mary and Anne, installing them in a nearby cottage and providing for them amply. Daily, William visited Mary Brennan in secrecy, and the enforced clandestine meetings added even more spice to their passion. He asked her once what she enjoyed most.

"Everything," she smiled. She listed for him her memories of fond rollings they had shared; the nakedness, the pinching, biting, licking, giggling, the kissing, the sucking, the rubbing, the savage thrusting, and the slow, teasing rises of desire—until he was ready to mount her on the spot. He had never known such vitality in a woman. And he could not keep away. When occasionally she grew querulous and anxious about her insecure status in his life, he promised her fervently that he would make her his wife as soon as his fortunes improved. For Cormac there was ever one rich fleet due in on the next tide. And Mary found it easy to believe him.

Anne, too, received an ample share of his love, for he saw himself and his future in her shining green eyes. She was growing quickly into a tall, sturdy, precocious child, highly verbal, with her mother's beauty and her father's quick wit. He often took her to town with him or down to the docks, dressed as a lad. She began to imitate the swaggering walk of the sailor and wore a small green cap over her sandy curls. To those who asked, Cormac passed her off as a visiting nephew of some distant relation. But few asked.

Eventually, of course, Elizabeth Sweeney Cormac discovered her husband's transparent ruse and his continuing support and love of Mary and her bastard. Abruptly, the embittered woman stopped his allowance and cut him off without a farthing in dependable income. Cormac ranted and cursed, but all his fits of anger could do little to staunch the growing tide of clients who were deserting him, too.

The final straw came when Cormac realized that Anne—the only rightful heir to his lands and heart—had reached the age of eight without ever having worn a pretty gown, tied her long hair in colored ribbons, played with a china doll-baby, or learned to eat with a fork. She seemed happy enough with her lot, dressed in boy's breeches, following her father about and aping his manner.

Cormac was adamant that Anne's future not be limited by the prejudices of this ingrown, stunted pack of hypocrites. He could see her young mind outgrowing the small community, just as her strong body was outgrowing tight breeches. Her hands were made for things finer than broken shells and gull feathers, now her favorite toys. Besides, she needed a nurse and a strong-willed one at that. Anne's spirit was stubborn, a full match for her mother in a shouting bout—of which there'd been too many of late. But a decent nurse would not go near the Cormac house, to serve under a mistress like Mary Brennan. Cormac saw that he could no longer stay in Cork with the Sweeneys and the rest of the community so set against him.

And so, like many of Ireland's finest sons, he began to think of leaving the Old World for the New. He felt the ambivalences of most colonists. He had looked over his shoulder at his English homeland, but had always felt himself a stranger to the land he left—as well as a stranger to the Irish land he usurped. But if a stranger, why not in a land full of strangers—the New World. The idea flamed in him like a haystack piled too damp, and it burned him from deep within.

Soon thereafter, a ship bound from the southern colonies made a quick stop in Cork to load Irish wool for Bristol. It carried with it packets of coarsely printed circulars that were passed from hand to hand along the docks and through the village. Cormac read one nailed to a tavern wall.

ADVERTISEMENT *for* SETTLEMENT *of the* CAROLINAS

If there be any younger brother who is born of gentle blood and whose spirit is elevated above the common sort, and yet the hard usage of our country hath not allowed suitable fortune, he will not surely be afraid to leave his native soil to advance his fortune equal to his blood and spirit. And so he will avoid those unlawful ways too many of our young gentlemen take to maintain themselves according to their high education but having small estates.

With a few servants and a small stock, a great estate may be raised. Although his birth, as a younger brother, have not entitled him to any of the land of his ancestors, yet his industry may supply him so as to make him the head of as famous a family, in Carolina.

The Chief Privileges

There is full and free liberty of conscience granted to all, so that no man is to be molested or called in question for matters of religious concern, but everyone to be obedient to the civil governor, worshipping God after their own way.

They are to have a Governor and Council appointed from among themselves, to see that the laws of the Assembly are put in due execution, but the Governor is to rule but three years; also, he has no power to lay any tax or make or abrogate any law without the consent of the colony in their Assembly.

Go to Master Wilkinson, Ironmonger, at the sign of the Three Feathers in Bishops Gate, London, where you may be informed when ships will be leaving and what you must carry with you.

Signed by the True and Absolute
LORDS PROPRIETORS OF THE CAROLINAS

The whitewashed tavern wall seemed to shimmer in the afternoon sun. Cormac read the circular through twice with ill-concealed excitement. Anne stood quietly at his side, watching his face.

"What is it, Father? Has our ship come in at last?" she asked in a low voice, mindful that no one was nearby. She knew she was not to call him father in a public place.

"It well may be our ticket to paradise, lass." He looked down at his growing daughter, her hair hidden under a worn tam cap. He made his voice deliberately gruff, watching her closely.

"We're leaving this godforsaken island. I'm full to the teeth with Sweeneys and constables and pious, hen-hearted numbskulls." Cormac did not know exactly what to expect from his daughter, but he certainly was not prepared for the look of total joy that illuminated her face.

"Leaving? Together?" The little voice grew gravelly in an attempt to mimic her father. "Good. They make me spew. We can surely do better elsewhere."

Cormac let out a cough of laughter, once more surprised at how little the small mind missed. "Ay, lass. That we can. But what do you think of going to sea?"

He took her hand and led her across the quay to the edge of the harbor. From the dock they could see the huge merchant ships lined up along the bay. There were fat merchant brigs, low in the water, their patched sails twisted like homespun scarves about their masts. Colored pennants and flags of all nations flew in the breeze. Trim sloops bobbed delicately on the tide, and gulls whirled and bleated in the sun. Vessels jostled past each other, and boatswains called out greetings over the creaks of the hulls. The bustle of the harbor caused Anne's body to tighten in excitement, and her father felt it in the firmer grip of her small fist. Anne took a deep whiff of the sea air.

William kept his eyes out to sea and asked carefully, casually, "You'd not be sorry to leave your home, then, and go to the colonies? How does the name Carolina strike your ears?"

Anne felt little confusion at his questions. He often spoke intently to her, though she rarely understood all of what he said. She had heard of the New World, of course—what child had not?—but the word Carolina was new to her. However, it fell liquid from her father's tongue, and she could not imagine a land across the sea that she would not love if he were there.

He swept Anne up into his arms and his voice turned soft and wheedling.

"Ah, Annie. You'll have tutors and governesses—gentle ladies to teach you of life and books and dancing—all the grand things a beautiful woman must know."

Anne grinned up in his face and tossed her head. "I don't want to be a grand lady. I shall be a seaman."

"Oho! So 'tis to sea you'll go! Well, before you're off, don't you think we should consult your mother on all of these fine plans?" William asked in a low, casual voice, "What will she say, do you think?" half to himself, half to Anne.

Anne answered without breaking stride. "She'll go where you go."

Cormac said nothing, once more startled by his daughter's perceptiveness.

~~~

*T*HAT EVENING CORMAC wrestled with Mary's mounting apprehension about this unknown frontier, Carolina.

"They say it's warm all year, with exotic fruits and hothouse flowers always in bloom. And a man can make a fortune in the space of five years t'would take a lifetime to build in England."

"Ay, but what can you spend it on, William? 'Tis a wilderness still. I hear they sleep on cornshuck pads and drink brackish water for lack of ale."

"Not in the southern colonies, my love. The houses are built of brick and all face the sea; the women wear the finest lace from London, and the land is all but free for the asking."

"Can you make a living on the law?"

"No."

Her eyes widened in surprise at his candor, and he went on hastily. "The colonies don't allow a solicitor to charge a fee for the law. They've a notion that the law belongs to all men for free. But there's fortunes to be made in merchant trade, and frankly I'm ready to give up a calling that depends so mightily on the personal whim and approval of every horse's ass in the county. In the Carolinas, if a man has money—and I mean to, pegeen—he's beyond reproach, whatever his past."

"Will we marry, William?"

He never hesitated a jot. "As soon as Elizabeth is dead and buried. Even in the colonies, a man can be jailed for bigamy, lass. But we'll keep our secrets to ourselves, and none need ever know. The minute we get word she's gone, we'll marry quietly. And she can't last long surely, as wretched as she is. She lives on bile and comfits."

Mary's eyes kindled with a sudden spasm of anger. "I hope she keels over soon, and the devil takes her to bed in hell."

William reached for her white round shoulders and buried his mouth in her neck. "She'll never touch us in the Carolinas, my sweet. No one will. We can do as we damn well please. No pimps of priests carving at each other's throats, no virgin dowagers pecking out each other's eyes—or ours. 'Tis a lawless land that cares little for manners and less for conventions. And the chink of a man's gold will set him high as any lord."

She twisted her hands through his hair. "Take me then, William. Take me to this new world of yours, to the Carolinas." She let a low moan move through her at the strength of his grasp. "On the next tide. I'm weary of feelin' a prisoner in my own house." She wrapped her arms around his neck and pressed her body to his, feeling all the secret places that she knew and loved so well.

Suddenly she pulled back and gazed up at him impishly. "I can be your whore there as well as here."

He laughed and threw her on the bed. "Better, I wager. Much better."

THE NIGHT BEFORE their packet ship was due to sail from Cork, Anne stood on the high upstairs windowseat and watched the lights in the harbor. Far to sea, she could see the dark black of the horizon layered from the lighter black of the sky. The blackest black of all was the encroaching land. To sea. To sail upon a fast ship to London. The grandest city in the world. And then, to sail the widest ocean to a new land. A land with room. For a pony and a new puppy, perhaps. A land where it never rained, and oranges grew in your garden all year. And to never hear again, "Cormac's bastard wench," from sliding, whispering mouths; never to feel eyes on her back as she followed her father. She watched a ship bobbing in the harbor, a lantern hanging on its bow reflected in the black water, and above it, a sister star that would follow her, just as the moon always followed her, to Charles Town.

The trip across the Channel was quickly over and a blur in

Anne's memory. Later in her life, she would remember only the furtiveness she felt, boarding the small ship at night.

"We'll be away at dawn, lass," her father confided. "The sooner I put the Channel between me and those goddamned Sweeneys, the better I'll rest nights."

Her mother was strangely silent through the short voyage and stood with her back to the coast of England shrouded in mist, facing Cork and the dawn light on the village. As the fog from the Channel enveloped the bay, Anne slipped from her spot on the bowsprit where she faced the open water to stand by her mother's side. She put her brown hand inside her mother's white one. Unconsciously, she mimicked a tone she'd often heard her father use and said, "Don't be afraid, Mother. Why, we'll have a far grander house in Charles Town than ever we had here. And you'll be its proper mistress."

Her mother yanked her hand away and hissed at Anne softly, "And what do you know of such things, you silly wench?"

At the hurt and the cool withdrawal in her daughter's face, Mary sighed in exasperation. "Ay, Anne. We'll see. Perhaps life will be grander there. But don't speak to me of mistressin' this or that. You're too green to speak of such."

She looked down at Anne's traveling clothes, a trim pair of breeches such as a young boy might wear, eminently practical for climbing about slick decks and in and out of dark, sulfurous holds. "And you can be sure you'll see a few other changes in Charles Town too, lass. There'll be no more breeches for you. Time you wore proper skirts. If you've a mind to talk above your years, you'd best learn to act above them, too. Young ladies of Charles Town do not haunt the docks like mangy wharf rats, I'm sure."

Anne started to reply smartly but thought better of it. There was little she could say when her mother was in such a mood. Just then she heard her father's approach and recognized the familiar creak of his boots. He came up behind Mary and put his arms around her shoulders. Her mother turned from Anne and laid her cheek on his coat. He murmured soft words to her that Anne could not hear. Anne went back to her place on the bowsprit and watched England loom large through the sea mist.

*T*O ANNE'S EYES, London was little more than an ugly stepsister to Cork. The London mist seemed colder, danker than any she'd felt in Ireland. Acrid smoke stung her eyes and nose from the forest of chimneys that crowded out the daylight. Soot and fog mixed together above the rooftops and fell in a black rain on every surface, fouling even the puddles in between the cobblestones. Narrow streets were pocked with taverns, and piles of offal and debris cluttered unswept wooden stoops. Lines of white-faced children, some no older than Anne, trudged to the mills at dawn like ghostly sleepwalkers, pulling their bits of rags about them.

Only at the docks did Anne feel at home, for the ships seemed the same she'd seen in the Cork harbor but sleeker, larger, and heavier in the water. She stood with her father on the riverbank of the Thames and looked down at the Pool spiked with masts.

It had taken a day and a night to settle her mother into a decent inn. It would take another month to find the sign of the Three Feathers, to learn of their travel needs, and to place their name on the register for their passage to the Carolinas. Her mother had felt the sway of the packet ship and fought down her bile with difficulty throughout the night. She was finally realizing the ordeal that lay ahead for her in the month-long passage to the New World. Her mood was foul. Cormac took Anne aside.

"She'll feel better when we're away from the old places for good. Leave-taking is always harder for a woman."

When he took her to the docks to watch the ships tug at their anchor lines, his restlessness infected her, but she wrested her eyes from the gulls who gackered and wheeled in the sun when her father tugged at her hand.

"Come, lass. We've much to do before we sail. A fortnight

would not be enough time to sell our baggage and pare us down."

She jammed her fists in her pockets against the damp river air. "Must we sell it all, Father?"

"Well, not everything. But three trunks are all we take aboard the *Profit*. That's a fine name for our ship, eh?"

"Ay. Point her out to me once more."

"There she sits, lass. Before you know it, you'll be smelling the orange blossoms of Charles Town."

There across the river Anne looked again at the ship that would carry her to the New World. It seemed almost her own vessel. She'd already picked several choice lookout posts, both fore and aft, to call her own.

The *Profit* was a three-masted merchant ship from Portsmouth. She was square-rigged with ten sails, all reefed now and waiting to be tested. Her decks were solid and wide and gently sloping up at bow and aft. Eighty feet from stem to stern, she was rubbed and oiled like a sleek lion. Her decks were dark and stained with sulfur and tar. Clean sand had been swept over her plankings and would make for a noisy progress from the boarding plank to the narrow passageway down to the cabins. Twelve cannons were lashed to the deck, six on each side on small wooden wagons, their snouts pointed out to sea. High atop the mainmast, just above the mist, an English Jack flew proudly in the sun.

AT DAWN ON their departure date, the Cormac family trudged down the steep riverbank to the dock to inspect the *Profit*. The night before, their trunks had been lashed side by side in their tiny compartment belowdecks. They spoke of it as "their" cabin, though they were to share it with the Beauchamps, a childless, middle-aged couple from Bristol. The reality of their confinement in a five-by-six windowless space for a month or more was all too apparent, even before their berthmates joined them.

When they had met earlier, the Beauchamps had seemed a nice

enough pair. At least they smiled at Anne and shook hands all around. Mary suspected that Mrs. Beauchamp was a Quaker from her speech and drab garb, but resolved to avoid the religious issue altogether in the hope that no reciprocally awkward questions would be asked.

William, Mary, and Anne walked up the ribbed plank onto the deck of the *Profit* and were greeted by a rough voice.

"She ain't ready for inspection yet, folk. Ye'll have to step off again." Captain Samuel Russell Nimrod strode up to the small party with an outstretched hand that at once seemed to welcome and also to usher them off the ship. His brow was clouded. Cormac stepped forward unhesitatingly.

"You said dawn, I believe, Captain. We're ready to board."

The captain spoke to Cormac, but his eyes appraised Mary all the while. "Ay. Well, 'tis true I said daybreak. We got an extra ton o'cording to load still. But I guess I can show ye to yer cabin at any rate."

Anne watched his black hair bristle all about his face like an angry bear's beard. Cormac made the necessary introductions.

"Captain Nimrod, this is my family. Mrs. Cormac and my daughter, Anne."

"Yer daughter, ye say!" He barked out a laugh. "She looks more a lad than a lass. Is that the way ye aim to keep her in Charles Town?"

Mary spoke up quietly, putting on her gentry speech. "No, Captain. This is only her father's idea of a more convenient garb for her aboard ship. I trust the crew will respect her privacy, regardless of her dress." She carefully ignored his eyes and the intense gaze she'd felt since she first stepped aboard the *Profit*. Anne watched her mother confront the captain's stare and then delicately turn it aside without ever acknowledging either its intimacy or its import. She had seen her mother do the same to men before. Regardless of his insolence, however, she liked the captain and his round brown forehead immediately.

"Ay, ma'am. Ye've no worry about the crew. They're rough, but they know their place. Well, come on then. I got little time, but I'll give ye the grand tour o' the finest ship in the harbor."

Captain Nimrod bellowed and gestured to this fixture and that cranny as he ushered the family down into the dark between-decks passage.

"She's got fine lines—finer than the old flutes o' her day. More sail, too. She can make the Carolinas in four weeks if the weather holds clear. We got a full crew o' nineteen able men, an' we're carryin' thirty-six passage-payin' transports like yerselves. An' a hold full o' goods for the colonies."

"Why the arms along her sides?" Cormac watched the captain's face as closely as possible in the gloom. He negotiated the cramped, steep hatchway as the ship rolled gently on the incoming tide. Mary clutched his arm tightly.

As soon as he'd asked, Cormac wished that he hadn't, for the captain was succinct.

"Pirates! I'll not lose this vessel to the bloody Brethren, the scum, not if I can help it. She's a sure prize, but she's no man's sport, not while I'm at her wheel. The *Profit* can hold her own and run with the best."

"Pirates?" Anne piped up.

"Ay, lass." The captain grinned down at her. "They've been plaguin' ships off the Albemarle for months now, but they don't spar with the *Profit*. Them guns point out to sea, ready to fight dawn to dusk. An' we never had to use them yet."

He shouldered aside a small curtain and gestured the trio inside. Their trunks covered all the floor space save a narrow strip eight inches in width down the middle of the cabin. There were four berths—two above and two below. Each berth was a small rectangular space, five feet by less than a yard, set into the side of the ship. All that separated each berth from the floor was a dirty canvas curtain that hung at its edge.

"Since yer messmates ain't aboard yet, ye can take first pick o' the pack. Upper or lower, ma'am?"

"Upper or lower what?" Mary glanced about in bewilderment.
She could scarcely see in the dank darkness.

"Berth, ma'am!" And his huge fist pulled aside a dirty canvas
flap. Mary tightened her lips when she finally saw the small space
that she and William must share, but she said nothing.

"Anne, do us all a favor and hop in the upper one," Cormac
said cheerfully. "Test it on for size."

Anne gladly climbed up in the upper berth and stretched her
body out, hands clasped on her breast as if in sleep. She felt close
and protected by the dark wood of the ship. The roll of the river
water made her anxious to be off.

" 'Tis a fine fit, Father. Shall I sleep here, then?"

"Ay, lass. And your mother and I will take the lower. The
Beauchamps can have the two on the other side."

The captain laughed. "Yer a sharp eye, Cormac! They're nigh
to six inches shorter on the port side." He appraised Cormac once
more and found him a likely adversary, then he deliberately swung
his eyes from Cormac's wife—at least for the time being.

"The area we just left is the public area, yer own fo'c'sle, where
the payin' passengers meet an' eat. Remember that ye cannot go
into the hold or the crew's fo'c'sle." He grinned. "Not that ye'd
want to. And as for the galley, ye must make yer own treaty with
the cook in yer own way. I shall tend to my loadin' now, so make
yerselves comfortable." He doffed his hat to Mary who merely
lowered her eyes in return, and he strode from the cabin, which
immediately felt much larger in his absence.

In his wake, the Beauchamps came down, towed by a small
ship's boy. There was an awkward silence when the two couples
realized that they'd be sharing this small space for over a month. It
had looked so much larger without their trunks, one couple at a
time.

Cormac breached the silence by bowing and offering his hand to
Mrs. Beauchamp. "It is an honor to share space with a lady,

madam. My wife and I shall do all possible to make the voyage a pleasant one for us all."

Mrs. Beauchamp, captivated by Cormac's gallantry, beamed her approval at him and at the masses of expensive bed linen that Mary began to extract from their crowded trunks. Anne noticed with a small smile that in spite of his bow, her father did not offer to switch berths with the Beauchamps.

Finally, the *Profit* was ready for departure. The sails were all unfurled as men clambered like monkeys up the taut ropes to the sky. There was a flurry of cording and sheet, and the canvas cracked and filled. The calm waters of the Thames gave way to the foam and lift of the gray open sea. Mary leaned on William's arm, feeling the full surge of dread and nausea overwhelm her all at once.

"I must lie down, William." She turned a whitened face up to his.

"Stay with me a while, lass. Let's say good-bye to England and the past together."

Mary stood the rolling motion a few moments more, just long enough to see the receding cliffs of land, then turned abruptly and made her way to the dark cabin where she was to spend most of the next month, near wishing for death.

The *Profit* spent the better part of a month in the North Atlantic—a great gray sea of drizzle and wind. No single day was the same as the next: gales of violent force alternated with days of eerie glass calm; red skies, green skies, blue skies, and black made Anne wonder at the vastness of the world. The ship seemed always in a struggle with an alien and eternal element—yet also one with the water upon which it rode.

The Atlantic encircled Anne like a living gray cloak. After the confines of a hidebound rural village, filled with searching eyes and wicked tongues, the sea represented a delicious taste of freedom.

After a few early skirmishes, Anne was accepted by the crew as a small adult and a plucky one at that. Because of her breeches and an unusual height for her age, it was easy to forget she was a girl. Soon she spent the days loitering in the company of the tars, following them about the ship. And Cormac, who had run out of proper ways to entertain her, was only too glad to let her entertain herself.

He would go belowdecks to kneel by Mary's bed, nodding curtly to the indentured servant, Clara, and whispering to his wife as he stroked her hands.

"Pegeen, you must come up and get some fresh air. This berth holds only the stink of bile."

But Mary was too weak to move and only lay groaning, pulling her hands away and calling Clara to bring the slop bowl again.

The rhythm of the sea fascinated Anne, and she felt she could stand and stare at its undulating currents endlessly. Raucous voices and ribald stories cast a spell of adventure on the high seas, which would stay with her always, and drew her just as surely.

She watched the seamen swinging high above the deck with their bare feet and strong brown hands, and she yearned to view the sea from high overhead in the lookout's perch. One day her desires got the best of her, and she started inching up the mainmast rigging. Suddenly, one of the burly tars grabbed her round the waist and hauled her off roughly.

"Hie there! Jes' where ye goin'!" He looked her full in the face. "Hell's bells, 'tis young Anne! Ye need a good hidin'!" His two angry eyes peered out of a huge black beard and startled her.

Anne screwed up her face as if to cry and mumbled, "I can climb as well as the best man here."

The gruffness faded from the sailor's voice as he took her hand and led her to the fo'c'sle deck.

"Ay, ye little monkey. If ye want to climb, go up an' down the hatchway!"

Anne scowled up at him. " 'Tis no fun in that."

"So yer bored with life at sea, eh? Well, 'tis not my job to keep young sea scamps amused, mouse. Just stay out o' me way, or we'll clamp ye in the hold with the rest o' the convicts."

Anne grinned at him. She knew the hold was full of hogsheads of nails, cloth, and tea—not convicts. She also knew that she'd found a friend.

Robin was a young seaman on his third voyage with Captain Nimrod aboard the *Profit*. He had left a young bride in Bristol and found Anne a captivating substitute companion. For much of the rest of the voyage, she followed Robin about, slipping in behind him when he went over the decks and even insinuating herself under his arm in the galley where the men gathered at night. As the only child under twelve aboard the ship, a child whose mother was always abed and whose father could not say her nay, she had a great deal of latitude and an unusual sense of freedom. With the men, she felt somehow connected, arm in arm as with kin.

Robin presented her with a wooden jointed doll he had carved for her. But at the look on Anne's face, he laughed and took it back.

"I can see ye prefer a sailor lad to a lass, eh?" He took his knife and shaved away the wooden curls, cut a moustache in the upper lip, and handed the doll back to her.

Anne chortled. "He's a regular tar now and needs his own ship to sail!"

"Ay. I'll carve one for him, an' he can be captain."

"I'll be captain one day."

Robin had learned not to laugh at the girl, but he did allow himself a small smile. "Ay, lass. An' I'll sign yer papers an' be yer quartermaster."

"But mark you, Robin. *I'm* to be captain, and I'll climb the rigging as I please, and you'll not stop me."

At night Anne would listen silently to the tales that spun themselves over her head in the crew's fo'c'sle. She'd learned that if she made herself small and silent, she'd not be noticed as readily and could stay unmolested a while longer. The instant she asked a question, however, she was quickly shuttled off to her own cabin. So much of what was said went through her undigested and misunderstood, but the tone of the words continued to enthrall her.

She heard of fights with huge sea lions caught in nets off in northern seas, of drowned villages whose sunken church bells still rang when the tide went in and out and warned sailors up on the surface of hidden rocks, and of gales where the sea was whipped to green butter, and men dove overboard to their deaths in panic. She heard hints of women unlike her mother with large white legs, hot pink kisses, and red open mouths. She heard tales of the great Spanish fleet with coffers full of gold, larger than two of her mother's trunks, and richer than all the Orient. She sat, half awake, half asleep, as the lanterns grew dimmer and the pipe smoke thicker, and the voices of the men wove in and out of her consciousness, swapping tales.

One night, as Anne watched quietly from a cave under the bosun's chair, she saw the sailors conduct a seance. Ghosts and ghost stories were commonplace aboard ship. On stormy nights, when the ship lumbered through the bowels of the Atlantic, even the most practical of men could be induced to talk of phantoms. To Anne, who was raised with the lore of Ireland always at the edges of her vision, such was the stuff of familiar pleasure, not terror. Once the men began, the anchor chain creaked more mournfully, the oil lamp flapped shadows into bat wings, and the swishing waves hissed past the hull with whispers of mysteries. Then, the sailors circled, joined hands on a small stool, and set it to turning around upside down on a table.

One brave tar asked, "Ghost, are ye with us?" and the stool moved with the dip and swing of the ship and answered questions put to it as truly as if a spirit twirled it at will. The proper mood was struck. Out were trundled the hoariest of tales—of ghost ships, of banshee captains who foretold the doom of passing vessels, of vampire rats and mythical albatrosses, and blood-red sails which turned to flame and lured innocent ships to disaster on hidden shoals. And the sea seemed the proper place for such stuff of men's minds.

Anne's favorite topic of these evenings was pirates. The men called them "that filthy pirate scum," or "those yellow dogs of pirate whores" or the like, in tones that caught her attention. In all, she sensed pirates were much reviled by the men but were also the object of some fascination and even secret admiration. For each of the crew, if seasoned, could tell of a particularly horrible passage with an unusually tyrannical captain who had made their lives a floating hell.

"Why, I seen one bastard force a bosun to swallow cockroaches live and wrigglin', an' then knock his teeth in when he gagged and choke him on his own blood by jammin' a marlin spar in his jaws. All for yawnin' at the wheel."

"Ay, an' I seen Captain Staines o' the *Rochester* flog a tar six hundred lashes with a tarred rope an inch thick."

"God's arse, ye sneakin' puppy, *I* was there, an' I don't recall *ye* aboard! 'Sides, I seen worse. I seen a captain's mate towed from the stern for punishment while the sharks munched him, inch by inch, an' he hollerin' for his life like a butchered sea cow. I can still hear him sometimes"—and his voice went up two octaves— " 'Save me lads!' An' his whole legs up to his hips gone in blood and froth."

"I swear by the Holy Virgin, did I see such a thing, I'd turn pirate meself. At least they run their own ships."

All of the men nodded in silent acquiescence and a secret understanding of the free men of the sea.

Robin said softly, "In honest service, there's poor rations an' thin at that. We put by but a pound a month and hard labor to get it. A pirate lives on fresh fruits an' wild game, an' can take a booty that'd turn a governor green with envy. A pirate ship runs in warm seas while we shiver up and down the northern coasts. Ay, 'tis worse things to think at than goin' on account."

"Careful o' yer tongue, Robin. Nimrod's a fine captain, but he'd split yer hide if he heard yer talk."

"I doubt it, mate. An' I do naught but talk. But one can look an' see that a pirate's life might well be merry."

"Ay," spoke up the bosun, after which all talk ceased. "Merry but short."

IT WAS NOON on September 17 when the welcome cry came, "Land ho!" and Charles Town appeared like a shimmering mirage on the horizon.

The *Profit* maneuvered through the harbor past Hog Island and Johnson's Fort up to the Battery to anchor in the warm, still waters of the Cooper River. Anne stood and looked at the city while her father helped her mother to rally herself to leave the ship.

In an almost cruel blaze of sunlight, fine houses faced the water; through the green park along the Battery walk, Anne could see delicately designed woodwork, high-walled gardens, broad porches, and decorous white houses that seemed to tremble in the heat. She saw dogs resting in the deep shadows, horses at hitching posts, and stray chickens fluffed in the dust of the road. Huge hogsheads awaited loading on the quay, and the air smelled of ripe fruit and decayed flowers.

Gadsden's Wharf was the main embarkation point for the city, and Anne counted close to thirty vessels clustered about this East Battery docking site. Beyond the broad tall gateways of the town, she glimpsed bricks faded by sun and sea air, smooth-trunked palmettos, and gray Spanish moss in the limbs of live oaks. As they boarded the small landing skiff, Anne turned and jostled through a few passengers to wave a final farewell to Robin who was leaning over the rail. They had said their good-byes the night before, but she had no doubt she would see him again. Indeed, he had promised as much, saying, "When yer a fine lady an' all o' Charles Town's at yer feet, Miss Anne, then I'll come round an' embarrass ye with old memories."

"You could never do that, Robin."

He had laughed and pinched her cheek. "You remember, I warned ye then!"

Charles Town looked very much a British colony in 1709. The ships in the harbor flew mostly British flags and were owned out of the large white or pastel houses that faced the East Battery docks. Charles Town produced indigo—then a new and experimental crop for which Britain paid a large subsidy—and silk. Indigo was a plant used to make blue and purple dye, the colors of royalty, and much sought after for its scarcity and prestige. The staple of Charles Town's wealth, however, was rice—grown on the large plantations that were spreading up the rivers, grown by the ton in this year and thereafter—shipped to England in large hogsheads aboard vessels much like the *Profit.* Charles Town was also renowned as a booming trade center, supplying ships direct to the northern colonies, London, Africa, and to the West Indies. Vessels from foreign ports brought back loads of sugar and spices, rum from the Caribbean, holds full of slaves from Africa, cloth and other luxuries from Europe, and much of what made life in the southern colonies more bearable than in the northern ports.

And the people of Charles Town were unusually colorful and cosmopolitan, particularly when compared to the more homogeneous and restrained Puritan settlements. There were expatriated noblemen from Europe, Caribbean pirates, and slaves fresh off the boat from Africa mingling with freed blacks from the islands. "Free-willers" who sold themselves to colonial plantations for five to seven years for free passage, food and lodging; indentured servants from England, Huguenots from France, Scots-Irish who escaped Cromwell's purge, religious fanatics seeking a refuge, and sensualists looking for an easy spot in the sun all surged like so much flotsam into Charles Town harbor.

The sailors reported that there were more women in Charles Town than in the northern ports because of the southern colony's reputation for beauty, cheap land, warm nights, and ample slaves. There were fewer churches, fewer jails, more doxies per seaman, and far more diseases than the twenty-four doctors within the city limits could ever contain.

Officially, Charles Town was owned and operated by the lords proprietors, remnants of the English noble families and the only aristocracy that the citizenry would tolerate. Practically, however, the town was truly the first capitalist colony in the New World and was run by money.

Merchants, privateers, pirates, and planters cooperated to overrule any but their own interests. A man needed only fifty acres to vote, and no one asked embarrassing questions of his religion, his politics, or his past. Many of the older planters were directly transplanted from Barbados and believed that to live in the West Indian style was the best possible environment for man. They brought an easy indolence to the city. But in most other ways, Charles Town was surprisingly, indignantly, more English than either Boston or Portsmouth and proud of that fact. The Charles Town settlers clasped the vestiges of the mother country firmly to their collective bosom as if to fend off the corruption of the colored folk in their midst.

The coachmen who maneuvered the shiny black rigs in front of the royal governor's mansion at 34 Meeting Street could have come right off London streets, even down to the heavy buttoned coats and full wigs they wore. The large, substantial hurricane-proof houses on Broad, Tradd, Elliott, and Church streets and Stoll's Alley were filled with family heirlooms and imported furniture from Sussex, Devon, or Kent.

Each planter maintained a town house in the city where he and his family might adjourn in the highly dangerous summer season, away from the flooded rice fields and the mosquitoes, and these summer respites often stretched through the Christmas holidays. Charles Town was known for its cotillions, assemblies, balls, receptions, cards and dice, slave auctions, taverns, horse races, cockfights, and hangings.

A hanging could pull an audience even from the lowland farms, since it usually included public speeches, floggings, and perhaps gibbeting as well. The laws of the colony were as brutal as those of the mother country. Men were flogged for minor trespasses of public decency and hanged for petty thefts.

Less than one-third of the population was white. Slaves, indentured servants, and a score of Indians made the outnumbered white citizens insecure, and they retaliated with frequent reprisals and harsh punishments. Thieves were branded on the face with a *T* if they were not hanged. A man could be pilloried for sleeping in the street. The rogue so charged would be hung with hooks under his arms in a public square for a full day, with his ears nailed to the scaffold to keep his face immobile. Witch trials and stonings were not uncommon, for the people lived with great fear as well as great beauty.

Local pride was running high when Cormac landed with his family, for just the month before, Nathaniel Johnson, colonial governor, and his militia had first tricked, then trounced the French navy. The people of Charles Town rejoiced, burned French flags in the harbor, and upended hogsheads of French brandy in the streets. When Anne first arrived in the city, there were still drunken sailors propped against the tavern walls, sleeping off the victory.

Under the rich tapestry of Charles Town, a savage barbarism simmered like the summer heat. To Anne, the narrow streets and fine houses looked like gates to the paradise her father had promised her.

PART TWO

~~~~~~

Charles Town,
The Carolinas, 1712

It is written. A daughter is a vain treasure to her father. From anxiety he does not sleep at night; during her early years lest she be seduced, in her adolescence lest she go astray, in her marriageable years lest she be childless, and when she is old lest she practice witchcraft.

Talmud

It is the beautiful bird which gets caged.

Chinese Proverb

ANNE CREPT DOWN the staircase. Daybreak leaked through the leaded window, but nothing moved out on the wide expanse of lawn, at the dock, or on the river.

"Damn that lazy whelp," she muttered to herself, switching her bow against her buckskin breeches in controlled irritation.

She eased out the huge mahogany door and made her way down the rutted path to the kitchen. Though Anne had often been frustrated by the plantation kitchen being so far from the great house—especially when covered dishes came cold and cloyed to the table—this morning she was relieved to know that hands would be up and stirring embers at the open hearth. No one at the great house would hear her impatient questions.

The door creaked on its wooden hinges, and Anne pushed into the kitchen, shuffling clean sand over her moccasins. The floor felt cold, even through her soles, and the fire in the hearth was barely alive.

The old black woman at the open oven turned with a practiced start, knowing full well it was her white mistress behind her.

"Lah, Miz Anne. You be up early this mawnin'. You give me a turn."

Anne ignored her pretended pleasantries. "Cassie, you see Charley Fourfeathers? He was to meet me on the front lawn at daybreak."

Cassie drawled out her reply, glad to carry tales. "I 'spect he's still sleepin', Miz Anne. He an' Jonah be up to the spring house 'til late, swaggin' tales an' smokin' greenleaf."

"Shiftless Injun's going to make me miss the best game on the river. And I can't wait much longer or the whole house'll be up."

Cassie slid her a sly glance, knowing just how much she dared taunt the girl. "An' ma'am find somethin' more fittin' for you to be at."

Anne stifled her quick retort and merely turned from the slave, peering out the single soiled window of the kitchen down through the graying mist off the river. She could just see a slouching figure amble around the line of live oaks up the path to the house. With no other word for the old woman, she snatched a handful of cold cornbread and dried apples from the larder and slammed out the door.

Anne ran down the broad lawn, fleet as a doe, her moccasins making wet prints in the lush grass. She looked back over her shoulder once. A single light shone in the upstairs chamber of the big house.

"God's breath, Fully's up. Now she'll be flapping and hissing like an old goose all morning 'til I return. A short hunt this'll be."

She hurried to the old Indian's side. "Charley, you're late this morning," she whispered, and grabbed his arm, pulling him under the cover of a live oak, shielding them both from any peering eyes at the house.

"Ay, Miss Anne. But I be here. The river is calm, and game be good."

Anne felt her impatience dissolve as she gave herself up to the pleasure of a morning on the river. They navigated sluggish streams of mirrorlike black water stained by the tannic acid of great cypress roots. She and her old friend stalked along the hidden wetlands of the Cooper, surprising small varmints who were out of burrows feeding in the quiet of the dawn. She drew her bow often, and almost as often relaxed its tension, never taking a shot unless she was sure to kill rather than maim.

At last after the sun was high in the soft air, Anne relinquished the river edge and the forest she and Charley knew so well and turned back to the house alone. She carried two fat rabbits over her shoulder and a dozen prickly burrs in her hair. She dropped the game off at the kitchen and walked unhurriedly towards the rest of her day.

*I*T WAS NIGH to eight o'clock, and the house was up in full throng. The shutters were all open to the morning air and looked like twenty eyes gazing down at Anne. She knew her mother preferred her to attend breakfast in a clean set of petticoats, but Anne decided just this once to take the chance she might be sleeping still. Breakfast alone with her father was a heady lure. She peered around the door of the morning chamber and saw him hunched over his desk, papers in his hands, and a table laid with covered dishes at his elbow. He looked up at her stealthy entrance, her bow still over her shoulder. He kept his face stern with an effort.

"Did you mean to fix me with an arrow, lass? I promise I'll not come quiet."

Anne grinned. "Two conies, Pa. I got them down at the marsh."

Her father appraised her and said dryly, " 'Pa' is it, then? You're sounding more and more like your niggers each day, daughter. Time was I was 'Father' to you, and glad to hear it, too." He deftly peeled an orange and handed it to her. "Your mother's right. You're getting too old to be romping about in breeches with bow and arrow and that crazy savage at your side night and day. Like an old hound, he is."

"He's my friend, *Father*." She stressed the word deliberately to tease him. "And you said I cannot pace the fields alone, so I must have him with me. Besides, he knows the trails like Fully knows the halls of this house. Is Mother up?"

"Ay. Just. And don't go running to her with tales of your conies, lass. She'll hear it soon enough from your servants. You think you get away with hellfire, but all eyes watch you. And they all report to me, don't be forgetting."

"Ay, Pa. As do the sun and the tide." She laughed and slipped up to her chamber before her mother could see her with wet breeches and bow in the dayroom. Enough that she had her woman, Fullborn, chiding her like an infant. She didn't need to catch her mother's slicing tongue as well.

Cormac went back to his papers, but his thoughts kept returning to Mary. He looked out at the verdant acres of lawn, the score of outbuildings, lines of trees, the pond, the dock, and the Cooper River beyond. He swelled with pride as he tallied it all in his mind.

Three years ago he'd come to Charles Town, a young lawyer with a serving maid as mistress and a hoyden of a daughter in a sea cap. He had taken enormous risks then, and each one had paid off handsomely. He'd quickly parlayed his legal skills for respect and some status in the growing coastal town. From a small house on one of the side streets of Charles Town, they had moved to a grander house on the East Battery. And then Cormac had begun to reap huge profits off the ships in the harbor. For three years he'd harvested those vessels like ripe fruit as they came in and out of the bustling sea roads. For three years he'd carefully courted every powerful man in the city, played the deferential newcomer to their established lines of control and now, after a handful of profitable voyages and slick favors, he was one of them at last.

He had found a hefty grant of good bottom land going to the

highest bidder and used his new influence to see there were few who bid against him. The parcel of four hundred acres in the fertile Cooper River lowlands—three hundred in fields, fifty in timber, fifty in grounds and outbuildings, all in the wealthy Goose Creek district—was the ideal spot for his rice plantation. Even though he used wenches to work the fields—cheaper at $45 a head than a buck at $60—he still laid out a pretty sum just to work the land that first season. But he'd pushed and mauled his finances into rigid obedience and managed. And now it was all his.

But Mary. She was his one source of real concern. Oh, she was readily accepted, brogue and all, by the best families of Charles Town. She had beauty and brains and knew how to use them to charm men and women alike. But her efforts had cost her, Cormac could see that now. Her health had not been robust ever since the crossing. After two years of entertaining the grandest petticoats in town, she stayed more and more in her chambers. And now she was with child. . . . He feared for her well-being. When he looked into her face, he thought he sensed a stranger hidden just below its familiar angles and curves. He felt a great weariness coming from her, a deep melancholy that no amount of company, gay silks, or rich wines could assuage.

Her constant companion, no matter where she was, continued to be the indentured servant, Clara. He felt uncomfortable with the closeness between his lady and this . . . drab. A servant of the lowest class. But when he approached Mary and asked her to discard Clara for another wench, she turned sulky and petulant.

"There's strong rumors going on about her, peg. You know there were on the *Profit* as well."

"What sort o' rumors, William? Never mind. I don't care to hear it. A lie goes round the world afore the truth gets its britches on."

" 'Tis said she dirked her own lover in a fit of rage. That she had to leave London with a price on her head."

"Ay. 'Tis said, no doubt, by some man. No woman would

believe it o' her. She's got a gentle good soul an' the softest hands in this God-blessed colony."

"Can no other woman serve you, pet? It makes my hackles rise to see the two of you together night and day—"

"Well, it's *my* hackles she tends, William! Now, I'll hear no more on it. She saved my life on that rottin' hellhole of a ship. And she's all I have of home. I'll not send her away. No, not even for you."

He shrugged off his defeat, but it vexed him now like a troublesome sting he could not soothe. Things had not been the same between them since they'd left London. Where once she'd been all pliant and hot-eyed eager, she was now ever weary, always irritable, and often absent. Now, when he bedded her, it was usually at his own request, for she rarely rolled his way of her own mind. Perhaps it was just the coming of the babe, he thought. Though he'd not recalled such a change when she carried wee Anne.

Well, at least on one point, he and Mary continued to agree. No matter how the old dowagers tried to lure her to first one parish and then another, she refused to be pulled into their soft entangling arms. He grinned to himself. She met—and bested them—at cotillions, receptions, and balls. But she'd step not a foot in either the Church of England, now christened St. Phillip's, or the First Baptist down the street, or the White Meeting House, or the Huguenot Church.

Ay, he recalled with fondness the figure she'd cut at the Draytons' reception last spring. The hall had been filled with lovely women, all dressed in the finest silks and newest velvets from the mother country. Her embroidered bodice was tight that evening, with a red silk stomacher, and her breasts were high. She looked much the same woman as she who'd captured his eye a decade before. She'd refused to wear a cap, said tight stays were quite enough confinement for one night. And her hair hung full and thick on her shoulders. Her scent was more enticing than the

Madeira in his glass. She drank sack and danced with him and laughed full in his face then as she still did in his dreams now.

Now . . . he sighed pensively. Now she seemed far away. And if he could bear to admit it, she was not loving, not passionate. Not as he'd told himself she was. He winced inwardly. 'Tis true, the land and the fields take my attention. As well they should if I'm to support this great house and all within it. Two new slaves were due from up the river today, bought by his overseer from Black Cypress Hall. The buck was strong and the wench wide hipped. T'would be a good breeding pair and good workers as well. And he'd need a wet nurse soon for the coming babe. His thoughts now turned to Anne.

She was growing so quickly and not in the way he'd envisioned at all. She was beautiful like her mother, with her red-gold hair and high color—but there all resemblance ended. He had to admit wryly that in all other ways she was more his child than Mary's. God's blood, she was nimble-minded. Her French tutor had proclaimed her the smartest head of her age he'd seen in the county. Too smart, he frowned. She'd not yet learned to hold her tongue or to ape the gentle manners she'd need for Charles Town beaux. Oh, she could dance as lively as a colt, but she cared not a fig for fine conversation. He'd watched one lad try to talk to her at the edge of the dance floor, and suddenly he went all red and sputtering. She probably asked him some unseemly question, Cormac grimaced, or challenged him to a rassle. Ay, she was wild still, like that damned Indian she ran with beyond the rice fields. Dancing, French, Latin, and needlepoint had done little to soften her young edges.

And she was spoiled as badly as a hold of ripe mangoes, he thought ruefully. She had her own room, her own niggers, her own dog, mounts, even her own Indian. He laughed inwardly as he recalled how she had told him she "bought" Charley Four-feathers, the plantation hunter.

Charley was the professional gamesman for the plantation, a

"civilized" Indian who bartered his skill with bow, pistol and musket, knife and tomahawk for free room and board. He was also Anne's bodyguard, since her father could not keep her within eyeshot of the house, and the Yemassee tribe still threatened the outlying edges of the county.

She'd informed her father that Charley was her brother. She had exchanged a vow of loyalty with the Indian, cut her arm, and mixed her blood with his over a filthy tomahawk in some secret forest glade. Cormac was amused when she claimed ownership of Charley. But he was insulted when she insisted that she belonged to him as well. Angered, and perhaps even a little saddened, for he felt he was losing Anne in some subtle way that he did not yet understand. Just as he was losing Mary. He shrugged and poured himself two fingers of rum. It was early in the day for fortification, but he felt little guilt. There was no one—not at Bellefield, not in this entire colony—to tell him what to do. Enough of this dinnling daydreaming. A new shipment of tools was due in an hour on the dock. There were other more plaguing problems to attend to just now.

That afternoon, over the long and heavy dinner that Cormac and his house took at three o'clock, Anne decided to prod her father once more with her latest notion. Cormac unwittingly gave her the perfect opening.

"Sam Brailsford has a good lot of slaves coming in to Gadsden dock in three days. We might take the chance to go to town and buy a new boat crew for the summer season. And perhaps a likely wet nurse for the wee babe."

Mary looked up from her plate and smiled her thanks.

In the pause that followed, Anne carefully placed her knife at the top of her plate, as she'd been taught, folded her hands and said, "Ay. And Anne can look into the new dame school at St. Phillip's." She sensed her mother's scowl, lowered her eyes, and added quickly, "Mother, I want to learn ciphering, and there's none to teach me here at Bellefield."

Her mother held up one white palm to arrest her flow of words and wearily held her forehead in the other. "Anne, 'tis better you put yourself to those talents that will serve you as a wife. You've neglected your needlepoint, your harpsichord, an' you've learned nothin' o' the management of a household such as this. You're far past the age o' rompin' in the wilderness like a wild beast." She sighed heavily and put a hand over William's. "I blame myself. Ye should have been in stays at five an' made to wear masks and gloves to protect your complexion. But I indulged ye. Now, you've got the hands of a field nigger an' just as brown besides. You're near marryin' age, child. But who'd have such a hoyden?"

"Perhaps nobody, Mother. Maybe I'll not marry at all. So I best learn ciphering to help Father."

"Not marry?" her mother scoffed. "Why of course you will, daughter, an' soon, too. Younger lasses than yourself are betrothed an' married inside a year. And mothers soon after, to be sure. No, Anne. 'Tis time you put away the fancies of a child an' learn the ways of a woman proper. Why, ye don't even know how to use a fan to signal your intentions to a swain. I saw ye fumble an' near drop it at Margaret's reception. There wasn't a lass in all o' Cork who could cipher, an' they never missed it, I'm sure."

Anne had listened quietly to her mother's complaints, but at the mention of the fan, surely the most senseless of all feminine foppery, her mind flamed. More useless than tits on a boar hog, she thought, and looked to her father for possible support.

He was watching her face as if he had read her mind. He turned to Mary with an opaque smile. "Perhaps, my dear, 'tis not such a bad thought. For surely ciphers cannot hurt the child. And she may well use them to good account to manage her own husband's estate some day. And surely, she'll learn all those other skills you mentioned by the by."

Anne beamed her gratitude to her father but knew well enough to hold her tongue.

"I will not see her leave Bellefield, William. She needs more supervision, not less."

"Ay. And she also needs the companionship of genteel folk as good examples. I heard tell that Elias Ball means to hire one Benjamin Dennis from Edinburgh to start a district school in Goose Creek. 'Twould be more convenient for the lass. And you or Fullborn could see to her training in the evening."

Anne's heart flew up at the news. She knew that her mother had no great desire to teach her, yet she did not want her gone from the plantation, either. Here, perhaps, was a loophole to freedom. But would her mother rear? As always, Clara stood over her, pressing food on her, glaring at Anne as she did at anyone who ruffled her mistress. Anne stared back malevolently, not caring who noticed. She sensed victory.

"But what gentle folk can she hope to meet in such a school? Darky children and poor relations. And how can she learn the proper accomplishments of a young lady from this Benjamin Dennis?" Her mother had not given up.

Anne could hold her tongue no longer. Ignoring her father's warning glance, she turned her sweetest smile on her mother. "But Mother, I already know the latest minuet steps, I can speak French, play a passable harpsichord, and do turkey work on tapestry when I've a mind. And ways are different here in the New World, Mother. Surely any man worth a farthing wouldn't want a wife with half a head. If I'm to be a true helpmate to a husband, then an ability to do ciphers should be an asset, not an obstacle to marriage. And, he need never know." She saved her best salvo for last. "Besides, Mother, I'm bored here at Bellefield. And you know when I'm bored I'm most likely to get to those things you find least proper for me. Let me go to this Goose Creek school, and I promise I'll not disgrace you. I'll put on stays and ride sidesaddle and put up my hair seemly."

Mary considered. She decided to press her advantage. "And will ye then begin to act like the proper young mistress of Bellefield? Will ye train yourself to your rightful role as wife to a worthy husband?"

Anne hated the very words of the extracted promise, but the

intoxicating bait of victory today allowed her to push tomorrow from her mind. "Ay, Mother. I'll do my best."

Her mother smiled and looked over at William. Her hand again enclosed his. She felt she'd won one of her rare victories from Anne this night.

THE SCHOOL AT Goose Creek had twenty-seven white students, two Indians, and one black child in attendance. Benjamin Dennis, duly imported from England and trained in Scotland, held court in a one-room hall above the spring house, the coolest part of the plantation on warm days at Elias Ball's estate of Kensington up the Cooper. At first Anne was overjoyed to be in a schoolroom and in close association with so many other children. She dressed for school more carefully than she had for any cotillion, laced tightly into stiff stays, with a full damask gown, sprigged petticoat, stomacher, apron, and cap. She rode to Kensington on her best mare, Foxfire, chaperoned by Charley in a clean leather jerkin. And she secretly wore at her waist, for protection and amusement, her own silver-mounted pistol.

For the first week she was in awe of her tutor. But she quickly found him wanting, and her contempt began to show. She baited him with questions in French that he could not answer. Her dream of learning arithmetic was soon shattered as she discovered that her teacher knew little past the rule of three in multiplication and no division at all.

She saw that she had not known true boredom before—not until she had to drone through a warm afternoon nodding over psalms she'd read a dozen times or more, waiting for the youngest student to lisp out a stuttered reply to an obvious question.

Anne lasted less than one year at the small school. During that time she learned far more about her peers than she did academics. At first she had reluctantly offered to help teach the younger children, anything to alleviate her intense boredom. But being refused, she openly dismissed Master Dennis as a fool and then ignored him. She began to make tentative overtures to the other girls at the school—there were only four—but was rebuffed as being too tall and too knowing. One ringleted young lady told her that she "lacked piousness" and was "too smart for her own good." When Anne retaliated by dumping her into a puddle, the girl organized a coven against her, and she found herself ostracized by the whole gaggle.

The boys at the school offered more diversions, but they too quickly paled. At the outset, they allowed her in their play as an equal. But when tales began to circulate between the great houses and the school, Anne was nudged out of male play as well. She did not really know why she was left out, and after a while she ceased to care, or told herself she did not. In one final effort to prove her worth, she challenged a boy to a battle. He gave her a black eye, after which she beat him to the ground.

At first Anne was able to shrug off most of her parents' questions about school. Even when she came home with the black eye, Charley supported her in her story that Foxfire had shied and she'd struck the pommel of her saddle.

And then, abruptly, all questions stopped. Her mother did not emerge from her chambers for seven days. The doctor came and went and came and left, quietly closing the doors to the study. William was alone within. When Mary emerged from her room, she was pale and listless, her eyes sunken deep inside her, seeing little. She had lost the baby. Yes, the doctor had said, there was some hope she might bear again; yes, she was well. But Anne knew otherwise. She looked at her mother's cloudy eyes, at her hair grown wispy about her temples, and sensed that she'd not carry life again.

Anne had heard the toasts at receptions and other grand affairs, when the men stood and held up glasses first to England, then to the queen, and finally to "our land free, our men honest, and our women fruitful." Indeed, great breeders seemed to fill the colony.

Anne knew of several families with ten or twelve children, and the mother no older than Mary herself. Many women were mothers at fifteen and grandmothers at thirty. Most only just recovered from their lying-in period when they were in the increasing way again. And Mary had collected her child-bed linen faithfully. She had a quilted satin child-bed basket, white silk damask gowns, and laced shimmies for infants of various sizes which Anne had seen. They were to be hers, Mary had said, when her own time came on her.

Anne wondered if her mother had lost the child because she'd been denied something for which she longed. She heard about a woman who was denied a piece of hog flesh and miscarried. Indeed, she suspected that such longings were the price a woman extracted for carrying the child.

Anne had deeply mixed emotions about losing a brother or a sister. She felt quite alone and sometimes yearned for a friend. Yet, in spite of her isolation, she was not at all sure she wanted to share her life and her home with another. And they would have been quite different, she and this new child. They might not even sound like siblings. She had been suckled by an Irish wet nurse and so retained some of the Irish lilt to her speech like her parents. Her brother or sister, however, would have been suckled by a nigger wench and would have copied her speech and manner. Perhaps, Anne supposed, they might not even look alike, so different did her mother look today than when she first had conceived.

After a short time Anne did not regret the loss. And there was little change in her mother's demeanor. She was perhaps more quiet and left the table at an earlier hour.

Her father was at first saddened, and then absorbed himself in amusing Mary however he could. He talked of trips abroad, a voyage back to Ireland, or up to Newport for the season. But at the lack of interest in Mary's voice, he dropped his suggestions. And soon, as always, Bellefield's business claimed him again.

Meanwhile, Anne did much as she pleased.

~~~

*E*VENTUALLY, RUMORS BEGAN to reach Bellefield that all was not as it should be at the Goose Creek School. William took Anne aside one evening into his study. Anne knew she could escape full disclosure no longer. Her father was angrier than she'd imagined he'd be.

"And what of your promise to your mother, Daughter? You have shamed me in the face of the whole county! 'Tis said my daughter brawls with young savages—and beats them!"

Anne made the mistake of letting a small smile slip across her face.

"Do you dare to laugh over such as this? Brute force you use on some young lad? Oh, don't try to deny it, miss. I'll hear none of your excuses this time. Brailsford himself took me aside at the auction last week to complain of your behavior! Am I to discuss my own daughter with the best of the county in the middle of a slave mart!"

Anne felt a sudden deep chagrin that she must be the talk of every drawing room in the county. "Does Mother know?"

"Only what she can see for herself! That you've not fulfilled your promise to act the proper lady! She's no fool, lass, though you try to make her so. She can see that you must be reined into petticoats and haltered constantly like a wall-eyed colt." He brushed his hair back from his forehead with an exasperated yank. "Now hear me, Daughter, and mark me well. To my mind, you have failed. You have broken your promise to your mother; you have learned naught in a year but cockfighting and brawling!"

"Pa, there's naught else to learn at such a place! Master Dennis is a fool!"

"And you begged to go there! You're digging with the wrong foot, Anne. The truth is, you brought disgrace to our name." He strode about the room, jerking and flapping his coat erratically.

"They don't fight fair, Father! They tease and torment and then won't fight back when I cuff them, but gang all together and push me out!" An old memory flared. " 'Tis like the Sweeneys, Pa!"

Instead of winning her father over to her plea, her remark made him grow livid with anger. Anne felt a chill of panic as a vein in his broad brow throbbed visibly. His voice was low and threatening.

"Dare you to throw up the Sweeneys to me? Shut your mouth, Daughter, or I'll cuff you myself! You still don't know what you've done! Years of proving ourselves, building a life! You've been spoiled too long, 'tis sure. You've turned to a field hand right under my very eyes! I've a mind to send you back to England to be sold as an indentured wench, just to let you see what you're throwing away with both hands!"

Anne was shocked to tears by his threat. Her fine resolve to defend herself crumbled before her father's rage, and she felt only shame. She stood tall and white with no movement. Only her eyes showed her pain. They burned over with tears and her cheeks grew wet. Her father was shaken by her tears, for she rarely cried even as a young child. And she was all he had. But he hardened his voice.

"Don't think to get by me with your sniveling either, lass. For I'll none of it this time. You've cut my expectations for you to the quick!"

But he looked again at Anne. Her head was down, her figure still as stone, as if awaiting execution. He could not bear her tears. He went to her and held her gingerly, speaking gruffly.

"There, child. Don't cry like a milksop. You've done me and your mother a bad turn and yourself a worse one. But I'll not be sending you packing. And from now on you'll be a model of young womanhood. You'll keep your promise to your mother. No more schools. We'll get a proper governess at Bellefield. No more talk of ciphers. You'll wear petticoats with pride and learn such housewifery exercises as you may turn to good advantage."

Anne held herself stiff in his arms. She felt at once loved and accepted, yet also somehow trapped. She closed her eyes and let his words roll over her like a warm coverlet. Perhaps it was time to grow up after all. She had been lonely. She could not endure the thought of being discussed by every old harridan up and down the river. Perhaps this was the best way. But deep inside, she wondered if it would be worth what she must give up.

FOR OVER A YEAR Anne strove to become the miniature grand lady her parents wanted. She struggled with stays, learned to use a fan to telegraph moods, practiced placing small black patches on her cheeks to set off her eyes or to cover a freckle, and turned her dressing table into an apothecary.

"Anne," her mother would say, while Fully stood by in awe of the proceedings. "Your fan is as important to a man as your eyes."

Anne blinked in disbelief.

"Ay, 'tis true, lass. Ye must know how to flutter a fan just as you must know how to curtsy. Each fan you have"—and she spread out half a dozen on the quilt to show her reluctant daughter—"each style means somethin' altogether different, an' ye must learn to choose the right one for the proper occasion. This is a Mecklenburg fan, here's a weddin' fan, a mournin' fan, a second-mournin' fan—"

"What's a second-mourning fan?"

"Why, that's if the dear loved one weren't quite so loved as for the *first* mournin' fan."

"Oh."

"Ay, an' here's a fan to tell a gentleman that you'll accept his attentions. You simply wave this red lace fan under his nose, an' he'll know."

"Why not simply tell him, Mama?"

"Because, o' course, to do so would compromise your virtue, lass. The fan does the speakin' for you."

"How convenient." She smiled to cover the edge to her voice.

"Ay. Quite. An' by the by, Daughter, I've told you not to call me 'mama' nor your father 'pa.' 'Tis vulgar and coarse. These country folk call the nigger wench who suckled them their mama. I am your mother, your father is your father, an' that's all we care to hear, thank you, in or out of company hearin'."

Mary proceeded to show her through the tangle of accouterments she'd need as a woman. On her bed were feather muffs and tippets, silver-mounted morocco leather pocketbooks, stay hooks, engraved smelling bottles in carved holders in case she got the vapors, genteel snuff boxes—not for her to use, but simply so that she might offer a pinch to a gentleman—an etui, and a housewife. The array was dazzling.

Mary took up a stay hook and fastened it to the edge of Anne's bodice. Fully beamed in pleasure to see her charge so transformed in such finery. On the hook, which was large enough to capture a flopping carp, her mother hung the etui, a small case, and the housewife, a larger case. She placed a bottle of smelling salts, a bone toothpick, and a silk pocket handerchief into the etui. In the housewife, she jammed a pair of small scissors, a thimble, and a packet of needles.

"Must I carry such with me hanging from my chest like so many anchors?"

"A proper lady does, lass."

"Then it's a wonder they can stand upright at all. Pockets make more sense."

Fully rolled her eyes.

"Perhaps," her mother said, unperturbed. "But we're not talkin' sense, Daughter, but fashion. Now, the articles of toilet are for your use also, my dear."

On the table were imported scented waters, powders, paints, lip salves, aqua vitae and tooth polish, waters to prevent tanning, almond paste for the face, and lavender—to take away the smell of sweat, Anne supposed, which she now felt running down her ribs and under her stays. She wondered if it was her long sickness or the loss of the babe that had made her mother hate her own body, had robbed her of her spine. Why else would any woman encumber herself so?

"I'll leave ye alone to sample all of these, Anne. Fullborn can help ye if you've questions as to their use."

"Ay, Mother." Anne watched her glide from the room, her skirts making taut and graceful rustles on the pineheart floor.

She eased herself down on the feather bed, her stays cutting tightly into her belly.

"Fully, take this set of chains from me. I can't breathe. And I'm soaked to the skin under all this blessed bone."

"Ay, well 'tis somethin' to get used to, lass. But ye should have started sooner. Now, yer waist is too big fer yer stays."

"Or my stays are too small for my waist. Fully, how do ladies walk and run or even speak in such a torture?"

"Mostly, they learn to do it slowly or not at all. Breathe up from the bosom an' not from the belly like an old woman wheezin' in the sun. Ye'll get used to it."

"And if I don't? If I keel over at every other step?"

"Well, ye got yer smellin' salts to fetch ye round proper. Remember, once ye got the eye of some man, ye can do as ye like."

Anne took small comfort from Fullborn's words for as far as she could see, no woman did as she liked at any time, regardless of her beauty, her wit, or her goodness.

Anne's debut as a lady was brief, and she finally backslid into her old easier habits. She simply took more care to hide her preferences from her parents than she ever did before. Increasingly, however, William and Mary were occupied with their own concerns. There were new, important guests at Bellefield as Cormac's money begat more money.

In Charles Town, pirates were being accepted into the best houses, as they were in many colonial seaports. They were called privateers, so as not to embarrass their patrons, and as business partners to the merchants, they filled the city coffers with gold doubloons from Spain, silver cobs, pieces of eight, pillar dollars and crowns, and plunder from ships all over the world. They attacked the Spanish shipping which competed with the colonial fleets, and then they sold the stolen goods more cheaply than those from England. Over sixty ships a year came from the mother country, and eighty more vessels plied between the Caribbean and the northern colonies. With Charles Town alone needing over a thousand new slaves each year, and trade with England amounting to over 160 pounds sterling annually, pirates were considered well-needed grease for the colony's economic gears.

For England was harrowing the colonies with taxes much as she'd repressed Ireland's trade. By England's navigation laws, all goods bound for the colonies had first to be sent to the mother country, taxed, and then shipped to the New World. At tables across the land, merchants, planters, and nobility, however loyal to the Crown, grumbled privately at the cost of their allegiance.

As Anne listened to her father's tirade against "home government" and "the poxed, money-hungry Whigs," she looked about the room and counted up in her head all the items that had been bought from the Brethren. The rum at the table, the velvet of her mother's gown, the lace at her own throat, her gold-damascened fowling piece, the wine in the cellar, the candlesticks and the candelabra they sat in, jewels, spices, even the table itself—all bought from pirates' ships at pirate prices.

In 1713, the most famous pirate captain in Charles Town was Paul Raynor. He often took supper at Bellefield with his companion, Con Kesby, a pirate who looked the part as Anne imagined it to be. While Raynor was tall, attractive, swarthy but suave, dressing for dinner in a fine frock coat with a full lace jabot and Dutch linen at his cuffs, Kesby was a vulgar ship's rat of a man—one-eyed, red-faced from rum and high wines, with red breeches and a single gold hoop in his ear. Raynor controlled a large and powerful fleet and a crew to match. He'd brought back a load of molasses and tobacco from the West Indies and had made a fortune for himself and William Cormac in the bargain. Tonight his pleasure and good favor were Cormac's highest priorities. And one of Raynor's greatest pleasures was telling sea stories and watching ladies' eyes spark at the adventures he wove for them.

"Tell us of your recent skirmishes, Raynor," Cormac encouraged his guest, and the pirate captain settled back in the great high-backed chair and lit up his Cuban pipe. His eyes squinted through the smoke, and the candles flickered as if the wind came up from the sea as he spoke. He addressed himself to Cormac, but his feral eyes slid from Anne to her mother.

"We're a hit-and-run bunch, Cormac. Speed and surprise are our weapons, terror our greatest advantage. I've seen men killed by a hail of oak splinters from a cannon on deck, six-inch daggers they were, and the butchery of a ship's surgeon awaited those who survived their agony. Gangrene in the tropics is not a pretty sight, ma'am." He bowed his head to Mary with a small smile.

"But we did have one great battle on the last sail. We were off Jamaica in open seas. The lookout spied a ship near twelve miles off with his glass and hollered 'ship ahoy!' off the starboard side. 'Twas a Spanish brigantine, flying Spanish colors, likely bound for Spain from the Gold Coast. We knew she carried a rich hold, heavy in the water. So we took a vote, man for man, and decided to take her. We tailed her for half a day to see whether the gunports on her side were real or painted on. You know, those false Spanish curs will paint fake guns aboard the smallest ship. But we weren't fooled by her tricks."

"Did you blast her?" Cormac could not wait for the tale to continue. Anne kept still so she'd not be noticed and sent from the table at the peak of the story.

"Nay. We rarely fire on a ship more than once, man. We mean to take her, not sink her. We put a single shot across her bow, hoisted our black flag, and she struck her colors without a fight. That's the sort of battle we like, of course."

Cormac was clearly exasperated. "But have you never seen battle then, man?"

Raynor smiled wryly. "Ay, milord. I've seen my share of sea fights and gore. Is that what you want to hear, then? I was on Tew's ship, you know. The *Amity* out of Bermuda in '92. He was a good captain and got up a crew of sixty men—even got a privateering commission from the governor of Bermuda, Isaac Richier, to plunder the French transports off Africa. That way, if we were caught, we had a passport to freedom. We could simply say we were after the enemies of the king, and we were heroes."

He held up a glass of red wine and peered into its glimmering depths. His voice took on a bemused tone. "Well, armed with this license to steal, we sailed out across the Atlantic through calm seas. Then Tew springs out his surprise. Did we want to go on account, says he. And make a fortune with or without the governor's permission? One bold push, he said, and we'd know ease and plenty all our days. Well, we all agreed to a man to follow him. A gold chain or a wooden leg, we said. So we shaped a course for the Cape of Good Hope and sailed into the Red Sea."

Raynor took a deep drag on his pipe then and gazed out the window for a moment as if remembering.

"For months we searched for the perfect catch, through the Indian Ocean, pocked with sharks and dead calms. 'Til we came on a vessel belonging to the Great Mogul of India. She was on the run between India and the Arab ports and carried a full load of riches and three hundred Indian soldiers to boot."

"Did they fight?" Again, Cormac broke in.

"Ay, man. They fought tooth and nail and well they should, for they carried a prize worth dying for. A king's ransom in elephant-tusk ivory and spices. Coffers of jewels and bales of smooth and shining silks. And over one hundred thousand pounds of gold and silver."

Cormac's eyes widened as he tried to picture such wealth.

"But we took her. With muskets and cutlasses, we boarded her

on the open sea; all eighty men of the *Amity* answered her three
hundred soldiers. Nary a pirate lost. We scoured that Indian bitch
and stripped her clean, sent the crew over the side to feed the
sharks, and then headed south, fetching up at St. Mary's off the
Madagascar coast. Tew split up the loot, and we sailed into
Newport in April '94 to a hero's welcome. Every merchant in
port ran over himself to provide us with the best. We went to visit
the royal governor of New York who threw us a ball at his
mansion. Mrs. Tew and her daughter Meg wore more jewels for
the occasion than the governor's wife and ladies all put together.
When we got back to Newport, the whole town wanted to sign
on Tew's next cruise, for each pirate had more in that year's time
than the governor himself did in a three-year term. They all
dreamed of sheiks and moguls and had Red Sea fever."

"And did you go again?" Cormac was leaning forward in his
chair, entranced. Raynor took his time with his reply, watching
Anne and her mother.

"Ay. I sailed with him again that year. But his luck ran out. And
luck's as vital to a pirate as his vessel. We took another commission, this time from Governor Fletcher, who was only too glad to
invest in such a venture. We sailed once more for the Red Sea.
And for the better part of a year we filled our ship's hold with
riches from the Orient beyond our dreams. Diamonds, gold,
silver, ivory caskets and hogsheads of wine—and then, while
boarding a small ship, Tew was shot in the belly. The bullet
carried away a foot of his flesh, and he died holding his own
bowels in his hands."

The table was silent. Cormac stared at Raynor and then, too
late, remembered his wife and daughter. He glanced furtively at
them both. Mary's face was calm and unmoved. Anne's face was
flushed with excitement. Raynor too followed his host's eyes
around the room.

"Your pardon for such a gruesome tale, ladies. I do hope I've
not offended your sensibilities. But those are the ways of pirates.

And war is what we wage out on the seas. Blood is the currency of war. You save yours and spend the other fellow's as best you can."

Cormac answered for his women, watching them carefully. Mary perhaps had heard only a piece of the story, and it was obviously too late to protect Anne from it. "I'm sure they've heard worse tales, Captain." He hastened to change the subject.

As the talk turned to business and trade, Anne's attention drifted. For all Raynor's glamour, she liked Con Kesby best. He both frightened and fascinated her, with his single gold earring and the ivory-handled dirk he stowed in his red breeches, even at her father's table. She rarely spoke to him, but she watched him under lowered lashes. And on occasion she felt he watched her as well.

Anne was growing up quickly. She knew it to be so when she stood naked before her glass and looked down at her body. Her breasts were mounding out slowly, but what she noticed first was her thighs. Always flat, they were beginning to round outward. She watched herself swell with a sort of detached curiosity.

By thirteen she was tall for her age, nearly as high as her father. Her monthlies started three months into her thirteenth year, and Anne was prepared. Fullborn had noticed her quick growth and told her what to expect. Anne could not believe she was to be so inconvenienced. One more set of restraints settled over her shoulders, as burdensome as the hated stays and the pointed moroccan slippers that cramped her feet.

"Ye cannot bathe, lass, when yer time comes on you. Ye cannot stand in cold drafts, nor eat pork, nor drink red wine, and if the pain gets too sharp—"

"Pain? Does it hurt, Fully?"

"Ay, lass. Some do. Why, I've known ladies who couldn't leave their beds for a week each month. And some went nigh crazy with the pain."

"Do *you* hurt with it?"

Fullborn laughed. "Nay, lass. 'Tis been gone from me life for years now. It no longer plagues me. That time o' me is through."

"Sweet Jesus. Well, at least it ends, then. How long do I have before it leaves me?"

"Many years, lass. Perhaps thirty or more."

" 'Tis a scurvy trick to play on women! Looks to me as though we get all the nuisances and men get all the fun, Fully."

"Lass, it does no good to rail against life like that or to talk like some tavern piece. Ye don't hear other women complainin' o' their lot, do ye? Now come here, an' I'll show ye the proper way to bind yerself when the time comes."

Anne came and listened, but she was not reconciled. When her flux came, she was relieved to feel little pain—only a dull heaviness that slowed her down and a plaguey throb in her forehead that made her restless and irascible. She soon found that the best cure for this was to mount Foxfire and ride her hard over the lowlands, urging her faster and faster until they both were spent. She often wished she were like her mare, fleet and surefooted, untrammeled by monthly blood and dirty rags wrapped at her loins.

Her father grew softer towards her as she developed. Anne felt him watch her, often with a small smile of love on his face. As she moved about the rooms, her skirts gracefully trailing after her, he never failed to notice some new bit of jewelry she wore or a new attempt at subduing her red curling hair.

"It's your flame, lass. Never cut your hair. 'Tis like the sun on your head. I could know you from a great distance, out of a herd of other women, by your hair." Then he stroked her curls softly. Anne quieted under his touch and determined once more to learn how to tame her unruly mane to his taste.

Her body seemed less her own these days, and she felt a stranger growing inside her. Anne noticed that the eyes of men followed her more, but that they often swiveled away when they saw her looking back at them.

When she attended the party at the Drayton's plantation, all heads seemed to turn towards her as she entered the ballroom—

and not just the heads of the men; the women's eyes slid enviously over her as well.

Phillip Drayton, youngest son of their closest neighbors, approached her, bowing over her hand. He whirled her on to the dance floor, clutching her waist gingerly. Anne had known Phillip since childhood, yet his hand, as it held hers, was damp, and she could feel him trembling through her glove. She frowned slightly in confusion, wondering what ailed the lad.

When John Drayton cut in, tapping his son's shoulder and putting his arm round her waist, she was even more amazed. Mr. Drayton was her father's age and yet she could have sworn she felt his fingers moving over her back, pressing gently, almost caressively, in a deliberately intimate fashion. She smiled slightly to cover her astonishment. So this, then, was the flirtation that went on between men and women. She took a deep breath so that her breasts appeared rounded against her bodice and watched Mr. Drayton from under her lashes. His face flushed noticeably as he followed the movement of her body. There is a lesson to be learned here, she thought, and I seem to be a fast study.

THAT WINTER MARY wanted to return to Charles Town for the holiday season. William was grateful for her renewed interest in a social life and bought a town house on a shaded street, back several blocks from the waterfront.

In the early morning, Anne's favorite time, she heard the hawkers through the streets, chanting their music over the sounds from the quay. The fish peddler carried gray shrimp, blue crabs, red snapper, pompano, and mullet. He sang:

> *"Day-O! Fisherboy's here*
> *Carry shrimp, an' snapper, an' she-crab, too!*
> *It all fresh fish an' won't bite you,*

Got all swimmin' things, high an' dry
Come an' buy, come an' buy!"

And ever after, the sound of "Day-O!" in the dawn light made Anne smile and feel ready for anything.

They owned one of the few brick houses on Bay Street. The brick was not red but pink, faded by the sun and sea air, and the roof was of heavy hurricane-proof tiles that shone black when wet. The wide piazzas and jalousied doors and windows caught the sea breeze and shaded the relentless glare of the sun. Trim black carriages with teams of two or four blooded horses clopped down the street; gentlemen on their way to jockey club meetings, octoroon beauties passing the gardens, peeping over the high walls on their way to Market Street, and silken ladies walking arm in arm, all paraded in front of Anne's window.

Anne liked the rabble of the city, loved the noise and bustle and movement. Turkey buzzards were so tame in Charles Town that they crept about the meat market under the feet of the customers. Mary thought them distasteful, but Anne found them beautiful and powerful birds with their useful naked necks. When the waters ran out of the upper harbor twice a day, the gulls and the buzzards cleared off the refuse, making the air less fetid in the heat.

Often, after the searing heat of midday was through, Anne sat out on the veranda and listened to the sounds from the harbor. The Indians called Charles Town "the mockingbird," after the bird of four hundred tongues. And in the streets one could hear a babble of Mother English, Scotch and Irish brogues, French drawls, Indian and African dialects, Spanish, German, and Gullah—an African dialect laced with borrowed French and English words. The black tongues couldn't pronounce certain syllables, so they dropped them and lengthened vowels instead. Of course, the children raised by these black mammys learned their speech patterns, so whole generations of white southern gentlemen and ladies spoke the same bastard English as their slaves.

One of Anne's favorite diversions was a trip to the market, where she might see the hunters from the inland mountains. They came to Charles Town in their buckskin leggings, no wigs, no lace, no shoes, only ragged moccasins and flintlock muskets. But they carried wondrous things: tiger skins, buffalo hides, the horns of elk, and huge bear blankets thrown over their shoulders like so many sheaves of wheat. And the stalls were full of ripe oranges, mangoes that still tasted of the sun of the Spanish Main, limes and other citrus; carcasses of beef, hogs, trussed chickens; healing herbs and those which killed such as baneberry, hellbore, and hemlock; brandies, wines, rums made from the finest sugars; and a thousand other remarkable testimonies to exotic places.

Gillah, the cook, took delight in collecting her wares fresh from the street hawkers rather than depending on shipments from the river or on Charley for game. With ample stores close at hand, she expanded their plantation bill of fare to include shrimp pie, stewed crabs, oysters and cream, blancmange and bavarian cream, all delicacies she could not concoct from Bellefield staples.

That winter two thieves were hanged in the Battery, and crowds gathered to watch. Anne could just see the scaffolding from the veranda. The rope was never long enough, it seemed, so the wretches always took a while to die, dancing in the air convulsively. When they were sentenced to be hanged, drawn, and quartered, their agony was even more prolonged. After hanging by the neck until almost dead, the victims were cut open and their entrails removed. Then their bodies were cut into quarters that were displayed in various public places on the wharf. Usually a large crowd gathered for such events, and children were held up on shoulders to get a better view and to learn the lessons of sin more thoroughly.

There hadn't been a woman burned in Charles Town since 1657; indeed, the royal proprietors frowned on such barbarities. There had been two who were pressed, however. Those punishments were not public, the better to preserve the criminal's modesty. As Anne had heard, the wench was made to lie flat on the floor naked, with only a mask for her face. Then a large stone was laid on her chest. Each day she was given only three morsels of barley bread and a small draft of water from the puddle nearest the gaol, just enough to keep her alive. And each day a heavier stone was placed on her. It was said that it often took three days to die in that manner.

Anne wondered sometimes at the brutality she saw around her and was dubious how such things could mesh with the fervent hymns she heard each morning rise from the six churches in the town. But it was all she knew—indeed, all anyone knew—and so she flocked with the rest of the crowds to White Point to see the executions, never doubting that Carolina justice was still more civilized and more genteel than that of the northern colonies, about which savage tales were told.

Anne would have liked to wander into the city every day, but her father had other plans for her future. After some deliberation and no consultation, Cormac sent Anne to the Widow Varnod to learn intricate embroidery, lace work, tapestry, drawing, and other city refinements. Since Anne was already reading Molière, Milton, Boccaccio, and Boileau, she quickly tired of the widow's emphasis on pastry-making and needlepoint.

One day a pink-cheeked young girl reprimanded Anne for her "irreverent" attitudes.

"If you do not learn to be a proper lady, Mistress Anne," the girl blinked at her, "you will never be a proper wife."

"Wife!" Anne replied in full hearing of most of the house. "Why would a woman of any sense wish such a fate? I wish to be handmaiden to no lord, thank you."

At the shocked faces around her, Anne knew that she'd made herself unwelcome again.

Soon, she was skipping school and spending her days down at the docks with her new-found companions at the sea wall.

∽∽∽

SHE ROAMED WIDE-EYED through the throngs of buyers and sellers, exploring all the harbor cast ashore, sampling the flotsam from every foreign ship. She peered into the darkened taverns, musty with salt, wine, and sweat. She saw doxies with breasts heaving over the edges of their bodices, sitting on the knees of drunken sailors or leaning out of windows, pandering their wares. She watched fights erupt and spill over the streets, men swearing and cursing each other over women and the price of rum. And finally, no longer content to merely watch, Anne joined a small gang of dockside toughs.

With her father busy at his warehouses and her mother rarely up before late afternoon, Anne now had more freedom than she'd known under the watchful eyes of all the servants at Bellefield. She learned to stow away a pair of breeches and a jerkin in the house of easement behind Widow Varnod's veranda. In the city, none cared what she did or where she went. The widow noticed only that Anne was increasingly absent, but assumed she was caring for her mother. As long as the tuition was paid, she asked no questions. When the Cormac carriage deposited Anne at the widow's door, she slipped around the side, shucked off her skirts, and yanked on her breeches. Then, as the young ladies filed into the widow's parlor, Anne pulled down her cap and headed towards the waterfront.

Two or three days a week she ran at will with a pack of nine boys, ages ten to fifteen, lads whose only aim in life was to become sea mice, or apprentices on a merchant ship. Many yearned most of all to be pirates and to be captain of their own ship. Each dreamed of the day when he might sail into the harbor with his own crew and see the quay thick with white bonnets and the skirts of women and feel their admiration like sunlight. That was what they played at, when they screamed and fought and ran like gulls over the docks. That was life, the world that lay ahead. The red banners, the screams of the wounded, the shouts of the brave, and the homecoming into the sunset with all of Charles Town standing on the dock, shouting, "Hurrah for the Brethren! Glory to the captain!"

Practice fights with wooden swords and stolen cutlasses were waged up and down the docks by every sea-bound boy, hoping to be noticed. Anne had an advantage over most, since she'd learned to handle a sword, a pistol, and a tomahawk at an early age from Charley Fourfeathers. She was also half a head taller than most of the lads she saw on the quay.

Her initiation was brutal but quick. She'd been running an errand for a doxy at the sign of the Green Gull who'd offered her a shilling for the deliverance of some vinegar from the midwife. Anne was dressed in her breeches, her hair pulled back in a pug and hidden under her cap, and her breasts bound and hidden under her jerkin. As she returned to the tavern, she was accosted by three young toughs, eager to jostle new blood.

"Hey!" One lean young lad stopped her, jerking at her sleeve. "Here's a chuckle-headed fool out takin' an airin'!"

Anne stiffened at the insult; her hand went instinctively to the dirk in her breeches.

"He looks a pitiful excuse for a man, eh Tom? His skin's as pink an' pasty as any whore's!"

With a low growl of rage, Anne snatched her arm out of the boy's grasp and swung it back again at his jaw. He was caught off guard by her quick blow, and he staggered back. But he quickly recovered, veered, and lunged for her head. Anne went down in the dust, grappling with the ruffian, pulling him over her and onto his back. She tried to sit on his chest, but he was slightly stronger than she and pulled her off, twisting her cap in his hands. Her matted hair fell loose about her shoulders.

" 'Tis a wench!" He lurched off her, dumbfounded, and pushed away to his feet.

One of his comrades jeered, "Ay, man. Can't ye tell a lad from a lass? Ye wouldn't know a horse's ass if it shit on yer boots!"

The boys clustered about them both, laughing, and Anne could not help but laugh too at the crestfallen look on her adversary's face.

Still, she was not accepted until she'd proven herself with several daring tasks. No more running errands for doxies; Anne was christened Andrew and taught to steal small items from the stalls that lined the quay and bring them to Tom, the group's leader. Taller than the rest and the oldest, Tom ran the young group of thugs with bluster, rage, and force. He could curse louder and hit harder than anyone else, so as with wild mustangs, he became head stallion by default.

After Anne proved herself by stealing fruit and trinkets from merchants, she was graduated to picking the pockets of drunken seamen who leaned against the tavern walls in the shade. At first such close contact made her heart jump and her hands tremble, but after she'd robbed a few and received the congratulations and greedy approval of her comrades, she took pleasure in her quick, light hands. As the only girl in the group, she had to prove herself sexually as well.

As in fights, Anne learned that bluffs must be met with action and that defiance counted for a great deal. The younger boys dared not affront her, for she had a fierce temper and a quick fist, but Tom was not afraid of her reputation and tested her at every opportunity. At the outset, she noted that he took frequent chances to jostle next to her, letting his hands brush over her bosom, keeping his eyes averted at all times from her own. She felt no fear, only anger at his clumsiness. Finally, he got her alone one afternoon and exposed his private parts to her.

"Look at this, lass. Have you ever seen the like?"

Anne looked warily over her shoulder and saw they were alone, that he had maneuvered her into a confrontation she must win or leave the gang for good. It was power he wanted, not pleasure.

She faced him boldly. "Ay, I've seen the like." As she watched, his tool grew and waved in the air in a jerky dance. "Am I to swoon with pleasure or what, you fool? You'd better tug on it each morning to make it strong, lad. For it looks like it'll bend in any breeze. A look at these may make it stand firm." Anne untied her jerkin slowly and let her breasts hang free. They were still small but ripe, pink-tipped, and pert. Tom suddenly looked less sure of himself.

"You crowing cock-a-jay! Your wit lags, eh?" She reached up and held her breasts out to him, taunting him with her soft smile, praying inside that he would back off as Phillip had done. Her husky voice grew even lower with threat . . . promise. "These are for a *man's* pleasure, boy. 'Tis sure you'll never touch them with your clumsy hands."

He sprang at her then, startling her, his pants still lowered, his chest heaving against her.

Frightened, she pushed back at him, "Be off, you idiot! Let go!" She twisted about, wrenching herself free of his grip. Tom was off balance just enough so that when Anne pulled herself free from his arms, he toppled over—and fell off the sea wall into the bay, his breeches still open to mid-thigh. Anne watched him tumble into the water, her hands furiously fastening her jerkin, her eyes wide in surprise. She hadn't meant to shove him so hard. The splash brought her back to some semblance of mind. She knew that he would endure no further taunting. She sensed that if she wanted to remain friends with Tom, she must save him from further embarrassment. So, smothering her laughter, she quickly walked from the dock and left him to repair his dignity alone. Neither of them ever referred to his defeat again.

Anne's sojourn with these amateur pirates was short but educational. She became better with a knife than she'd ever been with a needle. A year after she'd grown tired of their company, the governor of the Carolinas issued a warrant for the arrest of

"William Saunders, of ordinary stature, fresh-colored, black hair, about ten years old; Tee Weatherly, short, very small, blind in one eye, about fourteen; and Thomas Simpson, tall, squint-eyed, sixteen, for theft"—all running mates of her youth.

MARY HAD SOME hope that the trip to Charles Town might make her regain her energy. She remembered the social bustle and gaiety of their first few years in the city, but the reality of the present was quite different. Though Mary's social status was unchanged, and she was still considered one of Charles Town's elite, her physical ability to revel in that status was much impaired. She faced each day with a growing sense of dread, a deep weariness, and an almost chilling fear at the thought that she might be asked to leave the refuge of her private quarters. Anne deeply resented the gradual invisibility of her mother and the increased influence Clara held over her. Once, as she tiptoed to her mother's open door, bent on sharing a rare confidence, she saw the humpbacked wizened old woman holding her mother to her breast, rocking her, and crooning as to a bewildered child. Anne's face twisted in an involuntary grimace, and she stole away.

One day, Anne came bouncing in off the docks, heading for her room to change from her breeches back to her skirts. She had managed such a change twice in the last week, and no one seemed the wiser. As she paused at the stairs, she heard her mother's voice in the drawing room—with an accompanying murmur. The Widow Varnod was an unexpected guest in the parlor. A small shiver coursed up her back as she saw the inevitable confrontation waiting for her.

She quickly went up the stairs, taking them two at a time, and carefully easing past those boards that creaked. She crept into her chamber. Then she started and flushed. Clara sat on her bed, arms crossed, eyes narrowed.

"So," she hissed. "Ye been runnin' at the docks again. An' now ye think to sneak past yer mother once more, pretendin' to be the grand scholar in skirts." Her voice was low and threatening, and the very sound of it roused Anne's willfulness.

"Are you spying on me, you old witch?" Anne calmed herself with an effort.

"Someone must be yer mother's eyes an' ears, wench. Ye don't care if ye shame the whole house with your indecent ways."

Anne turned her back to Clara, drawing herself up with dignity. "My mother has her own eyes and ears, old woman. And certainly her own mouth. I'll not hear such from a hired drab." Losing control, she whirled around, her green eyes flashing. "Get out of my room and don't come back!"

Clara stood up slowly, deliberately mocking Anne's command. "Oh, ay, mistress. Whatever ye say, mistress." She turned at the door. "But ye won't be givin' orders much longer, brat. When yer mother hears how ye spend yer days an' yer father's money, chasin' after dockside trash like a common whore, she'll pack ye off to a convent where nobody'll care fer yer fancy ways." She laughed viciously. "Ay, ye can give all the orders ye like then, behind high walls. An' ye won't see the light o' day 'til yer wed proper. 'Tis the only way to deal with the likes o' you. An' if I were yer father, I'd beat ye 'til ye screams an' begs for mercy."

"I'll tell my father, and he'll sell your papers to a slaver! You old scut," Anne snapped.

Clara grinned, a slow taunting smirk. "We'll see who tells who, milady." Then she turned on her heel and stamped from the room.

Anne took several deep breaths, trying to compose herself. Her body quivered with rage. It wasn't enough that she had to face the widow and her mother, she must also be plagued by meddling servants.

She yanked off her breeches angrily and pulled a muslin gown over her head. Damn that old woman! How she found out all she did, Anne could not tell. But she had eyes everywhere and a mouth to match. Anne felt suddenly helpless, knowing that there was little she could do to keep Clara from telling the household. But she vowed the gossip would end there. In the meantime, she did not relish the scene that must be played out downstairs.

As she went into the drawing room, she heard her mother's voice, as cold and hard as a stone wall.

"Well, here's our Anne, Widow Varnod." Her mother turned a gaze on her—a measuring, far-off look, with nothing in it of love.

She's going to cast me to her, Anne sensed. I'm going to get out of this one myself. She sat down demurely in the chair farthest from the two women and folded her hands, silent, steeling herself for battle.

After a pause, in which it was clear that no one else would speak, Mary began, in her most cultured tone. "Anne, the widow tells me you've missed some days of school. Where have you been spending that time?"

Anne decided to take a chance. "Down at the docks, Mother."

There was another pause, during which her mother's eyes turned glacial. "And how have you spent your time there, Anne?"

Anne silently cursed her mother for humiliating her before the widow, a gossipy old droll who'd spend the tale like so many guineas up and down Charles Town by nightfall.

She looked deeply into her mother's eyes, and suddenly she understood. Her mother did not want the truth. She wanted absolution—in the eyes of all the city. That is why she had the widow witness this farce.

"I've been reading, Mother. I sit in the shade at White Point past the noise of the docks, and I read."

The widow's eyes flew open in suspicion. "And what do you read, mistress?" She did not believe Anne for an instant, yet she had to hear this tale to its end.

"I read all I cannot read in your school, Dame Varnod. I read Shakespeare, Molière, Milton, and the classics." She smiled. "I long ago finished with the Bible, excellent though it may be, so you see, 'twas time for me to go on to . . . other things. If you like, I shall read aloud for you, and we can discuss a passage or two."

The widow stuttered out her incredulousness at such a brazen defense. "You read Milton? Molière?" She turned to Mary. "You allow such books in the hands of a child?"

Her mother laughed, a tinkling, icy sound. "My dear widow, the classics are for those who can digest them, of any age. Clearly, we have underestimated our Anne." Her green eyes flickered over Anne appraisingly. "We shall have to find a tutor for her who can keep up with her quick mind." She turned to her daughter, her smile frozen. "Daughter, I'm glad to see you've been using your time wisely. Though I would have preferred to supervise your progress, of course, I cannot fault your . . . taste. You may be excused."

Anne got up leisurely and bowed to the two women. She knew by her mother's face that she was not believed, yet she also knew she was impervious to any further assaults. She had taken the responsibility for her own fate with her lie, and her mother had washed her hands, preferring not to know.

Anne was secretly pleased at the way she had covered her tracks and so, a week later, circling the house from the back to avoid the parlor, she felt secure in her game. Suddenly she heard a series of strange sounds. A steady thumping noise was coming from the side garden, and as she stopped to listen, a whimpering wail rose through the air. She followed the sounds and found Clara, her arm raised above her head, beating Anne's dog with her cane.

Lady was the only animal she'd brought from Bellefield, her oldest and most faithful hound. Her nose was no longer keen, and her eyes were glazed with age, but Charley had placed her in Anne's arms as a pup, and now she waited out her life, lying in the sun on the kitchen steps.

Anne was frozen by the scene. Clara had the dog by the ears and was beating her about the haunches furiously, silently, her mouth twisted in rage. The only sound was the rhythmic whack of the cane and the keening yelps of the dog as she desperately tried to twist loose. Lady gave one last gasp and sank to the ground in a heap.

Clara turned and saw Anne standing there, her mouth hanging open in horror.

"That lazy bitch best learn to lie somewheres else! I dropped a full plate, trippin' over her carcass!"

Anne turned slowly, as though in a daze, and saw the shattered plate on the steps. She wrenched the cane from the woman's hand, raising it above her head to strike. Then she felt an icy control settle over her fury, and she hurled the cane far over the garden wall. In almost the same movement, she whirled and slapped the old woman as hard as she could.

"Don't you ever touch anything of mine again, do you hear? Anything!" She jutted her jaw close to Clara. "Next time, I'll not stay my hand." She dropped to her knees and examined the dog carefully, crooning softly.

Clara laughed mirthlessly. "All this noise fer an old hound. When yer mother's pitiful sick upstairs. Ye care more fer that old cur then fer yer own blood! She's been calling fer ye all day."

Anne's attention was momentarily diverted. "And where's my father, then?"

"That ruttin' cad's off as usual, never here when she needs him."

Anne's eyes narrowed. "How dare you speak that way of my father! When I tell him, you'll be out of this house by nightfall."

"Tell him an' welcome, brat. He knows 'tis true. Yer own mother told me. He got her with child, a poor servin' wench, an' his folk chased him from Ireland. An' yer nothin' but a bastard besides. 'Tis no wonder yer common as pig tracks," Clara said calmly, almost gleefully.

Anne's face flushed and then whitened; her hands twisted at her side. "My mother told you that?" she asked, her voice low.

"Ay, brat. An' even yer father can't buy that truth!"

Anne's mind whirled. The whispers, the sly glances, the pain of her childhood ran before her like a tidal current. Damn her mother and her pitiful confessions. Clara's tongue knew no bounds, and she was not above blackmail. She could ruin them in Charles Town forever if she chose.

"And who else have you told?" Anne asked, trying to control the quaver in her voice.

"No one, ye silly baggage. An' I keep my tongue long's I keep my place." She turned idly to pick up the pieces of the platter as though she had all the time in the world. "Now get to yer mother," she threw over her shoulder. "An' don't be plaguin' her with things she don't need to know."

Anne climbed the stairs in confusion. It was a breathlessly hot afternoon. Her breeches stuck to her, prickling her skin. She felt her flux starting, a low ache in her back, a restlessness added to her anger. She heaved a bewildered sigh.

She waited outside her mother's door, listening for a moment, but she could hear nothing within. She gently pushed the door and saw her mother lying in a pile of twisted lines, her hair spilled about the pillow, her face white and still. Anne felt part pity, part irritation at her weakness. It seemed to her that she had always been sickly like this. Anne went to her mother's side, knelt by the bed, and took her frail hand in her own large one. Her mother opened her eyes but did not smile.

Instantly, Anne felt a hard anger at her mother's weakness, her need to confess family secrets to a servant. Mary coughed and shivered with the fever. She glared at Anne.

"Clara says she's . . . seen you. How could you shame me so?"

"Oh, Mother, I wish that trull's tongue would strangle her!" Anne's anger stiffened her voice more than she intended.

Mary's own pride strengthened her. "Anne, your *own* tongue is your undoin'. You will never be of any worth 'til you learn to curb it!" Her eyes shone with fury but she fell back weakly on the pillow. She was still in command, and she felt her power keenly.

Her voice turned venomous.

"Clara says you've been seen down on the wharf, Daughter. An' not readin' but runnin' with a pack of wild dogs like some bitch in heat."

Anne was shocked by her mother's vulgarity. She felt a moment of confusion, but her strength rallied with the heat of her own anger. "Aye, Mother. And you believed her, did you not? It's true, I have made my own friends down at the waterfront. But I am no bitch in heat! How could you say it! I am as maiden as I was when you birthed me. Perhaps Clara would like to put me to the test? She's had her filthy prying fingers in all else in our lives!"

Now it was her mother's turn to be shocked. "Anne!" Her eyes filled with quick tears. "What have you become, Daughter! A trull? You sound like a servin' wench in some tavern!"

"A serving wench, Mother? And you complain of my tongue? When it's you who told such a secret as you should have carried to your grave! You told Clara you were just such a serving wench, my father a rutting outcast, and me a bastard born on the wrong side of the sheets! And you chide me for my tongue! You've ruined us, Mother. Ruined us all with your pitiful confessions. Clara will tell all she knows!"

Her mother began to cough and wail. "Get out! Send Clara to me! I'll see you no more!"

Anne rushed from the room, anger and despair filling her heart.

She found Clara in the kitchen, bending over a pot of hot broth. Anne shouted, "You cursed witch!"

Clara moved quickly and hurled the contents of the kettle over Anne's feet and legs.

Anne gasped and hopped frantically, her skin reddening before her eyes. She screeched in pain and swung at the old woman savagely. Clara deftly pulled a knife from her skirt and raised it above her head, her mouth working, her eyes white. She jabbed it into empty air as Anne ducked. Clara shifted hands for a second thrust. In an instant, Anne plucked her own knife hidden in the folds of her skirt and plunged it into the old woman's chest. She felt it catch, grate on something hard, and then slide deeply into her breast.

Anne leaped away. Clara stumbled, her eyes rolling back in her head as she slid slowly to the floor at Anne's feet.

Anne stared in horror at the crumpled heap that had once been Clara. She sank to a bench at the hearth, watching for movement, waiting for Clara to groan or stir. But she was still. The fire snapped suddenly, and Anne jumped, her heart in her throat. Then, a deep sorrow flooded her...not for Clara's death. For Clara, she felt only a quiet shuddering awe—but sorrow for her mother's face, sorrow for her father's shame, and wrenchingly painful sorrow for herself. Her mother's voice dinned in her ears, "You will never be of any worth...."

She searched for her anger again, reached for it deeply within her mind, trying to recall the power it had given her. But it was gone. She cried then, from grief and rage and fear, weeping for the perfect things, broken.

THE HEARING INTO the circumstances of the death of Clara, indentured servant, was swift and almost casual. A bonded servant was technically a criminal and had no rights of a free citizen. Cormac himself acted as Anne's defense counsel, arguing that the old woman was a quick-tempered, foul-mouthed wench who'd poisoned the minds of too many in the household. Anne's blistered skin was displayed to the court, but Anne testified to little else.

She sat through the inquest, her head down, her mouth set, her hands folded. She looked the picture of sober sorrow and, indeed, she felt so at the time. There was some hint that Clara had taken possession of her mistress's mind, possibly by witchcraft.

In a final attack on Clara's character, Cormac brought a witness who swore that Clara had been seen on the streets of Charles

Town after sunset and she had owned a dog, both crimes for a bondswoman.

When such evidence was added to her reputation as a double-tongue, the judge decided that Charles Town needn't worry itself overmuch on the death of a serving maid. He declared Anne's action self-defense and the inquest was closed. Her father escorted her home, grim-faced. She waited for his explosion of rage and the inevitable constraints on her behavior. But none came. Whether he sensed her sorrow and regret and hoped for a new sobriety or simply did not know what to say, Anne never knew.

He said only, " 'Tis said she stabbed her lover in the back in London. Well then, she's perished by the sword as well."

Anne ventured a remark, more to feel close to her father than to converse, for she really did not want to hear more. "Perhaps it's for the best, Pa. Perhaps there was reason to it all."

Her father barked a harsh laugh, more a sob than mirth. "Perhaps. Perhaps if the dog hadn't stopped to take a shit, he would have caught the rabbit. Reasons are whores, Anne. And none knows it better than a lawyer. 'Tis better forgotten."

Anne lowered her head, her eyes filled with tears at the bitterness in her father's voice.

"I shall never forget it, Father. It blinds me still. I can still feel the knife twist in her guts."

Her father raised his hand to her, as if in protest. "Tell me no more of it. I do not wish to hear of your trials, Anne. I've my own to bury." He sighed deeply and turned from her; his eyes and voice were flat and lifeless as he continued in a low whisper.

"We live with a number of rooms within us, lass. There's a best dayroom where we show our finest face to neighbors and relations. There's the bedroom where few are allowed in. There's a small attic chamber where no one comes in save ourselves, where we share nothing with anyone. And there's a final cellar, so hidden away in the ugliness of our souls that we never even go inside ourselves. Down there, we lock up all our failures, our pains, and our trespasses." He looked up at his daughter, his face bleak. "Now you have a secret for your cellar, lass."

Nonetheless, Anne felt unforgiven. The night Clara died Mary had come out of her room, her hair wildly disheveled, her nightshift soiled, and her legs bare. She crept along the hall, feeling her way and shuffling her feet. Anne knew before she even opened her chamber door why she'd come. Her mother suddenly appeared in the doorway, the shuttered light from the moon making weird patterns on her nightshift, her voice quavering.

"So ye murdered her, then."

Anne sat upright in bed, for the first time frightened of her mother, an apparition of borderline madness. She kept still in her bed, not daring to approach this wild thing she scarcely recognized.

"Mother, it was an accident," she said quietly.

Mary's harsh laughter shattered the stillness. "An accident? Did she fall on your knife then?"

"No. But I did not mean to kill her."

"No, o' course not. Neither did ye mean to split my heart, but so ye have. I've housed a harlot. A harlot and"—her voice rose in a shriek—"a murderess!"

Anne tried to raise her voice above her mother's to get her attention, to calm her hysterics, but Mary would not hear her. She paused at the foot of the bed, wringing her hands, and glared at the girl as she huddled under the quilt.

" 'Tis your father's sin as well as your own. Coddled ye an' spoiled ye rotten—'tis rotten ye are to the core, harlot!"

All of a sudden she stopped and whispered to Anne, cocking her head like a beady-eyed bird to hear the buzzing of an insect.

"Do ye have a plan?"

"A plan, Mother?"

"Ay! A plan! Don't be daft, lass. Ye must have a plan, or they'll hang ye sure!"

At her words, Anne froze. Before she could think of a reply that might move her mother out of her room, Fullborn appeared at the door, her wrapper pulled about her body. With one quick glance, she took it all in.

"La, mistress! 'Tis too cold an' late to be traipsin' in the dark. An' no shoes, my Lord." Clucking like an old hen, pretending deep concern and some vexation, Fullborn led the unprotesting woman back to her own chamber. Fully did not return to her again that night. That was her single note of censure, Anne knew. But neither did her mother plague her again. Anne was glad of the reprieve for she did not want to speak of it anew or think of it at all.

THE NEW YEAR began soberly for Anne. She was continuing to ripen and looked more womanly than the other girls her age. She was taller than most, standing quite as high as her father. And her breasts had nearly doubled in width overnight. She often stood before her glass, bemused by her own reflection. Coarse hair had begun to grow thickly in tendrils between her thighs and under her arms. When she put her hands under her breasts and held them out as if to be admired by her own image, the nipples grew hard and flushed with blood, and she felt a warmth move down her body. She found such fondlings pleasant and imagined that such was the sort of sin the clergy warned against. She was comfortable with her own body. In spite of its unpredictable fluctuations, she began to trust its secret whisperings to her.

After the notoriety of Clara's death, Mary rarely came from her chambers, at least not when Anne was around. And Anne did not seek out her mother's company.

In an attempt to mend her ways, she willingly left off the docks and her old comrades, assumed a skirt and a dozen petticoats, allowed herself to be thrust unprotestingly into the tightest stays, and to all eyes seemed to welcome the mantle of young ladyhood about her shoulders. She spent two hours each day practicing her harpsichord, another two hours on needlepoint and French, and declared herself available for whatever else her father cared to bring on.

She even acted as hostess at a small gathering Fully pressed upon her—a tea for some visiting relatives of the Darcys, old friends of her parents. The Misses Darcy had been once-in-a-while scholars at the Widow Varnod's school, and Anne thought them the least unpalatable of all the young ladies present. She found herself looking forward to their visit, especially since they were bringing two sisters, cousins, who were visiting from Norfolk. Her mother made one of her rare appearances just long enough to plead a headache, then left Anne alone with Mrs. Darcy, her two daughters, and their two cousins. Only Fullborn attended Anne, sitting quietly in the corner of the room.

When the ordeal was over, Anne analyzed her performance objectively and felt she'd done quite well. The conversation rarely stagnated; the four girls were loquacious. Anne had memorized a dozen questions to ask her guests. No one seemed to notice that she became glaze-eyed at their answers except for Fullborn, who shot her a small twinkling grin now and again.

"Fully, is it necessary to go through such maneuvers simply to cultivate women friends? They speak of such dull things!"

Fullborn chided her softly. "They speak of their lives, lass."

"Well, their lives are pitifully small things, to be sure. When I asked them what they thought of the Yemassee threat to the South, they simply parroted back the digestions of their elders. And old Mrs. Darcy looked at me as if I'd just raised my hoops over my head to even suggest such a topic. As if war and murder and savages shouldn't concern young ladies." Anne laughed as a thought struck her. "I'd like to see Rachel Darcy fend off a war party with her little gloved hands! 'Why tell me, sir. Do you think it dreadful warm this month? Shall the hurricane season be upon us soon, do you suppose?' God's blood, what simps!" Anne ignored Fullborn's frown and her enormous sigh.

"I shall find friends in other ways, Fully. At balls and races and the like. No more tea parties for me, thank you."

By the age of fifteen, Anne was the sauciest, most provocative belle in Charles Town.

The young men found her more appealing than those delicate ladies she had been trained to imitate. When they escorted her on buggy rides or walked her in the gardens at a private ball, she had to pluck their hands away from her waist, her arms, and her breasts. Her low bodices plumped her body up invitingly. Her red-gold hair continually escaped her bonnet, winding its own way down her throat and into the hollow her breasts provided. Her eyes were deep green; her lips large and sensual. Several high-born young men of Charles Town sought her out, much to Cormac's delight, but few were able to arouse her passion. For the most part, she felt nothing but disdain for all their clumsy attempts to squeeze her bosom or rub against her as they passed. She was not surprised that the "best" families had sons who were as lusty as the wharf rats she'd run with. She began to feel some slight scorn for men in general. Each seemed to be ruled by his private parts, however much he might plead finer feelings.

At her pleading, her father hired a fencing master to teach her the intricacies of swordplay. When her mother argued that such an activity was inappropriate for ladies, Cormac wisely countered her.

"She needs some outlet for her energy, Mary. She's used to riding free over the fields at Bellefield. Here in the city she'll come to no good without some . . . similar exercise."

"She can walk. She can ride sedately, William. She can take the carriage out with Fullborn."

But Cormac knew that these would not appease Anne's active nature. Some part of him understood her, though he did not recognize why.

The fencing master, Paul LeVey, was a lithe and swarthy Frenchman with a courtly air and a provocative sneer. He quickly appraised his young student and found her equal to all he might ask of her. Within a month they were lovers.

Anne felt the magnetism between them and reveled in the tension she felt whenever she entered the drawing room where their lesson was to take place. Dressed in breeches and a soft white blouse, her hair bound in a tight knot, she knew she presented a striking picture. M. LeVey had the back of a field hand and the muscled legs of a seaman. Only his quick hands matched the fineness of his foil. One afternoon after each had eyed the other warily, they began their usual banter, circling their cork-tipped swords.

"*En garde, mademoiselle.* Watch my tip closely...*d'une épée, non?* Carefully, carefully...." He circled her cautiously, his eyes gleaming at her, a taunting smile playing over his mouth.

Anne felt a great surge of power go through her as she parried his thrusts, reaching for a vulnerable angle, looking for an opening. Once, he let her come too close, and she barely missed his shoulder. Then, he forced her back and recircled the room. He teased her, bantering with her, provoking her pride.

"Can you not reach me, *ma poulette?* Here I touch you and here and here!" He thrust firmly, moving faster than Anne could predict, flicking her with the tip of his sword first here on the shoulder and there on the thigh.

She circled him warily, watching him closely, trying to see the movements of his hands and his body before he made them. He twisted away. She lunged once, twice, and finally flicked his blouse under his breast.

"*Ah, monsieur!* You are touched! Here!" She circled him, laughing incautiously, her tension feeding her joy.

"*Eh bien, mademoiselle!* But *there,* I touch you once again! And there!" And he flicked off the tie that held her blouse closed at the throat. Her shirt fell open and exposed the roundness of her unbound breast. She thrust once more, then lunged under, too close to the curve of his arm, and he sliced his sword at her again.

She whirled just in time to avoid his blade. He never took his eyes from her body.

"You are beautiful, *ma poulette*. A Diana." LeVey breathed harder now, and Anne felt her own breath coming in ragged gasps as she feinted and dodged.

Suddenly Anne saw that his attention was distracted by her open blouse, and she lunged, flicking her sword at his own shirt, opening it just above his stomach. His eyes widened at her audacity.

"*Très bien, ma chère!*" He grinned and circled closer, flicking repeatedly at her blouse, her breeches, intimately touching her lightly over her body, tearing open the silk more and more until it hung from her shoulders. She felt warmth flood her loins and was giddy with the tension and excitement that fluttered in her belly.

"Come then, LeVey," she gasped. "Take what you can."

He threw down his foil and grabbed her shoulders, bending her back over the couch where she'd cornered herself, pressing his mouth to her throat. Anne felt her own pulse beat under his lips; her blood seemed to want to leave her body and go to his mouth. She curled her arms over his head and pulled his face to her breasts as, half naked, they grappled on the floor.

It was over in a moment. Anne came in waves of ecstasy at the instant he entered her, urgently, hot and wet, with a quick lunge as he had moved with his foil. She felt some pain, then a liquid bursting of heat within her that left her sweating and shaken. He hastily pulled her to her feet and glanced at the closed door between them and the rest of the house.

He whispered, "Have I hurt you, *ma poulette?*"

She looked up at him grinning, her hair wild about her face. "*Non, monsieur.*" She wrapped her arms around his neck and pulled his mouth to hers once more, feeding on his lips, plucking at them gently with her own. Under his mouth, she murmured, "I bested you on that match. Say it."

He pulled back his head and grinned at her, his breath warm on her face and still coming quick. "*Oui, poulette*. You bested me. I shall best you next time."

Anne pulled his chest to hers and gently rubbed her naked breasts on his, watching his eyes follow her nipples. "We shall see, LeVey."

Word quickly spread among the Charles Town beaux that the Cormac wench could be had—and not for the price of tender words and a marriage proposal—but for passion. If a man could only find the proper levers and handles to caress. And, surprisingly, her reputation as a woman of passion, as a spitfire, did little to dampen their ardor.

Now, if a young man approached her, she watched him carefully, observed him move, marked how he danced, how he touched her. When he asked her to join him in the garden away from the ball, she went willingly, silently, waiting for him to test his mettle against hers. If, when the opportunity came, he held her clumsily or she sensed that he did not know his way with women, she pushed him away with dignity. Sometimes she would even let a man maneuver her into the back of a darkened phaeton or beneath a secluded arbor, let him even explore her beneath her skirts . . . but if he performed awkwardly or did not arouse her, she refused him any further liberties.

Often Cormac found himself sequestered in his study with one or another of the eligible young stallions of the town, explaining that Anne was still too young to wed. When Cormac cautioned one young man of her tender youth, he was shocked to see the lad smirk.

"She's far older than her years, sir. Some are made to marry young, and Mistress Anne is such a one."

"You forget yourself, sir!"

"No. I will tell you the truth, sir. Your daughter will be made a mother before the year is out, with or without your blessing." And he turned on his heel, leaving Cormac red-faced and spluttering. Inside, he feared it must be so.

∾∾∾

STEPHEN ARCHER was the son of a wealthy planter and had been smitten by Anne the first time he saw her at the races. He approached her tentatively, in awe of her manner and her beauty, but was relieved to find that she welcomed his advances—at least at first. He saw her often, gradually working up his courage to insinuate a hand around her waist in the carriage, to brush his palm over her breast in the garden, to squeeze her arm when they walked dockside in the afternoon. To his surprise, she seemed to be waiting, calmly, for him to do or say whatever he had planned to do or say next. In a frenzy of desire, he invited her for a carriage ride knowing that if she accepted, it would be a signal that her desires matched his own. She agreed. When he had her alone, he reached for her and burst out clumsily, "Oh, Anne! I must have you or die! You must be my wife!"

She pulled back from his arms and looked up at him. She had enjoyed his caresses but had not yet decided whether he was going to be able to carry out their promise. She knew that he didn't know her at all. That in fact, none of the men who had grappled her knew her.

None of them wanted to know her, only to have her. She was not disappointed by such a discovery, but neither did she intend to give herself without due payment. So far, Stephen had done little to arouse her. Perhaps he was one who needed a bedding or two before he could relax. She opened her arms and drew him to her silently, ignoring his words. She took his hands and placed them gently on her breasts. She feared he might swoon, but instead he feverishly burrowed into her skirts. Actually, he quite adequately acquitted himself, she thought later. He had possibilities.

But Stephen was in love. He sensed that he would have to trap Anne to have her, and he could not bear to think of her in another man's arms. He spread the word about Charles Town that he had bedded her repeatedly, had rolled her behind barns and in her own father's house. Then he went to Cormac to offer his hand in marriage to protect Anne from herself and her reputation.

The hardest part of Stephen's plan was facing William Cormac.

"You say you have bedded my daughter, man? And you have the goddamned gall to tell me to my face!"

"I came to propose marriage, sir. To offer Miss Anne my life and my name and estate. I think it an honorable proposal and one which Anne might do well to accept, considering her...tendencies." He put his head down in what he hoped was a portrait of humiliation and some shame. "I will protect her, sir."

Cormac paced silently, casting an occasional baleful glare to the handsome stud before him. Oh, he'd heard the rumors, but half-hoped that they were only envious lies. Now, in his heart, he knew they must be so else this young hot-blood would not dare to make him such an offer. He sent for his wife. If their daughter must be bartered off in such a way, she should have some say. Mary was ushered into the room, her hair smooth, her dress subdued. Stephen could hardly believe that this sober matron was Anne Cormac's mother, so striking was their difference. He felt increasingly uncomfortable.

"My dear," Cormac began gruffly, "young Archer here has made an appeal for Anne's hand in marriage."

Cormac waited for Mary to protest that her daughter was too young, but she did not. She merely folded her hands and said, "Well. And 'tis a pretty honor for our Anne, to be sure. The Archers are a fine family. I shall leave it to you, William." She stood as if weary of the subject. "Sir," she said and bowed to the young man.

But Cormac would not let her loose so easily. He quickly took her arm and sat her down again. "My dear. Stay with us a while and listen to your daughter's fortune. There are details we should discuss together."

Archer felt himself to be in the middle of some intricate dance that he did not understand. Mary sighed and leaned against the chairback, gazing up at Cormac with resignation.

He went on, half to himself, half to his wife. "She is young, of course. But perhaps not too young. She is...old for her years." He pulled himself up with dignity and continued. "She is also beautiful, intelligent, well educated, and of considerable estate. Of course, Bellefield shall have to go to a future male heir, you understand, but Anne shall have an ample fortune settled on her when she weds."

Archer knew his role at this point and was relieved to be able to help move the conversation along more habitual lines.

"Anne herself would be sufficient estate for any man."

Cormac grinned wryly. "Ay. 'Tis true, lad." He looked an air of dismissal to Mary who rose once more to leave, again with her small bow.

"I shall send the lass to you, good sirs."

When Anne came in, she glowered at Stephen and at her father in turn. Both men were uncomfortable with her cold dignity.

"Sit, Daughter. Mr. Archer and I have been discussing your future fortune."

Anne did not smile but only gazed at her father, waiting.

Ignoring Archer, Cormac dropped to the chair next to Anne and took her hand. "Lass, if what he tells me is true, 'tis best you be wed as soon as we can post the banns. Your mother agrees. What do you say to the matter?"

She turned a frozen smile to her father. "What he says is true, Father. But give me leave to speak with him alone."

Cormac looked crestfallen at her admission but brightened when she offered to speak to Archer at all. "Ay, lass. That's a good plan. You call me back when you've set the date." He got up to leave and chuckled, "I guess I can safely leave her alone with you lad, eh?" and went from the room.

Anne turned to Archer, and the cold glass in her eyes turned to a hot glitter.

Ten minutes later Cormac was pulled back to the study by great crashes and the sound of muffled cries. He threw open the door and saw Anne—a hard-backed chair lifted over her head—bludgeoning the screaming young man to the carpet. He was whimpering and bleeding, and it took Cormac and two servants to pull Anne away from him. She was stiff and cold with anger and stalked from the room, never looking back at her erstwhile lover. She said only, "He who kisses and tells deserves a beating. Had I a brother, he'd have done no less."

That night, after Cormac had allowed his own anger to cool, he went to Anne's chamber. He found her sitting up in her bed, waiting for him.

"Lass, your mother took to her bed in a swoon when she heard."

"Ay, I know, Pa. She shouldn't have been told."

He once more reined in his temper, discomfited by her composure. He went on with his intended speech. "Anne. My Anne." He took her hands. "Have I sired a whore? Can you not find a single man to wed? 'Tis time you did. I'll not have a daughter shame me and your mother. You're the talk of all Charles Town, lass."

"If I married now," Anne said slowly, "I would rue the day and so would he. There's something in me that cannot stand a bridle, Pa. No matter how pretty."

Her father looked down at her hands, now soft from the months away from Bellefield. "Ah, lass. I've half a mind to send you back to the country. You got in less trouble there."

She smiled gently. "I was younger there. I expect I'd do the same wherever I was now, Pa."

"Well, I cannot leave the city now, at any rate, and you best stay here where we can watch you. At least a little. Why will you not marry?"

"I can't be some man's titmouse yet, Pa. And I've not found a man who makes me want to stay with him. When I marry, t'will be for more than love."

"What more is there, pet? Your mother and I took each other for love, and many said we were wrong to do so. What else would you be looking for?"

"A certain knowing, Pa. A certain strength. I don't even know for I've not found it yet. But until I do, t'would be wrong to bind myself to any man."

"Well, you best take care, Daughter. Or you'll find yourself with child and then, by God, I'll marry you to whoever'll have you, bag and baggage. Do you hear?"

"Ay, Pa. I'll take care."

Her father's face was stern. "I'll give you your head, lass. For one year. If in one year, you haven't found the man to wed, I'll find one for you. You can't dance with luck forever. People will forget and forgive the fancies and flights of a young girl, but if by sixteen you've not settled on one man, you shall settle on the one I choose. Agreed?"

"I could never agree to such a bargain, Father."

"Well agree or no, that's how it shall be."

He rose and left the room, and Anne knew he would fulfill his promise. She would be wed in a year, one way or another.

The next day Anne wasted no time but went directly down to the docks, followed by Fullborn as an emblem of propriety. There she waited calmly outside a tavern until a protesting Fully could bring back the information she sought. Fullborn returned muttering darkly of "rude vinegar-soaked sponges" and "the middle days of the moon." Now Anne knew what she needed to protect herself. She never again was able to feel her body was her friend, but she settled for understanding it as a complex adversary to be wooed, pleasured, and tricked into obedient barrenness.

A FREQUENT VISITOR to the Cormac town house was Captain Benjamin Hornigold. Hornigold was a successful privateer turned pirate. He handled his ships and crews as effectively as any Royal Navy captain and took no guff from the sea or his men. He was tall and strapping and, like Con Kesby, wore a single gold hoop in his ear.

Many Charles Town ladies vied for his attentions covertly, and the doxies at the wharf openly struggled among themselves to see who would share his bed when he was in port. Cormac had bankrolled several of Hornigold's early successful expeditions, and the two men considered themselves friends as well as partners. Hornigold's coat was embroidered with gold, and his hair laced with silver. He was a commanding figure at any table, and Cormac welcomed him to his own.

Anne heard again, as she had at Bellefield, of bags of diamonds, smoking cannons, ships in flames, the click of dice on deck, and the screams of a gale in the riggings. Hornigold entertained the Cormacs with tales of his ribald adventures. As he spoke, Anne could almost see the golden doubloons, feel the heat of a long Guinea night, hear cries of "A sail! A sail!" from the crew. "Ay," Hornigold said, " 'tis a sweet trade."

Anne often plucked at him with teasing questions, unconsciously drawing his attention with her open admiration and curiosity. Now that she was older, and Mary so withdrawn and silent, she was never sent from the table.

"And what, pray tell, is this vast difference between a pirate and a privateer? You make one sound a scoundrel and the other a hero," she bantered.

Hornigold laughed and slapped the table, ignoring Cormac's groan.

"Ay, mistress. Depends on whose ox is gored, of course! Pirates go where the profits be. If it's profitable to offer their services to nations at war—well then, a proper pirate will volunteer to do her routing for her, with a royal commission signed by the queen herself. And they'd be loyal privateers for the Crown. With letters of marque, you see. The queen, she saves some money, and the pirate, he gets a share of the loot. Money's like dung, you know. It must be spread about to be of any use."

In the pregnant pause that followed Anne drawled, "And then?"

"And then he turns back to pirate when the war is over and takes the British ship along with all the others as prey. Why, when Sir Henry Morgan led the raid on the Spanish for the queen, she dubbed him knight and governor of Jamaica, though he was as likely to go a rovin' against her own ships as the Spanish on the next tide. Ay, the line between pirate and privateer is a fine one. The smartest be pirates one day and heroes the next."

Anne watched him move and speak, barely hearing his words but fascinated by his manner. She was so weary of the dandified coxcombs of Charles Town, leering husbands, and old psalm-singing widows eager to disapprove of her every move. She had danced with most of them, kissed a few, and allowed some of them to explore her, experiencing it all with a detached mixture of curiosity and barely roused desire. Now, she recalled them with an impatient shrug.

But Hornigold stood head and shoulders above them . . . a man's man. His shoulders were broad and well-formed as a hunter's. He wore tight breeches, and his black curled hair seemed always damp with sea spray. Unlike the merchants who usually frequented her father's table, Hornigold's face was dark and lined, and he made no attempt to hide either his wealth—wearing gold and heavy stones on each finger—or his frankly appraising stares at Anne and her mother. It was no accident that she'd worn her amber-colored taffeta gown with the low bodice this night. And he'd been properly appreciative. His eyes had dipped into her cleavage several times, though he'd not said a word.

After the sour-cream tarts had been finished, Cormac lit his cigar and leaned back in his chair, smiling expansively at his women.

"Did you ever wish to marry, Captain? Surely you miss the comforts of home and wife and a fine daughter such as my Anne here."

Hornigold winked his eye like a mischievous parrot. "You've two beauties to be sure, sir."

Mary smiled softly and inclined her head slightly in acknowledgement. Anne rolled her eyes, waiting for the twist to come.

"But there's an old saying amongst rogues. When the candles are out, all women are fair. And I'd not give up all those beauties in darkened rooms for twice the lot at my table."

Mary's face turned cold, and Anne felt her own eyes widen. Hornigold seemed oblivious to the impact he'd had on the women.

He grinned. "And some of us would have them no other way."

At that, Mary could ignore his vulgarity no longer. With a chilly smile, she interrupted him. "Why Captain, you astound me. Surely, in all your travels, you must have seen more good unions than bad. And I would wager enough to convince you that good wives are plentiful. And faithful." She arched her brows. "Unfaithful beauties must certainly exist more in the minds of bachelors than in reality. I, for one, have never been unfaithful to my marriage bed."

Anne grimaced internally, embarrassed at her mother's piousness.

Emboldened by the wine and his reception, Hornigold refused to take the hint. "Plenty are, ma'am. And most with rogues like me."

Mary gasped. Cormac waded in, plucking defenses from the air and hastily making amends.

"A joke, merely a jest, my dear. I'm sure the captain means no offense."

Anne wondered if he had heard of her own reputation.

Hornigold smoothly interrupted his host. "Indeed no, madam, I was merely defendin' my bachelor state. Frankly, I find the utmost delight in women. All women. But they're at their best when they run free like the sea."

Anne could not resist tweaking him one more time. "You say you like your women free. How could any woman be free with a pirate? Pirates themselves are scarcely free. You buy women like slaves, I hear."

Mary's face assumed her usual blank smile when Anne said something she'd rather not hear. But Hornigold ignored her father's wince and answered her readily.

"I've never had to buy a woman yet, mistress." He smiled silkily. "And as for the freedom of the pirates, why I'd venture that democracy had its very start in the hold of some pirate vessel."

"Anarchy, you mean. Do you not force captured men to join you?"

"We never have to. There's plenty of volunteers clamorin' to share the profits. When we take a man on, the quartermaster gives him a paper saying we forced him just in case the matter should ever come up in court. And men who volunteer often ask the quartermaster to force them to save their necks at some future dates, should they be asked. I've seen a mate swear bloody oaths and curses and wave his cutlass—all in show—so the man could swear later, with witnesses, that he'd been pressed into service against his will. Mark me, lass. There's no freer life than the sea."

He paused and leered at Anne as if no one else was in the room. "You'd not abide an anchor, I wager, mistress. You'd buck and founder."

Cormac quickly changed the subject and asked Hornigold about the earthquake at Port Royal.

"Ay, 'twas a mighty roll. But the ship rode the swells like she was born to it, unlike some which heaved and broke on the rocks. I'd rather 'av been on her decks than on the docks, for they sank 'neath fifty feet o' water. What they say is true—the Devil loves his own best. And the sea loved me as well. Rocks me to sleep each night like a favored child." He grinned. "Like a landless gull, we pirates be. At nightfall I furl my sails, lay me to rest, and under.

my pillow herds of walrus an' whales rush by." He inclined his head towards Cormac. "Though I do look forward to a chance at clean linens and a soft bed, and I thank you for your hospitality, sir."

Anne became instantly alert, turning private pictures over and over in her head. It was not the first time Hornigold had stayed the night under their roof, nor would it be the last. But it was the first time she cared. She carefully arranged her features in a casual placidity, disguising her interest lest someone notice.

The women left the table so that the men could relieve themselves comfortably in the chambers provided for them.

Once in her chamber, Anne removed her clothes and held the candle close to her face. She stood before the mirror, watching her movements, loving the feeling of air on her body. A specter of a smile played about her mouth. She shivered as the light nightgown fell over her body, grazing her limbs. She knew that part of her allure was her innocence. And tonight, as she pictured him waiting for her, she felt trembling and virgin as any maiden.

She turned before the glass and examined her legs. They were long and lithe, but they could never be shown. Some women even considered their limbs unsightly, Anne knew, and wore their petticoats even when bedding with their husbands. Anne guessed that her mother had never strutted naked before her father, though their lust for each other had been obvious when she was young. The rules for love seemed suddenly as restricting and intrusive as Widow Varnod's chilly parlor.

She thought of Ben's talk of the sea and felt a strong yearning to be away from Charles Town, off to some place where she could run, speak, and dress as she pleased.

She eased the door open. The pirate captain was under the sheets, sitting up, and the bed seemed small beneath him. His massive chest loomed black against the white linen, and his prominent muscles were clearly outlined by the moonlight. As she stood in the doorway a deliciously musty odor wafted towards her. Hornigold's eyes glittered as they feasted on the sylphlike image of Anne in her gossamer-thin nightdress. He extended his hand in a courtly gesture.

"I'd have waited all night, lass."

Anne felt panic thrill down her legs. Now that she'd made the step, it seemed ridiculously dangerous. If her father should hear a sound... but she glided quietly to the bed and took his hand without a word. He looked tense, almost predatory. He wore the smile of the wolf just before it closed hungry jaws on the rabbit. Anne trembled as she recklessly slipped her gown over her head and moved over on top of him naked, watching his eyes. They turned soft as he moaned in pleasure at the touch of her skin. She put her hand on his thigh where his muscles tensed. With a sure grip, he rolled over and stretched himself on top of her. Hornigold lowered his mouth to her face. He kissed her gently on the eyes, then on the lips; one hand cupped her breast softly. He pulled back and looked at her intently.

"You're an intoxicating wench. Do you know what it means to be here with me?"

"Ay, Captain. I do... and as I please."

He laughed low in his throat. "By Christ, I wager you do."

Those were the last coherent words they spoke for a long while. She moved down, and he leaned into her. Such a hard man, she thought. She eased her hand up to his groin, outside the sheet, and felt the force and fierce heat of his member. She thought of him inside her, moving hotly within her, and she shivered. His fingers seemed to leave cool traces on her skin like fingers of the wind. She put her arms around him and slid down on the bed, pulling him on top of her. She pressed her mouth to his, crushing her lips and her body against him, licking, biting softly. Her breasts felt taut and full. He lowered his lips to her stiffened nipples. Her belly fluttered like a caged bird. She felt all fluid and heat, like open wet palmetto leaves swinging in the sun. Her hands roamed over him, stroking, squeezing. She kissed the corners of his mouth, and he quickly, eagerly, returned the kisses, full and hungry on her open lips.

The moonlight seemed to love Anne. It caressed her skin, fell softly over her hair, added luster to her eyes. She felt she had bcome a night creature, felt Hornigold was melting into her, blending into her own skin as he cupped her firm buttocks in both hands and found her warm pubic lips. He spread her damp thighs and licked her moist center, opening those secret folds with his mouth. Finding her hidden core, he held her arms to her sides, pulled her to him, and softly penetrated her with his tongue. She gasped with pleasure and writhed under his mouth. She arched her back, clutched his shoulders with both hands, thrashed, and whimpered ecstatically. She had never felt so possessed in her life. Her quivers grew to tremors and then to quakes of throbbing, wrenching waves of delight. She gasped for breath, tossed her head like a wild thing, and cried out softly, riding the waves within her on a crest of foam, her lithe muscles contracting, relaxing, contracting, relaxing, until finally she was spent. She collapsed within his arms.

He raised his head, kissed her heaving belly, and then moved up over her, teasing her hard nipples with his tongue, smiling softly at her in the darkness. She reached down and grasped the hardness of him. Suddenly, she was filled with a new and heady tension. She pulled him into her. He filled her completely, and their eyes locked; she felt him stare into her, through her to her soul. She closed her eyes as he began to move rhythmically inside her. She sensed him holding back, but also knew that he could not wait for long. She felt him tensing inside her, felt his tight slickness hot against her skin. Her breasts crushed under him, but she was not aware of his weight. She lifted her hips and ground her body into his. As he thrust faster, he began to spurt uncontrollably, laving her insides thickly, in her deepest, darkest reaches. As he emptied himself, she felt a vast tide of joy fill her and her contractions matched his own.

Later they lay side by side, under the damp sheets, her hand resting on his furred chest. Anne no longer thought of the other people in the house, of other people in her life. She knew she was changed from this moment on. I've had nothing but boys in my life, she thought.

He broke the silence. "You were worth waiting for, lass. I wager you didn't learn such tricks in Dame Varnod's school."

She rolled over and trailed her fingers over his ribs, watching as slow goosebumps rose on his flesh at her touch. "You made it happen for me, Ben."

He grinned. "Pretty words, Anne. Save them for those who need 'em."

" 'Tis the truth," she whispered, arching her brows in mock indignation. "I've had boys and their clumsy thumping in cramped phaetons. They've never moved me at all."

"I don't believe it for a moment, but I'll let it pass." He played with her soft breasts, tweaking the nipples, and then asked her softly, "Do you need to know what'll happen next, lass?"

"Nay," she smiled.

"Good," he said. "For no one does, and I can't promise you much."

"Pa says I must marry in a year, or he'll find a man for me himself."

He pulled back and looked at her thoughtfully. "Is that a proposal?"

She laughed for the first time since she'd come to this room.

"No, Captain. I'm not ready to be reined, as you said. And when I am, I'll choose my own master. Fine a trader as you are, I doubt my father would want me to take you for a husband. But we can share a bed when you like."

He took her in his arms again. "That suits me, lass. But my father told me never choose a mare with a blanket on." And he drew the sheets back slowly, gazed at her body, and began to caress her skin once more.

THE MORNING STAR was rising in the east as Anne's shadow traced a hasty retreat along the wall and back to the safety of her own room. She slipped under her sheets, which felt cold and virginal after the warm damp linens she'd just left. She pondered this night's actions. She had felt lust before, but never such passion. The thought of forsaking these sensations forever was unbearable. The threat of marriage to some distant "gentleman," some safe choice of her father's, loomed ahead of her like a sort of death. Still, she felt more in control of her destiny than ever before.

After a time, Anne awaited Hornigold's visits as eagerly as she yearned for her freedom, indeed with the same part of her mind. She began to fancy herself almost in love.

She accompanied him to the waterfront, on his arm like a grand lady in silks, attracting the envious stares of tavern bawds from one end of White Point to the other. Charles Town was growing quickly, spreading back from the sea with eager fingers into the mainland. Anne no longer needed to dress as a boy on the docks or to wear her hair in a pug. Women were beginning to be seen in many parts of town that they had not frequented before. Indeed, it was unlikely she could have passed for a boy anymore.

As if by osmosis, the young swains of the city seemed to know that Anne had an ultimatum, a paternal edict to fulfill. And they flooded, one by one, to the drawing room on Bay Street. But Anne was drawn to none of them. Some of the finest families in the country sent their best prospects, but she could no longer imagine herself tied to a plantation, mistress of a household of slaves and children. The only slave she wanted near her was Fullborn, not slave but servant and white-skinned as herself, ever silent and devoted. Oh, Fully fussed at Anne continually about her dress and behavior as she always had, but at least she was loyal. She never carried tales to her mother and never prated at Anne more than she could bear. In fact, she was the only woman Anne had ever trusted in her life. It was she who taught her to stain her brows permanently dark with tannin from the roots of the cypress tree; she who told her to use the seeds and bark of the toothache tree to make a hot astringent to ease her pain when she ate too many macaroons; and she who always looked the other way when Anne slipped in late from a carriage ride.

But Fullborn did not approve of Captain Benjamin Hornigold. When Anne left the house in his presence, she said nothing and only compressed her lips into a tight, grim line, glaring balefully at everyone who crossed her path—everyone except Anne. The other servants learned to stay out of her way when the mistress walked on Hornigold's arm.

Cormac seemed to draw an invisible shade over Anne's willful disregard of propriety. Anne waited tensely to be yanked into his study for yet another angry reproach, but he said nothing. His own problems with Mary, who grew more irascible and physically frail by the day, consumed his attention.

The Green Gull was Hornigold's favorite watering hole when in port, and Anne often sat at a corner table with him, watching the men drink themselves into oblivion in the arms of willing whores. One golden afternoon, the captain introduced her to a man he called "the finest smuggler on the docks." Unlike most of the men who frequented Hornigold's table, this young rogue paid scant attention to Anne. His name was James Bonny.

He barely glanced at her but only shifted in his seat so as to present her his back. Anne eyed him indignantly. His frock coat had an expensive cut, but his slim shoulders barely filled it. She wondered if he'd had it off a friend. He wore a gold cuff on his right wrist, and his hands had the look of a man who was more used to counting money than wrenching the wheel of a schooner. His piercing gray eyes studiously avoided her. But as he raised his glass, his eyes swiveled towards her, and she felt an electric current pass between them.

His yellow hair curled about his shoulders, and Anne was surprised to find herself wondering what it would feel like to run her fingers through those blond waves. She quickly turned her smile on Hornigold and her shoulder to the young man.

As Hornigold rambled on about his business, she noticed that Bonny's face rarely changed. The young man seemed restless and would not linger over amenities as the elder pirate wished. He listened carefully, relentlessly ignoring her. Anne felt her anger rise and stared at him all the harder. For some reason, it had become increasingly important for James Bonny to notice her, even to want her. Bonny, however, did not suffer her attention gladly.

He shrugged his shoulders like a horse plagued by flies. "I wonder you bring such a . . . lady to talk business, Captain. She ought to be home safe in her parlor."

Hornigold chuckled. "This lady goes where she likes, Bonny. And glad I am of it, too."

Bonny stared back at her now frankly. "She's a handsome piece. Does she speak?"

Before Hornigold could even glower, Anne snapped, "Ay, sir. She can speak. And you're apt to rue your question if you call me that again." Her eyes flashed.

"Handsome?" Bonny's lips showed just the glint of a smile.

Anne glared at him, disdaining to answer.

"My mother often told me, handsome is as handsome does," Bonny continued unconcerned. "Your own would take to her bed if she saw you here."

"Are we talking of mothers now, or can we finish our trade!" Hornigold hollered impatiently and turned the conversation back to his goods. When he finished, he said, "I sail on the tide, Bonny."

Anne glanced at him in surprise, for she had no idea he was leaving so soon.

Hornigold smiled sideways at her and then said, "And you can deliver my gold to Mistress Cormac at her father's house on Bay.

"And Bonny," he leaned forward intently, "the bag best not be light, or I'll be visiting Tilda Redhose's rooms soon's I beach next. And if I find you there, I'll break both your thievin' arms."

Anne's eyes widened, and she watched Bonny carefully. He stiffened for an instant, and then he laughed, a forced, boyish chortle. "Your gold will be safe, Captain. At least until it reaches the lady's hands."

As they left the tavern, Anne asked Hornigold when he'd return.

He took her chin in his callused hand.

"Don't look to me for wedding papers, miss. I'd not share your halter. For I could never hold you—nor could any man, I believe."

Anne gazed up at him, her eyes glowing green in the sunlight. "You fool!" she grinned. "You think you know a woman because you've seen her naked, do you? The man I want will hold me just as surely as I hold him—but *you're* not that man and never will be, Captain Ben!" She laughed then, as he picked her up and swung her around.

A WEEK PASSED, and Anne was called to the parlor to receive James Bonny. He was dressed more elegantly than before, and he bowed deeply over her hand.

"So, you can offer a decent bow, sir." She said daringly, brave enough to mock him on her own turf.

"I hadn't realized you came to the Green Gull seeking bows, milady." He smirked and waited for her to sit. Instead, she led him to the veranda where they could attend to their business privately. Once there, she held out her hand, watching him. He bowed insolently again and pulled a small bag from his coat, dropping it into her palm.

She heard the chink of coins and resisted the impulse to count them. He turned to go.

"Stay a moment, sir," she said quickly, not at all sure why she spoke, unconsciously letting her eyes wander over his body . . . his yellow hair.

He turned smoothly and arched an eyebrow in question.

"I would ask a favor." Anne persisted.

He eased into a chair languorously, watching her. She blushed slightly under his scrutiny and looked away over the garden. "As you know, Captain Hornigold is at sea. I need to go to the waterfront at times. Often, in fact. And I dislike walking the docks alone."

"You mean, you want to go to the Green Gull." He grinned. "And of all of the escorts in the city, you chose me?"

She bit back a sharp retort. "I'm told you know the docks well."

"And the doxies . . ." he laughed. "What else do you know of me, mistress, that you'd walk on my arm so brazenly?" His voice was hard, but his eyes were soft.

She made her own voice match his in willfulness. "I know you live off whores, buy cheap and sell dear. And, I know Captain Hornigold trusts you. Because he does, I choose to as well. I'll not be cloistered in this house just because he's sailed. I need . . . no, I *want* to go to the docks, say, twice a week. Will you be here for me, or not, man?"

He laughed again, low in his throat. "Ay, I'll be here. 'Twill cost you, mistress, but I'll barter with you for my services."

"And what will it cost?"

"That remains to be seen," he said smartly.

For the next month, James Bonny appeared regularly at her door, always immaculately dressed, to escort her anywhere she wanted to go. As she grew to know him, she was more and more drawn to his wry grin, his insolent shrugs, and his general irreverence towards all that Charles Town held dear. He made her laugh with sly stories, circulating the waterfront, about the best-placed ladies in the county. He listened quietly as she told him that her father swore to marry her off within the year, unless she could find someone suitable. And he mocked her lightly as she tried to describe her father's definition of "suitable."

Gradually, Bonny's cynical defenses gave way to grudging

admiration as Anne shone on him like a determined sun. One day, as they strolled towards the house, he stopped and stared wistfully at the imposing brick columns. He turned and gazed into her eyes. "And what then does a fine lady want with me?"

Anne pulled him into the shadows of the wisteria, heedless of any eyes that could spy on her from the veranda. She wrapped her arms around his neck hesitantly, watching his eyes for permission, for she could not take his sneered rejection again.

"James, I want to help you."

"Help me?" he grinned.

"Ay," she said. "You could be a merchant in your own right, without taking alms from such as Hornigold or pocket money from whores."

"And how am I to accomplish this grand dream, eh? By taking alms from you instead?"

"I've enough for us both, James. In time, your ship will come in . . . your own ship, James. Not another's."

"And what would Hornigold say about his woman offering to stake another man's venture?"

Anne dropped her arms and looked searchingly into his eyes. "I am my own woman, James. I was when I took up with the captain and I am now . . . that I leave him. It's you that I want."

"Why?"

"You ask too many questions of a lady, man. Do you not want me?"

His hands eased around her waist warily. "Ay. What would a man have to do to have you?"

"Again, too many questions, lad," she said throatily, and she led him deeper into the shadows and tentatively went into his arms, losing all hesitancy when she felt his mouth on hers.

Anne flickered about James Bonny like a bright moth. She cajoled him, petted him, and hungered for him—but she did not bed him. Each time their lust for each other led them close to a rousing consummation, he would pull away and declare that he had too much respect for her to so compromise her future. Anne could not bring herself to upbraid him, for she was touched by his unusual gallantry. She sensed a quick intelligence under his rude demeanor. Often, when he looked at her, she felt he knew her better than she knew herself.

Anne guessed correctly that Ben would take his ousting with a laugh. But when her father heard of Anne's latest companion, he yanked her into the study for a final, furious edict.

"Daughter, your time is up and so is my patience!"

"Father, you gave me a year. It's been but half of that."

"You were to find a suitable mate and instead you waltz around in broad daylight with a tavern pimp! You scare off any decent man who might be willing to wed you!"

"Pa—"

"Do not interrupt me, Anne! I shall hear no more! I'd hoped you'd come to your senses and find a man worthy of your status. But 'tis clear you have no eyes for gentlemen, only for poxy bastards and tavern whores. I'll not give you any more time, or rope, to hang yourself. You're more than fifteen, nigh a woman, and half a devil besides. I'll not share your shame, nor will your mother. You've all but killed her with your brazen ways. I've given you my best, and you've thrown it in my face! Like a wanton!" He slammed his fist on the table and then brushed his hair back with a shaking hand.

"Well, 'tis done. George Pringle has come to me, offering his son. 'Tis not quite the match I'd hoped, but you're lucky to get an offer at all, brazen as you've been." He opened his hands hopefully. "Think of it, lass. He's a sober, healthy boy with a good name and will come to a large estate in time."

Anne felt she would gag on her rage; she could not speak.

Her father met her indignation head-on. " 'Tis done! I shall hear no more! 'Tis a fine match, and you'll not be offered better!" He turned away from her searching white face. "Your mother and I are agreed."

"Oh, are you then?" Anne's voice was low and husky. "It is all arranged, is it?" It took all her self-control to lift her head and leave the room, quietly closing the door behind her.

She fled the house, running to the room at the docks she'd rented for James. She burst into his chamber. He stared at her in alarm, caught with his hand in midair, pouring a tumbler of rum. She grabbed the bottle from him and took a quick gulp, grimacing. She felt cold in spite of the liquor's heat. "My father's gone back on his word!"

James stiffened and glanced involuntarily to the door.

She smashed the glass to the floor. "No, you fool! He said he'd give me a year! A year to wed someone "suitable." Curse his "suitable" to hell and back again! And now, before I can do it, he's betrothed me to some idiot boy who needs both wife and nursemaid!" She stalked the floor, switching her skirts in frustration. Suddenly, she stood erect, her eyes flashing. "But I've found my man, suitable or no. James, we must run away!"

"To where?" he gasped.

"To Bath!" she shouted, grabbing both his hands and whirling him around. "We can be married before he can stop us!" She stopped and held him, gazing into his eyes. "If you will, we can be happy, James. If not, I'll be on a packet ship in a fortnight, and you'll be back in some whore's bed. Will you do it, man?"

"Shouldn't we think a bit, Anne? . . ."

"There's no time to think, James. Just speak! I'll take some of mother's jewels for a dowry, and by the time he can catch us, we'll be legally wed. Are you game?" She held him in a passionate grip, her hair falling down about her shoulders, "Oh, James," she cried, "When the risk is out, life's not worth the trouble. Aren't *I* worth the trouble?" And she sealed her lips to his.

*T*HE OLD PREACHER at Bath was startled out of sound sleep by a heavy pounding at his door. The couple in the lamplight looked an incongruous pair—the bride dressed in a fine traveling suit of expensive brocade, a bulging valise at her side, the groom equally feathered in a luxurious coat—but each was bedraggled and bore the signs of a long journey. The press of coins in his palm and their hurried reassurances convinced the clergyman to do his duty... and Anne was married to James Bonny.

They spent their wedding night at an inn outside of Bath. Bundled into a small chamber together, the newlyweds faced each other almost reluctantly. It seemed that their passion had fled now that they were united legally. All that Anne really wanted in the world was to sleep. Preferably alone. But Bonny was determined to play out his role as eager groom. The vows he'd just heard her demurely recite seemed to fire him to a new arrogance.

He waited until they were alone and installed within the best chamber, a cramped and dimly lit wedding-night closet. Then, to Anne's amazement, he approached her like a swaggering bull. He boldly drew her into his arms and put both hands on her bosom with a grin of proprietary satisfaction.

"So, wife you be. Of James Bonny, Esquire. There are worse berths you might have picked."

She smiled up at him, rather pleased by his attentions but wary, too. "Ay. And better, too. But wed we are, and no one can say nay to that."

James kissed her then, hard and wet, moving his mouth slowly and insistently from side to side over hers. She did not feel the sly, warm, curling response in her stomach and throat that she usually felt when he kissed her, only fatigue. The tongue next, she thought.

But under his lips she sensed a hard smile, an almost feral power. Startled, she drew back, trying to see into his eyes.

"Don't play the coy maiden now, Anne. You bound and bought me. I'm yours now, will you or no. And I'm ready to see firsthand what sort of mare I'm to gallop through life." He picked her up bodily—Anne wondered briefly where he'd got his newfound strength—and in that instant she did not struggle. He tossed her on the bed, and her skirts flew up to her thighs. Before she could choose to go to his arms willingly or resist, he was on her, ripping at her gown, burrowing coarse hands beneath her skirts, and tearing open her linen, groping for her sex as if she herself had long denied him. Any spark of desire was quickly drowned by her quick rage at such a bruisingly rough tumble. She struggled to push him off her, but he jammed one knee between her thighs and opened her legs forcefully while he pinned her arms above her head.

"Get off me, you fool!" She panted with fury, and her breasts heaved. They were scratched and mauled by his hands. "We'll both enjoy it a hell of a lot more if you'll let me—"

But he only squeezed his eyes shut and gripped her all the tighter. Anne wondered whom he was mounting; it was surely not she for he never once looked in her face. In a half-choked growl, he cut her off.

"No! You've had it all your own way! This one will be my way! You're wife now and mine! And I'll make you know it!"

In his angry passion he was stronger than she, and though she tried to throw him off, he forced his hip between her thighs and with one free hand pushed his member inside her. Anne instantly quieted. She knew that any further struggle would only give him more to savor. She lay inert, her body passive, her will defying him through every pore. He seemed not even to notice her flaccidness, but only pumped away briefly, arched his back, cursed hoarsely, and fell, spent upon her.

When she knew he was done and she felt the power fade from his grip, she rolled him off abruptly. She felt violation, like a poker-red infection at the core of her being.

He smiled at her, and she sensed pride in his now-soft solicitude. "Did I hurt you?"

Anne laughed in spite of her repugnance. "Hurt me? With that mollywort? 'Twas over and done before I knew you were there."

But she saw his brow tighten and feared a new assault. She took a new tack. "Why did you take me in such a way, James? I'd have come to you willingly."

He hid his face under his arm, his mouth sullen. She waited, but he said nothing. The tender inner lips of her private parts still burned from his coarse friction. But she fought down her resentment and reached over to stroke his arm, sensing that he needed her compliance. She wondered briefly what he feared, to be such a bully.

"You're my wife now. I can take you as I please."

She kept her patience with an effort. "Is that what you want then of a wife?"

"Ay. And there's plenty who like it."

She shrugged, her scorn showing now. "Well, you picked yourself the wrong woman, lad."

"I didn't pick you, mistress. You picked *me*. And a good bargain it was for you, too. You used me just as surely as I used you." He scowled. "Well, the fine lady has her mount now. And a good ride into the bargain."

"Oh?" She made as if to rise from the bed, tossing her hair behind her.

He grinned at her, reaching for her again. She slapped his hands away viciously. He fought her down, heaving his body over hers, and pulled her hair back on the bed so she could scarcely move. His voice lowered silkily. "Ay. And if you'd settle down and decide to be a woman instead of so hell-bound manly, you'd enjoy it yourself."

She laughed angrily.

He glared at her. "I'll be husband, wife. And I'll be master besides!" He reached for her once more—and this time, realizing that she must endure him to tame him, and that she was not yet ready to let him go, she willed herself to relax and bide her time.

Mr. AND MME James Bonny took the overland route home to Charles Town, in no hurry to face Cormac's wrath. After nearly two weeks' absence, Anne found herself standing outside the house on Bay Street, a plain gold band on her hand and no great sense of elation in her heart.

The house was shuttered, the windows draped in black crêpe. Anne knocked, while James waited in the carriage, unwilling to come inside until he knew what his reception might be. To her surprise, Fullborn answered the door. She said nothing, only put her arms around Anne's shoulders and drew her inside. Anne stiffened for the shock she knew was coming.

"Fully, why is the house shuttered?"

Fullborn shook her head. "Yer mother's passed, child. They buried her yesterday. Yer father's at Bellefield mournin' her like a mad thing."

"Mother's . . . dead? How?" Anne's face was rigid; her hands shook as they flew to her face as if to ward off the words.

"She miscarried the babe. The doctor couldn't save her this time."

Anne's head whirled in confusion. "The babe? I didn't even know she was with child!"

Fullborn's face was pained. "Ay, lass. I know. Few did, save her woman and yer father. She took to her bed after you left and we heard. . . . She didn't have the fight in her."

"Jesus, Fully! Oh, Mother!" She fell into Fullborn's arms, and her stomach cramped with pain. She felt a deep sob well up in her, but she choked it back.

"And Father? Does he know I'm wed?"

Fullborn's face grimaced shortly and then smoothed, bland as any field nigger's. "Ay, lass. The news that Cormac's daughter was wed to . . . such a man as James Bonny traveled fast."

Anne slumped in a chair, bewildered. Mother dead. A babe . . . another babe . . . both gone. She realized how little she had seen her mother in the last few months and wondered, her mind erratic, if she would notice a difference in the house now that she was gone. But her father... her father must be torn by grief. And then she remembered James. Abruptly, she stood.

"I must go to Pa, Fully. To Bellefield."

"He'll not see you, lass."

Anne brushed her aside absently, her mind already on the reunion. "Not see me? Of course, he'll see me. He needs me."

"No, lass. He...he thinks you killed yer mother."

Anne's eyes widened in shock. "I? Killed Mother?"

"Ay. With yer elopement. 'Tis but the ravings of a broken heart, but he's stubborn and says he will have ye arrested on sight. 'Tis best not to go until—"

Anne's sorrow shrieked into life as anger. "I *will* go to Bellefield, Fully. Wed or no, I am his daughter and he will see me! He needs me! We need each other. I loved Mother, but you know she has been dying for years.... 'Tis hard, but Father must go on and make a new life. We both must." She turned and opened the door, her hand hesitating on the latch. She looked out at the waiting carriage, her voice low.

"Did she suffer?"

Fullborn bowed her head, her eyes turned away. "They tried to save the babe. The doctor couldn't get it out of her belly... whole. She died two days later."

Anne moaned and her eyes misted over—the street rose and fell as if in a heat wave. She left and closed the black door softly behind her.

BELLEFIELD WAS CLOSED and silent as though no one had lived there for years. Anne knocked, but the door remained fast. She called out, but no one answered. James pulled at her arm and suggested that they go and send a letter instead, but Anne yanked her arm away.

"Father! It's Anne! I know you're there! Open the door!"

There was only a deathly silence. Then she heard her father's muffled voice shout feebly, "Get off my land! Get out of my sight!"

He must be drunk, she thought. She glanced at the slave quarters but could see no movement.

"Father, you must see me! I mourn her, too!"

"That's fine talk from a murderess! And a thief! You took your mother's jewels. You broke her heart. I warned you! You killed her, and I'll no more of you! Go to hell, you and your pimp!"

"Father! Open this door and listen to me! We'll break it down if we have to!" She pounded hard and listened as the hollow echoes rang through the vast halls. Suddenly a shot blasted out of an upstairs window, and the wooden porch splintered at her feet.

James cursed and jerked back, crouching under the stairs. Anne glared at him, her anger rising like a delicious fire.

"Father, I know you'll not shoot me! I'll stay here until you open this door!" She banged again. The next shot buzzed by, dangerously close to James' ear. He shouted more curses at Anne, bounded down the steps, and slid behind a tree, cowering.

Cormac's face appeared at the upstairs window. He looked a demented, crazed thing—his hair wild, his eyes red and puffed. He shrieked down at his daughter, "The militia's looking for you and that whelp!" She heard him pacing mindlessly.

"Your mother would have died before she'd let that dog in her house! I'll shoot myself afore I'll pass a farthing to a whore and her pimp! A gibbet at White Point is where you'll end, and I'll not watch it!" He slammed the shutter, and Anne heard the sounds of reloading from upstairs. A silent sob choked her throat, and she shook her head in disbelief.

She heard a twig snap behind her, and Charley Fourfeathers appeared at her shoulder. She almost cried out his name, but he silenced her with a finger to his lips. She followed him away from the house with James trailing behind her. Charley had two cabins, one by the river and one in the woods. She stumbled along the paths, numb with shock, plucking the honeysuckle vines off her arms, glancing behind her to see that James could keep up. It was dusk when they reached Charley's place.

"What he say be true," Charley said. "Master Cormac signed the warrant. Soldiers find you here and you be jailed or worse. For murder, he say. And theft."

James interrupted him scornfully. "They'll never take me. I'll join a press and get to the islands 'til they forget my name."

Charley silently turned gray eyes on him. Anne felt her viscera surge with contempt. She grabbed his collar and then, with a weary gesture, let it go. She wished she had the nerve to shake him as savagely as she wanted.

"Damn you," she said. "You wed me and bed me quickly enough. Now, you'll stand at my side like a proper man or I swear I'll tell them you abducted me, and you'll not leave Charles Town with your skin!" She turned from him. "Charley, can we go north?"

"Ay. But Cormac has friends in all ports. He be mad enough to haul you home in chains."

Anne sat down on the floor of the cabin, searching her mind for a solution. Finally, a tight smile played on her lips. Con Kesby... her father's old friend. And hers as well, she hoped. She sent Charley to the docks to find him.

That night, Kesby came to the cabin in the woods and offered to take the newlyweds to New Providence Island on his sloop, passage free.

Bonny spat disgustedly. "New Providence! That's a pisshole for dogs! There's nothing lives there but Brethren and bandits!"

"Would you rather face the king's soldiers?" Anne asked quietly.

Con Kesby smirked and turned to Anne, his eyes narrowed and shadowed. "Ye'll find no king's men on New Providence, lass, an' the Brethren take care o' their own. 'Twill give yer father a chance to becalm himself an' withdraw his warrant. But mark me, 'tis a lair for outlaws." He watched her intently, more openly than he had over her own table when she was but a girl. Anne was suddenly aware that she had few choices at the moment. She tightened her jaw stubbornly and felt something inexorable open its fist inside her and spread tingling fingers from her stomach out to her arms and legs.

"What do ye say, lass? Yer not afraid, are ye?" Kesby asked quietly, glancing at Bonny and then back to Anne.

Anne felt weary and far older than her sixteen years. "When do we sail?"

He grinned at her, his eyes gleaming in the shadows. "We sail at midnight. On the tide."

"We'll be there."

When the moon was up full, Anne and Bonny made their way over long-familiar trails to the Cooper River. Charley Fourfeathers had a small canoe waiting. Silently, they paddled down the black water, past the houses of Charles Town and the plantations of Goose Creek, past the bastions of all Anne had ever known and out to the breakwater where Kesby's sloop was tethered. As soon as Anne and James were aboard, the anchor was lifted, and the ship set quiet sail for New Providence.

PART THREE

New Providence Island,
1716

I have observed, onboard a ship, how men and women easily give way to their instinct of flirtation, because water has the power of washing away our sense of responsibility, and those who on land resemble the oak in their firmness behave like floating seaweed when on the sea.

RABINDRANATH TAGORE
Letters to a Friend

Adam must have an Eve to blame for his faults.

Old Italian Proverb

FOR ANNE, the sea was as a long-remembered womb. She watched the dappled coastline recede as the darkness swallowed Charles Town. As Kesby's sloop broke away into open sea, the smells of the land—ripe fruit, boggy lowlands, rotting fish, tarred wood, and green palmettos—all faded and were replaced by a crisp tang of salt and spray. The genuine smell of green, a cold, foam smell found only on the open sea, replaced the warm, vegetative odors of land. Anne felt exhilarated once out and away from the searching lights of the city. She was relieved to turn her face to the open sky and see only the twinkling of a million stars.

The sea was her main, indeed her only consolation in this banishment. She had left with little more than her personal clothing, a few toilet articles, and some of her mother's jewelry. No longer Anne Cormac, Mistress Cormac, belle of Charles

Town, daughter of Bellefield—but only Anne Bonny. Bereft of a fortune and a family. And yet, she did not feel so much regret as relief. She would have preferred her fortune and her freedom, too, but if she had to lose one to gain the other, then she felt it was a fair trade. At least for now. Besides, in her heart she knew she could move her father to compassion if and when she was ready to return alone—but never on the arm of James Bonny. For now, she would ride the current wherever it might lead.

As the Atlantic Ocean gradually ebbed into the Caribbean, Anne watched the sea change color from deep blue to cerulean. Around the fringes of the Florida islands she saw the ocean's currents melt into translucent jade green, revealing many feet down the pure skeletal whiteness of the shifting sandbars, the waving brilliance of a thousand underwater plants, and the sudden flashing underbelly of the barracuda. The shores of the cays they passed were scalloped with thousands of coves and bays, inlets and anchorages, ponds and hurricane holes—some with hospitable, gently sloping beaches and some with jutting reefs lurking just below the surface, alive with layers of poisonous, spiny sea urchins.

Kesby's sloop, the *Shark*, was a sleek and handsome tern over the waves. An ideal pirate craft, she had a spear of a bowsprit almost as long as her hull. Stabbing through the water, this bowsprit held a parade of canvas that made her swifter than any schooner or heavily laden brigantine. In a favorable wind she could mount a square topsail for an extra burst of speed up to eleven knots. Not too small for battle, the *Shark* drew eight feet of water and carried a crew of sixty men and fourteen cannon. She could still slip in and out of channels where a man-of-war would founder.

Kesby's crew was the usual motley tribe Anne had seen down at the docks, yet they seemed as one in their general admiration of their captain and each other. Their camaraderie was such that Anne found herself drawn to their tight knots of after-hours gossip and tales, just as she'd been as a child. Surprisingly, the men did not accost her but seemed to respect her married status and treated her with a certain rough gallantry.

They did not afford Bonny the same respect. Most of the pirates edged around him as they would a powerful but diseased dog, and Anne could not ignore the disdain she observed in their eyes when they addressed her husband. She finally asked Kesby why the crew seemed so united in their dislike of James Bonny.

"He has a reputation, Anne. And if ye'd asked me afore ye wed, I'd a put ye off him. But ye didn't ask."

"And what sort of reputation does he have, man? He's surely nothing next to your own talents?"

Kesby glowered briefly and then his brow cleared. "I'll forgive ye that, since ye do not know better. But never again compare the likes of Con Kesby to a cunt-struck rogue like Bonny—not on me own ship. And never while yer a guest on any vessel not yer own."

Anne felt chagrin at her blunder. She softened her tone and looked the contrite spouse. "Pray, do tell me, then. What is his crime?"

"He's a snot-nosed sucker. He plays both ends against the middle an' betrays all hands he shakes. 'Tis well known over the docks that he cheats Brethren and merchant alike. An' neither side has much use for him."

"Why did Captain Hornigold deal with him, then?"

"Ben Hornigold has a weakness for dockside trash, be they male or female, an' he owed Tilda Redhose a mighty favor." He appraised Anne shrewdly.

"Why help us, then? Why not leave me and my husband to be netted by the militia like so many herring in a hogshead?"

He grinned. "Not for yer sake, lass. Though ye are a toothsome piece an' have been since ye were old enough to crack a walnut. No, not for you—for Ben Hornigold."

"For Ben?" Anne did not believe the old pirate for a moment.

"Ay. He said ye were a craft worth savin' once. An' he's been a friend. So for him, I'll deliver ye out o' the hands o' the law. But if ye rile me crew, I'll put ye off on some deserted shoal like so much excess baggage. I'll have no brawlin' in the fo'c'sle or whorin' in the steerage."

Anne looked out over the waves and smiled thinly at his threat. "I'll cause no trouble, Captain. It's no small relief to me simply to be away from land."

Kesby laughed heartily, startling the gulls that wheeled over them. "Ay. Ye got the thief's disease. I saw as much at yer own father's table."

"The thief's disease?"

"A fear of the quiet life. It kills more pirates than musket balls. An' I should know, for I'll die of it meself."

*I*T WAS SAID that once a band of buccaneers forced their way up to the vaulted gates of heaven. Saint Peter was quite anxious to rid himself of these uninvited intruders who had obviously arrived at the wrong refuge for eternity. He hit on a sham worthy of the Brethren themselves. "A sail!" he cried, pointing out the doors of paradise. "Where!" demanded the pirates, craning their necks to see. "To leeward on the port quarter!" replied Saint Peter. "Go for her lads! Boarders!" they shouted as they hastily rushed out of the gates of paradise . . . which were then slammed securely behind them.

Anne heard this and other tales from Kesby's crew and felt part of a special family, sensing the solid fraternity that work at sea can forge among men. She strayed from Bonny's side often during the day, seeking private spaces to gaze out at the water or to watch the men at work. And at night she left their fo'c'sle reluctantly to berth with her husband, wishing that she might stay to hear one more of the pirates' ribald adventures.

Bonny's swiving had improved. He obviously felt he had tamed

Anne now and could afford to be gentle. Anne found his embraces tolerable, though scarcely the practiced pleasure that she remembered with Hornigold. She had to admit that her groom had a pleasing countenance. With his blond curly locks, he looked more like a fallen angel than a man. When she teased him about his resemblance to some winged spirits that she'd seen in paintings, he told her that angels were above men, just as God was above angels, men above women, and women above children and dogs. Therefore, he could not be confused with an angel. James Bonny believed in the proper order of things.

Anne learned something of the sea on this trip to the West Indies. The crew speared a hammerhead shark off an island one morning and hauled the great gray beast on decks. It was over twelve feet long, with a thrashing tail, a huge planked head like a cross, and two glassy white eyes on the ends of the crossbar of its snout. Anne ventured closer to watch the men club the creature, then skin it from tail to gills. They later dried the sharkskin for leather and used the fish's liver as a source of oil to rub on blistered fingers or toes and for cysters or enemas to rid themselves of rotted meat in their bowels.

She learned that the coral banks were the most treacherous pieces of land in the hemisphere. Ships that were driven by storms off their course thought themselves in the relative safety of deep water. Their sounding leads found no bottom; their drafts sliced effortlessly through blue waters. They felt safe to ride out any squall, worried only for their riggings. And then some alert watch would hear, above the howls of the winds, a strange rhythmic roar. It sounded like surf, but it couldn't be—not in open ocean. Suddenly a lookout would see the impossible: an explosion of towering breakers dead ahead. By then it was too late. The men would curse and pray and wrench at sails and rigging, but often the ship would smash into the rocks, splinter in the surf, and be gone within moments.

The carpenter told of just such a wreck off Deadman's Cay

three years before. Twenty-seven men survived the rocks. They drifted over the sea for thirty miles on a section of decking and washed ashore on Grand Caicos. Twenty-one died of thirst or exposure. Four committed suicide, driven mad by bugs and the fear of sharks. Two lived.

"Ay," warned the carpenter. " 'Tis a sea of deceptive softness. A man can die easier here than in the Atlantic, mother of all death an' all life."

And so the crew prepared for both. When not servicing their ship, they practiced with a variety of weapons up and down the decks. Anne heard the noises of the flintlock pistol for several hours each day as man after man fired rounds at targets in the sea. They would sneak up on one another with a garotte, a thin wire with two wooden handles, and feign slashed throats and noisy deaths.

Dirks flashed in the sun, and cutlasses clanged together with regularity, yet rarely was there an accidental wound. Each pirate carried and cleaned his own cutlass and pistols. The cutlass swung at the hips; the pistols were thrust in a string of leather across the chest; and each took pride in the brute strength and skill such weapons demanded.

Anne took delight in wearing her dirk openly and in using a cutlass with the best of the crew. Her fencing lessons stood her in good stead when she strode on deck, for the men were not above challenging any woman to a mock duel who wore her weapons so openly.

Kesby's men prided themselves on their many rich catches per season . . . but they told of a parcel of failures besides.

Once the bosun related how they'd had a ferocious five-hour battle with a tall brigantine and took her—only to find the hold full of Newgate felons, a worthless cargo, for they already had all the crew they needed. For spite, they ran the ship aground in Jamaica and let all the convicts loose to pester the governor.

After booty, belly timber was the most popular topic among the crew. They ate only two meals a day, one at midmorning and a second at midafternoon. Messmates clung together like two brothers, each knowing the other's peculiar tastes and sharing all victuals equally. The cook fire was kindled in a low-sided box of sand fastened to the deck at the foot of the mast and watched religiously, for fire on board was feared more than the king's men.

Meat, fresh or salted, was stewed in a large iron pot and then dished out into wooden pannikins or eaten with the fingers. Each man ate all he could hold when stores were full. Each took a lesser ration uncomplainingly when they were low. Fresh water was carried in casks belowdecks for emergency drinking and cooking only. Beer was the common beverage. When beer was scarce, it was watered down and called "belly vengeance" or "chowder beer."

Anne's favorite pirate mess was salmagundi—a salad made with palm hearts, oil, garlic, eggs, and any loose pieces of salt fish available. Most of the crew craved turtle when they could get it. Green turtles were a staple aboard most Caribbean ships. Easy to catch, they were plentiful, nourishing, and could be kept alive for weeks by simply turning them over on their backs. To catch the turtles, the men used remoras, or sucker fish, attached to long cords. The remora swam into open sea and then attached itself to a turtle. The men then pulled them both aboard.

Dysentery, called the flux, was an ever-present problem for seamen, especially to those crews pressed from English ships with bellies unused to fresh fruit. Anne noticed that the pirates were surprisingly modest. The tars fixed a head on the bow of the vessel—out of sight of the decks and often the most secluded piece of the sloop. There, over the open sea, a crude seat was rigged, and the men simply hoisted themselves out over the waves, sheer muscle holding them over the foam. The splashes of salt water wiped them clean, and the sun dried their nether parts. Usually after a few weeks, the sun, salt, and sweat turned all seamen a dark mahogany color. It was said that for those poor bastards suffering from the flux, their color extended to parts unseen by any but the unblinking sun.

Anne, of course, used her own cramped, sour quarters and her private chamber pot, yet she often envied the tars their fresh air and brisk natural approach to such chores. She pinned up her skirts often on that crowded sloop to avoid nettings and bilge water, but she dared not exchange them for breeches and blouse, heeding Kesby's warning of "whorin' 'tweendecks." Besides, Bonny would have become more disgusted by her conduct than he already was.

He scolded her frequently for loitering round the men as they took their ease. At first she tried to explain that she found them interesting, a needed entertainment on a tedious voyage. But when she saw that he did not trust her, she snapped at him to leave her be, she would speak with whom she pleased and only the captain could say her nay. Sensing that he could hardly beat her without arousing the ire of the crew and his host, James soon lapsed into a sullen silence. Anne spent more and more time perched on a damp hogshead in the corner of the fo'c'sle, grinning at the tales they wove for her delight.

AFTER TEN SHORT DAYS the *Shark* sailed into New Providence harbor. To Anne the island looked a perfect pirate haven. It was twenty-eight by eleven miles of well-wooded land with plenty of fresh-water wells, fruit, fish, turtles, pigeons, wild hogs, and cattle. After haphazard possession by both the French and the Spanish, it had become the capital for smugglers and pirates from all over the southern hemisphere, and from that capital vast plunder was taken to the Carolinas for resale to the highest bidder.

To the distant eye, New Providence appeared to be a paradise. Certainly from out in the harbor, the white beaches and green waters, the high coral hills, the waving palms, and the blue cloudless sky seemed a wide scope to Anne. She had heard it said that New Providence was cut from all moorings of society, and that when a pirate slept he did not dream of heaven but of pulling into New Providence once more.

When Kesby handed her a glass and she put it to her eye, the beach came alive like a cankerous boil. The shore was crowded with drunks, crippled beggars, pimps, and bawds on the lookout for clients. The blue water when it rolled on the sand was clogged with remnants of broken spars and casks, smashed fruit, and dead fish. The bay held vessels of every kind. Some were well-kept ships, others neglected half-rotted hulks. All showed the scars of plunder and hard use.

"Is this the infamous pirate fleet?" Anne grimaced at Kesby.

He shrugged. "They don't waste time over appearances. When one ship's wore out, they take a new one. Ye want to change yer mind?"

Anne grinned as bravely as she could manage. "No. It's still better than a Charles Town gaol."

A longboat was dropped unceremoniously into the bay, and Anne, James, and Kesby were rowed to shore. A crowd gathered on the littered beach.

James sweated in his velvet suit. Pale and wary, he eyed the town with open apprehension. Anne sat high up in the longboat looking serene. Her copper hair was piled on her head like a glorious beacon. She wore an emerald gown with the bodice cut daringly low, even for Charles Town society. Kesby appraised her.

"Ye mean to be the belle of this godforsaken island as well?"

She shot him a tight smile. "I mean to try." But her stomach was rigid beneath her skirts, and she felt a sudden urge to row back to the *Shark* and go far away.

The boat rowed closer, and she could see the ramshackle dwellings dotting the shore and lining the hillsides. The heavy smell of rum, sweat, and garbage greeted them, and Anne wrinkled her nose in disgust.

"Got yer pistol, lass?"

"Ay. It's handy." She patted a fold of her skirt.

"Good. These louts are trickier than they look. Show them fear, an' they'll be at yer loins like ruttin' dogs."

Now they were close to the docks, which were spilled over with barrels of rum, bales of silk, bags of spices, and other windfalls. Spanish plate, silver mugs, and gold coins were scattered carelessly amid the loot. The plunder was guarded only by a couple of besotted pirates. One was unsteadily pissing into the harbor. A body, obviously dead for some time, floated nearby. Crabs fought for space on the head. Bonny muttered angrily and put the back of his hand to his nose.

Anne conquered her own queasiness by sheer will, determined not to show her hesitation. She forced her eyes to keep moving and tried to concentrate on the vistas of land and sky. They docked, and Kesby helped her over the side. Anne thought she felt him squeeze her hand as if for support.

By now word of her arrival had spread, and the inhabitants of the pirate republic were traipsing down to inspect this new bit of fluff. Sailors came hurrying in their loose cotton trousers. A peglegged seaman stomped alongside a giant black slave. Gawking children like beach fleas were slapped out of the way, and yelping dogs were kicked aside by those who jostled for a better view. The crowd quieted as Anne stepped ashore. She neither smiled nor frowned at them but held herself tall and proud, staring boldly back at those who stared at her. Her breasts were rounded and white next to those of the slatterns in the crowd, and her dignity and tall beauty held her audience transfixed for an instant.

Then a bedraggled little man stepped nervously forward. He wore the remains of buckled shoes, a tricorn hat, tiny spectacles, and no leggings. He peered at Anne closely and attempted a ragged bow.

"Major Thomas Walker at your service, mum. Welcome to New Providence."

The bow was too much a temptation for the pirate behind him, who planted one bare foot on his backside and pushed him into the water. The major splashed and gulped as his hat and wig floated off with the tide, leaving his bald head bobbing in the dirty foam.

The crowd erupted in howls of glee. Someone fired a pistol in the air as salute.

Kesby took Anne's arm and muttered, "Come, lass. Let's adjourn afore they be on us like ants."

The crowd parted for them, but then followed the trio closely, hooting and hollering. Some of the men attempted to attract Anne's attention with leering antics and whistles. One toothless hag kept plucking at her skirt, cackling in mindless glee. Anne finally shoved her away, and the crowd laughed all the louder. They came to a narrow street lined with taverns and brothels. At an upstairs window a bare-breasted trull paused in her sweating labors over an unseen client and gaped at Anne's red hair and gown. The crowd milled around them, and finally they were blocked completely when they came to a bend in the lane where two large hogsheads were set one on the other.

On top of one of the barrels was a brace of pistols and two filthy, large-handled mugs. Behind the barrels skulked a scar-faced brute of a man, bleary-eyed with rum. One ear had been hacked off to a scarred stump. He waved a pistol at the crowd and bellowed, "Avast! Nobody passes who don't raise a mug with me!"

Kesby leaned down and whispered to Anne, "Take a swig. He takes a toll from all newcomers."

Then the old troll leered and belched fumes towards Anne. "And the price of passage for this beauty is a kiss!"

The crowd whooped as one, eager for any diversion, particularly one that might involve the debauch of a beautiful woman.

Anne's eyes glittered green with anger. "Get out of my way!" she snapped. "I'd rather kiss a horse's ass!"

"Oho!" the brute sniggered. His eyes turned squinty and cruel, and he reached for his pistol again. "Kiss or die, wench."

Kesby cursed and reached for his musket but before he could move, a shot rang out. Through wisps of pistol smoke, he saw the pirate standing stunned with one hand cupped over his good ear. He took his hand away and stared at the blood in his palm. What had been his remaining ear was now hanging by a grisly shred, torn by Anne's quick shot. His other hand was still outstretched for the pistol he never touched.

Anne calmly put her pistol back into its hiding place in the folds of her skirt and appraised the bleeding pirate. In a low, throaty voice she asked, as though surprised, "My God, was that a head? I thought it was the handle of a rumpot." She turned then to the crowd and flashed them a brilliant smile. They exploded in glee. The joke was passed up and down the twisted street, and Anne's tormentors quickly became admirers. A grizzled old man in a captain's frock coat stepped forward, bowed, and swept off his hat at Anne's feet.

"Brave colors, milady! 'Tis the grandest entrance I ever seen in my domain!"

Anne cocked a quizzical eye at Kesby, and he solemnly nodded.

The old man extended his arm, and Anne took it gingerly. "I be Captain Henry Jennings, founder and number one citizen of the pirate republic of New Providence."

Anne felt as if a legend of her childhood had come to her rescue. "Captain Jennings of the Spanish Plate fleet? I have heard of you, sir. Hornigold has sung your praises. The fame of Captain Henry Jennings is widely known."

He gave her another courtly bow. "No wider than your own, I'm sure, milady. You're a friend of Ben Hornigold, then? And who am I havin' the privilege of addressin'?"

She grinned at him. "Anne Bonny, Captain." She threw a glance back to James who brought up the rear. "This is my husband, James Bonny." James tossed him a curt bow and glowered at Anne, who blithely ignored him. Jennings patted her hand on his arm and turned on his heel, leading her uptown.

"Delighted, delighted. Hornigold will be pleased to see you, no doubt."

"He's here?" Anne's face must have showed her interest.

Jennings guffawed. "The dicey rogue! Nay, ma'am. He's taken his new mate, Teach, on a voyage to the Albemarles. I doubt we see his flag 'til the blowin' season."

"Then we'll wait."

"Wait in style, then, at the House of Lords."

Anne smirked. "A House of Lords in a pirates' den?"

"Ay, to be sure. Even pirates have their betters . . . and you, milady, must mingle only with the best!"

Anne smiled and let herself be led through the crowd, up the twisted street, followed at a safe distance by Kesby and James.

As Jennings babbled on, pointing out various landmarks for Anne, she remembered what Ben Hornigold had told her of the old pirate.

"Hell, the man was honest to the bone 'til the king's justice drove him to it!"

"You sound like Father in his cups," she'd said. "He says the law is nothing but a bauble for the rich, the firstborn, and the puffed-up legal thieves who steal with writs and settlements instead of pistols."

"And damned true he is, too! Jennings was the respectable master of a trading sloop, see, and he happened to salvage a Spanish galleon. And what do you suppose he cached but near three hundred and fifty thousand pieces of eight for his pains! Well, he took the gold back to Jamaica, his home port, and the niggardly sons o' bitches who ran the island, honest government men all, demanded his gold by the rights of the Crown! When he refused, they called him pirate and clapped him in irons. 'Twas enough to turn a good man bad, lass. So, Jennings took off with what of his own gold he could steal back from the government dogs and turned pirate for good. Better to hang as a wolf than a sheep, he said, and hoisted a *jolie rouge* over New Providence for all who felt the same!"

And now she was walking on his arm under that same flag to inspect the House of Lords.

The House of Lords, for all its fine title, was little more than a dockside slosh. It was the largest tavern on the island and the hub of all pirate business. Jennings pushed aside a drunk who was puking near the door and ushered Anne inside its musty interior.

It was dark. There were no windows, and the high ceilings made the room seem almost medieval. There were pirate shields and flags nailed to the wall, and a number of smoky oil lamps hung from the rafters. One large gilt mirror mantled the bar. The wooden planks that served as a counter gleamed like some sanctified altar with huge golden chalices plundered from Spanish churches and the Plate fleet.

In the middle of the room was a long, heavy table and a score of stained benches. Seven men sat and stared at Anne as she entered, and several even rose, compelled by some long-forgotten but instinctive reflex. Jennings gestured to the littered table and the company.

"These are the lords, milady. The best the Brethren has to offer. Pirate chiefs all." He went round the table, and the men nodded and stared at Anne with sea-squinted eyes.

There was Thomas Barrow, known rogue of the Caribbean; John Martel, who commanded a pirate sloop of eight guns and eighty men and had taken the *Berkeley* and the *King Solomon* off Cuba a month before; Thomas Cocklyn, who commanded the *Rising Sun*; Samuel Charles Bellamy, who called himself the "Free Prince of the Seas" and commanded the *Whidlaw*, a galleon of twenty-eight guns and 150 hands; John Auger, captain of the *May*; Richard Turnley, an expert pilot; and an Irishman named Edward England, who plundered the seas in the *Fancy*. Anne dropped a deep curtsy to them.

"I am proud to meet the royalty of the republic, gentlemen."

Her cheeks dimpled winsomely. The pirates barked out a chorus of cheers and called for rum.

As the crowd began to push into the tavern, two large bouncers moved among the mob carrying boarding axes. "No coin, no rum!" they shouted and hustled the more obvious derelicts out the door. The proprietor of the House of Lords ambled from behind the bar to make Anne's acquaintance, wiping his hands on a wide apron made of old sails.

Jennings said, "Milady, we've a fine cook from the mother country, all the way from the Lords' tables in London—Albert Balser. He took a meat ax to his lover, and now he cooks for pirate lords."

The huge man giggled like a young girl. Anne could not suppress her own laugh. "Were you betrayed, poor cook?"

"Ay. The filthy bugger couldn't keep his ladle out of other pots!" The company guffawed, and the cook fluttered his beefy hands and swept back to the kitchen.

Jennings seated Anne at the head of the table as the guest of honor and relegated Bonny to a small table at the rear. Other pirate chiefs around the room began to approach her to introduce themselves, and Anne met—in quick succession—Thomas Robinson, Howell Davis, John Carter, and Thomas Burgess. Finally, as a second round was passed, Governor Sawney struck a courtly bow and toasted Anne with a flourish. He was a ragtag old gentleman whom the pirates suffered to be official toastmaster and host.

"Fair lady, we are honored to have such beauty in our midst. We trust you'll excuse our harsh manners in the presence of one so genteel."

At that moment Anne could no longer suppress a demure burp. It was heard round the room and was the signal for more raucous belches. Jennings whacked her on the back and called her a born pirate queen.

The feast lasted into the night with turtle soup, beer, ale, salmagundi, and haunches of roast pig. Anne got her first taste of bumboo, a pirate drink of rum, water, sugar, and spices, and found it much to her liking. There were four barmaids serving, and they flounced from table to table, their skirts pinned up at their hips and their bodices open and stained with sweat. As the pirates got drunker and grabbed at their breasts, they slapped them aside with only token resistance. Finally all service had ceased, and they lolled from one lap to another, drinking with the customers. Then the doxies joined in the fun, and before long each man had a woman on his knee or was grappling with one in the corner. A few heedless couples rolled under the tables, ignoring the kicks and shouts of the crowd.

Anne felt the need for some air but when she looked to find James, he had disappeared. She sought out one woman who looked friendly, Bess Budd, Jennings' whore. Bess was a plump tart with cheeks that were red with burst veins from the London cold she'd left. She seemed brash and outspoken, and Anne liked her at once.

Bess walked her outside the pub towards a deserted stretch of beach. Along the water was a trough marked by upended turtle shells. Bess hiked her skirts and squatted over the trough, motioning Anne to do the same. In such a sisterhood of relief and darkness, Bess told Anne her story.

"I've not been happier, lass, than here in this scurvy pond. 'Tis just the spot for the likes o' me. An' for you, too, I wager."

Bess had been a seamstress in London but could not make ends meet. She inevitably turned to the easiest livelihood for a pretty woman but was still discontent. She saved her coins carefully until she was able to buy a small pub, but she was soon heavily in debt because of high taxes and low profits. Faced with a choice of gaol or emigration, she shipped to Jamaica where she fell in with Jennings who carted her to New Providence as his woman. Anne saw her teeth gleam in the darkness and heard her laugh over the splash of the waves.

Anne slapped at mosquitoes on her bare shoulders. "Will you

help me settle in, Bess? Show me all I need to know?"

"Ay. If you promise to keep off me man." She grinned.

Anne laughed. "Jennings? You have my promise. Why do you want him?"

"Oh, he's old, but he's less trouble than most. He don't need to oil his truncheon often as some, an' after my life, the fewer pokes, the better."

Anne took her arm. "All I want is a safe harbor, Bess. And a little space to breathe."

"Well, you'll find it here. But"—she picked her way delicately around the edges of the open trough—"if it's free breathin' ye seek, let's move upwind a mite."

As they walked through the darkness, Anne told some of her story, at least those parts she cared to share.

Bess asked, "What of your husband?"

"I wager he can look out for himself. He can stay if he chooses ...if not..." She shrugged eloquently.

"You can do a damned sight better. The best of the seas come through this island at one time or another. You can take your pick."

Anne surveyed the littered beach and the crumbling hovels thoughtfully. "I intend to choose more carefully next time."

"And your plans?"

"Just to do the best with what's at hand."

"You must have a man here, lass. And by the looks of it, he best be strong enough to hold off the rest."

"Then I shall have one...the best available."

"The best are already spoken for."

Anne laughed. "You show me the best, Bess, and let him decide for himself if he's taken. Aside from yours, all are fair game, to my mind."

"You're a regular female rake, miss!"

"No. Just tormented with an everlasting itch I can't reach."

Bess shot her a wry smile. "It'll pass, lass. It'll pass."

Bess went through the door of the tavern, pulling Jennings out behind her. The three of them ambled through the darkness towards the hut that she shared with the old sea captain.

Breathing the melange of green and ripeness that was the perfume of the island, they passed the tavern and meandered down the twisted street to the beach. Anne saw a rag-tag child, bent over a sprawled drunk. He was carefully carving away at a finger, trying to remove a ring from the unconscious hand.

ANNE SPENT THE next few weeks setting up what passed for housekeeping on New Providence. She picked a spot on a slope behind the town and away from the harbor's conflicting scents of spices and refuse. There, she and James built a thatched hut from flotsam washed up on the shore and furnished it with pirate plunder on sale at every tavern in the town.

James signed on a turtle boat and sailed off for the surrounding bays, leaving Anne home alone. Actually, she preferred her solitude and soon fell into a pleasant routine.

The morning in New Providence was her favorite time. The air was clean, and the blue harbor was glazed with sun. The bright tropical flowers half hid the shacks, and the tide had swept the beach clear of debris and excrement. Each new day Bess and Anne strolled down to the docks, attended by a young black boy owned by Jennings. The slave toted a parasol for the two women, a basket with coins, and a brace of loaded pistols.

Daily, one ship or another sailed into port piled high with plundered treasure. Auctions were held on each corner. Booty was strewn this way and that, and Anne and Bess could pick, choose, and barter as they liked. As Bess was the woman of the island's most respected citizen and Anne was its most beautiful, the two were accorded uncommon respect.

After the women had made their purchases for the day and sent the slave boy home with their loot, they went to Madeleine's parlor on the hill.

Madeleine was a Frenchwoman from Martinique. An oddity in more than one way, she could dress a woman's hair as well as the finest nigger wench in Charles Town and employed the only seamstress on the island. Madeleine preferred women in all places, including her bed, and so her hut and its adjoining veranda became the gathering spot for the female elite of New Providence.

There, Anne met Emilie Cerise, who had been one of a shipload of whores sent by the French government to civilize the pirates of Tortuga. When the pirates began to marry the whores and turned to farming and fishing rather than going out to sea, Emilie left and came to New Providence to seek her fortune in her usual manner. Another wench, Margaret Hutchens, had been sold by her husband in Virginia in a bill of divorcement. When she could not abide her new spouse, she fled the colony and sought refuge on the island. If she returned to the colonies, she was likely to be made a bond servant for life; on New Providence she was her own mistress. The fourth trull, Jenny Hardy, had owned a brothel in Bristol but fell in love with a pirate and followed him to the West Indies. Once there, her lover found another skirt more to his liking, and now she was more or less marooned on New Providence until she could find another man to take her off.

Anne's favorite was a strapping, sporting girl named Meg Moore, who had worked as a midwife and was reputed to be the most talented abortionist in the islands. Her tools were little more than serving spoons and awls, but her skills were often sought and highly paid. She could also cure syphilis with a mercurial preparation she'd learned to make in London, and could ease gonorrhea with a West Indian plant called *guaiacum*.

None of the women were beautiful. All bore the scars of their lives like banners, for each had learned to survive in a hostile world.

Madeleine fawned over Anne as she stepped over her stoop. "So tall! Such eyes of fire! Enough to make a man swoon with delight!" And she looked as if she might do just that, much to the amusement of the other women. "Why, I've heard nothing but Bonny this and Bonny that all morning and could not wait for you to call!" She kissed Anne on the cheek resoundingly. *"Tu es si magnifique,* I may try for a toss myself!" At that, Anne dissolved in laughter and felt entirely at home.

From Bess and the others, Anne learned much of pirate life ... and how to best profit from it. For these women had not learned three hundred different figures and tunes for country dances, or how to flip and flirt a fan, but they knew how to mold beeswax caps over the mouths of their wombs to prevent babes from growing, and how to use suppositories of black hellbore to start the monthly flux and to kill an unwanted fertile seed early on.

Anne learned to use hot grease to keep off the bugs, to make cassava root mush with bananas and nutmeg, to blend ink from fish blood and berry juice, and to eat citrus to keep her teeth from becoming loose as dice in a cup. She got her clothes white by boiling them in seawater and learned to watch for signs of a hurricane from the west. When the sky was full of mist, the sun rose ruddy through the vapor, and the sea was full of long swells, the women knew to pull up all boats and to coop the chickens.

In return, Anne taught her friends to swim. It was surprising to learn that none of the women knew how to move through the water efficiently, and most feared it. Consequently, they washed but rarely bathed. She went to a secluded cove with Bess, Meg, and Jenny and was amused to see them wade with their long shimmys tied around their legs for modesty. Anne swiftly stripped to the skin and dove headfirst into a white breaker. Their shock turned to admiration as they saw her stroking through the current, moving as she pleased through the green water. She dove to the bottom of the inlet and brought up a piece of coral to comb her hair, and they all clustered about her, eyeing her figure, and clamoring for lessons on how to master the waves.

She watched them shuffle through the sand to kick up any

hidden sting rays and imitated their steps out to deeper water. Then she dove shallowly into the waves and beckoned them to follow. But when she came up, she blundered right into a man-of-war. Its tentacles wrapped around her bare legs and left stripes of fire on her flesh. She felt she was being sliced with a hot cutlass each time the waving arms brushed her skin. She cried out, gulped for air, and struggled to the shore. When she reached the sand, she collapsed, moaning, and the women ran to her side.

"'Tis a man-o'-war got her. See the red welts raisin'," cried Bess.

"Ay. Who shall do the honors?"

"Me. I'm full nigh to burstin'." Meg pulled aside her linen and kneeled over Anne's legs. Anne writhed, trying to inch her red inflamed limbs to wet, cooler sand, but Meg pulled her back and held her still. Before Anne could protest, she squatted and wet directly on the welted skin. Everywhere that the urine splashed, Anne could feel the burning leave her flesh. Finally, Meg was drained and looked up at Anne with a grin.

"Ye need more?"

"Nay," Anne croaked. "The pain is gone. You must have a powerful water to drown such a fire."

Meg laughed. "Must be the rum, lass, for we all can do it. I seen a man beg to be pissed on when he stumbles into a field o' them devil fish. An' that same man'll put a dog to the sword for liftin' a leg on his boot." Meg pulled Anne to her feet. The women gathered their belongings and ambled back to town, their voices lifting over the waves like warbling tropical birds.

Bonny HAD BEEN gone most of a month, coming off the turtle boat just long enough to provision and to pull Anne into the hammock for a fast tussle. In his absence she had kept the rest of the pirates at bay only by dint of her fiery temper and the protective influence of Jennings. When Anne complained to James that she needed him, he shrugged and reached for more broiled pompano.

"You can keep them off, wife. Just do as you did with me afore we wed."

"And what was that?"

"Why, talk of honor and your fine name and your father's fortune, of course. You're the one wanted to ship to this besotted nightmare. And I'm the one must put bread in our bellies. I don't mean to do it by risking my neck and going on account. So suck up to Jennings, and he'll look after you proper."

Anne said nothing as she gazed out to sea.

Gradually she felt her whole body respond to this island like an opening blossom. Her skin turned pink, then golden brown; her hair seemed to grow overnight and cascaded down her back in flaming waves. Her muscles lengthened, and her hips developed a swing from walking in the sand. She placed flowers in her hair and gold hoops in her ears and used her stays to prop up a thatched canopy for shade.

The sun made everything grow more quickly on the islands. Flowers budded, bloomed, and died in a day. Fruit ripened while she reached for it. And yet the island itself had a slow, leisurely pace. Because there were no seasons to chart, time had little meaning and one day melted into the next. Anne felt as if a decade had passed since she had seen her father or danced at a Charles Town ball.

One afternoon as the sun was setting, Anne dozed in the shade of a towering palm. The air was turning cooler and she stirred, rousing herself lazily. Off in the distance, she saw a mighty sloop rounding Hog Island.

Anne decided to head towards the harbor and as she came within eyeshot, a large group was already forming along the wharf. She picked up her step and went in search of Bess, her curiosity piqued. As she watched, black flags flickered as they were hoisted up the mast.

She quickly found Bess in the crowd. "What on earth is going on?"

Bess laughed. " 'Tis Ben Hornigold!"

Anne beamed with pleasure as she remembered the last time she'd bedded with Hornigold. Her knees shivered and sent small thrills up her thighs. He was right—the devil looked after his own.

She dashed back to the hut to dress, choosing the gown which he'd often remarked made her eyes turn a sparkling green. Anne strode regally towards the House of Lords, a fitting place for her entrance. She opened the door and paused, knowing that she was backlit in gold.

Hornigold was seated at the main table surrounded by a bevy of admiring ladies. Anne stiffened and her eyes went dark, but her smile remained intact. The noise of the crowd ebbed as she walked to Hornigold's side, her head high.

She put her hand on Hornigold's arm, "Welcome home, Ben."

Hornigold jumped as though he'd been brushed by a tarantula. "Jesus Christ! Anne Cormac! What are you doing here?"

Anne smiled her best at him, inwardly amused by his shock. She knew she must look to great advantage in this scurvy setting.

"I came to bring you your gold." From out of her ample bosom she drew a plump bag of coins, took his hand, and dropped it in his palm. The sound of gold seemed to break the spell of quiet in the room. The crowd began to laugh and discuss the scene among themselves. No eye turned away from the drama, however.

"Ay, 'tis Anne Bonny now," Ben mumbled. "Well, I heard you wed that scum and lit out, showin' the militia a clean pair o' heels."

"You heard the truth. Did you see my father?"

Hornigold twisted his face in a wry grimace. "Indeed, I did! He blames me for introducing you to that wharf rat."

Anne laughed, though his words hurt, and replied throatily, "Well, you should have told him I showed you a thing or two."

The pirates closest to the couple whooped at that.

"I'm here at any rate, with your goods intact, and glad to see an old friend." She wrapped her arm round his neck. She felt the desire, the need to rub against him in a feline movement of invitation and pleasure. But he stayed stiffly seated. Nell, one of the doxies at the table, came to life screeching. "You filthy cunt! You can take yer claws off him."

Anne glanced at Hornigold. His eyes had gone cold as the Atlantic in a winter storm. She turned cooly to Nell. "Oh? It looked to me . . . as I'm sure it did to all these gentlemen"—she gestured to her rapt audience—"that you belonged to everyman." Anne's mouth went hard and she steeled herself for assault.

Hornigold slammed one big paw on the table so hard that the tankards jumped into the air. The room fell silent. "Avast, woman. Leave her to me."

Anne turned her emerald eyes on him. "You want her, Captain?"

She carefully smoothed the folds of her gown and made her face bland.

Hornigold smiled silkily, his eyes expressionless.

Anne tossed her head and turned to Nell. "Never fear, girl. He's yours with my blessings." She turned back to Hornigold, her eyes flashing.

A voice from a corner said, "God's breath! Whose woman is that! One of us is a dead man. Bring that beauty to me naked!"

She whirled to leave, but an arm reached out and grabbed her before she could reach the door. A man loomed out of the darkness, and Anne stared up at the owner of the voice. He was tall with huge shoulders, no neck, merry eyes, and a demonic black beard. He had it tied in braids with ribbons, and it hung about his chest and shoulders like a tatted black curtain. He'd be a fop but for his size, Anne thought. He wore a sling across his chest with four loaded pistols, an assortment of knives and daggers stuck into his waistband, and a cutlass at his shoulder.

But what diverted Anne's attention most forcefully was the stench of him. He smelled of the sea, rotted fish, sweat, rum, and those private places of a man that cloy the fastest. The effect was somewhat like bad cheese left in the sun.

"Kindly unhand me, man. Who—or what—are you?"

"Ned Teach, mum! I like a piece with fire!"

"Do you now, Mr. Teach?"

"Ay!" The crowd laughed, waiting for the next volley. Anne wanted to go, yet she could not seem to make herself move towards the door. Her eyes still strayed to Hornigold.

"Strong words, Teach. Matched by a strong smell. But words don't make the man or move a woman."

She turned to Hornigold, flashed her best smile and slipped from the tavern to the fading whoops of the pirate chiefs.

Her heart took little pleasure in the scenes she played out in her mind as she walked back to her hut. Hornigold had been her only hope for passage out of this place. Clearly, Bonny was happy to stay a turtler all his days, content to come home long enough to provision himself, comfort his cock, and then leave. But Anne knew such a life would not sustain her much longer.

Depressed, Anne trudged back to her hut. She missed her father, her mother, Fully and Charley. Her heart was heavy and she was homesick.

Hornigold visited her later that night, but Anne could muster little of her former warmth for him.

"Why did you elope, Anne?" he asked, humbler than he'd allowed himself to seem in public.

Anne signed. "I'm not sure, Ben. Guess I thought I was ready for one man." She looked at him searchingly. "Ben, it could have been you. But not now."

Hornigold reached out and touched her lips lightly with his calloused fingertips. Then he turned and walked away.

MIDDAY, when the trade winds seemed to die and the air was still, Ned Teach made a formal call. He approached Anne's hut in full regalia. Not a leaf was moving, no birds called, and the reek of human waste lay heavy on the air. In spite of the heat, however, Teach was outfitted in his best pirate breeches, a full jacket, a tricorn hat, and armed to the teeth. That he still had not washed was all the more apparent in the sweltering heat. Anne felt heavy and bored, as lifeless as the sea, which looked as if a thin, watery veil wavered across it. He sauntered up to her, oblivious of her yawn.

"We're in for a blow, mum."

Anne said nothing but only cocked a weary eye in his direction.

"I've come to ask ye formal to take me on. Let's weigh anchor an' hie us to Ocracoke. 'Tis cooler there."

"Not for me, man. Anywhere in the Carolinas would be too hot for Anne Bonny." And, out of boredom as well as a strange sense that he deserved to know, she told him her story.

At first Ned did not believe her, but when she pointed out to him that there was little other reason she'd stay in New Providence were her story not the truth, he spilled out a stream of foul epithets.

"Damn their scurvy eyes! 'Tis injustice pure an' plain! Set upon by yer own pa! To drive a female . . . a fine lady as yerself, mum, to such is damned knavery!" Anne could see his heart was open to her, and she smiled at him like a grateful child. But the woman in her knew he was better left her friend.

Ned Teach had made himself a legend, and from his reputation alone took victory after victory, often never needing to fire a single cannon. He was impetuous, wildly competitive even with his own crew, and rabid to win whatever prize he could catch. Anne had heard that one day at sea, Teach had grown bored and decided to challenge his crew to a test of endurance.

"We shall make a hell of our own, lads, and see how long we can bear it!"

Two or three of the more impulsive of the crew accepted his challenge, and they all went down into the hold. There they seated themselves on the large stones used as ballast, and their captain ordered several pots of fuming brimstone carried down into the depths of the hold. Then he commanded that the hatches be closed tight and the brimstone set on fire. The men sat there in the dark, peering through the dense, sulfurous fumes with watering eyes and sweating nerves. One by one, they each gave out, finally crying for air, and the hatches were opened. Teach never called out at all but merely sat half-baked by brimstone, leering at his weaker companions. When he finally emerged from the hold, black-faced and bellowing in triumph, one of the crew cried out that he looked as if he'd come straight from hell itself, right off the gallows. That gave Teach a new idea.

"My lads!" he roared. "Next time we'll play a wager at real gallows and see who can swing longest without being throttled!"

Teach's unpredictable violence kept his crew in superstitious subjection. They never knew what he might do next. One night, while drinking in his cabin with his navigator, Israel Hands, and others, Teach covertly drew two pistols under the table. While all but he had their mugs raised, Ned fired his pistols and wounded Hands on the knee, crippling him for life. When the man asked why he had done such a thing, Teach replied, "Hellfire, Hands! If I don't kill meself a seaman every once in a while, the rest will forget who I am!"

Teach's beard was the single most dramatic element in his mystique. It was a frightful black cloud covering his whole face. Only his fiery eyes poked out from the dense bristles. To emphasize his unique feature, Teach called himself Blackbeard, and plaited his growth into little tails, some of which he festooned with ribbons and others he trained back over his ears. When in battle, he stuck lighted matches under his hat. The matches were slow-burners made of hemp dipped in saltpeter and limewater. The effect was both terrifying and magnificent. His face, with red eyes and matted black hair, seemed wreathed in smoke; to his prey he looked a demon from hell. To complete the effect, he always wore a bandolier with six pistols, three daggers, and a huge cutlass at his waist.

She gave him a quick hug in spite of his rankness and sent him on his way.

Anne took to walking over the island for hours, watching the wind and the tides, learning the ways of the weather, and the paths of the birds. Often she glanced up at the huge old mansion on the hill, the crumbled pink stone attesting to the absence of its owner, Chidley Bayard.

He was a powerful merchant in the Caribbean whose bribes and cargoes had wrangled him political leverage. His headquarters was in Port Royal, and he had homes and offices in Cuba, Hispaniola, and on the island of the pirate republic. It was said that his mansion on New Providence, cared for only by a brace of imported slaves, was the least impressive of all his estates. Yet it was the finest home on the island by far.

Bayard commanded a fleet of a dozen fine sloops and several hundred privateers, seamen, agents, slaves, and private assassins. Though his manners were foreign and thus suspect, he was welcome in the finest houses because of his wealth and power. It was also said that he had never married. He had a succession of mistresses, and his latest had reigned for four years, a long tenure in the islands.

Her name was Maria Renaldi, and from all reports she was his match, vice for vice. A mix of Spanish and French blood, she was tall and vividly dark. She had a habit of carrying a small whip on the streets of Havana and slashed imperiously at unlucky slaves and servants who did not please her. It was rumored that once she had grabbed a cutlass and decapitated an old beggar woman who had inadvertently dirtied her skirts. If the rumor was true, then Bayard's power had saved her from arrest, for she traveled with him still.

Anne sighed deeply and turned her gaze back to the waves, walking on down the sand. She knew she must take some action soon or decay here like a beached mullet.

The next month, when Bayard and his mistress returned to the island, Anne made it her habit to ride her wiry pony up the beach directly under the walls of the mansion. She wore tight breeches that Madeleine had made for her, and her bosom bounced under her loose blouse. Her hair streamed out free behind her, and she laughed frequently and urged her pony faster. She galloped the horse up through the shallow breakers, wheeled him, and rode furiously back up the sand to the trees.

Within a week Bayard knew all of Anne Bonny's habits, even when she usually dined at the House of Lords. He chose one evening to dine there, too. When Maria saw the extra plates set at her lover's table, she bristled.

"What is this?"

Bayard shrugged. "I have business to discuss with Jennings. Of course, we must invite his woman and his guest to join us...."

Maria smiled tightly and took out her cutlass, laying it gently at her place.

Bayard laughed. "Is that to cut your roast, my dear?"

Maria glared balefully at Bayard and at the rest of the company who listened covertly.

"It is to split that Bonny bitch from brain to buttocks if she dares sit at my table." Her threat circled the room loudly, and all were hushed.

"You will do nothing of the kind," Bayard warned softly. "Unless I give you leave."

Albert Balser, hearing this exchange, hurried out and met Anne as she strolled to the tavern with Jennings and Bess. "Maria awaits you with a cutlass!" Albert wrung his hands. "She swears to cleave you in two!"

Jennings cursed softly. "She can do it too, lass. She's a demon with a sword!"

"So I've heard." Anne smiled wryly. "But I'm a devil with a foil. As discourteous as it seems, it appears I must go to dinner armed. Can you get me a rapier?"

Jennings shrugged and slipped away. He came back with a fine-bladed weapon. Anne flexed it and lashed it twice through the air as Albert's eyes grew huge and glassy. "Jesus save us, you look the wrath of God."

Anne grinned. "No. But I am ungodly empty. It's time to sup, my friends. Shall we go in?" She led the way, her foil dangling casually at her waist.

When Anne came through the door, a tense silence settled over the small crowd. All drew back, leaving a clear lane between Anne and Bayard's table. Bayard rose and began a sweeping gesture of welcome to Anne, but Maria stood and clapped her cutlass resoundingly on the table. She towered over him.

"You may take your meal here, woman. But not at my table. If you dare, I swear by God I will cleave your head to the ground."

Anne laughed easily. "I shall find it hard to eat without my throat."

The crowd grinned as one maniacal fool, their sympathy clearly with Anne, yet eager for a fray. Her voice turned hard and quiet. "I shall sit where I choose." She glanced at Bayard. "This is not Havana. And I am no weak old woman."

Maria exploded with rage. White-lipped and trembling, she leaped across the table and lunged for Anne's throat, swinging her cutlass over her shoulders. Anne was prepared for her and deftly sidestepped her rush. She grabbed a stool with one hand and her foil with the other. Twisting between tables, she used the stool to keep Maria back and flicked at her with the foil. Again, Maria swung the cutlass, shouting curses in Spanish. Anne ducked, and in warning nicked the woman's arm with her foil. Maria swung again, as spectators dropped to their bellies to avoid her wild arcs. Maria was clumsy but strong; for a moment Anne's foil looked no match for the heavier weapon. Maria swung a fourth time and splintered Anne's stool like a piece of driftwood.

Anne felt a skitter of panic lash through her stomach as she dodged the woman's powerful thrust. Jennings hollered at her from a corner, shoving a cutlass towards her.

"Take this, lass! She's too strong for you!"

But Anne moved with her back towards him and kept dodging the mad woman's fury. Finally, the weight of the cutlass began to tell, and Maria took shorter, less frequent arcs with the murderous weapon. Now, Anne moved in. She began to flick her foil in and out, darting nimbly about her opponent, cutting the bodice ties on Maria's blouse. Maria lunged, and her bodice slipped to her waist, revealing hard brown breasts with molasses nipples.

Still circling, dodging the cutlass, moving swiftly between pirates and tables like so many hip-high cattails, Anne flicked her foil at Maria's skirt and it fell, entangling the woman's legs. The crowd shrieked with glee. Even Bayard smiled thinly behind his oily spectacles. But Maria kicked free of her skirt, clawing and spitting like a singed cat. Her dark nipples rolled like angry eyes as she swore and screamed and lunged again—too late.

Anne slipped aside, and Maria nearly fell on her own linen. Anne moved in deftly and lashed Maria's bare shoulder, laying open the muscles near to the bone. Maria yelped in surprise and pain. She stared for an instant at the ribbon of raw meat exposed on her arm and then charged at Anne with new strength born of fury.

Coolly, Anne stepped around behind her and severed Maria's underskirt. This time Maria tripped and sprawled on the floor, with nothing but her underlinen about her ankles. The roof nearly split with pirate laughter. Bayard did not laugh but only watched the spectacle with gleaming, feral eyes. Maria screamed curses and rolled on her back, wielding her cutlass with both hands. Caught off guard, Anne's shoulder was slashed open, and the sword served her a glancing blow on the forehead. She rocked back against the wall. Maria sprang to her feet and picked up the cutlass once more for another fatal rush.

Now Anne fought for her life. She balled her bloody fist, and her face was white with strain. Her shoulder felt useless to her, but she knew if she faltered she was dead. Maria lunged, hoping to decapitate Anne, who was pinned against the wall. But she swung too far and wide, and Anne bent at the knees, came under her arm, thrust upwards with her foil, and neatly cut Maria's forehead open wide.

She turned then and faced the crowd, sure that the fight was over. The crowd gave a shout of approval, and Anne lowered her foil. From behind her, Maria rushed at her again, her sword held high, the blood flowing down her contorted features. Anne moved just in time to avoid her thrust, whirled behind her, and fell to the ground. She rolled to the side, as the woman stabbed viciously into the planks beneath her, and Anne saw that she would not give up.

Though Maria was near-blinded by the blood streaming down her face, she hacked wildly in all directions, determined to fight to the death. She swung for Anne again; Anne slipped under a table desperately; Maria's sword hit the table leg and clattered from her hand. In a flash, Anne was out from under the table, foil in hand, her weapon at Maria's throat.

A pirate shouted from the corner, "Put the bitch to the sword! She'd have done you!"

Anne glanced at Bayard—a quick flick of her eye. Bayard slowly nodded once, his eyes black behind his glasses. Anne looked into Maria's face for some fear, remorse, or compromise. She saw none. Maria pulled back her head and spat full in her face. Numbly, Anne fixed the point of her rapier beneath Maria's left breast and quickly ran her through.

LATER THAT NIGHT after Anne had bound her arm, ignoring the dull ache which leadened her body, she joined the carousing at the

House of Lords which was still going at full tilt. After just a few tankards, she was exhausted and, when Bayard approached her with his silky manners, she went home with him. There, he tossed her on his huge bed and tore passionately at her clothes, murmuring throaty words of wonder at her beauty. Anne laughed and let him take her, while one piece of her mind watched as from across a wide, black sea.

When Bonny returned, he had already heard of Anne's victory at the tavern and did little to conceal his disgust.

"So, you murdered again, eh?"

Anne was shocked at his attack. She did not know quite what she'd expected, but certainly not shouted accusations.

"Murdered? It was self-defense, James. If you had been about, you would have seen as much!"

"I was out earning your bread, madam. And while I was, you were gaming and whoring with the likes of Bayard and his Spanish piece!"

Anne's anger flew to her face and mottled it red. "She came at me with a sword, husband! And what would you have me do? Accept my death meekly?"

James closed his eyes as if he could not endure her face. "You can try that bait on the others but it won't work on me. I know the wench you are. I know you went to that tavern with foil in hand, hoping for a fight. And you didn't just best her did you, miss? No. You had to run her through."

Anne faltered at his accusations. In her mind's eye, she swiftly recalled the times in her attack when she might have finished Maria without killing her. He had gleaned a partial truth. He saw self-doubt and was quick to lash it.

"Ay. You needn't protest your innocence to me. You were roused to blood, and blood you would have. You always get your way, don't you?"

Anne began a quick retort, but his next taunt stopped her. "Just like Clara. Ay, I heard the talk. 'Tis not the first woman who's felt your sword."

Anne's eyes grew flinty. "Get out, then. If that's what you suppose, go elsewhere, you cowardly whelp. I can make my own way."

"I don't doubt it. And I go with pleasure, madam. I for one don't intend to spend my life as outlaw from one hellhole to the next. And bound to the likes of you, that's all I'd ever see." He bowed sarcastically. "I leave you . . . to your pleasures. Split whom you like with impunity. There'll always be someone to believe you didn't mean it." He strode from the stifling hut and did not look back.

Anne marched furiously in the opposite direction, lashing her skirt with her hand. The wind was brisk at the shore, and she walked forcefully into it, defiant. James' words stung at her mind. Finally she stopped, away from all eyes.

She stood and looked out to sea—to the slow rollers that rhythmically crashed on the reef, one by one. She felt a terrible ache in her throat, and her mouth twisted involuntarily. Against her will, the tears slicked down her cheeks. She could not stop them but could only wonder at the small, uncluttered patch of fear that she felt in her heart. Suddenly she felt cold, and shivered. As she looked up the hill, the lights of the Bayard house were lit and seemed to be the first stars in the sky. She pulled the gold band off her left hand and dropped it on the sand. She watched the small wavelets tumble it over and over. Just before it was pulled away by the sea, she reached and retrieved it, putting it back on her finger.

ANNE TOOK OVER as mistress of Bayard's house. She could not stay on the island without a man, and there was nowhere else for her to go. She was glad to be within four walls of comfort again, but was more eager than ever to be away from New Providence.

As Bayard's paramour, she had ready access to his various caches. She outfitted the house and herself with every bauble a pirate ship could steal. Silks and velvets for herself, gold-woven tapestries and Oriental carpets for her rooms; jewels from every nation's plunder filled the cases on her dressing table. In one corner of her chamber she set up a small shelf with gold and clay idols stolen from the South American Indians. When Bayard teased her for her pagan idolatry, she reproved him.

"These have a great feel of life to them. Unlike this dead cross." She lifted a silver cross emblazoned with garnets from her case. "These have the gods still living in them at least." And she insisted that they stay.

Life with Chidley Bayard was not the refuge Anne expected nor did it provide the excitement she seemed to need. Bayard, like many grasping men, did not desire Anne for herself but to have and display her as a reflection of his own prowess. He was a feeble lover, and Anne soon wearied of all the games he required to fuel his passion.

At first he seemed to feed off her vitality, drawing his desire from her natural exuberance. But that quickly jaded. He then had her wear black masks to bed and took great pleasure in "guessing" her identity. Anne first thought such imaginative complexities rather novel and even fun. But after the dozenth mask and the hundredth ludicrous guess—"Are you then perhaps a young virgin fled from a Spanish convent?"—she began to get irritable.

Just about the time she was ready to rip off her mask and slap him with it in exasperation, he invented a new game he called "Pig in a Poke." She was to pretend that he had overpowered her completely, that when he threw himself on her body, holding down her wrists over her head, she was overcome and could not buck him loose. Then he would grip her buttocks in his sweaty paws, kneading her flesh furiously, and tell her to squeal. "Squeal for mercy, my little piglet, and I shall perhaps spare you the sword." But, of course, the more she squealed, the more demanding his sword became. Finally Anne could not keep from laughing as she pretended to squeal, and he rolled off her in disgust.

If I do not play his games to his satisfaction, she thought, with luck Bayard will find a different playmate. The man's a child whose head is full of dinnling make-believe. And he prefers his fantasies to any real woman. But she knew that for now she could not afford to leave Bayard's sanctuary. So she played what games she must, with as little obvious scorn as she could manage, watching all the while for a better opportunity. And Bayard continued to flutter around her like a sickly moth about a bright flame.

Anne had to go to such lengths to please Bayard in private that she was loath to extend herself at all in public. He took her to Jamaica to attend the governor's ball and to gloat over his ownership of her.

Sir Nicholas Lawes was the titular head of the Jamaican government, His Majesty's captain general and governor in chief, chancellor, commander in chief, vice admiral, and president of the island. Bayard had frequented the governor's home and looked forward to flaunting his new mistress. Maria had not attracted the admiration of the society women of the island, and Chidley had soon left off taking her to functions at the governor's mansion. He hoped, with Anne on his arm, to recover some of his old prestige. He knew that whoever the governor's wife favored was automatically part of the elite of island aristocracy.

From their very entrance, Anne was the compass point of all masculine eyes in the room. She wore her dark jade watered silk, low in the bodice and the shoulders, and her copper hair, burnt gold from the sun, was curled in tendrils down her neck. Her breasts were high and round, and she swayed gently with her heavy hoops like a tall hibiscus in a warm breeze. A wreath of brilliant emeralds nestled in the hollow of her bosom and set off her eyes to dancing glints of beryl fire.

After being introduced to the governor and his lady, she pointedly ignored the stares of various men in the crowd and made her way quietly to a group of ladies huddled in the corner of the ballroom. She introduced herself courteously and then stood by, waiting to be included in the conversation. The women were polite, but they did not make an effort to draw Anne into the group, continuing to discuss people and subjects of which she had no knowledge at all. Anne sensed no hostility, only dismissal.

She resolved to stand at the perimeter of the women's circle as long as she must to be accepted. But finally, getting no response, she grew bored and raised her eyes to the small clusters of men that dotted the room. One man had been waiting for just such an opening. Glancing over to Bayard who was in deep conversation with two merchant acquaintances, he bowed elegantly and walked across the empty ballroom to Anne's side. She set her face in a bland and formal mask, but he ignored her disguise. Bowing and grinning, he drew her away from the fringe of the women and out to the dance floor. She looked to Bayard, and he smiled at her over a merchant's shoulder. He seemed to welcome her step into the center of attention. This stranger had his hand at her waist and her feet whirling before she had time to even plot her course.

"Peter Currant, mistress. At your service. You seemed too fine a flower to wither in that barren soil." He looked askance at the tight knot of women. Now their eyes were following Anne's movements as they continued to speak to one another. They see me now, Anne smiled to herself. Right through me when I'm alone and right at me when I'm on a man's arm. The music whirled faster.

She smiled slowly at the man. "Captain Peter Currant, you might have said. For I've heard of your exploits, sir."

Currant was a pirate whose adventures in Cuba had pricked the pride of even New Providence rovers. The men said he was the devil's own in courage, and the women said he was poxed to the hilt but worth a roll besides.

He grinned immodestly at Anne. "Ay, and I've heard of yours as well, Anne Bonny."

She looked surprised at that. Were tales of her spread as far as Cuba?

He leaned down closer and whispered, "And I wager those old clams in the corner have heard of you as well."

She glanced quickly at the women. Their eyes swiveled away from her as on one pivot and then back again as she turned her head. She muttered in exasperation, half to herself, "God's breath. What can they have heard of me here?"

He laughed, a curiously boyish bray. "Only that you are toothsome—which you are. And that you're deadly with a foil—a prowess which you can't imagine they'd approve."

Anne frowned. "And now you've added fuel to their petty little fires by leading me to the dance floor ahead of them all."

He whirled her faster, defiantly. "You're sailing a sinking ship, madam. They will never accept you anyway, so why not enjoy your freedom?"

She drew back from him frostily in the middle of the dance and bowed stiffly. "Thank you, Captain. I believe I shall give it a final effort."

She walked back to the knot of women, her head high, a confident smile hiding her uneasiness. This time the circle tightened even more surely, and Anne found herself facing a row of white shoulders.

She stood there again, fanning herself gracefully, hoping that her face did not disclose her humiliation, and turned slightly towards the window as though she sought only a breath of air. She started slightly when she felt a hand on her elbow. One of the women had dislodged herself and had taken her arm.

"My dear, let me introduce myself. I am Sara Sutcliff Lawes, the governor's sister-in-law. Allow me to welcome you properly to Jamaica."

Anne beamed at her in gratitude and bowed graciously. "Thank you, milady. It is kind of you to do so, I'm sure. For I know no one here."

The woman smiled grimly, the skin over her eyes creasing like parchment. "Oh? Then you are not acquainted with Peter Currant, your dance partner?"

Anne laughed softly. "Oh, no, madam. I but danced with him as an accommodation. I have heard of him, of course, but we've not met."

"I see. And have you visited the island before?"

"No, I've not had the pleasure."

"And you hail from . . . ?"

"Charles Town, madam. Perhaps you've heard of my father, William Cormac?" Anne watched her hopefully, sensing that she was in deep water.

The woman assumed an air of formal bewilderment. "Cormac? No. I cannot say I know the name. But, of course, we are all acquainted with Mr. Bayard. A relation of yours, perhaps?"

Anne stiffened. Not a friend but a spy. Sent by a committee of harpies. Her smile froze. "No, Mr. Bayard is no relation. Have you lived here on the island long, then?"

"No relation. I see." The woman ignored Anne's questions and raised her brows in eloquent censure. "Is it true you have no wedding papers, mistress?"

Anne all but laughed in release. A glance at the flock of women told her that they were busily filling in any conversational lags and pointedly ignoring the inquisition they'd arranged. She smiled. "Of course, I have wedding papers, madam. Rest assured."

"To the man with whom you are consorting? With Mr. Chidley Bayard?"

Anne sighed and let her weariness show. "No. But then you knew that, did you not?"

"Yes." The woman drew back her skirt as if a dog had shat on the rug. "I fear that you are horribly out of place, my dear. I find you neither droll nor particularly nice to know."

"Indeed." Anne stepped closer to her and whispered conspiratorially. "Would you perhaps find it nice to know Captain Currant? The way you watched him move, I am sure you've heard of his prowess as well. Perhaps we could arrange a midnight toss. That should prove most entertaining for the ladies."

Madam Sara Lawes's face froze in a sneer of disdain. She said loudly, "Please keep your distance, harlot!"

Anne lashed out as quickly as a cat o' nine and slapped the woman square in the mouth. Taken off balance, the governor's sister-in-law wavered, then toppled to the floor with a hysterical scream. The women parted like a tide of sheep, fell back, and bleated in shock. Bayard was suddenly at Anne's elbow as she stood over her adversary, surprised as any at her fall. He hustled her out the door and to the safety of his ship.

It took most of Bayard's power and all past favors called in to keep Anne from arrest. The governor, appalled that such a scene could occur in his own home, considered a charge of assault and disorderly conduct but settled for a florid apology from Bayard, several lucrative concessions, and a deep grudge.

The most immediate effect of Anne's action was the sudden curtailment of her movements. Now most knew that she was wanted in Charles Town, so any British territories in the West Indies were potential danger spots for her. Spanish colonies such as Cuba were also off-limits, for news of her duel with Maria Renaldi had spread over the islands like a hot sea breeze.

Consequently, one of Bayard's chief attractions for Anne was diminished. She could no longer leave New Providence on his arm bound for some glamorous port. He could no longer flaunt her beauty—in Jamaica, Cuba, Port Royal, or Hispaniola. And because he had to travel to oversee his holdings on these islands, Anne found herself often alone again.

THE MIDDLE OF the year in 1716 brought the hurricane season to New Providence. Anne watched with an ominous sense of foreboding as the swells rolled higher on the sand and the feel of the water took on a turbid chill. A few of the pirates cursed and worked frantically, trying to haul this or that wreck into sailing trim, but most sat morosely in the tavern, snapping at the doxies and each other. It was too late to heave anchor for safer ports. The entire island waited and listened.

Anne rode her pony to the back of the island, searching for fruit and game. There was little to be had in this season; even the birds seemed to have deserted their nests—still, there was little else to occupy her time. She had listlessly moved from her own hut to Bayard's mansion and back to her own hut again, until she felt rootless as kelp.

She maneuvered her mount up the beach and into a circle of palms, flopping down into the coarse grass. The fronds were strangely still—not a breath of wind set them rustling—and the usual jabbering flocks were silent. She rolled on her side and watched a sand crab scuttle from one hiding place to another. She barely noticed the wind rise.

Suddenly, the pony snorted and lifted his head. She followed his eyes and saw a roiling mass of clouds collecting over the horizon. While she watched, they flattened and seemed to coil like a black snake. The wind had already begun to whine as she galloped back to the settlement.

She tied her pony to a stout spar and then, thinking better of it, loosed his reins, slapped his haunches, and sent him trotting to the safety of the palms. The clouds were racing inland now, pushed by a moaning wind that slashed her hair about her and made it hard to breathe. The beach palms rocked and trembled like wet cables, yet there was no rain. The waves were whipping the shore, and she had to lean into the squall, gripping her arms to her sides to keep them from flailing behind her.

Her hut was already thatchless, and her hammock was flapping in the wind like a mad thing. A few people were racing up the beach, heading for the tavern, the strongest set of walls on the island. She looked at what was left of her possessions; a few items, nothing worth the effort of salvaging. She grabbed a swatch of red as it swirled by—a favorite gown—she tied it frantically to the nearest tree, knotting it savagely.

She groped her way to the tavern, embracing palms to keep from being shoved back down to the sand. The wind tore great waves apart and hurled the spray over her. All at once, the clouds split and rain pounded her, stinging her skin. She heard a grinding noise above the clatter of the rain and looked towards the harbor.

A sloop had snapped its anchor cable and ploughed into two smaller craft near the docks. In a terrible crash of flapping sail and spars, the ship smashed through the hull of one vessel and then into the other, shoving both into the sagging planks. The winds and waves, heedless of the litter before them, swept pieces of wood and canvas into the sky. A chicken, squawking wildly, fluttering helplessly, whirled in the midst of sail and wood and torn fronds, and then was gone.

By the time she reached the tavern, Anne was shivering violently in spite of the heat. Her clothes were torn, and her hair blinded her. As she flung open the door of the tavern, a ragged child wailed and a hoarse voice cursed at her to shut the door. The walls themselves pulsed with the storm, and Anne felt her body all over, expecting to find bruises from the fists of rain and wind that had pummeled her to shelter.

Bedraggled pirates and rogues leaned against each other, bemoaning their luck. Anne slid down next to Jennings and Bess, exhausted.

"I'd hate to meet this blow on the seas!"

Jennings handed her an uncorked jug. " 'Tis worse on land, methinks. At sea a good ship'll ride the wind if ye rig her tackles to the tiller. On this godforsaken island there's nary a tree to hold to nor a cellar to hide in."

The wind moaned and shrieked, and the people listened as with one ear.

Anne drifted off to sleep, trying to ignore the noise and chaos around her, willing herself to think of warm beds and hot food.

She started awake suddenly, wrenched from her sleep by the sound of silence.

The tavern's single window was gone, and the roof let in small patches of light where none had intruded before. She raised herself stiffly and stretched. Jennings and Bess were tangled together, drunk and snoring. Suddenly, a baby squalled fretfully, and Jennings raised himself up on one elbow and cocked a bleary eye at the cask in the center of the room. Balser had provided it for the refugee's convenience, and it now reeked with raw sewage. Anne picked her way towards the door.

"It's only the eye," Jennings called. But Anne could no longer stand to stay in the room another moment. She pushed aside a drunk from in front of the door and waked out into the strange hush. Somewhere, she thought, a palm must still be standing—a secluded palm—so she could relieve herself in privacy. No bird called; no insect buzzed at her loins; not a frond moved. The air was heavy and rank, as though no winds had been through at all. Even the sea seemed motionless. She remembered her father's warning about her "fierce and resolute temper."

Our emotions are no more constant than these winds, she thought. She wondered if the storm had hit Charles Town. And she felt the breezes begin again, stirring what was left of her skirts. She hurried back to the tavern just ahead of the tail of the hurricane.

When the winds had passed, Anne picked her way over the sand and the litter, back to where her hut had been. There was little to note that her dwelling had ever sat between these two trees.

Women filed past her, some of them weeping tiredly. They stooped to pick up bits and pieces of wreckage, looking for any remnants of value. Gulls, their beaks agape, washed loosely up and down on gentle waves, oblivious to the dead fish on the sand. Vessels of every size had smashed on the rocks and lay in mangled heaps on the beach. Some larger ships straddled smaller ones like huge bulls in rut.

Everywhere, Anne saw the havoc wrought by the storm. She crouched in the sand, letting the heat soothe her. Then she thought of her pony and set off for the patch of jungle behind the settlement to find him. She wondered idly if James had survived the storm.

The first ship to lay anchor in the bay after the storm was the brig under Ned Teach. And the first stop for the man after a quick tankard at the House of Lords was up the beach to Anne's hut.

Anne saw him coming as she was mending her hammock. She'd seen his ship sail into harbor and sensed that he would visit her without delay. She was wearing no flowers over her ear. The wind had stripped them all. But she had saved a silken blouse with lace sleeves that Madeleine had made. She did not bother to improve her appearance but waited, hands on her hips, as he strode over the sand like a huge bear. He would have taken her into his arms, but she backed away in mock terror.

"Ned Teach, you polecat! Don't you dare implant that stench on me!"

He laughed heartily and plopped down in the shade. "So you survived the blow I see, lass. I swore ye'd tame even a hurricane, but they tell me it near carried ye off."

"No more than everyone else on the island, Ned. The Brethren need a good blow each year, I guess, to cleanse their souls. And your ship sailed it smooth?"

"Ay, she gripped the sea like a young hellkite and held on fast. An' I've a new bride for me troubles!"

Anne laughed gaily. "A new hen, you old rooster? How is it possible? Did the winds sweep the nose from her face?"

"Nay, lass. She's a beauty, too. I bumped her up at a dockside pub an' she rocked back, bared her bilges to me, an' gave me a fine gallop 'til dawn. She's a good craft, but I don't care much for the meat inside the bones."

"You're not in love, then?" Anne asked with a sly wink.

"Sweet Jesus, no, lass! Ye know I'm savin' me scurvy heart for you alone!"

He patted the sand next to him, and Anne sank down, relaxed and enjoying their easy cajolery. He looked out to sea for a long silent moment and then stared full into her face. "I got bad news, lass. Stiffen yerself for the blow."

Anne felt a chill of foreboding flood her. Somehow, she knew before he spoke.

"My father?"

He did not look at her but out to sea. "Ay. He's taken himself a new wife. 'Tis said she's with child."

Anne had not expected such news. Death, perhaps, or disease. But remarriage? And so her mother's old rival, the Sweeney woman, must be dead as well. Her mouth twisted at life's ironies. "So soon?" Her brows arched up in surprise and pain.

"Ye've been gone more than a year." He paused. Still facing the sea, he clutched her hand and squeezed it tightly, then let it go. "That's not the worst. The talk in port is that he's disavowed ye for good. An' the warrant for yer arrest still stands."

She felt her throat tighten like a hundred cords pulling her off her feet into the air, swinging helplessly. So, she thought. A new bride. A new family. And I'm to be swept from his life like . . . the dregs of a bad meal. Oh, God. What a black wrath. And now I am truly alone. Disowned by the only man I ever loved. From the only home I've ever known. And I am to be dismissed from his life, then, like dirty linen.

For one blind instant she felt a murderous hatred for James Bonny, her father, for all men. She felt a great aching loss. She remembered something her father once said. "When you allow love to fall from your hands, lass, then they are forever empty." She knew in her heart that he would never relent. That he had turned his back on her as completely as though she had died with her mother. No law would recognize any claim she might have. No one in her father's new life would give her a passing thought.

"Hie aloft yer heart, lass." Teach spoke quietly. "We all sleep in a single bed sooner or later."

She pulled her shoulders in and lifted her chin. "And who is she? This new bride?"

"Mistress Susanna Ball. 'Tis said she brought a handsome dowry."

And the blessings of her father as well. Since Ball's land, Kensington, abuts Bellefield. Such a merger makes a mighty fortune for them both.

Anne's mind screamed. She is but nineteen! A scant two years older than I! She searched her memory and recalled a young girl, somber, dark-haired, pale, and demure, with clasped hands and slight shoulders. Carrying her father's seed. So he suffered little from my sins. He shrugged my disgrace off his shoulders and me along with it.

She traced an aimless pattern in the sand with one quivering finger. In her mind she was back at Bellefield, riding free over the lowland pastures. Her father stood watching her, laughing, his hands on his hips. A tall man full of strength and pride. A lined face full of love. She could feel his arms around her, holding her small body up over the gunwales so she could see the great Atlantic before them.

She struggled to return to the moment. Her mind lurched back, and she realized that Ned was waiting for her signal to go or stay. She stood abruptly, brushing off her skirt.

"Well, I wish him well of her." She lifted an invisible glass in mock salute. "May his donkey ever be in foal."

Teach smiled gently at her. "Now may not be the best time for an old offer, Anne. Since I shot off me cannon 'bout me new wife. But if ye'd have me, I'd set ye above all others. I'd see to yer comforts an' take care o' you proper."

She shook her head. "You're a good man, Teach. I'm grateful for your offer. But I cannot accept your bounty."

"What will ye do?"

Anne pondered for a moment, turning her options over and

over like cold stones in the sun. What would it profit me to cast my lot with respectable society? I am set adrift, that much is certain.

"What have those in high quarters ever done for me? I wager my fate is with outlaws, Ned. Perhaps I shall go on account myself."

He laughed and slapped his knees, his black beard bristling with each jolt. "Ay, lass! That's the wench I know!" He lurched to his feet. "Then I'm off." He leered at her. "You'll be in good hands I wager afore the sun sets twice. And while I'm at it, I'll send Charles Town your regards."

Before she could dodge him, he grabbed her in his burly arms and pressed a huge kiss on her mouth. She staggered backwards when he released her from the sheer force of his embrace and laughed weakly.

"Watch out for your wedding tackle, lad." She grinned. "A woman'll forgive much, but lose that lot, and you're naught but food for fishes."

He smirked and strode off down the beach. She watched him go, her mouth drooping. When she was alone once more, she slumped to the sand, her head in her hands. She could not hate her father, try as she might. Men were not against one, really. They were merely for themselves.

*T*HE NEXT TIME Anne saw Ned Teach he had a fine gentleman in tow. She was at the House of Lords with Jennings and Bess when the door blew open as if pushed by a squall. Ned stomped in the room, his eyes fiery and reeking of rum. Behind him loitered a tall, bewigged man in a long frock coat.

"Anne! My favorite Jezebel!" Teach shouted, clasping her by the waist and whirling her about. Anne finally pulled free, straightened her hair and her skirts, and heard a mild voice say, "More like Aphrodite, I'd wager."

Teach guffawed and shoved the man over to Anne. "This is the hellkite I told you of, lad. Anne, this is Major Stede Bonnet, a gentleman farmer from Barbados who aims to join the Brethren!"

Anne looked at him more closely. All the while Teach bantered, Bonnet watched him carefully as one would observe a chained bear. He clearly liked the pirate and just as clearly knew him for the rogue he could be. Teach slapped him on the back. "A pirate! And under my expert teachings!" He winked at her.

Anne appraised Bonnet quietly. He had the pink face of an aristocrat, not the mahogany color of a seaman. He wore a long, blond wig that had gone to damp tendrils at his cheeks from the heat. Next to Teach's black bristles, Major Bonnet's clean-shaven chin looked almost boyish. Anne grinned to herself; his knee breeches, silk stockings, and buckled shoes would send Madeleine into moans of ecstasy.

Bonnet bowed low over Anne's hand and kissed it softly, meeting her eyes with frank interest. She dropped a quick curtsy almost reflexively. Something in his manner reminded her of the gentlemen she'd known in Charles Town light-years before. As Teach elbowed them to a vacant table, he told her Bonnet's history. Major Stede Bonnet had left his Barbados estate and sufficient wealth to keep most any man satisfied.

Stede said little, only smiled intently at her, watching for reactions.

"His shrew of a wife drove him to it, lass! Let that be a lesson to all vinegar tongues!" Teach bellowed.

Bonnet all but blushed. "Teach has generously offered to take this farmer in hand and make him a sailor."

Anne became suddenly aware of the makeshift vision the House of Lords presented. For the first time, she was embarrassed as she imagined what she must look like to a gentleman with Bonnet's breeding.

"The dog wants to go on account!" Teach was beside himself with glee and howled his way drunkenly over to a neighboring table to investigate a likely looking trull.

Anne found herself suddenly alone with Stede Bonnet. She smiled slowly at him, glad she had taken the time to put a fresh flower in her hair. "On account, Major? I should think a man in your position would scorn the company of such as these." She indicated the rabble of the tavern with an expressive shrug.

He leaned forward and took her hand, then dropped it as if remembering himself. "I've come to recruit more men. That should prove my intent."

Bonnet continued softly, watching her eyes. "They tell me this island is the place to find anything I need—free of the constraints of hidebound aristocracy."

"And the law," Anne added, grinning. "Ay, Major. The republic could be a paradise—" she grimaced as two drunken pirates erupted into violent battle in one end of the room—"but one must watch out for the wild beasts."

"And what, may I ask, could possibly hold a rare lady as yourself in such a . . . lair?"

She laughed, delighted with his quick wit. She scanned his face intently and saw, in the lines about his mouth and his small, finely etched nose, the dignity of generations of breeding and taste. Even the arch of his brow suggested a steady intelligence, reminding her of rows of bound volumes, cultivated voices, and dimly remembered sonatas.

"I'd rather endure the company of rogues," she said softly, "than that of starched ladies who can talk of nothing save their gowns, their babies, and the latest court gossip. Ladies who pretend to swoon at the least touch of . . . life." She laughed throatily. "And besides, at the moment, I've nowhere else to go."

He smiled and offered his arm. "Perhaps you'd show me a bit of the island?"

At his side, she felt as though she were strolling the gardens of a fine estate instead of the back yards in a makeshift pirate lair.

" . . . Now I take my chances for myself. And the risk is all the more exciting."

"A short life but merry?" Anne asked.

"Indeed. I have been the model son, perfect husband, and loving father. For the rest of my life, I intend to be impious, profane, and indiscreet."

Anne laughed softly, her hand gentle on his arm. "Commendable goals, sir! But can a gentleman shed his skin so easily?"

Bonnet's face turned meditative. "When Adam delved and Eve span, who was then the gentleman? As God is my judge, once the risk is taken out of life, there is little left. I want fair winds, a fleet ship, and the dizziness of freedom."

Something in his voice jarred Anne, left her stirred in a way she'd not felt for a long while. The man seemed to voice many of her own yearnings and stepped into a lonely spot in her heart that had been growing daily since she'd come to New Providence.

"I used to climb the plantation palms to watch the ships move along the sealanes. My father often scolded me for my empty dreams."

They sat down on the sand in a secluded cove and stared out over the waves together. Anne asked a question she'd never found an answer for within herself. "What lures us, do you think? What is it about the water that so draws some souls?"

He did not laugh at her question or turn it away but seemed to be eager to share her thought. "You remember the legend of Narcissus?"

Anne nodded, at once delighted to be exercising her mind in a way she'd not done for over a year.

"Well, Narcissus could not grasp his own image, as you recall, and so he dove into the deep water and drowned. Thus it is with some souls and the sea. We see ourselves in all oceans. It is the image of an elusive phantom life we see in each wave, the key to all meaning."

Anne felt a deep comfort in his presence. In spite of his figure and his dandified attire, this displaced gentleman touched a familiar chord in her.

Bonnet's father had died at forty, burdening him with a fortune, a large plantation to manage, and an invalid mother. Before she passed away, she arranged a prosperous marriage for him that produced three daughters. Then Bonnet's younger brother died of a fever. His widow and four daughters moved to his household, bringing a total of nine dependent women under his wing.

"I could no longer stand the sound of their voices, no, nor even the hissing rustles of their skirts day in and day out. I was not raised to leave women helpless, but neither could I entomb myself in their arms. I left it all to them and took to sea. I wish them well." He sighed. "And myself far away."

He looked at Anne sitting on the sand, her bare feet resting in the warm waves, her hair blowing free as any native's, her skin glowing in the setting sun. "And now, here I sit with a woman who depends on no man." He gestured over the broad expanse of beach. "Who's mistress of her own estate."

She smiled. "I never wanted to mistress anything. Were it offered, I'd likely run, just as you have."

He took her chin in his hand and turned her face towards him. "You need nothing else. You are a complete and perfect woman, a goddess in her own realm." He lowered his lips to hers and kissed her, at first gently, then more insistently. Anne's mind whirled to James. How could I have married him? she grimaced inwardly. Thank God he's not here now. And then she realized that he might never be back again. And if he did come back, what allegiance did she truly owe him? And then she thought no more, but merely let her lips loose to swim under Bonnet's mouth, while the waves chuckled a thousand soft secrets.

His kisses were more and more searching; his mouth probed hers and found a willing well of pent-up desire, of loneliness, of a bewildered sadness that matched his own. And yet Anne felt a slight hesitancy from the man. He reached for her breast timidly at one point, touched her wonderingly through her silken bodice, then abruptly pulled his hand away. After several moments of kisses, Anne drew back her head and gazed into his eyes.

"What is it?" she asked huskily.

He dropped his eyes and flushed slightly. She could see her own wetness still on his mouth.

"I cannot pretend that you are not another man's wife."

Anne frowned in frustration. "And you another woman's as well?"

"No. That troubles me not at all." His voice was as soft as the water under her feet. "But I would put any man to the sword who touched you, were I your husband. I cannot do less than reproach myself for seducing a lady who belongs to another."

"I belong to no one, Major. No one but myself. My husband has taken it into his head to better himself on a turtle boat. And he's made it painfully clear that he doesn't care to keep me as his wife." She paused delicately, wondering how much he knew of her life. "Surely, you are aware that I've lived with another man in his absence?"

Bonnet lifted his head and looked at her intently. His blue eyes seemed to bore into her, yet gently. "Yes. Of your own free will?"

"Ay. And I left him just as freely." She smiled at him, caressing his arms softly, pulling his mouth to hers once more. "Come." She coaxed him to his feet and to the cover of a private glade. "We cannot help ourselves, you and I. 'Tis part of what we've become."

There, under a long-branched palm, the fronds making a natural umbrella from all eyes, he laid her on the sand. With eager, trembling hands, he gently pulled her skirts up to form a blanket for them both. He threw off his coat and lowered himself over her, his mouth buried in her neck. Anne felt a great tenderness well up in her, a strange blend of sorrow and joy that caused her eyes to water with its power. She gripped Stede's hands and pulled them to her breasts, gazing into his eyes. There were no words left to say; indeed, she could not speak for the tightness in her throat.

He loosed one hand and ran it tentatively, delicately, up her inner thigh, and she felt her muscles quiver as with a chill. His other hand, still with hers entwined, cupped her head, gripping her hair. The heat in her belly grew now, moving down her limbs, and she began to murmur and moan low in her throat. He moved his hands faster now, hotter and more insistently until finally, with a wild cry, she wrapped her arms tightly around his head and pulled him into her. For just an instant she stopped, gasping at the heat and fullness of his body, and then she saw he was moving once more, throbbing, arching her agile hips under his loins. They were gliding together, echoing the cries of the waterfowl. When her last shudder was complete, she clenched him tighter, willing him to stay within her, beyond all words, past any thoughts save the moment. Abruptly, she felt his desire rise again, and she tightened her legs around his hips and strove to meet him until they once more spasmed, this time his own cries mixing with hers. Afterwards, as the light left the sky and the mosquitoes began to find them, they rolled themselves in their clothes and slept locked tightly in each other's arms.

Stede roamed the island with Anne, heedless of the passing tides, and would not be taunted by Teach or his crew to turn his head to business. Yet Anne felt a strange reserve develop inside herself that would not allow her to love Stede. When she was with him, she was carried away by his voice, his manners, his caresses. But when they were apart, she found herself wondering what she saw in such a bewigged dandy. Meg frankly called him a fop and could not understand her attraction to him. Stede was growing to love her deeply, but she was drawn to his feelings for her more than she was to the man himself. His tenderness made her feel more cherished, more feminine than she ever had before. Yet even when he began to write verse for her and weave flower chains for her hair, she could not muster up a passion to match his own.

And as the weeks passed, Bonnet began to spend more time gazing out to sea with an anxious frown hovering above his brow.

Anne knew that their time together would be short, but she was determined that it be gay.

"My crew is complete. My sloop is loaded. No prey, no pay, they say, and well I know it, my sweet."

"Ay," she said calmly. "Soon you must be off."

He looked even more anxious. "But you must come with me, Anne! I cannot leave you here in this cesspool."

She hesitated, wishing that this moment had not come. She wanted to go from this island urgently. She knew now that one of Bonnet's chief attractions for her was his passport from New Providence. And yet, now that he was asking her, she knew that she could not leave with him. He would never survive as a pirate. She took his hands gently.

"Listen to me, Stede. I don't want to dash your hopes. But Teach has expressed grave doubts that you'll ever make a pirate. You don't know the sea, he says. You'll tire of it, or the king's men will make you rue your choice. Perhaps you should consider returning to Barbados."

She winced at the pain she saw in his face. She did not want to hurt him, but neither did she want to place the reins of her life in his hands. As much as she wanted to leave the island, she did not wish to escape with Stede Bonnet.

"Do not dissuade me, Anne! This is one dream I'll not barter— not for you, not for any woman!"

"Oh, Stede. Much as I care for you, I can't encourage you to such a course. You're a man of honor. Your sins will haunt you."

He grew florid and cursed, yet even in his anger, he picked his words carefully. "If I were a pirate, you would not hesitate, by God. It makes my head whirl to think how fast you would run off with me then."

"But you're not a pirate, Stede. And I doubt you ever will be. Besides"—she lowered her head—"someday you'd see you couldn't manage me. And you'd hate me for it."

"Never."

She saw she would have to hurt him. "I want off this island. But not with you."

Bonnet looked crushed. "I shall be a pirate, my dear. And a good one. And when I am, I shall sail back to this hellpot and pull you off, away from your errant husband and your sporting friends." He lowered his head and glowered. "You can't think too highly of me if you doubt my word."

Anne laughed and pulled his head to hers. "Oh, my dear. I think very highly of you. I think you're far too good for this lot, to be sure. But I am a practical woman, Major. Do what you must and so shall I. And in the meantime"—she urged him closer—"let us both be practical and not fret away what time we have left."

*B*ONNET LEFT IN a fast-lined sloop with a full and eager crew. Ned Teach's brig followed him into deep water, then the two, master and apprentice, sailed away from New Providence. Anne stood on the beach and waved both of them good-bye. She missed him once he was gone, her major. But not quite enough to wish him back again. She wondered privately if she was ever to be almost in love, always to feel a shallow sea between her heart and another's like the half-light that comes from an unformed moon.

Stede Bonnet and Ned Teach split up once in open water, and the major sailed on his new sloop, the *Revenge*, to plunder the Caribbean. He captured the *Anne* out of Glasgow, the *Endeavor* out of Bristol, and the *Turbet* from Barbados, all bound for Virginian capes. He burned the Barbadian vessel to prevent news of his piracy from reaching his wife and set the crews ashore to fend for themselves.

He then sailed for Charles Town; he wanted to be near Anne once more. The harbor had two deep-water channels. The smaller ran to Sullivans Island; the main channel ran southward past Morris and Folly islands. A pirate sloop waiting between the two channels could effectively monitor all sea traffic and follow those out to sea that looked most choice. Like sharks to a feeding, the pirates gathered to prey on the richest vessels, watching for those lying so low in the water that the crews could wash their hands at gunwales.

Bonnet's luck was good. He took a brigantine from New England, plundered her, and sent her on to Charles Town. He closed with a sloop from Barbados, stole her cargo of sugar, rum, and slaves, pressed her crew into service, and added the vessel to his growing fleet.

Bonnet's prizes swelled his reputation, though his crew still grumbled about his unseaworthy and clumsy sail techniques. But with a rich flotilla and an opulent cargo, he made ready to sail back to New Providence to reclaim Anne. On the way, he stopped at Turneffe off Honduras for fresh water. There, he once more met with Ned Teach, who was provisioning his new forty-gun French guineaman that he'd christened the *Queen Anne's Revenge*.

Teach eyed Bonnet's fleet, particularly his sleek *Revenge*, and said, "I could damn well use such a sloop in my assault on Charles Town, lad. Let's join forces an' make 'em howl for the sake of one red-haired wench back on the beach!"

"Actually," Stede demurred, "I'd planned to sail to New Providence with the next good wind to see her."

Teach thundered, "Well, by God, if ye mean to move a spitfire like Mistress Bonny, ye must show some fire yourself! Come with me an' devil her old port. 'Tis no accident I've named me own vessel after the lass. Together, our two *Revenge*s will bring them to their knees. That'll show her!"

Bonnet was not at all certain that he or his crew needed another excursion. Secretly, he was already tiring of the discomforts and boredom that were the mainstays of a life at sea. But he went aboard the *Queen Anne* to share a tankard with his old friend, leaving his crew behind on his own sloop. After a few rounds of bumboo, Teach blandly announced, "I've taken the liberty of puttin' a man or two o' me own aboard your sloop, Major. 'T'will be a better crew all told, and ye will be more comfortable aboard the *Queen Anne* with me. Come! We'll drink on our new partnership!"

Bonnet's face flushed with quick anger and humiliation. His crew had easily accepted a new commander, and he was now virtually a prisoner on Teach's brig. His own men were party to his demotion.

There was little Bonnet could do but agree, with all grace, to stay aboard the *Queen Anne's Revenge* and sail with Teach. Their reputations preceded them when they sailed into Charles Town accompanied by a flotilla of five ships and four hundred men. Laying off harbor, Blackbeard and Bonnet took nine vessels, among them a ship bound for London commanded by Robert Clark, a sloop, two pinks out of the Indies, and a brigantine with fourteen slaves aboard. Their most important prize was a merchant ship bound for Bristol. Among its passengers was Samuel Wragg and his young son.

Wragg was a member of the council in Charles Town, a prominent and respected citizen. He was dragged on board the *Queen Anne's Revenge* together with his son and closely questioned about the number of guns in port, cargoes in and out of Charles Town, and, finally, his acquaintance with a certain Cormac and his daughter, Anne. Teach cursed them roundly, threatened them with instant extinction, and their town with total devastation. After the inquisition the prisoners were hustled back aboard their ship and locked in the hold.

Sitting in the blind darkness, they were convinced that at any moment the ship would be burned and sunk with them trapped belowdecks. After giving them several hours to ponder their fate, Teach hauled up Wragg and another prisoner, Marks, and announced his intentions. His crew needed medicine, he said. Mercurial preparations for the pox. All would be held hostage save Marks who would go ashore with two pirates to demand a chest of medical supplies from the city council. If after two days the pirates, their prisoner, and the medicines did not return, all the hostages would be put to death, all the captured vessels burned, and the town terrorized.

Marks and the two pirates were then put in a small skiff and rowed to shore with Blackbeard's threats ringing in their ears.

While the council debated, Teach and his crew tormented the town. Members of the crew strutted about the streets, jostling women and brandishing weapons, knowing full well that the colony was all but defenseless. With a population of about ten thousand blacks and six thousand whites, mostly living out in the lowlands and unprepared for such an attack, the people could think of little to do. With no man-of-war in sight, they abandoned themselves to despair.

Charles Town had just endured a two-year war with the Yemassee Indians. Then, after six months of relative calm, pirate Captain Christopher Moody had taken his pleasure, leaving looted warehouses, burned homes, and debauched women in his wake. Now Blackbeard and Bonnet webbed the harbor like two fat spiders waiting for hapless flies. There were eight sails in the bay ready for sea, but none dared venture out. No inbound vessels would cross the bar with the pirates in place, so all trade was frozen.

Governor Johnson was furious at the pirates' audacity and recommended battle, but the council finally decided to yield. When the chest of medicines was rowed aboard the *Queen Anne's Revenge*, Teach cursed Marks and Wragg in lieu of the general citizenry for "inhospitable and rude manners to weaker folk," relieved them of their money, stripped them naked, and set them ashore.

The pirate captains howled at the thought of council gentlemen sent back to the city stripped of their pride, their watches, and their breeches. New Providence rocked with Teach's revenge, and Anne was a heroine.

"And Bonnet, that fop, rowed to Bath-Town to apply for a

king's pardon! One week with Teach, an' he's ready to feel the rough side of a woman's tongue again!"

Anne smiled sadly to herself. So he had given up the dream after all. Now that the memory of his caresses had dimmed, she felt relieved that he'd escaped back to where he belonged. But her face warmed when she recalled that first night under the umbrella palm, and she hoped that wherever he sailed, the wind would be at his shoulder.

ONE OF THE most skilled and audacious corsairs operating in the straits of Florida, Captain Charles Vane, brought his ship into New Providence harbor to auction off his plunder and to give his crew an opportunity to relax. Vane himself was a man of moderation. A few hard drunks and easy doxies, and he was content to be back aboard his sloop. But he tarried long enough at the House of Lords to brag about his new quartermaster, Jack Rackham, who had stopped off at Cuba and would not be along to New Providence for a week.

Anne had already heard of Jack Rackham, the infamous Calico Jack, named for his theatrical garb: a shirt, jacket, and breeches made of colorful calico cloth. He was something of a legend in the Caribbean, not for his piratical prowess, which was adequate, but for his sexual conquests. He had bedded, it was rumored, titled ladies in England where he'd been a liveryman, French duchesses in Hispaniola, and Spanish beauties in Cuba. Rackham was said to be unusually handsome for a rogue.

"Ay," Vane laughed. "He takes a woman as he takes a ship! No time wasted, straight alongside, every gun brought to play, and the prize boarded."

Two days passed, and James Bonny returned. He went brazenly to Bayard's estate, after checking to see that the governor was not on the island. Anne had the mansion to herself as usual. James burst in on her and found her playing with her pet parrot, surrounded by the luxuries that Bayard's ships provided in his absence. She looked up as he stalked in, his hands on his hips. Her face went slightly pale, but she squared her shoulders and faced him calmly.

"So. You survived the hurricane, then. We thought you were lost, James."

"Ay. I see you did. One boat was lost. We've been marooned on a godforsaken cay for most a month. I'm lucky to be alive. Wouldn't be at all if we'd not hailed Rackham's sloop."

Rackham again. So he's arrived as well, she thought. But she kept her face bland.

He glared at her. "I see you found a new master."

She bristled, but only her eyes flashed. She was determined to keep her temper in check. "Not master, James. He's been a friend. And as you can see, he's rarely here at all."

James closed his eyes in weary contempt and lifted a hand to stop her. "Please, woman. I don't need to hear your tales. Get your things and come along."

What else had he heard? Of Bonnet? Of Teach? Of her father? She realized then what he'd said.

"To where?"

"I have found a decent house in this hellhole. 'Twill do us 'til we can collect enough coin to take us home. We lost the turtles on that last trip out, but as soon as we can, I mean to get back to Charles Town."

Then he had not heard of her father's betrayal. She felt a quick indignant anger at his commanding tone, but also a deep sadness that they had come to this moment between them. Her mixed emotions must have showed on her face, for he said, as soft as he had ever been with her, "Come, Anne. You are still my wife, for good or ill." He went to her and took her hands. "Let us start again. I'll ask you no questions. I'll not plague you for your conduct in my absence. I'll stand by you if you'll come with me now."

She gazed about at the riches in the room, the wealth of a dozen countries and countless cargoes, all for her pleasure. And then she remembered, with a quick grimace, each gesture, each invasion she'd had to give and accept to earn every silken thread or golden bauble. She knew she could not bear Bayard another night. She glanced at James. He looked far more dignified than when he'd left. He has met death head-on, she thought. And now he wants to go home. To Charles Town. Perhaps they could build a life together now. Impulsively, she gathered up as much as she could carry and followed James down the beach to the settlement.

For almost a week Anne attempted to make of James' "decent house" a livable shelter. They occupied the second story of one of the few wooden structures on the island. Half of the floor was a cluster of rooms used by doxies who lured clients from the tavern below, and half belonged temporarily to Anne and James. It was definitely better than a thatched hut, or so Anne thought. After several nights of late-night noise and the accumulated filth of many hot, sweaty bodies, however, she began to yearn for the breezy solitude of her beach shack. She watched James warily, waiting for some signal of a new start between them. He kept his word. He never reviled her for her actions. He never asked her questions—but he never touched her, either.

He was grave and cheerless. After a week he packed a few provisions and went turtling again, leaving without even a parting embrace.

For two nights Anne confined herself to her rooms. On the third night of James' absence, she walked out on the beach, disconsolate. She felt empty and old, as if every sense were numbed. The stars were just as bright, she knew, but she took no pleasure in their dappled constellations. The full moon threw silver on the water as always, but tonight it looked cold and metallic rather than inviting. From far down the beach she heard the usual carousing at the House of Lords, and she turned her head to catch the sounds of laughter. She was suddenly filled with restlessness, a twisting resentment that she should be such a watcher, a listener, and not one of the laughers herself.

As she neared the tavern, she realized that most of the noise was coming from the beach in front of the old stone building. A pirate crew was crowded on the sand dividing plunder from a long and profitable voyage.

Business was over now, and the women from the village drifted in to join the merriment, share the free rum, and dance to the music. Anne walked to the edge of the beach; for a moment no one noticed her. The bonfires lit her face to a glow, and her hair falling down her shoulders looked like flame licking at her skin.

Bess moved towards her quickly, pulling her into the fringes of the crowd.

"Calico Jack's brought in half the wealth of the Indies, lass! Come an' choose yerself a trinket!" She turned to the pack of men picking through chests spilling over with gold, plate, and silks. "This is Mistress Anne Bonny, you lot! She's spoken for an' wed legal! If ye trifle with her, me own man'll clap yer ears to yer head!"

From the opposite edge of the crowd, a deep voice rang out. "The lady's welcome, Bess. I myself will answer for her safety." The man strode through the mob that parted for him, eager to return to their celebration.

Anne watched the man approach, wondering why Bess stayed stubbornly at her side. He stepped up boldly, swept his hat from his head, and took her hand. His eyes searched hers in the firelight. Anne felt a blush start from somewhere inside her body and flood her face. She was glad that the glow of the fire hid her flaming cheeks.

Rackham stood out from the rest of the crew like a three-master in a bay of skiffs. He was tall with no beard at all, and his dark hair hung to his shoulders in tangled waves. Somehow he looked elegant and saturnine at once. His style of dress distinguished him from the other pirate captains—he had disdain for silks and velvets, preferring cotton calico, freshly washed and loose fitting. Anne felt rather than saw that his chest was large, hairless, and rippled with muscles. His major adornment was a huge cutlass, encrusted with rubies and emeralds along the hilt, tied to a leather bandolier at his waist. She saw no impudence, no arrogant sensuality in his gaze, yet she sensed that she was quite naked before him.

Suddenly resentful, she withdrew her hand. "Bess, my thanks for your welcome. I'm sure I can fend for myself." Bess glanced at her warily, then shrugged and walked back to Jennings' side.

In the center of the crowd, the musicians began to play, and the women raised their voices in song and swayed while the men stomped to the sounds of drums and fiddles. The torches flickered wildly in the warm wind. Women from the brothels quickly paired with the pirates; couples danced and whirled and then lurched off into the palm groves, leaning on each other, drunk with rum and the balmy night breeze.

Anne and Rackham stood and watched the dancers, each wrapped in separate thoughts. Out of the corner of her eye, Anne saw him reach into a side pocket of his pants. Before she could react, he was reaching slowly under her hair and winding a magnificent rope of pearls around her neck, his fingers brushing her throat softly. She stiffened at his touch, but her lips smiled as if they willed themselves.

"I have sailed halfway around the world searching for a woman whose beauty is equal to these. They are the sea's own." His eyes devoured her as he murmured, "Please accept them with my compliments."

She picked up the strand of beads, which hung down between her breasts, and held them up to the light . . . pearls, smooth and lustrous, glowing with fire from the light of the torches. Her skin looked opalescent under them, softer to the touch.

"Captain Rackham, you take my breath away with your generosity . . . yet, I wonder. Are you in the habit of bestowing beautiful gifts on complete strangers?"

"They belong to women like you." He grinned. "And I'll not ask anything in payment . . . you'd not willingly give." His eyes laughed, and his lips looked inviting.

"I belong to another, sir." She was surprised at how difficult such an admission came to her mouth.

"Do you now? You look like a woman who never belongs to any man. No one could ever own such a beauty. Any more than a man could own the sea, though he may lay claim to a favorite cove or two."

Anne laughed in spite of her tension. "You have much pretty wit, sir, for a pirate captain."

"Newly made captain, milady. And so not yet jaded by great beauty. And besides, 'tis no wit. 'Tis truth." He took her hand again gently and laid it on his arm as he wheeled her towards the music. But she stopped at the edge of the crowd and pulled her hand away. It was all happening too easily, too fast. If I dance with him now, it will be a tacit admission to all who watch that I'm fair game, she thought. No Bayard. No Bonnet. Just a woman alone.

"Please, Captain. I am grateful for your gift, but I cannot barter my reputation for it."

He glanced at her intently and seemed to grasp her meaning.

"I can wait, milady. The best prizes one must have patience for." He turned with a chuckle and left her there alone, at the edge of the firelight.

ONE DAY MELTED into the next, and Anne had established a leisurely life for herself—of surf and sunny days. She would bathe in private coves, swimming nude in the warm water. She climbed up into the huge turtle shell she used as a canoe and curled up to dry in the sun, letting the wavelets rock her into a lulling slumber. From a great distance she heard her name called over and over. She peeped up over the shell's rim and saw Jack Rackham standing at the water's edge. From his vantage point she doubted he could see much of her, but she was instantly aware that there was no place else to hide but in the water. Tipping the shell forward, she poured herself over the side and into the green depths, her back to him. The water enveloped as it clearly revealed her, beautifully nude. Rackham, with the long strides of a cat, walked out to the end of the coral point and grinned down at her.

"Good morrow, milady. I found you." He doffed his hat and glanced at some location beneath her neck.

"How?" Anne felt uncomfortable, but she also knew she must look to a great advantage. She felt no real shame at the display she made.

"Actually, I followed you. A goodly walk, I must say, in this sun." He lowered his eyes a few inches more. "But it was worth it."

Anne blushed again, her feet feeling for some purchase on the sand. She glanced around; they were completely alone. "Well, you might be a gentleman and leave me to my pleasures, sir. I can't get out and cover myself with you here."

"I am gentleman. But I'm no fool, lass. I would not steal your pleasures from you; I want only to share them." With that and a bold laugh, he quickly stripped off his clothing and dove cleanly into the water.

He moved so quickly that Anne had only a fast glimpse of hard, brown loins and muscled arms before the water splashed over her head; he surfaced next to her, not touching but close. He shook the water from his face like a great spaniel and laughed into her shocked face. Now Anne realized how clear the water was as she saw his strong legs pump the water. He moved closer and put an arm around her waist, drawing her body to his.

She felt his hand on her waist; his legs grazed hers. She had to put her hand on his shoulder to keep afloat. Somehow she could not summon up the outrage she wanted to feel.

"Are you mad? My husband will run you through if he catches you."

Rackham put back his head and laughed merrily. "The turtler? I have heard all about the man. All of New Providence knows of his prowess with a weapon."

That remark roused her to some anger. "And have you also heard of my prowess, sir? *I* will defend my own honor whether he cares to or no!" But it was hard to be angry while bobbing in the warm water clutched by such a man.

He smiled gently. "Ay, mistress. I've heard of your prowess as well. And if you wish it, I shall set you free as any mermaid." He waited, his hand softly stroking her waist, smiling down at her, staring into her eyes. Again her mouth betrayed her and twitched into a smile involuntarily. She lowered her eyes, silent. He pulled her close then, his belly cleaved to hers; his feet found sand and so did hers. Anne felt his hardness against her thighs as he bent his mouth to hers.

Later in the shade of the palms, she lay in his arms, twining her fingers in his black hair. She had lost her independent resolve beneath the waves, sometime before he carried her out of the sea and onto the sand pressing his body to hers. His body felt hard and demanding on hers, yet strangely familiar, intimately a part of her blood and sinew.

Then on the soft moss beneath the palms, he held her hands above her head. Raising over her with his body, he hovered just above her, barely brushing her skin with his own, moving himself up and down in between her legs softly, softly, light as any ocean breeze . . . until finally she could bear his teasing touch no more and, wrenching her hands free, pulled him down into her, moaning, her tongue sliding wetly past the salt on his face to the hot darkness of his mouth.

Now the breeze cooled their bodies as they lay twined together. She pulled herself back to the present to hear him say, "My God, woman. You are as warm as you are beautiful. Is there no pleasure you don't know?"

"Many," she drawled lazily. "But I'm young yet."

He grinned. "Ay, you are. Young and old—tart and sweet. Does your husband know what a treasure he has?"

"No. He finds the tart not to his taste."

"Well, I like vinegar with my greens. I cannot let you go back to him, that's certain. Now that we've pinned him with horns, the least he can do is quietly withdraw and leave the spoils to the victor." He squeezed her gently. "Is there a chance a pirate could lure you from your turtler, milady?"

She felt the strength in his arms, a strength she had not known in a long while. Certainly not with Bayard. Or Bonnet. And when she pictured James, all she could remember was a scowl and a petulant whine.

"You know my past, Jack. Have you no...questions of me?"

He laughed. "Who am I to question your past, lass? 'Tis your future I prize. The world is broad, and I mean to have the soft parts as my own. I ask you to share them with me."

She stroked his neck, her eyes far away, remembering old dreams. "I *am* ready to leave this island."

"Excellent! I shall take you to Cuba where I have land and a house fit for a queen!"

She was suddenly hard with old determination. "I swear, I'd choke to death under another roof. I'm sick to death of being left behind on the beach while all the world spins by."

He opened his eyes in mock terror. "Oho! The hellkite shows her claws! Teach told me you were an outlaw born for sin." He watched her as he fondled her breast knowingly. "Well then... what say you to a life at sea? With me. And your only roof shall be the open sky."

Anne caught her breath in her throat. For the first time she actually considered her inner dream from some practical place in her mind. At sea. Moving from island to island, taking plunder at will, free from James, from any restraint, free from the heat and the filth of the island, to taste different winds each morning and to see new stars each night. She wrapped her legs around him and pressed herself up to him teasingly.

"A tempting offer, sir. I shall think on it," she purred.

"Do, lass." He murmured throatily as he lowered himself on her, once more hard and eager. "Yes. Do. I can wait."

ANNE KNEW little of her new lover. Jack had been given the honorary title of captain by his crew, though he did not yet command his own ship but one of Vane's. She had heard that he was the illegitimate son of a London merchant, the black-sheep rogue son of an English duke, and a member of a famous theatrical family, but she did not know whether these tales came from Rackham himself or were woven by his many admirers from mere loose ends.

Increasingly, however, his past was less and less important to her. Just as he vowed to ask her no questions of her earlier life, so she asked no questions of his. One rumor did unsettle her though, and it persisted in her mind long after she'd tried to will it gone. It was said that Jack was, like many handsome young men in the king's navy, a great favorite with certain known sodomites in the officers' fo'c'sle. But since Anne could see no present evidence of such a sexual detour, she scorned the gossip as the result of flaming envy.

Jack Rackham and Anne Bonny used the island of New Providence as a lovers' paradise. They bathed together in secluded coves and frothy breakers, washing each other's hair with rainwater, rolling as one through the waves, and splashing each other like two young otters. They rode bareback up white sugar-sand beaches and away to the far side of the island. They ate juicy mangoes and made love under palm trees, then dozed in the dappled sunlight as their bodies cooled. Jack played his hornpipe, and she whirled and danced in the moonlight for him, a bright swath of cloth over her hips, her breasts and her hair free. And they held each other gently, murmuring through long, lazy afternoons in the shelter of a convenient banyan tree.

"Why are you so bound to go to sea, lass?" he asked her one day.

She tried to tell him of Narcissus, of phantom souls, of the self she felt was out there somewhere, beyond the horizon. But he did not catch the flavor of her yearning. Finally, she asked him, "Well, then. Why do *you* like to go to sea?"

"I don't. I've no great longing to live my life in bilge water and sour holds, but I've not discovered another way to be a pirate. And I do like goin' on account!"

"Why?"

He looked amazed that she would ask such a question.

"I mean, besides the money which is an obvious lure, why else be a pirate? Why not a merchant?"

He made a horrid face.

She grinned. "Well, piracy is more than fancy thievery."

"Ay!" he laughed. "But thievery is the most honorable profession you can name! Even the good Lord stole Adam from the earth and Eve from his side!"

"Off with your twisted carcass, you rogue!" she growled. "I can see I'll get no sense from you this day." She playfully slapped his buttocks. He made as if to rise off her, and she quickly pulled him down again, muffling her laughter in his neck.

But he continued, soberly recalling the execution of nine pirates he'd seen in Jamaica the year before.

"Nicholas Lawes, the scurvy bastard, had the gall to haul the lads in and hang them for the very same activities they'd been heroes for during the queen's war. And they had no counsel! Under the law of the king, unless they be up for treason, they have no right to counsel at all, yet treason they were hung for, not piracy." He shivered slightly, though the air was warm. "I hid in the crowd and watched the lads go to their deaths, wondering all the while if I'd be spotted as one of them, for I'd known five of them and served with three more. 'Tis a sorry thing, lass, to see a comrade die, dancing in the air. Simply because he won't share his plunder with the king's man!"

Anne told him then of her own confrontation with Sir Nicholas Lawes and his hospitality. Rackham howled. "Knocked her to the floor, you say? Sweet Jesus, I'd have given my arm to see it!"

"Ay. But now I can't set foot on Jamaica, or he'll clap me in irons."

"Oh, he's a charmer, he is. And he comes by it natural, too. Sir Nicholas's father was a snake. But mark me, lass, we'll tweak his grizzled beard yet, we two. For Dan and Andrew and Solomon— and for your honor as well. Sir Nicholas Lawes will suck my wake afore I'm through."

Jack and Anne were inseparable for the next few weeks. Jack showered her with attention and treasures. He brought her brocades, watered silks, embroidered slippers, laces, fans, and jewels. And in return, she lavished him with passion. When she was with him she thought of nothing, of no one else.

And then James returned.

They were resting in the hammock, drinking rum with limes. Anne was completely comfortable and at ease, her eyes were closed, her head resting on Jack's arm, her hair fanned out over his chest. Loincloths were all they wore.

She sensed James' presence before she heard him. Her eyes flew open, and there he stood, grim-faced and pale, his fists clenched and his mouth tight.

"I might have known I'd find you here with him, you faithless harlot." He spoke low and threateningly, his eyes boring into her. Jack started and then deliberately leaned back in the hammock, his eyes hard and his hand on his sword hilt which rested against the tree. He said nothing, but only stared at Bonny.

Anne found her voice. "James. I'm sorry you found me like this. I would have told you." She got up from the hammock and faced him. Rackham rose silently to stand by her side.

Bonny turned on him with a sneer. "So you drag me off a godforsaken cay; you save my life. And now you steal my woman. A fine sense of honor, that."

Rackham stood steady, never taking his eyes off Bonny or his hand off his sword. "I did not steal your wife, man. From all accounts, she's been her own woman for some time. She made her choice." He put his hand out as if in truce. "Can you not live with it?"

Bonny lashed out at Anne with venom in his voice, his face contorted with jealous rage. "You whore!" He turned to Rackham. "Did she tell you that you're not the first, Captain! Did she tell you of Bayard and Bonnet and Teach and all the rest? Her scabbard's been open to any sword on the sea. And probably poxed them all in the bargain! Did she tell you you're not the first or the last she's rutted with!"

Anne glanced at Jack. She had not told him all, but his face was expressionless; hard but steady. "Ay. She told me all. Do not abuse her, man. You cannot keep her, will ye or no."

James laughed, a bitter snarl. "Abuse her!" He held up his stiff middle finger in a vulgar salute. "Abuse her—ha! I but took her measure!" He clenched his fist and took a step closer to her, his eyes squinting with rage. "'Twas too crowded a hole for me, man!" He threw a final curse over his shoulder and stalked away. "Enjoy her while you can, you poor bastard. Until the next ship comes in!"

Anne stood for a moment, her head down, her ears ringing with James' curses and her shame. Nothing he said was true . . . yet neither was it false. She turned from Jack, her arms wrapped around her body as if for warmth.

"I did not expect him back. At least not so soon."

Jack watched her wander aimlessly from hammock to hut and back again, putting on stray pieces of clothing.

"That much is evident. But would you have changed it if you could?"

She looked up at him, her eyes full of unshed tears. "Ay, I would. I hate to have a man see the evidence of his own horns so clearly. I'd have spared him that. I'd have told him myself."

"Well, it's done now, lass. You're mine." He went to put his arms around her and pull her to him, but she twisted away, her face pained.

"Yours. Why is it that every man needs to say that word?"

She brushed her hand over her eyes and walked towards the beach. "Leave me to myself for a bit, Jack. I'll come back. But let me think alone for now."

ANNE DID NOT see James again after he strode from her in anger—at least not for a good while—and she was soon so involved with Calico Jack that she was able to put that final painful parting from her mind. Chidley Bayard had come again to the island and left just as quickly. Clearly, he had little use for his errant mistress. If he noticed her absence, he made no flap. Doubtless, his women in other ports consoled him, Anne thought, and she was grateful to avoid yet another encounter with a cast-off lover.

She and Rackham loved again as honeymooners, reveling in the sensuous delights the island had to offer. But their refuge changed dramatically overnight when bales of royal proclamations were unceremoniously dumped on the docks of the pirate republic.

It was late in April, and rumors had run before the arrival of the royal parchment for several months. The crowd quickly ripped open the bales and sent a runner with a fistful of papers to the House of Lords. Anne and Jack sat over a cup of grog as the lad burst in, waving a long rumpled paper excitedly. " 'Tis news of the king's pardon! Who can read it?"

Jack looked up from Anne and laughed. "Who cares to? 'Tis another scurvy bait for a king's noose!"

Another pirate in the corner bellowed out, "We'll have it read, Rackham! Some of us be loyal subjects still!"

Jack shrugged and returned to his cup; the proclamation was posted on the wall as a group of pirates struggled to make it out. Anne left her seat and went to the wall, drawn by curiosity to this first piece of civilization she'd seen in almost two years.

BY THE KING

A PROCLAMATION FOR SUPPRESSING OF PIRATES

GEORGE R.

Whereas we have received information that several persons, subjects of Great Britain, have, since the 24th day of June, the year of Our Lord, 1715, committed divers piracies and robberies upon the High Seas, in the West Indies or adjoining our Plantations, which hath and may occasion great damage to the merchants of Great Britain and others trading in those ports; and though we have appointed such a force as we judge sufficient for suppressing said pirates, yet the more effectually to put an end to the same, we have thought fit by and with the advice of our Privy Council to issue this our Royal Proclamation; and we do hereby promise and declare, that in case any of the said pirates shall, on or before the 5th of September, in the year of Our Lord, 1718, surrender him or themselves, to one of our principal Secretaries of State in Great Britain or Ireland, or to any Governor or Deputy Governor or any of our Plantations beyond the seas; every such pirate and pirates so surrendering him or themselves, as aforesaid, shall have our gracious Pardon, of and for such, his or their piracies, by him or them committed before the 5th of January next ensuing. And we do hereby strictly charge and command all our Admirals, Captains, and other Officers of the seas, and all our Governors and Commanders of any forts, castles, or other places in our Plantations, and all other our officers military and civil, to seize and take such of the pirates who shall refuse or neglect to surrender themselves accordingly. And we do hereby further declare that in case any person or persons on or after the sixth day of September 1718 shall discover or seize or cause or procure to be discovered or seized any one or more of the said pirates so refusing or neglecting to surrender themselves as aforesaid so as they might be brought to justice and convicted of the said offense, such person or persons so making such discovery or seizure to be made shall have and receive as a reward for the same, viz. for every commander of pirates or any pirate ship or vessel, the sum of 100 pounds; for every lieutenant, master boatswain, carpenter and gunner, the sum of 40 pounds; for every inferior officer, the sum of 30 pounds; and for every private man, the sum of 20 pounds. And if any person or persons belonging to and being part of the crews of any such pirate ship or vessel, shall on or after the said sixth day of September 1718 seize or deliver or cause to be seized or delivered any commander or commodore of such pirate ship or vessel so said that he or they be brought to justice and convicted of the said offense, such person or persons as a reward for same shall receive for every such commander the sum of 200 pounds which said sums the Lord Treasurer or the Commissioners of our Treasury for the time being are hereby required and desired to pay accordingly.

Given at Court at Hampton Court, the fifth day of September 1717, in the fourth year of Our Reign.

GOD *Save the* KING

As Anne read, Jennings burst in from the docks. "We must counsel, lads! I sent word to all ships in the islands to hie sail for home. The king has sent to us, and we must decide as one voice, ay or nay!"

Jack's laugh drifted lazily from the corner of the tavern. "Be you ready to beach yourself then, Captain? Do you itch to take up a plough, old sir?"

But few listened. The pirates in the tavern clustered in tight knots of excited conjecture as Anne watched with silent interest.

The pirates had chafed all coasts in the southern Atlantic and the Caribbean and brought shipping in the Leeward Islands to a complete standstill. The guard-ships employed by the king to protect trade could take little effective action against the vast pirate tribe.

The governors asked for some action against the pirate republic of New Providence, hoping to wipe out the outlaw refuge. Finally, the Crown appointed Captain Woodes Rogers as a new governor in chief over the Bahamas with an expressed assignment to "wipe out piracy by whatever means he thought fit."

Woodes Rogers had sailed around the world in command of a privateer in 1708 and brought back Spanish treasure worth eighty thousand pounds. He was a driven, grimly compulsive Royalist, and New Providence's first real threat.

In a week the harbor at New Providence was crowded with vessels. Small snows and large sloops, pinks, brigs, and flutes all crowded into the shallow water, and those who could not dock sent convoys onto shore. Teach was not among them, but Anne knew that he would make his own decision and do as he pleased, vote or no vote.

In the ruins of the Old English fort on the island, a council convened of pirate chiefs. Anne sat at the fringe of the light, pulling her skirts around her legs. Because of her reputation, she was allowed far closer to the hub of the crowd than most women. Calico Jack sat at her side rather than taking his place with the rest of the captains. He feigned disinterest, but Anne could see that he followed the proceedings with thinly disguised curiosity. Jennings held up his hand for silence, and the crowd turned to face him as one.

"Well, then, lads. Ye all know the news! Woodes Rogers has rented the islands from the lords proprietors and is the new governor! Ye've all heard of the king's offer! And Rogers is on his way to New Providence at this moment to settle the island and make it a capital for King George."

There was a ripple of murmured conversation through the crowd.

"Belay that noise, lads! Ye all know we must meet him as one mind when he comes. Are we to give up the island then to the king and his men? Are we to surrender and take the king's coin and land and be pardoned? Or are we to fight and maybe die for this bloody piece o' beach? What will ye say?" He waved the proclamation in his hand, and the edges glowed in the firelight. The buzz of the crowd increased.

A voice from the rear shouted, "Goddamn the king! Let's build up the fort an' blow the governor to hell when he shows his lily-white ass in our waters." A small cheer erupted around the man.

Anne looked at Jack. He's enjoying this, she thought. And she wondered how such a raucous group could ever hope to agree on anything.

"Read the proclamation, Captain! Read it to us now!" shouted another voice.

"Blast ye, man! Ye know I can't read such a blister!" A few chuckles surrounded the old man. "I can tell you, though, that we got 'til September fifth of this year to pay it heed. Ye can deliver yerselves to any officer of the king and find full pardon for all yer scurvy sins at sea. Or ye can refuse an' be hounded from island to island 'til yer caught!"

Hornigold stood up in the circle of light, looking older, more tired than Anne had ever seen him. She compared his profile to Jack's and found it wanting. Her moments of pleasure with him seemed part of another lifetime now.

"What it means, you fools, is that we must sign the law an' take the pardon or run to deep water and keep runnin'!"

Another voice interrupted him. "God's breath! We've too many guns an' the fastest sloops in these waters! How do they mean to catch us all?"

Jennings held up another hand and waited for silence, a hush that was much longer to come. "Before ye vote, ye should know what they'll bring against you! Rogers is no pimp, lads. He'll bring the best in the fleet to bear on all who refuse his offer. An' they're navy ships all, manned and fitted with the best the king's coin can buy!"

One pirate made a rude catcall, but Jennings ignored him and went on. "All but three of his ships are full-rigged an' those three men-o'-war! There's the *Adventure*--she's got forty guns in all, an' the *Diamond*'s got the same. The *Winchilsea* has fully twenty cannon and so does the *Swift,* an' she's in Jamaica at this minute.

"Rogers himself will be on the *Ludlow Castle* with her full forty guns, and the *Scarborough* will sail nigh him with thirty more. The *Seafor* has twenty, the *Lynne* has twenty, and the *Phoenix* has thirty more! Then the *Squirrel* and the *Rose,* both with twenty, await him in New York. Face it, lads, he's got the fastest fleet and the most guns on the seas!"

The crowd was dead silent for a moment as the pirates visualized the full force of the fleet coming for them. Anne glanced at Jack, but his head was down, his finger tracing aimless circles in the sand, a faint smile at his lips. Jennings looked wrung out, as if he were weary to the bone.

"And why send all those English ships against Englishmen, eh?" An angry voice lifted out of the silence. "And now we're just so many blisters on the king's arse!"

"Ay!" bellowed Jennings. "But we kept the Royal Navy out as well! When Teach an' Bonnet raided Charles Town, they fired up our own against us! They're givin' us a chance. If we don't take it, they'll bring the gibbets next!" His voice dropped so that only those close to him could hear. Anne watched Bess's face as she heard Jennings grumble. "As for me, I don't relish a dance at the end of a noose. I'm too old to fight the whole damned navy." Bess glanced at Anne and smiled softly.

A younger tar spoke up with quiet intensity. "You old men can take the pardon. The rest of us will take the seas."

"Ay, ay, ay!" echoed round the circle. But most of those who shouted the loudest looked askance at the pirate chiefs who kept silent, their eyes sliding moodily to each other under their hats.

Con Kesby stood up slowly, his cutlass gleaming softly in the light. Jennings watched him warily, sensing his mood, then sat down, giving him the floor.

" 'Tis time, lads," the pirate chief said roughly. " 'Tis time to sound yer minds. But afore you speak, remember, the king's men got little to do now save harry us from port to port. England's at peace. And know too that your own will turn against ye for the reward. Perhaps 'tis good to take the pardon now, while 'tis offered. A wise man knows when to hove anchor and move to other seas." He sat down. Only the sound of the waves broke the silence.

Jennings rose once more and lifted both hands in the light. "Ye heard both sides, lads." He looked around the circle. "All those for pardon and a new life say aye." A full chorus of voices spoke as one shout, including most of those of the pirate chiefs.

Jennings grinned. "And those hands for blowin' the governor to hell an' sailin' into a noose, say ay." A small defiant knot of voices started to shout, but dwindled as most looked to the glowering chiefs in the darkness. Suddenly a lone voice cried out, "Hell, boys! We can take the pardon an' if we cannot abide it, well then, we can always go on account once more!" A solid roar of laughter arose from the circle.

"A pardon it is, lads! Ye've decided your fates!" Jennings looked around in satisfaction. Jack abruptly stood and walked away from the group, his back stiff. Anne glanced back at Jennings who stared sadly after her, and then turned and followed Jack out of the firelight.

She hurried to catch him and slipped her arm through his, kicking at the sand, waiting for him to speak.

"I'll not take the king's pardon. Not before I've had a ship of my own. I'll not be made captain only to deliver my ship to the king's hands."

Anne quickly thought. If they were pardoned—a large if, since the proclamation made no mention of other crimes save piracy— she could perhaps return to Charles Town with Jack, maybe start a life together. But what sort of life would this man build in such a city? And what sort of life would she share with him? Her mind flitted over her Charles Town home, the fine linens in the cupboards, the wines, the long white tapers, the rich brocades, the niggers, all clean and obedient, and her gowns laid out end to end on her soft feather bed. And then she thought of the dreary stifling afternoons of gossip and manners, of small children clinging to her full skirts, of tight stays and the sliding glances of all she knew, of Jack—her Calico Jack—in a merchant's frock coat with gold watch and chain and a powdered wig. He could never endure it. She would lose him. She stopped suddenly in the sand and drew her arm from his.

"Do you remember what you asked me, my love?"

He smiled and pulled her to him. "Ay. Have you decided to go on account with me, then?"

She smiled, tilting back her head so that her hair fell down on his hands about her waist. "I have. A tempting offer it was then and is now. Woodes Rogers be damned. We'll take your ship to sea, my Captain." She laughed lightly. "Now that all the rest of the dogs are clearing the field, there'll be more for us."

He bent her back over his arm and kissed her throat, his lips moving slowly, slowly up her neck as if feeling for a pulse. She whimpered softly and put her hands to his head, pulling his lips up to her face. Swiftly he covered her mouth with his own and searched for her tongue. She tasted rum, firesmoke, and saltspray. And in the back reaches of her mind, she knew that whatever was coming for them was worth this moment.

WITHIN A MONTH Captain Woodes Rogers' large flotilla cautiously felt its way into New Providence harbor. The *Delicia*, his own flagship, led seven ships, two brigs, three men-of-war, and two sloops. The fleet carried a small knot of soldiers, a rather bedraggled group of colonial pensioners, and a hard crew of cast-off navy seamen. All together, they did not create an impressive display. Richard Turnley, a pirate favorite, was himself the captain's pilot, and news that Turnley had taken the pardon early did much to sway dissenters over to the side of the new governor. Turnley had been eager to insinuate himself into the winning side. He had volunteered to lead the flotilla past the dangerous Bahamian reefs, and now he stood at Rogers' side as he gazed over the harbor with his glass.

Rogers was in full regalia, with a naval captain's frock coat, the purple sash of the Crown across his chest, and a jewel-encrusted cutlass at his side. His long curling wig did not hide the scars of his former life, however. A cutlass slash ran through one eyebrow, and his upper lip had been torn away by a Spanish musket ball. This wound had drawn the flesh away from his upper teeth, exposing them in a constant snarl.

Within minutes the news of Rogers' arrival blew through the outlaw settlement like a tropical squall. Pirates and prostitutes, children and dogs raced down through the streets to the docks. Some of the seamen, anxious to begin on a favorable footing, sent up ragged cheers to greet the lumbering flotilla. But the ships came no farther into the harbor than its mouth. Slowly as the people watched, the line of warships moved out across the horizon, trying to block the entrance to New Providence entirely.

When Charles Vane heard that the governor had arrived, he whipped a small defiant crew into a frenzy of leave-taking. "I'll not be taken by some white-palmed government fop!" he shouted. And many agreed, at least enough to man a small sloop. His ship was almost ready to sail and had attracted the few men on the island who chose to reject the king's pardon.

As Anne watched, she saw that one of Rogers' ships had wedged between a pair of large submerged rocks out in the bay, affectionately known by the pirates as the King's Bollocks. These protrusions were now effectively keeping the governor's ships from bottling the harbor. Vane's ship was making ready to sail.

Anne raced for the House of Lords, wondering why Jack wasn't on Vane's ship, why he'd not taken any steps to leave the island before now. Jack was dicing with friends, and she drew him aside to whisper urgently in his ear. "Jack, the governor's here, and he's blocking the harbor!"

"Ay, I know. I guess we're stuck fast."

"No! We're not stuck at all if you move! Vane is weighing anchor now! He'll sail right past the flotilla if he hurries. We could go along!"

He looked wonderingly at her. "You'd sail right now? Right past the king's men?"

"Ay! But only if you step and go! I'll not be taken in midharbor for all the island to see."

"I haven't even a proper pistol on me, lass!"

"Well, get one, man! And hurry! I'll meet you on the beach in a quarter hour!"

She ran to her hut, threw on a striped cotton shirt and trousers, bound her hair up in a kerchief, and jammed two loaded pistols in her belt. In one hand, she carried her cutlass; in the other, a small bundle of everything she cared to keep.

When she got to the docks, the shadows were lengthening. Vane's ship still sat in harbor, and way out at the skyline there was still a large hole in the line of king's ships. Jack shouted to her from the shallows. He had a small skiff loaded with what he'd been able to carry. She splashed through the waves and climbed aboard.

As they rowed to Vane's ship, Anne glanced again out to sea. The wedged brig had finally broken loose from her moorings and was pulling into line across the mouth of the harbor.

"Jesus save us. Now we'll never get past," Rackham groaned.

But Anne did not answer. She was studying the ships and watching the breeze that was blowing offshore.

Rogers, aboard the *Delicia*, was also carefully observing the ships in the harbor. As a former naval officer, he was appalled at the clutter of wrecks and near-wrecks that littered the water. He saw that he could not move closer without risking damage to his own ship. The wind was against them, and night was coming on. He knew even Turnley could not maneuver the flagship nearer the shore. But for now, none could escape the net he'd laid across the bay.

"Lay anchor here," he called to Turnley. "Any ship that comes close, we blow from the water. At daybreak the wind will shift and we can move in."

"Oh, ye needn't worry, Captain," said Turnley smoothly. "No one will dare rebel against the king's proclamation and your guns."

Rogers smiled at him and sneered inside. That oily bastard will be the first off my ship and the last on, once we secure this foul vipers' nest, he thought.

Vane was glad to see Anne and Jack and immediately made Rackham his quartermaster, just like old times. Vane then called for a council of war. The best plan seemed to be to wait until dark and attempt a dash for freedom. All aboard knew that dawn would bring a forced surrender if they did not escape this night. Anne eyed the guns that flanked Vane's ship and felt her stomach tighten. Suddenly she stepped into the circle of pirates and spoke up.

"I've a bet—" She started again. "*Another* plan. If you'll listen."

"I'll take orders from you 'tween the sheets, wench, but not 'tween decks!" a sailor cried out lustily. The crew guffawed. Jack grinned.

Vane said, "You're here at Rackham's sufferance, mistress. 'Twould be better if you stay below."

Anne threw back her shoulders and glared at Vane. "My life's at stake here, Captain, as well as yours. Are you afraid to hear a better plan?" She looked around with fiery eyes at the rest of the crew. "Are you so anxious then to feel Rogers' sword that you'll not waste a moment to hear me speak?" She put her hands on her hips. "Go then. Rush to your deaths, you fools."

Vane looked at the circle of men and rolled his eyes in mock exasperation. "God, woman. Spit it out. Or 'tis sure we'll die of your tongue, instead."

"Here it is, then." And as she began to detail her plan, Vane grinned. Soon he was way ahead of her and chuckling craftily as he ordered the crew to put her words into effect.

The men hopped to Vane's orders and kept low, trying to stay out of sight of Rogers' glass. None of their activity was detected by the lookouts on the flagship. Vane's sloop was hidden amidst a tangle of other ships along the docks and was slowly moving closer and closer, without seeming to, toward an abandoned French brigantine. The brig carried twenty guns. It had been captured by Vane on his previous cruise, and he was familiar with the ship's limitations and possibilities. Night fell; in the confusion of torches and flares from shore, no one in Rogers' flotilla seemed to notice the sails of the French brigantine slowly flaring into life.

Rogers himself was preparing to go ashore in a longboat. He intended to establish order at once. He was nearly halfway down the ladder when a call from one of the lookouts brought him back to the deck of the *Delicia*.

"What do you see, lookout?"

"Sail, Captain! Dead ahead and fast bearing this way!"

Rogers grabbed his glass and peered out over the dark waters. The French brigantine, under full sail, was plying straight for the flotilla. There was a strange glow on her decks. Although the big ship was approaching briskly in the offshore breeze, it seemed oddly canted to one side. Rogers chuckled to himself. Those fools. Did they suppose that darkness would shield them from his twenty-pounders?

The brigantine came relentlessly closer. It was not yet near enough to present any danger, and Rogers, more curious than alarmed, turned to Turnley with a grin.

"What sort of craft is this, pilot?"

Turnley strained to make out the ship. "I swear I haven't the faintest, sir. It could be one o' the sloops left in the harbor, but 'tis movin' right well in the wind. Don't know who's manned it. Not pirates, I wager. They'd surely pick a smaller, faster sloop than this fat bawd."

"Well, damn it, Turnley! If that barge comes any closer, I'll blow it to splinters! My men have orders to fire on any ship that looks hostile or tries to leave port!" A thought struck him. "Could it be a welcoming party, do you think?"

But Turnley was absorbed by the strangely canted approach of the brigantine, which carried it dangerously close to other ships in the harbor. It gouged against one anchored sloop, then bounced off the bow of another.

"My God!" exclaimed Turnley. "If it's a welcome, sir, they're drunk as fiddler crabs! The wheelsman on that craft must be crazy!" Suddenly the glow on the decks of the ship flared up, vividly illuminating the ship and wrenching another exclamation from Turnley. *"Christ, she's got no wheelsman at all!"*

In the dim light he could see no crewman aboard the brigantine. Vane's crew had turned it loose under full sail, the wheel lashed so that the ship would be blown by the offshore breeze directly at the line of ships across the harbor mouth. With no hand at her wheel, the vessel canted under the night breeze, but kept on coming dead toward the flagship.

And as Rogers watched in amazement, the second half of Anne's plan burst into effect. A slow-burning mixture of sulfur and gunpowder laid down along the brig's decks had finally reached pools of highly flammable oil that had been spread around each of the vessel's loaded cannons. In a fearful eruption, the cannons all blasted forth in a tremendous volley, belching musket balls, shot, assorted ammunitions, belaying pins, chunks of scrap iron, and anything else that Vane's crew had been able to jam down their black throats.

The spectacular fireworks were devastating to watch. Although little of the shot actually hit the flotilla, the smoke filled the air, and the sulfur singed the nostrils of every man in Rogers' crew. The effect was just enough to divert attention from Vane's sleek little sloop which was now coming out of the harbor in the wake of the flaming brigantine.

Rogers and his officers faced the assault calmly enough, but many of the soldiers, unused to sea life, were beginning to panic. The brigantine, now a ship of fire, was still bearing down relentlessly on the fleet. The sky itself seemed aflame. Several of the crew began to scramble over the decks in confusion.

"Cut the anchor cable!" cried a seaman aboard one of the ships. "Get out of the way!"

The blazing brigantine was almost upon them. The governor was still holding his flagship fast, scowling out to sea. He knew that if he broke and ran now, with all of New Providence looking on, his prestige would suffer among the pirates, and he'd not be able to hold position on the island.

"Gunner, blast that brig with a broadside!" he ordered the crew.

The mate stared at his captain with goggled eyes. "But sir! There's no one aboard, sir!"

"Fire, I say! You dare to question me, you fool! She's in range now, and we'll scatter those flames afore they roll over us! Now, sink that ship!"

In a second the guns roared from the flagship. The burning brig shivered under the broadside, and the flames were momentarily scattered. But then the breeze picked up unexpectedly and Vane's decoy, blazing like a huge torch, canted once more into the path of the flotilla.

There was a stunning detonation as the flames finally reached the powder magazine deep in the hold, and the brigantine was shattered in the water. The explosion was so severe that the waves themselves parted. Huge fragments of burning ship flew high in the air and rained down on the flotilla. Men scurried up and down riggings and decks, trying to protect the sails and dodge the debris.

In one final surge of panic, the flotilla broke. Two brigs cut their cables and ran out to sea, leaving a gaping hole in the net of the blockade. Out of the sulfurous mist, Vane's sloop slid through the waves, firing its four-pounders at the nearest warship as it ran.

Not a gun was fired in reply; the surprise was complete. The bulky men-of-war could not maneuver about in time to take up pursuit. Vane's fast sloop sliced into the night, leaving behind a flaming bay and littered waves. As it sped past the last straggling man-of-war, Rogers' crew heard pirate laughter wafting back on the breeze. And above the rough shouts of the men, a lone woman's voice was raised in triumphant song.

PART FOUR

On Account, 1718

When a woman takes on some of a man's attributes, she must triumph, for if she intensifies her other advantages by an excess of energy, the result is a woman as perfect as can be imagined.

GOETHE

Give me a spirit in life's rough sea,
Loves to have his sails filled with a lusty wind,
Even 'til sail-yards tremble and masts crack,
And his rapt ship runs on her side so low,
That she drinks water and her keel ploughs air,
'Til her keel ploughs air,
Oh, heigho, and a lusty wind!

Welsh Sea Shanty

ANNE STOOD ON the top deck of the *Seahorse* and scanned an endless horizon. Once more, she knew the sigh of the wind and the steady thrumming of the stays and riggings. Finally she felt she had room to think and space to act, and the broad plains of water gave her peace. Vane's sloop had been on the water for a scant two days; already, Anne knew every plank of the fifty-ton ship.

Anne and Jack shared a small cabin off the mess, one of the few private places on board. The *Seahorse* could carry a crew of seventy-five pirates and fourteen cannon and was severely undermanned with only thirty-two hasty rebels and four guns.

Accordingly, Vane's first stop after escaping New Providence was a small inlet off the Cuban coast for provisions and fresh water. There, hidden by palms and protected by a shallow reef, the crew stripped the sloop and made her an even more dangerous predator.

Anne worked alongside the men as they lopped off half the fo'c'sle, trimmed the pilot's cabin, and stripped off pounds of railing to lighten the vessel. In a last defiant gesture, Jack ordered twelve more ports cut along her sides for new swivel guns—guns which he intended to capture at the first opportunity.

When the *Seahorse* was ready to leave Cuba, Vane called for a council to sign new articles. Anne sat alone in the cramped cabin, waiting to know her fate. If the crew wished, they could put her ashore and never look back. She knew the traditional bans against women aboard a pirate ship. She had hoped, by working uncomplainingly alongside them, to counter their prejudices. There were some, she sensed, who were indignant at her presence, who resented her each night she slipped away to join Jack in his narrow berth. But there were others, she hoped, who had accepted her as a valued pair of hands on an undermanned ship. She huddled in the darkness, her knees drawn up to her chin. If they did put her off, how long would Jack be content to be beached in Cuba? How long could she safely stay there herself?

Her thoughts were cut short by Jack who burst in the door, snatched her hand, and hauled her on deck. He said not a word, nor did he meet her eyes. Only when she reached the quarterdeck where the men were gathered did she trust herself to glance at him. A tight smile played over his mouth.

Vane came forward. "Anne Bonny, step to center deck."

She strode to the middle of the circled men, her head high, her eyes straight ahead to the sea.

"The men have had their say, woman. They'll have no weepin' an' wailin' in battle, no faintin' in the fo'c'sle, and no whorin' in the hold."

She looked about at the men, her face flushed.

"And if ye promise to abide by these rules, ye can stay on as one of us."

She broke into a dazzling grin.

"Be you ready to sign the articles of this ship?"

She laughed in relief. "With my life, Captain."

The men gathered about her then, clapping her on the back. One by one, each stood over a barrel, placed his left hand on a hatchet, his right on his heart, and pledged loyalty to the ship, the captain, and all his Brethren. Each man then made his mark on the ship's roster. When it came Anne's turn, she stepped proudly forward and signed "Anne" with a flourish, refusing to hang James' tail at the end of her name.

THE SEAHORSE SAILED for Barbados, the crew anxious to be away from Spanish waters. The heat was building in a cloudless sky; the sun almost straight up. Suddenly, the watch called, "Sail there! Off starboard bow!"

There was an instant flurry of men to the gunwales, and Anne stood by Jack, scanning the horizon. Far out over the waves, a small speck broke the even line of the sea, scarcely visible. As she watched, the dot swiveled, and Anne could see a white flash of sail.

The gunner, Noah Harwood, called for action. The men clustered about him grabbing weapons and preparing for a good fight.

"Come, lass!" called Jack. "Pick your battling tools!"

For an instant, Anne did not move. The moment she'd visualized at least a dozen times in her dreams was now upon her. One small voice of disloyalty pricked her heart. If Jack loved me, she wondered, would he let me . . . ? But she shoved it from her mind. He loved her enough to let her do what she wanted, what she had claimed she wished for all along. She shook off her hesitancy and joined the men pawing over the axes, pikes and hooks used for boarding.

There was no further time for thought. Jack, Vane, and Harwood filled the air with shouted orders. The cannons were primed and loaded with huge black balls; the decks were cleared of all debris, the sails tightened, muskets loaded, and dirks flashed in the sun as their edges were tested against callused thumbs. Anne's hair stuck to her head, dark with sweat.

"We'll see her soon enough, lass! Stack these muskets closer together, an' keep yer eyes to yer business!"

Jack glanced at her and grinned. " 'Tis a merchant, lass. Near thirty ton or more. A tidy bitch and ripe for the plucking."

At Vane's command, the great cannons were trundled into place, their black mouths gaping at the sea. Fenwick, the mate, came up behind Anne and squeezed her elbow. He was keen-eyed and wiry as an eel.

"First time, lass?"

Anne said nothing, but her trembling smile gave her away.

He laughed softly. "Well, after the first, all the rest's easy. I recall I stumbled about like a whore at a weddin', my first take. Wrap a rag round yer head afore we start to blast else ye'll have no eardrums left."

A few moments later, Jack yanked her aside. "You all right?" he hissed. She nodded woodenly. "Good." He peered at her. "Stay behind me if you can; if not, stay aft."

She shook her head. "I won't let you down, Jack."

His face hardened. "You can't, lass. They'll maroon us if you do, with nary a look back."

She pulled away and hurried off to make her weapons secure.

The little sloop skimmed the water like a hungry shark. Within an hour they had closed on the merchant ship, and Anne saw it looming large as a cliff, at the bow. Her determination moved her up and down the decks as if in a heady dream.

Now, half the pirates crouched beneath the rails, keeping their heads down. Anne hid under the lip of the cannon, her thighs trembling with excitement. Her mind flitted back to her last gown and hoops, and she smirked as she imagined herself jumping over the decks dressed as a lady. The thought distracted her. God's breath, she cursed silently, keep your mind here where you need it. Harwood stood in plain sight, calmly whittling, watching the approaching ship. She felt another icy touch of terror, and she knew that if she had her knife in her hand, she'd likely impale herself, so clumsy did she feel.

Suddenly, she heard a voice shout across the water, "Ahoy! *Destiny*, Norfolk! Stephen Crandall, Master!"

Anne peeked out. The ship was before her; the topmasts slashed across the sky like crucifixes. Jack glanced at her from his station on the quarterdeck and winked.

Once more, the voice called, "Your colors and your port!"

In a split second, Jack pulled both pistols, hoisted the black Roger, and shouted, *"From the sea!"*

Immediately, the drums began to thunder, and Harwood reached down and fired off the cannon. The sloop rocked as the guns roared, and the shot whistled through the air. Anne popped her head over the gunwale in time to see the ball explode in a fiery burst on the merchant's decks.

An animal howl rose from the pirates as they surged from their hiding places, waving cutlasses and shouting threats. Anne felt a savage growl of triumph rise in her throat, and she was carried along with the tide of battle.

The *Destiny*'s own guns answered the blast, and a hail of musket balls came screaming onto the decks. There was a volley like thunder, and the sloop shuddered as splinters flew from the plankings. Anne ducked and ran for the bulwarks. In one corner of the deck, Jack shouted orders; Vane commanded a group of pirates from the other side. Large billows of foul black smoke rose out of the chaos.

The deck canted beneath Anne as she stood and fired over the bow. A man dropped out of sight, felled as easily as a pigeon on a branch. She turned to see if anyone saw her shot but was overwhelmed by the din around her. The cannons that had been leashed to the decks like great dogs were all firing now, one after another, and the noise was deafening. Return shots from the *Destiny* hit riggings and shrouds and landed whistling and hissing into the water.

"Let's take her, ye whimperin' old women!" shouted Vane and led the way to the port side where the two ships had closed, their hulls butting against each other like two angry rams.

"Boarders! Boarders!" cried Jack, rushing to the bulwark. Anne's sword rasped ominously as she pulled it from her scabbard; the blade held the sun like flame. She rushed to join Jack. Another broadside hit the *Seahorse*, and Anne staggered back; the deck heaved and bucked, and Jack grabbed her arm, wrenching her back to his side. Choking smoke billowed around them. Anne's eyes were filled, and her lungs ached, and the only place that seemed free of the smoke was up above her head in the riggings. She threw her grappling hook up and clambered aloft frantically, coughing and sputtering.

She was caught then in the tide of pirates rushing onboard the merchant, and a cry of "Boarders!" wrenched from her throat. A grenade whizzed past her ear and exploded on the deck behind her, but she never paused. She jumped over the *Destiny*'s bulwarks and charged through fighting seamen, cutlasses swinging, dirks clashing, and muskets roaring. With a jarring thud, the *Destiny*'s mast crashed on deck, pulling down a mass of lines. Anne leaped aside just in time, but a dozen men were netted beneath it like squirming herring.

Finally, the captain of the *Destiny*, seeing devastation and defeat all around him, called for quarter.

Anne was clashing swords with a seaman on the fo'c'sle and had edged him into a corner. At the call for quarter, the tar's eyes cleared and he seemed to see Anne for the first time. His jaw dropped when he realized he'd been battling a woman. Wide-eyed and dazed, he stumbled to join the rest of the crew.

Anne looked about to see Jack. He was standing at the captain's side, directing traffic back to the *Seahorse*. He grinned at her and motioned her off.

She felt exhilarated but close to tears. She squared her shoulders and went to work unloading the booty with the rest of the crew. Carter made a batch of bumboo, and both crews joined to share pipes and tankards. The captured men peered at her sharply in the shadows, but no one asked questions. Four men had been killed in the fray: one pirate and three seamen. Their bodies were promptly wrapped in torn shrouds with bullets at their heads for weight and slipped overboard into the sea.

Vane stood on the quarterdeck and solemnly intoned, "The sea heals all wounds and covers all tracks. May ye find a new ship with the wind at yer backs."

The *Seahorse* had taken little damage, nothing that could not be repaired in a day. Vane and Rackham decided to take the *Destiny*'s guns and those of her crew who wished to join them and set the merchant ship adrift.

Before she slept Anne took one more look at the sea. It was empty now, a great desert of silver and purple hues with a horizon like a knife edge. As she gazed, her mind whirled with fatigue. Jack came up beside her and took her in his arms, holding her gently. He said nothing but turned and led her below to the welcome silence of their berth. In her dreams that night, cannon balls ripped through blinding smoke like phantoms from hell, and she jerked spasmodically with fear.

IT TOOK ANNE several days to recover from the battle and to wrestle her mind to some ease. Staring out over the waves helped, as did the refuge of Jack's arms and the easy familiarity of the crew. Each man had learned to live with battle—with its heart-stopping fear, the shrieks of the bullets, the tangles of nets and shrouds, the blood, the crowded din of bewildering noise. Anne resolved to harden herself like the others. And as Fenwick reminded her, "After the first, all the rest's easy."

Now the *Seahorse* carried a crew of forty-two and twelve guns. Rackham introduced each newcomer to the crew with the words "And this is Anne Bonny, our own pirate queen. She can raise a cutlass with the best of you and shoot the eye from a gull at one hundred paces. Insult her, and you will feel her sword—and mine."

At first the new men edged around Anne as they would a black widow, but soon they came to know her as a comrade.

Except for Fitch. A new recruit from the captured merchant, Fitch could not believe his good fortune to be aboard a pirate ship, complete with a pirate moll. At every opportunity he brushed against Anne in the dark passageways. Finally, she whirled and slapped the ugly ferret of a man, challenging him to a duel.

Vane heard the commotion and came to investigate. "What's the melee, Anne?"

"This pimpled, pockmarked lout has done his best to squeeze me at every opportunity! He bumps my bosom and rubs his parts against me in every passage, and I've had enough! I'm a member of this crew, and I won't be treated as a common whore. I demand satisfaction!"

Fitch just leaned against the gunwale and grinned at her, his eyes glinting under his filthy cap.

Vane realized that the men had clustered about his back waiting to see the outcome of Anne's challenge. "Well, Anne, under the articles, you got such a right." He turned to Fitch. "What's it to be, man? Apology or duel?"

Fitch sneered. "I don't aim to cross swords with no wench. She don't belong on a proper ship, no how."

Anne took a step towards him, her fist clenched. "By God, you hound. You'll fight or be branded a coward to all eyes here. I'm a damn sight more pirate than you'll ever be. I'll avenge my honor or shoot you down like the dog you are!"

Fitch looked nervously around the circle of men. He knew he had to fight or suffer disgrace. "All right! But when I blast her arse, don't blame me! And go get Rackham so he'll see she started this!"

As one of the pirates turned to fetch Jack, Anne snapped, "Belay that! He was on watch half the night and needs his rest. I can handle this myself. 'Twill not take long."

Two barrels were set up on deck twenty paces apart. An unloaded pistol together with ammunition for one shot was placed on each barrel, and Anne took her place at the keg farthest from the crew.

Fitch swaggered to his barrel and turned to glare at Anne. "Get on with it, then," he growled.

Vane held a hand aloft and looked at the two adversaries. Anne nodded that she was ready. Vane dropped his hand. Anne quickly reached for the gun, no movement wasted, loaded, primed, and cocked the flintlock, and then looked up to see Fitch still readying his pistol. She stood, her hands in front of her holding her pistol pointed at his head, waiting disdainfully for him to finish. He looked up at her, saw that she could kill him at will, and blanched painfully under his swarthy skin. As he frantically lifted his hand to fire, she pulled off one quick shot, and Fitch's pistol clattered to the deck together with a piece of his thumb. He yelped, more in surprise than pain, and looked up at Anne with disbelief.

"Perhaps you can manage to keep the rest of your fingers to yourself," Anne said calmly.

The men parted in awe as she walked away to take her place on deck for watch.

*T*HE *JOHN AND ELIZABETH*, a lithe frigate bound for New Providence, was easy prey for the pirate sloop. She carried a quantity of Spanish pieces-of-eight, and Vane stripped the ship clean. Now that he had funds and a full crew, his first instinct was to run for the Windward Islands to careen and carouse. Anne and Jack preferred to stay at sea, knowing that the gold would scarcely last a week once the men found willing whores and cheap rum. But Vane was adamant, and the *Seahorse* dropped anchor at a small island in the Windward chain and settled in.

It was there on the hot beach that Anne made a frightening discovery. The days at sea had passed, seeming to vary little from one to the next. On the water her body was part of the rhythms of storm and calm, the ebb and flow of the currents. But here on land she became suddenly aware that she was tied to time, however much she sought to forget it. Her body was immediately, jarringly, separate from the elements, alone and of itself, and had—she discovered as she counted the days—betrayed her. She was with child, pregnant with Jack Rackham's seed. And as best as she could remember, she had been without flux for at least two months, possibly three.

Frantically, she cast her mind to those days on New Providence when she and Jack had known such naked joy, such untrammeled freedom. All the while her body was preparing a trap for her. She wondered why the human spirit must be housed in a body at all.

Her flesh had never felt her own. It was too hot or cold by turns, alternately willfully detached or the slave to any stranger's touch. Better to be a breath of wind or an unseen melody than a body. Yet there was no escape, no matter how she drew her mind away. The babe was his, of that she was sure. Probably he had done this to her in the very first week they'd loved together. And she had loved on, over and over, never knowing what lay inside her, festering.

For one long moment, she felt stark panic. A child. She would blow up like a melon, the heavy disfigurement, the long tedious waiting, the pain of labor, the ripping of flesh, the blood, the agony—perhaps even death. Her mind turned doggedly to her mother, killed finally by a child within her. Barely under control, her thoughts spun to Jack. Jack, who liked his women fleet and slender, hungry with passion and life. Then her fear was replaced by a dull anger. She felt bound and tied just as surely as if she sat in a Charles Town gaol. And Jack had said she was like the sea itself.

"Like the waves, Anne. Free and strong and changeable as the wind. You can be a tempest, but for the man who knows how to board you, there's nothing finer."

Jack. Well, he had boarded her, that was certain. And now she'd bloat like a tethered cow. She looked down at her belly, still fairly flat, and at her breasts, full and high. She imagined she could see beneath her skin to her womb and the bloody, blind parasite clinging to her insides, sucking the life from her muscles, pulling them slack and stretched. She thought of Meg Moore, the skilled abortionist at New Providence. Perhaps she could rid her of this burden. But then Anne remembered the tools of her trade—the sewing awls, the bent silver spoon—and she shuddered. She could endure an outside wound, a cutlass slash, a knife cut—but the idea of those cold relentless instruments probing her insides made her knees weak. She knew she could not endure such a violation. Besides, Meg always said past three months the risk of bleeding to death was too great. Might as well take hellebore and nightshade, she'd said. Suddenly Anne felt overwhelmed by the prospects before her and she hurried to find Jack, needing his arms and some comfort.

She found him in the hammock they'd strung by their make-shift hut. She climbed into the swinging net and stretched her body alongside his.

"Jack," she murmured hesitantly. "I've something to tell you."

He opened one eye and lazily drawled, "Are we all out of rum? That's all that could mar my humor today."

"No." She rushed out the words impatiently. "I'm with child. At least two months, maybe three. I just now realized."

For the longest moment, his eyes remained closed. Then he opened them and said tiredly. "Is it mine?"

Anne's face mottled red with indignation. "Of course, it's yours, you bastard! And don't think I welcome it, either!"

He put his arms on her shoulders and pulled her close. "Hush, lass. Calm down. Easy . . . easy." She quieted under his touch. "I just wanted to be sure." He stroked her hair and tilted her face back so he could see her eyes. " 'Tis not such a problem, you know. You can hie yourself to a midwife and rid your belly of the thing before the week is out. I know a woman in Cuba who'll do it."

Anne squeezed her eyes shut against the visions that floated up in her mind. She sighed. "No, Jack. It's too late. Meg Moore told me—after three months, it's suicide to tamper with it."

"Meg Moore was no expert. We'll find someone who knows what to do. 'Tis sure you can't have the babe. Not and sail with me."

Anne's anger rose again. "Jack, I'll not risk death or mutilation at the hands of a butcher. 'Tis too late, I tell you. The babe will be born, like it or not."

He pulled away from her coldly. "And what do you intend to do in the meantime? Take prizes up and down the seas with a belly hanging over your belt? The lads agreed to let you stay on as one of them. But a fainting, puking brood mare's something else again."

"They'll never know. At least not for a good while. I'm flat even now, Jack. Likely, I'll remain flat for a month or two more, and my blouse'll hide much. I won't faint or whine. It's for sure I'll not be stowed away like some housewife! The day I wait on the beach for some man, the waves'll run backwards. I can ship with you 'til near my time and then we can careen the ship, and I can deliver the babe all at once."

"And then?"

"And then I'll give it up as a foundling to some trader's wife. With luck, the crew'll never know I was with child at all."

Jack yanked his hair back in exasperation. "Christ, Anne. What a job this is. I thought you were barren, but I guess it was Bonny 'twas lacking. What scurvy luck."

She put her arms around him. "It will work, Jack. I promise you. I'll make it work." She soothed him then, murmuring endearments into his neck, fighting back her tears and bitter resentment.

VANE SEEMED happy to stay on his Windward Island forever. His small purse of gold was sufficient to buy him an occasional trull and all the rum he needed. He was content to while away his days in a hammock and his nights swapping sea tales with the men who were still impressed by his title of pirate chief.

But the crew grumbled at their enforced idleness. Anne was especially anxious to be once more at sea, fearing that the time allotted to her was all too short. Finally she and Rackham agitated the captain into setting sail, and the *Seahorse* weighed anchor once more.

Vane took the fleet sloop into the trade lanes of Florida, looking for prey, taking care to stay well off New Providence and Woodes Rogers' domain. Twice the lookout shouted "Sail ho!" sighting large merchant ships, and twice Vane took the glass, perused them carefully, then announced they weren't worth the chase. The second time, as he turned the sloop away from a potential prize, Anne's restlessness goaded her into defiance.

"Hell's teeth, Captain! The articles read no prey, no pay! 'Tis sure they're not going to sail up and surrender!"

Vane turned a baleful eye on the woman. "Ye need not quote the articles to me, mistress. I wager I know them well as any here—surely more'n you. When yer captain of yer own ship, then chase phantoms to yer heart's delight. Those ships weren't worth the risk."

She wanted to challenge him further but knew better. At sea the captain's word was law. She sensed the only reason she'd been allowed even that small rebellion was because she was a woman.

And she was increasingly aware of that distinction daily. She was grateful she felt no nausea, no weakness, but her belly was alive now, and she could not ignore it. She felt a steady humming through her body like the low singing of the rigging in a freshening breeze. Her breasts were stretched and sensitive to even the touch of her blouse, and her nerves were taut with expectation. She felt more alive, more joyously robust than she ever had before.

*I*T WAS THE end of November, provisions were low and the crew was restless, when they sighted a ship, a small white speck breaking the clean edge of the water. They gave chase and caught her in half a day. As they came close to the vessel, Vane stood on the quarterdeck, peering through his glass.

"She's not hoisted her colors, nor asked for ours."

Suddenly, the lookout screamed, " 'Tis a French frigate, Captain!" At the instant he cried out, a blast of cannon whistled off the frigate's fo'c'sle.

"Hoist French colors!" hollered Vane. A stolen French flag was hastily run up the pirate mast. Another burst of cannon exploded right in front of the *Seahorse*.

"She's not deceived! Run for it, lads!" Vane cried.

Astonished by the command, the wheelsman obeyed. The sloop lurched aside, and men scampered to their stations, some pausing to peer over the nettings at the French ship which was bearing down on them, guns blazing. She was perilously near, and her bulging courses and topsails revealed her captain's eagerness to do battle.

"Goddamn it to hell!" screamed Rackham as he raced to add his own weight to the wheel. "Helm a'lee!"

Anne felt the ship heel and tilt madly as it responded to the thrust of sail and rudder.

The *Seahorse* twisted round with the wind, flapping headsails and canvas. Men were sloshed over the deck like rag dolls as the waves crashed against the bulkhead and over the rails.

Vane stood transfixed in wide-eyed bewilderment as the French frigate loomed closer. His coat was wet with spray, and he absently wiped his eyes. Rackham took one look at him and yelled, "Braces, lads!"

"Make them think we want a fight, Jack!" Anne shrieked across the confusion. She saw the frigate was barely a half mile off and still closing fast. Miraculously, because of the sloop's erratic twists and turns, the *Seahorse* was unhit by the frigate's relentless barrage.

Vane was jolted from his shock by the sight of the enemy's topmast rising above them like a forest. Unless they took immediate action, the two ships would collide.

"Starboard guns!" yelled Vane. Anne helped haul the great cannon to its port. With the ship so canted, it was like fighting uphill.

"Fire!" bellowed Vane. The *Seahorse*'s guns barked a sharp retort at the pursuing frigate, all the while running for its life. The shot sailed far wide, but the ruse had worked. The Frogs were pulling her in, dropping sails eagerly, ready to battle this insolent pirate ship.

Vane looked as though he might call for yet another blast, but Rackham strode to him and grabbed his shoulder. "Run for it, man! Forecourse up and loose topsails!"

Vane turned, distracted, and repeated Jack's commands like an automaton; this was not lost on the crew. They jumped to his orders. The foresail filled, and Anne felt the *Seahorse* pick up the thrust. When she looked at the French frigate again, she let out her breath in a gasp of relief. The sham had worked. The French ship was frantically trying to load on sail again as she saw their new tack, but the delay was too much. She was bucking behind the *Seahorse*'s stern almost at a standstill.

By the time she could catch the wind again, the *Seahorse* was away. In one last attempt at revenge, the frigate fired a final round. With a shuddering crash, the pirate ship was struck. As Anne watched in horror, the long spar snapped and fell over the rail, dropping the sail into the water, dragging rigging and canvas behind them. The lookout was trapped in the lines, tangled impossibly in the shrouds; towed by the fleeing sloop meant certain death. Vane looked about.

"Cut us free! Axes, there!" he called.

The lookout shrieked, "No! Save me, lads! Don't let me go to the bottom," and his eyes bulged from his head in terror.

But the crew, driven by the chaos and deaf to the cries of one more pirate, frantically hacked the spar away. With a hiss like a breath releasing, the sail swept to the stern and faded past with a trail of rigging behind. Anne ran to the side. The lookout's eyes locked with hers, his mouth open in panic. Then the spar twisted and rolled, and last thing Anne saw was the man's jerking hands sinking beneath the water, desperately reaching for life.

Rackham said hoarsely, "Poor devil! God rest his soul!" Anne, appalled, could only nod.

THE MEN WERE incensed at their close call. Rackham maintained that they might have taken the frigate had they been prepared and not turned tail at the last moment.

"She may have had more guns, but we could have taken her. The time comes I cannot take a frog at sea, I'll hang up my pistols and take up a plough," he boasted.

Vane defended his decision and then closed the issue. "By God, I command this ship! I'll tolerate no cabal and no second-guessing."

As they sailed into Bermuda for fresh water, the muttering of the crew came to a head. Vane was last off the sloop and rowed ashore to find the pirates clustered together under the shade of a palmetto.

"What's this?" he asked, striding into the middle of the group.

Anne looked as if she were about to speak but controlled her impulse.

Jack glanced at her and then at the rest of the company. "Sit down if you like, Vane. We're taking a vote as to whether you stay on as captain."

Vane opened his mouth once, then closed it grimly, sinking to the sand, his eyes darting poisonously from one man to the next.

" 'Tis time then, lads, to speak your piece. There's some that say Vane turned coward on us in battle and lost us a good man—that we could have taken the French frigate and should have, too. And more, that he's passed up less risky prizes on the sea when the store was low and each man in need of coin. Those who agree, say aye."

The vote was conclusive. Of forty men, thirty-two voted Vane out of command. It was decided that he would be put ashore on Bermuda with a small captured sloop, those men who had voted with him, and sufficient ammunition and provisions to man a new enterprise. Vane stood up at the verdict with cold dignity.

Rackham looked up at him. "I'm sorry, Vane. Your season here is through. 'Tis someone else's turn to command."

Vane sneered. "You, perhaps? And yer wench? You think ye know all about command, but ye don't. Somewhere along the way, in the teeth of a gale or facing an enemy's cannon, or becalmed with the crew near mad with thirst—*then* ye'll know command. When you need help, there's none. When every bugger's looking aft at you, and ye hold life and death in yer fingers, *then* ye'll know, mark me. I be well rid of ye all." He stalked away, and his few followers straggled after him. Anne felt sorrow for the man, but she was too proud of Jack now to let her joy be sullied by pity.

Jack shrugged off Vane's departure. After the remaining group had settled down, he called for a new question.

"And for the next business, gentlemen? Who's to command in his stead?"

The vote was all but unanimous. In the relief and hope that comes with change, any change, most of the men voted for Rackham as new captain of the sloop. Three jokingly cast their votes for Anne, remembering her call for the cannon against the frigate. But Anne only laughed.

"I give my votes to Jack. He'll run the ship, and I'll run him."

The crew guffawed and slapped him on the back. He had the good grace to grin.

THE SEA WAS even more beautiful from the deck of their own sloop. The countless spans of cays and reefs, the treacherous sandbars and islets seemed a personal tapestry to be explored now that Jack was in command. The sloop ran before the wind like a bird. Anne knew that some eighty miles to the west lay the coast of Florida and to the east the main routes used by ships going to and from the Indies and New York. But all of that seemed far away. Her only world was this small swift ship. All that mattered was the *Seahorse*, Jack, the crew, and the growing sense of a stranger inside her body.

Her belly was beginning to bulge slightly now, but she wore her blouse outside her breeches, loosely belted, and, so far, none was the wiser. She noticed that Jack did not mount her with nearly the robust enthusiasm he had before, but she put his reluctance down to a new protectiveness he must feel for the child within her. Sometimes she forgot completely that she carried life—and she climbed the decks and worked and fought alongside the rest of the men. Other times her body overwhelmed her, and she was suffused suddenly with a hot sense of wonder at what—or who—was growing steadily under her heart.

The change of command seemed to bring the *Seahorse* luck, for out of Bermuda she immediately ran alongside a heavily laden trading schooner. Anne was eager for a fray now; even the decking beneath her feet felt alive. Jack maneuvered the *Seahorse* up close to the schooner, while Anne helped to keep the crew hidden under the bulwarks. Now, she heard the captain's voice call out across the water, "What ship? Where ye bound?"

And Calico Jack's hoarse cry, "From the sea!"

The two ships met at right angles with a lurch. Anne could see riggings and spars ripping loose, scattering men like frightened birds.

"Boarders away!" cried Anne, and with raucous yells, the pirates surged up and onto the bulwarks, their cutlasses slashing through the enemy before they could recover.

Jack shrieked, "We make widows tonight, lads!"

Anne jerked the lanyard of another gun. She saw the packed cannon ball explode on the trader's deck.

Running to join the boarding party, she pulled herself up into the shrouds, slashing at a man who tried to pull her off. She dimly heard shrieks of pain and rage, the blasts of muskets and the clang of swords; she was dazzled by the fire and smoke.

Jack stood on the trader's decks, clashing swords with a seaman, the hiss of their steel reaching her ears. He stabbed him through the chest, and he fell. The seaman's mate keened a war cry, his cutlass aimed at Jack's belly. Jack downed him easily, with a nauseating thunk like a dull hatchet opening a wood keg.

Jack shouted, "Cut the lines, lads! Cripple the bitch!"

Anne ducked as a ball whizzed past her face. Suddenly she felt a weakness in her legs, a flutter in her belly. She grabbed her stomach and silently cursed herself as she slid down the rigging and onto the poop deck. In relief, she heard the trader's captain call, "Quarter! Goddamn yer eyes! Quarter, I say! Damned insolence! Yer all a pack of thieves! Picaroons! No better than niggers!"

He was still sputtering, "No damn gentlemen!" as his crew gratefully threw down their weapons.

The men began to fall away from one another; the chaos changed to calm. In spite of the fact that the decks looked like a charnel house, there were few men killed.

The pirate crew set up a ragged cheer, as Jack, like a heroic spector, his pants red with blood, cried, "She's ours, lads!"

In the trader's cargo were several huge hogsheads of wine. The pirates swarmed over them like water beetles. They found a few bottles of rum, broke off their necks with their swords, and the celebration was soon in full swing. As the pirates and their new recruits drank, they exchanged gossip and news from up and down the coast. Anne sat on the edge of the group, her hair tucked under her cap, her blouse pulled down. Few of the recruits even noticed her, much less guessed her identity. But she started when she heard one man's news.

"Ay, 'tis true. Stede Bonnet's been taken and twenty-two o' his men besides."

"And Blackbeard?" someone asked.

"Ah, that scurvy bastard got off scot-free. He pulled Bonnet back into his troops after the damn fool got a pardon! Then they plagued the Carolinas together 'til Teach tired o' the sot. He took all the booty, tricked Bonnet, an' left him an' his men stuck on the sandbar holdin' their parts in their hands! Well, Bonnet got off an' tried to catch Teach. Though what he'd do if he caught him, I don't know. But anyhow, Bonnet ran right into a warship out o' Charles Town, Colonel William Rhett at yer service! Course, he was still boilin' over Teach and Bonnet's siege o' that harbor. An' he plucked Bonnet out o' the sea like a drunken turtle an' hauled him to Charles Town in chains!"

Anne sat in a reverie. She started when a wave suddenly smacked a porthole. Green foam drooled down the glass. Oh, that damned fool! she thought. He was safe away and pardoned and then to be lured back into it by Teach. That knave!

She turned from the knot of men and went to the rail, gazing out to sea. She pressed her belly to quiet its ache. Stede Bonnet

...all the while she'd pictured him safe in his wife's arms, he'd been out on the seas somewhere. She wondered how he could have been so stupid as to be gulled by Teach—not once but twice, from the sound of it. She was overwhelmed by anger and sadness. Her heart felt crowded in her breast. She looked down at her blouse—still no discernible bulge unless one knew what to look for. It seemed a decade since she'd heard Bonnet's voice. She recalled the touch of his lips, soft on her own, perhaps the gentlest love she'd ever felt. It was he who'd first given her the words to tell of her feelings for the sea; he who'd understood her before she spoke. And now he stood in the shadows of the gallows.

Vividly she remembered the last hanging she'd seen in Charles Town, the futile kicks of the dying man, the rude jostlings of the crowd. She could not bear to think of Stede—with his fine frock coat and his Belgian lace cuffs—subjected to such degradation and pain. In an instant, she made up her mind. Her thoughts whirled with the possibilities before her. She hurried back to the hold to collect more information.

Jack was drinking with some men on the poop deck when she found him. His eyes were already bloodshot with the rum and wine, but she pulled him aside.

"Jack, Bonnet's been captured!"

He looked at her calmly. "Ay, lass. I just heard the like. 'Tis a shame. He was a good man, though not for the sea."

Anne smiled up at him. "Ay, he was. And I'm glad to hear you say it. Jack, we must rescue him from the gallows!"

Jack's eyes widened. "Rescue him? Don't be daft, lass! He's in a Charles Town gaol with all of the town at the door!"

"No, Jack!" she said urgently. "He's not! They're keeping him at the marshal's house. I know just how to get him out; I've been to balls at that house as a girl. I know we can do it! We can't let him hang!"

"I don't know why not, Anne. He'd let *me* hang, I wager."

"Perhaps. But *I* wouldn't. Nor will I let him." She paced to the rail once, twice, and back again, her arms crossed firmly.

"Jack, I'm going to help him. Are you coming or not?"

"You are *not* going to Charles Town, nor am I! Jesus, you're as flighty as a nesting sparrow! I'm captain on this ship, and I say you'll not set foot off these decks! No, and I'll not risk my neck for some bewigged fop who once bedded my woman! By God, you ask too much, wench!"

Jack's eyes blazed, and she saw none of his early tenderness there. He glanced at the men on deck who were watching them. She withdrew coolly.

"Jack, I understand your feelings. I'll not ask you again. But neither can I let the man go to his death without lifting a hand. No one can help him but me. If you won't help me, I'll go it alone."

He began to holler once more, but she stopped him. "Jack, I *will* go!"

He yanked her arm and pulled her aside where fewer could witness their words.

"You go, Anne, and I swear I'll not have you in my bed again! I'll not have it!" he hissed. He lowered his head and his eyes bored into hers, his pupils contracting with rage.

"What is it, Jack!" she whispered back harshly. "Are you afraid? I swear I've a plan—"

He snapped off her words with a quick jerk on her shoulder. "I'll hear no plan to save some old lover! He's been taken, and he's through! He should never have started the life and you know it! He hasn't the stomach or the nerve! And I'll not risk my ass for him, nor will you!"

She narrowed her eyes and seemed to see him for the first time. A part of him she could not fathom, could not reach. Did not want to.

"I believe you are afraid, *Captain*." She stressed the word; he did not wince. "But I am not. And I'll still say where—and when—I'll risk any part of me I choose." She jerked her arm from his grasp and stalked belowdecks, feeling his glare pierce her shoulders like a hot blade.

ANNE TOOK her case to the crew. By the slimmest margin they voted to sail to Sullivans Island, south of Charles Town, and lay offshore to wait. Several argued against such a plan. Mathias Bench, the ship's carpenter, complained, "Ay, an' we all be taken by the king's men waitin' for that damned dandy and the lass!"

But Hestor, the quartermaster, countered him. "Bonnet's a good man, Bench. I'd damned sight rather go after him than Teach, the madman. If it weren't for that devil, he'd be safe on the seas yet. I'll not go ashore, but I wager we can lay up one night for a mate to do her work. 'Tis a gallant effort." He turned to Anne. "Ye must be back well afore dawn, lass, or we're off. I wager if anyone can pull that poor bastard out, ye can."

Two night later Anne guided the sloop to a hidden inlet south of Charles Town and was rowed ashore, towing a small dinghy behind her. As she stepped into the skiff, she turned to wave one last time at Jack. He stood on the quarterdeck, his eyes shrouded in the darkness. He was motionless, his face set. Anne turned her back to the ship and peered over the water to the black live oaks bunched on the beach. She had just twenty-four hours.

IT TOOK HER most of the night and part of the morning to reach Charley Fourfeathers. She traipsed along the back trails by the river, keeping out of sight, her mind full of nostalgic thoughts of her father. When she arrived at Charley's cabin in the woods, he scarcely recognized her for she was dressed as a seaman, scratched and scuffed, her hair hidden under a dirty tam. Quickly, she outlined her plan to him as she pulled two of her most beautiful gowns from a small bundle.

That night the sounds of revelry could be heard up and down Broad Street, where the marshal's house stood. Black carriages rolled up to the front of the mansion and discharged small clusters of stylishly gowned ladies and their gentlemen. Liveried black servants lined the streets, keeping back the riffraff. Across the road a crowd had gathered to watch the glittering spectacle of the governor's ball.

The town was particularly elated because the capture of Stede Bonnet and his men meant a fine display in the weeks to come. The trial would undoubtedly be well attended, and the inevitable hangings would pull visitors from all over the county—perhaps even as far as Carolina to the north.

The front of the marshal's house was festooned with every available lantern, making a wide wash of light up the steps to the ballroom. Only a single lantern, however, hung above the side door to the cellar. Beneath the lamp, shadowed by the bushes and trees which grew close to the house, two soldiers shared a vigil, leaning against the wall.

As the chimes from St. Phillip's church clock sounded ten, the soldiers stirred restlessly. They turned to listen to the music pouring from the ballroom.

Stockdale, the younger of the two, stamped his feet to keep them from tingling with fatigue. "Christ, this is a long shift. Don't know what made us so damned lucky as to pull watch on this night."

"Ay," replied his companion, Maulby. "If I can't dance, I'd as soon sit."

"Now, that'd be a sight, seein' you dance with those fine ladies, you fool. There's not a one let you touch her sleeve."

"Pox to them all, I say." He laughed. "And from what I hear, plenty's got it, too."

"Ay," grinned Stockdale. "Under those fancy skirts 'tis all the same in the dark." He hastily stuffed his pipe in his uniform pocket as he heard soft footsteps up the path.

"Who goes there!" called Maulby. "Halt and be identified!"

The liquid sound of feminine laughter wafted towards the soldiers, as Anne stepped out of the shadows into the light of the lantern. She was precariously laced into her richest emerald gown, her red hair twisted down her neck and shoulders like a mantle of fire, and diamonds nestled in the dark furrow of her breasts. Her waist was loose, but her bodice was low. As she walked, she wove unsteadily from one side of the path to the other. She half-glided, half-tripped up to Stockdale, her hands softly grasping his arm for support.

"O la! You startled me, gentlemen!"

"Madam, I believe you've lost your way," Maulby stuttered, his eyes going to Anne's breasts. "The ball is up those front steps."

Anne giggled, an enchanting warm burble of joyous abandon. "Why, I've *been* to the ball, Captain. And the ball's been to me as well. I believe"—she leaned unsteadily into Stockdale, her hands fluttering at her throat—"why, I believe I'm tipsy as a . . . trull!" She whooped, "Oh! Pardon me! My lords, I'm much too wild tonight to be loose."

Stockdale took her arm and began to lead her to the light. "I'll escort you back, madam. You cannot stay—"

But she wrenched herself from his grasp with a lovely petulant pout. "No, my lord. I won't go back to that stuffy place. I need some air." She moved towards the bench down the path, half-shrouded in bushes. "Must sit for just a wink and rest. And *then* I'll go back and dance and dance."

She put up her arms to Stockdale, smiling softly. "Do you dance, milord?" She swung him around the path, giggling, and then fell suddenly in his arms. "Is there no place I can rest for just a minute?"

Stockdale eyed his comrade with a small grin. "Ay, milady. I'll help you to the bench." He took her arms, and she leaned into him again, her breasts brushing full against his chest. Suddenly she seemed to trip on her skirts and, throwing her arms around the young soldier, she pressed her body to his. "Oh, milord. You're so strong! Not like those fops upstairs."

Now Maulby grinned openly as he winked at the young soldier. "You go on, lad. Take your time. Then come back and relieve me." He chuckled. "Since the lady's in no hurry."

Anne grinned silkily at him. "No hurry at all, Captain. No place to go, and no one to watch if I do."

She giggled again and let herself be drawn to the bench around the corner and out of sight. Stockdale plopped her down on the bench and hesitantly reached for her, casting a nervous eye over his shoulder. He was trembling with anticipation, and Anne could feel the sexual heat rise off him like a galloped horse. She drew his head down to hers, murmuring, "Take off that silly helmet, lad, so I can run my hands through your hair." He hastily tipped his helmet off his head, bent to grab her, and Charley Fourfeathers came from behind the bushes and cracked him on the head with a club. The thud of the muffled wood on Stockdale's skull was followed by a sigh as he crumpled at her feet. Anne and Charley quickly stretched him out on the ground behind the bench, and she ambled back up the path to the light.

Maulby was amazed at what he saw. This beautiful woman was drunkenly staggering right into his arms, her hair wild, her bodice pulled open; one breast winked at him in the darkness.

"Where's my mate?" he gulped.

Anne laughed softly. "He's resting, milord. He was not . . . quite the man he looked." She glided closer and winked at Maulby with warm promise. "How about you, good sir? Shall we show him how it's done?"

Maulby licked his lips nervously. "Ay, milady. I won't fail ye. Just as soon as me mate gets back."

Anne shrugged disdainfully. "I wait for no man." She turned and weaved down the path towards the shadows.

Maulby hesitated for a split instant, torn between desire for the wanton creature before him and his duty. It was an easy decision. He ran after Anne, calling, "Wait, mistress! Wait for me!"

Anne turned, and he all but ran into her arms. She laughed and leaned into his body, putting both hands on his backside. "I can tell, sir, you're worth waiting for." She casually tipped off the soldier's helmet as Charley eased from the shadows and saluted him as he had his comrade. Now both sentries lay in the darkness, oblivious to the beauty who had lured them there.

Anne hugged Charley quickly and took the other gown from behind a bush. She bent and searched Maulby's pockets for the key. She tripped up the path, smoothing her skirts, unlocked the side door, and slipped inside.

Down the dark corridor a door stood ajar, a ribbon of light at the bottom. She pressed herself against the wall and eased down the corridor, holding her skirts so they would not rustle. She peered into the room. Inside a single candle burned on a table. Stede Bonnet sat, his back to the door, writing.

Anne's heart thumped wildly when she saw him, and she pressed her hands together to calm herself. The creak of the door caught his attention. He looked up. Anne stood in the doorway framed by the glow of the candle. Bonnet was struck dumb.

Anne smiled; her mouth trembled. " 'Tis I, Stede. Anne. Come to save you." She looked over her shoulder hastily, and went to him, shoving the gown in his arms. "We've no time to talk, my love. Get into this." As always, action calmed her.

Stede pulled the gown up over his breeches, yanked off his shirt. Thank God, he's still clean-shaven, Anne thought, as she tucked a bonnet over his head, arranged his curls to show at the edge, and tied a bow under his chin.

"Come!" she whispered, tugging him out the door. "I've help waiting!" Anne and Stede crept along the corridor, out the door, down the path, into the darkness, and away.

Anne, Bonnet, and Charley stole down the back streets of Charles Town until they reached the inlet off the Cooper River where they'd hidden a plantation dinghy. Once there, Anne threw on a sea coat, letting her hair hang free. Stede ripped off his gown and embraced Anne with passion.

"My dear God, Anne! My love! To risk so much for me!"

She kissed him fervently. "I could not bear to think of you strung up for all the world to see." She pulled away, looking over her shoulder. "But, come. We're not safe yet." She hurried

Bonnet into the dinghy; he and Charley rowed the skiff through the darkness to Sullivans Island. The tide was against them and rather than row against the current, they decided to land and continue on foot across the island.

COLONEL RHETT had been jerked from his bed by the news that his pirate prize had slipped from his hands. Furious, he quickly organized a massive manhunt, determined to recapture his prisoner.

After plunging through the myrtle thickets and over sandhills, Anne sensed her mistake, but it was too late to go back for the boat. They had to cross the long island to reach the pirate dinghy hidden in the shoals and then row to the *Seahorse* waiting beyond the bar. Anne had thrown away her dress and changed to breeches, but Stede had badly twisted an ankle and was unable to keep up their pace. They heard their pursuers behind them.

She heard the signal shots, the shouts of men, the baying of dogs, and knew they were trapped. Even if they could reach the dinghy in time, they would lead Rhett right to the *Seahorse* becalmed outside the bar. Anne knew Rhett was smart enough to have his men-of-war circling the island to back up his land party. Besides, as the sounds grew closer, she realized they'd never even make the dinghy at all.

"Hurry, Stede! You must move faster!" she cried as they crashed through the brush. He groaned. Charley was helping support him, but Bonnet had been exhausted by his ordeal in prison and was near the end of his strength.

Bonnet himself finally called a halt. With the sounds of their pursuers growing near, he stopped, panting, leaning against a tree.

"This is no good. I'm the leg of mutton they want; you're just the gravy. If they catch us, you'll hang, too. Stay here and I'll lead them away."

Anne glanced at Charley in the darkness. He only shrugged. She walked calmly into Bonnet's arms, but her heart was desolate.

"I'm sorry, Stede. We did our best for you."

He kissed her once. "I know. I'm grateful. I've got my memories of us—and they'll fortify me to the end." With one last look, he turned, veering off in a new direction, dragging his ankle behind him.

Anne turned to Charley, her eyes glistening with tears. "They'll take him sure," she whispered. Charley took her arm and led her away towards the beach.

As they reached the dinghy, a cry of triumph went up in the distance. They have him, she thought. A picture flashed through her mind's eye of Stede hobbling over a sand dune, clearly outlined in the moonlight, a pack of dogs at his flanks.

As Charley rowed her to the sloop, Anne tried to talk him into turning pirate, rather than risking capture. He looked over his shoulder at the black ship, waiting like a patient beast. The sea was a sheet of silver under a cloudless black sky, the edges turning green as weathered brass with the impending dawn.

"Here, you're all but a slave, Charley. At sea you'd be free."

"Who be not a slave?" he replied solemnly. "All be slaves to something. We each choose our master." He smiled slowly, a rare reflex for his creased brown face. "You be of the sea. I be of the land."

He took a small starfish from out of his jerkin and handed it to her. "This be your talisman."

She smiled gently at him. "Thank you, Charley. It's beautiful." She gazed at the red five-fingered creature for a moment, then reached over the dinghy and dropped it into the cove. "So I shall always know where it is." He nodded.

As they reached the ship, she turned and waved once to him, then climbed the rope ladder to the decks.

As she neared the top, she was dazzled by a sudden pain in her back. She stopped, closed her eyes, and willed the ache away. She wondered if this night had taken more from her than just Stede Bonnet.

ᔕᔕᔕ

ANNE KNEW NOW that her time at sea was limited. She did not feel herself at all. Her breasts felt stretched and taut, and her belly was beginning to get in her way. Finally, Hestor, the quartermaster, approached her, hat in hand. Such a rare posture from one of the crew immediately put Anne on her guard.

"There's no use ye tryin' to hide it, lass. 'Tis whispered all over the ship."

"What, man?" She knew already, but she wondered if she dared bluff his challenge.

"That yer with child."

"Did Jack tell you that?"

"He didn't have to, Anne. Yer belly's creepin' out to blare the news itself. 'Tis time to take to land. The men won't take a prize with you on board and risk yer life . . . and Rackham's bairn."

Anne thought of Jack. He had been glad to see her when she returned safely from Sullivans Island, but she sensed a growing distance between them. They still shared a berth, but she wondered if they still shared hearts. She often caught him watching her as she moved from one place to another on deck, his eyes impossible to read. Before, she could always see her own reflection in his eyes—now she saw only shadows.

She felt weary now of the constant movement, of the heat, of the work. The thought of a white warm beach seemed all at once a welcome haven.

" 'Tis true, Hestor. I am with child. And when we reach Cuba, I'll beach myself willingly. But for now, can you keep this to yourself? I can't bear the stares of the men."

Hestor smiled. "They never stopped starin' at ye, lass, an' I doubt they will now. But I'll keep mum. If I have yer word."

"You do. Does Jack agree I should be put ashore at Cuba?"

" 'Twas he who sent me."

ᔕᔕᔕ

So ANNE WENT ashore in Cuba. Rackham set her up in a small house at Zagoa beach, a ramshackle Spanish settlement sprinkled with a few taverns, brothels, and native markets. She deeply resented Jack's indifferent attitude, which she saw as desertion. Oh, Jack was with her—for now. But she knew he would not stay in Cuba for the four months it would take her to deliver. Almost immediately he was restless and talked of lost prizes, missed chances, and the dangers of resting too long in Spanish seas.

In a rare gesture of placation, Jack sent for Meg Moore to stay with Anne during her confinement. When Meg heard that Anne was holed up in Zagoa, awaiting a child, she slipped aboard a trader bound for the island and came to her immediately.

Anne embraced her on the beach, laughing with joy. Meg brought a welcome smile and willing hands—but bad news. Stede Bonnet had been hanged November 18, 1718, at White Point.

When she saw Anne was strong and could take the details, Meg told her all she'd heard. Anne cringed at the images but pressed her to continue.

Bonnet had been recaptured and taken to trial immediately. His comrades, all twenty-two of his crew, were hung before his eyes on November 8. Yet the people were reluctant to deal so summarily with a man who'd been a gentleman of some estate. One group of townsfolk, headed by Colonel William Rhett himself, surprisingly backed a suggestion that Bonnet be transported to England to stand trial.

The move was blocked by Sir Nicholas Trott, presiding judge at the piracy trial, who refused to read Bonnet's plea for clemency and sentenced the pirate captain to death. Meg said she'd heard that some of the ladies in town wept at the trial to see Bonnet at the dock in his wig and lace frock coat, gripping a book of his poems.

Bonnet was led to White Point by a rope tied to the tail of a cart that hauled his coffin. The waterfront was thronged with spectators, and one young girl skipped up to the condemned man and placed a nosegay of wild flowers in his manacled hands. When the cart reached the gallows, it was obvious that some sympathetic rogues had sabotaged it in the night, for the yardarm was cut. A hasty construction job was done, and Bonnet was made to stand on his coffin so that he might reach the scaffolding. The noose was fitted about his neck, and Bonnet waited while ministers prayed over him and dignitaries gathered.

"Damned insolent dogs!" Anne cursed when she heard, her eyes stinging with unshed tears. "If there is a God, may He shrivel their hypocritical souls in hell!" She passed her hand over her eyes once. "Did he die well, Meg?"

"Ay, considerin'. The rope was too short, so when he dropped a few fellows had to grab his legs an' pull 'til he was quiet. But afore he went, they say he said, 'Hell must be a merrier place than this!' "

Anne shook her head. "That's like him," she smiled, her mouth quivering. "As if hell's nothing more than just an indigestible biscuit. He so loved the sea that land seemed scorching to his feet." She sighed. "And who else did that bastard Trott send with him?"

As Meg recited a few names, Anne moaned and covered her face with her hands. Bob Tucker, an old friend from Jamaica; John William Smith, a pirate guest at her father's table; and Jim Levitt of New Providence. She'd raised many glasses of ale with Jim at the House of Lords. Friends, companions . . . twenty-nine hanged, fluttering over the waterfront like laundry in a breeze, buried at the low-water line, so their bones were uncovered in a sink tide.

Two days later, the shock of Bonnet's death still fresh in Anne's mind, Jack came bursting into the house with more bad news.

"Teach has been killed off Cape Fear! Some king's pimp name of Maynard got him! They say he was shot five times and took twenty-five cutlass wounds before he died."

Anne felt an unearthly calm settle over her. Ned gone, too. Rogers' net was closing fast. "He lived hard, and he meant to die hard as well."

"Ay," Jack nodded, his face somber. "But the dogs cut off his head like savages and fed the rest to the sharks."

"He always said, better the fish than the buzzards." Anne turned away. "He got his wish at least."

Jack looked hollow-eyed. He slumped in a chair. "Christ, Anne. The sea's crawling with king's men and ghosts. Maybe we should've taken the pardon when 'twas offered."

Anne remembered his boldness at the council campfire, when Jennings suggested just such a chance, recalled how he had defiantly stomped away from the circle of pirates, vowing to take his ship to sea. Now, the wind had been knocked out of his sails. He looked up at her. She only shrugged sadly and retreated to her room.

Ned Teach's fate proved to be a warning to pirates in and out of the Caribbean seas. "The sweet trade's going sour at last," Jack said.

Anne was deeply depressed, and for days later, she sat on the beach, facing stolidly north to the colonies, remembering the men who were gone.

THE *SEAHORSE* STAYED at Zagoa for over a month, long enough to sound the bottom of the crew's pockets. Though Jack tried to keep Anne company, she began to realize that she looked forward with relief to her solitude, to being alone with the life growing inside her. Nagging at her to amuse him, Jack was becoming a damned nuisance.

"God's breath, this scurvy hole is boring!" he said with an irritating frequency.

Anne looked up from stringing some shells for a necklace. "Well, heave anchor, then! I wish I could leave, too. But I can't. And you're no good to me pacing back and forth like a caged wolf. You make me wish I'd never let you near me!"

"Ho! You wanted me just as much as I wanted you!" He tugged her out of her chair and kissed her lightly. "You want me this minute, I can tell it."

She grinned wryly. "Ay. It's not crowded enough in there now. Be off with you, fool!"

He dropped her readily. "Ay, I'll go to town and see if I can lure some innocents to the dice."

"There are no innocents left, Jack."

Grinning, he went on his way, distracted now from his ennui.

Anne put down her handiwork and headed for the beach. As she walked along the shore, she felt the baby turn within her, that rolling motion that made her feel she was an ocean holding a wave. Yesterday, she'd noticed a broken blue vein running behind her knee that she'd not seen before. She'd seen matrons with many children whose bellies were as flaccid as old spaniel bitches.

Two months ago the seed within her seemed an anchor; now it made her feel like an open door to all life. Sometimes when she touched her belly she felt a lightning current, a shock of recognition run through her skin and up to her breasts, as if tiny hands curled inside her stomach had somehow grazed and grasped her fingertips for an instant. Some days her fears crowded in on her and pressed her in places where she'd never felt fright before. Fear of pain, fear of death, fear of being swallowed up by the very life she carried. Other days she felt impervious to any harm, totally inviolate, as the life force itself.

CHRISTMAS IN ZAGOA had a solemn religious feeling with little of the abandonment and pagan frivolity she knew in Charles Town. The Spanish erected a huge altar made of palm fronds and broken spars; in the middle they placed a small cradle with a clay figure of the infant Jesus. To the left of the clay babe the natives constructed a tall figure of fronds and cord and belted a blue shawl over the top. Then they placed a ring of clams about the whole display and hunkered down to sing the praises of the Virgin and Child.

Anne and Meg had strolled out to the small settlement for diversion. Their little house was quiet since Jack and the crew had taken the sloop out to a nearby sea lane to ambush any stray ship. Anne's stomach bulged ominously now, and even her loosest gown would not hide it. She'd given up breeches over a month before. It was almost as if the child had not quite been sure if it wanted to grow for the first six months, and now was attempting to make up for its delay. She rubbed her back lightly as she walked back to the house. It had ached all afternoon.

That night as she lay in bed listening to the waves, she was stirred by a humming through her flesh. Perhaps it was the rum she'd had at dinner. But then she'd had the same rum every night. Suddenly she felt a small dimpling sensation in her loins and a pop, a slight burst in her belly. Before she could wonder what it was, a gush of water flooded her thighs and her linen.

My God, she gasped. The baby. She elbowed her way up to a sitting position and hunched over, staring at the tufted cleft between her legs. She could barely see herself under the mound of her belly. Her sheets were drenched. The ache in her back intruded forcefully now into her consciousness.

"Meg!" she cried out. "The baby's coming!"

She heard a quick patter of bare feet, and Meg was at her side. "So soon? You're not due for more'n a month."

"Ay, but look!" Anne showed her the sodden linen.

"Jesus Christ, your water's broke. Your time's come, then."

Anne felt a stab of fear clutch her bowels, but she fought it back. "It's too soon! Can you stop it?"

Meg frowned. "No one can stop it, lass. 'Twill come soon, will ye or no. And the sooner the better, you'll be thinking once it starts. 'Twill be fine, you'll see."

She hauled Anne to her feet. " 'Tis better to walk now, lass. Walk while ye can. Pay no mind to the pain. Is it bad?"

Anne shook her head, her eyes wide. "Nay, but it's there. Feels like gas from chowder beer."

"Ay," Meg smiled. "That's it. Walk now!"

For three hours Anne walked and sat, sat and walked, her hands clutching her belly, her brow sweating, until she could not place one foot before the other. The pain had built to a honed-sharp edge now, and it twisted her belly like a hot coil. She could scarcely breathe as it rose in her, rhythmically slow at first, then harder and faster until it gripped her mind and welded all her thoughts on her flesh. Meg helped her to bed again, but she could not be still. She crouched on her hands and knees, her hair falling about her back and grazing her clenched fists in the bedclothes.

"Oh, Jesus, Meg! It rips through me like hot lead!"

"I know, lass. I know."

"How could you know?" Anne writhed in angry pain. "You've never had it! Oh! My God, here it comes again!"

She gasped and grunted, squeezing her eyes shut against the red-scorching ache that knotted her body. Some part of her mind wondered from what caged animal such sounds could come. Some part of her mind cursed Jack, free on the open sea and absent when she needed him. Some part of her mind felt shame at the picture she must make, crouched and helpless with her naked flanks and heavy belly exposed. But just as quickly, all of her mind spun back to focus only on the awful pressure bursting in her. Long pieces of time slipped by, unnoticed except as they were punctuated by her pain.

As she struggled, she heard Meg shout, "Bear down, lass! Can ye push?"

"I can't—*not* push!" Anne gasped, straining to breathe and knotting every muscle for the effort. It seemed she must push her entire womb out onto the bed, so hard did she shove with everything in her. She was on her back now, pushing, straining, and she felt no movement within her—no help from the babe. She heard Meg muttering something, her head and hands down between Anne's flanks; she felt a pulling, a tearing inside her, and then she slipped off the edge of the high lonely place to which she'd been chained, off into a gray sky, off into the sea, and heard nothing.

She awoke instantly. She knew it had only been moments, for Meg was still at her feet slowly wrapping a small bundle in a bloodied sheet. The room was as silent as the moment Clara had died.

Through a gray haze Anne saw death crouching in the corner of the room; she heard its slow silent hissing and saw its great eyeless face. Anne's lips drew back from her teeth in a silent involuntary snarl, and then there was only Meg. She shook her head as though to clear it, drawing in her breath sharply to stave off her panic.

"Is it born?"

Meg looked up, startled. "Ay, lass. It's over." She shook her head sadly. "It never breathed once, Anne. I think it died inside you."

Anne stared at Meg. Then at the lumped linen in her hands. She forced herself up on her elbows and wordlessly reached for the bundle.

Meg began to weep silently. "Ye don't need to see it now, lass. There's time later. Ye should rest now."

"Bring it to me," Anne said quietly with the last bit of her strength and fell back on the bed. Meg brought the tangled mass she held, and Anne pulled back the flap of the sheet. A girl. Tiny and gray as an unopened clam. Her eyes were shut tight, thin blue lines, as if she could not bear to view the world even once. Her legs were twisted about each other, and there was blood in the creases of her body as though she'd been dipped, then dried by a careless hand. A gray and white cord hung from her tiny stomach—a lifeline to nothing. Anne touched her skin, hesitantly at first, in wonder. Then she untangled the cool damp legs, and wrapped the sheet carefully about the little body.

She looked up at Meg who was sobbing quietly in the corner of the room. The sheets of the bed were bloodied; a dark mass was partially wrapped at her feet. Another piece of my body, thought Anne.

"It's over, then," she said dazedly.

Meg moved as if to come to her, but Anne stopped her with a look.

"I want to be alone now. Thank you, but leave me."

Meg said, "Anne, try not to think—"

"Leave me!"

Meg went without another word out the door and closed it quietly behind her.

Anne carefully placed the tiny body on the bed and lowered herself beside it, gently pulling it close to her breast. As she lay on her side, gazing at nothing, she felt a seeping wetness down her arm. She looked and saw that her right breast was leaking a thin clear fluid, an aimless rivulet which trickled down her skin and into the sheet that covered the infant's head. Her body's last offering to a dead dream. Anne began to weep then, and she sobbed as if her body labored to birth yet another burden.

FOR A WEEK she lay, dispirited and lifeless, her eyes dull and unseeing. When she got up at all, she merely wandered aimlessly down to the harbor and back again. She had no more tears. Indeed, she wondered if she could ever cry again, so completely did she empty herself over that small still mass. Meg did her best to console Anne.

"You'll have other babes, Anne. You're young yet and strong."

But Anne barely heard her. She sat on the beach for hours, staring listlessly out to sea, watching the waves break one after another until the wind stung her face like hot sand. Her eyes were dark and haunted as if she'd seen a place inside her, the cellar of the mind her father had described, and even the sunlight felt different now.

When Rackham returned, he was appalled at her condition.

Her cheeks were pale and thin, her whole body seemed smaller by half.

"You need proper care," he said firmly. "We're going back to New Providence."

She merely turned weary eyes to him. "How can we possibly go back there? Rogers will be waiting for us with a gallows."

"Nay, Anne. I met Hornigold off Coxen's Hole. The pardon's been offered for another year."

"And you believed him? Maybe he's just out for the reward on your mangy hide."

"If he was, he'd have taken me then and there, for he could have. No, Rogers got the word from the king himself. We're to come in and be pardoned. He'll not arrest us if we come in a month."

Meg piped up, "That sounds likely. There was talk o' such when I left. 'Course, those who took the pardon first time around are screamin' fit to burst 'cause they wasted a year on the beach." She smiled. "But ye could go back, Anne. 'Twould do you good."

"Why are they giving us such a chance now?"

"Because they need us." Rackham laughed. "England's going to war with Spain any day, and she needs us by her side! One more reason to get off this poxed island. If war comes, we'll not be able to bribe our way to safety anymore."

Anne pondered it for a moment. "Well, Rogers is a man of his word, I wager. We'll go, then."

Jack grinned. "Good. I've already put it to a vote, and the men agree. We sail tomorrow."

As they left Cuba with the evening tide, they rounded the inlet to Coxen's Hole. There, anchored beyond the bar, they discovered twelve Spanish men-of-war, their forty-pounders all pointed to the sea like the jaws of crouching dogs.

"Jesus, the whole fleet's gatherin'," whispered Mathias as they slipped by in the night.

"Ay," smiled Anne for the first time in a week. "Thanks be to

Rackham, we escaped that scurvy island just in time."

NEW PROVIDENCE had endured some radical changes in their absence. The fort had been strengthened and repaired. The cluttered harbor was cleared of most of the wrecks, and the docks were missing their usual piles of debris and booty.

"What hit this place?" asked Anne of Bess when she saw her.

"A hurricane called Woodes Rogers!" she laughed as she told Anne what had transpired.

"When Rogers beached, he ladled out the king's papers like honey. Right there at the House of Lords."

"And the Brethren took it?"

"Took it? They fair stood in line! Six hundred o' the best— Davis an' Cochran, an' Auger, an' Burgess, an' Carter, an' ay, your own Ben Hornigold. An' he made the rest official as well."

"Official what?"

"With titles fine as any London stiff! Robinson was named provost marshal, my Jennings is now the special aide to the governor, by yer leave, an' that scum Turnley was given the job of chief pilot."

Anne rolled her eyes. "You mean he picked out those most likely to revolt and got them sotted with pretty feathers."

Bess laughed raucously. "Ay, lass. Ye should have seen old Ben Hornigold, Davis, and Burgess, hats in hand, being sworn in to protect the peace. An' yer own Bonny beside them."

"James? Well, I'm blowed."

"Ay. He lined up right behind those bandits with his paw out, and now he's one o' the militia."

Anne shook her head ruefully. "That man always knew which side buttered his bread."

"Ay. An' then Rogers closed the taverns down."

Anne gaped. "And the man's still standing?"

Bess grinned. "Standin' an' struttin' still. He told the men that 'til this pisshole was cleaned up good, they'd get no rum. Didn't take long for even the doxies to join in then. When a few revolted, he put 'em to work in the heat o' the day. When they tried to bribe him, he put those at digging trenches. And when Chidley Bayard offered him half the profits if he'd let his own smugglers in an' out o' the harbor, Rogers kicked him out an' burned down his grand mansion."

Anne whirled and looked up at the hill. The pink walls were gone; only blackened, crumbled stone remained.

"Bayard will be back," Anne muttered.

Bess laughed gaily. " 'Tis said he's got plenty of troubles with the Spanish now, an' got no time for the likes o' Woodes Rogers."

"Sounds like Rogers is just asking for open rebellion. I'd have thought those devils would have mutinied by now."

"Oh, a few did, to be sure. But the governor set bandits after bandits. Hornigold and Cochran sailed after those that lit out and captured thirteen—and Rogers hanged 'em high."

Anne was amazed that the rest of the island had allowed such a proceeding on their own beach.

"Ay," said Meg. "Well, old Rob Morris—you remember him, Anne—the one-eyed drunk. He stood on a barrel, wavin' his pistol, callin' for a rope for the governor!" She shrugged. "Rogers shot him down like a dog as he stood. He fell right into the crowd, dead as a mullet. And Rogers left the rest hangin' for two days."

And as Anne walked over the island she could see that Rogers meant business, and the pirate republic was perhaps the better for it. Though she missed the old freedom, the House of Lords and the easy, carefree days, she was glad to feel she could walk the streets without fear of being accosted by some drunken seaman or another.

She was happy to see Jennings, Hornigold, Emilie, and the rest. They seemed little changed in her absence, yet she felt like a completely different person now. She wondered if life would ever seem so full and free again.

She went with Jack to be pardoned by Woodes Rogers. He remarked, "I have heard much of your beauty, mistress. But you look the worse for wear. I hope you see now that a life at sea is no life for a woman."

She nodded mutely.

He said to Rackham, "You have your pardon for all crimes before this date. I expect you, Rackham, to report for the work detail as soon as you're settled. And you, mistress"—he turned to Anne—"find a safe place to heal."

Thus assured, Jack took Anne to a house Jennings had obtained for them. After several weeks of rest and loving care by Bess and Meg, Anne's health improved and more of her old friends came calling. The most fascinating topic of conjecture among the woman was Governor Rogers' celibacy. He had been on the island for nearly eight months and as far as any could say, no woman shared his bed.

"No doubt he's keepin' himself for you, Anne!" laughed Bess. "They say he fears nothing."

Anne smiled wanly. "The man who fears nothing is more dangerous than a coward. I'll take Rackham, thanks."

Nevertheless, when Anne had taken to walking the beach again, she received a message from Rogers asking her to call. Rackham was included in the invitation. They arrived at the governor's quarters, and Jack hurriedly took her aside.

"Let me do the talking, lass. I don't trust this knave as far as I can spit."

But Rogers greeted her cordially and introduced them to a naval officer of the Crown, Captain Charles Lewis.

"Captain Lewis is stationed at Jamaica," Rogers explained. "He has obtained information that the Spanish are gathering warships and sloops in Havana together with an army of some size." He looked at Anne quickly, then away. "He feels the invasion is headed for New Providence. During your stay in Cuba, did you hear or see anything that would suggest such a move?"

Anne glanced at Jack, then stepped forward. "More than once, good sirs. The Spaniards often insisted that the Bahamas belonged to them. In fact, just before we left Zagoa, we heard that a certain official had arrived in Havana from Madrid. He was given the title of governor of New Providence." Jack frowned slightly but said nothing.

Rogers nodded, thinking to himself. "That would certainly indicate that they intend to move against us. What else?"

Anne and Jack then told him all they knew about the strength and location of Spanish troops in and around Cuba. Because Jack had been on the island less than Anne, he often had to fall silent while she pieced together a tapestry of information. When they were ready to leave, the governor thanked them and bowed slightly over Anne's hand.

"Today you have belied your reputation and earned your pardon. I consider myself in your debt."

GRADUALLY THE PAIN of her dead child faded from Anne's mind. She tucked the memory of the birth into the dark recesses of her consciousness; soon the infant seemed only a dream, a pale specter that floated up before her on sleepless nights, a tug at her heart when she saw a child playing in the sand. She tried to believe as she always had that what happened to her was for the best. Such a view was her only religion, a hope that had often buoyed her during bleak despair. But this loss strained her capacity to believe in her future. When she tried to talk with Jack, he was sympathetic for her pain but not for her loss.

"What would we have done with a babe, lass? Perhaps 'tis best it was lost."

One part of Anne's mind focused on the practicality of what he said—it was true, the two of them had little time or space for a child in their lives. But a secret core of her mind withdrew in a cold rage from such thinking. Soon she stopped talking of it altogether. When she saw a child splashing in the waves on the beach or clinging to its mother's skirt, she turned away.

JAMES BONNY had prospered under Rogers' new regime. Before Anne and Jack arrived, he had ingratiated himself into Richard Turnley's affections and was soon promoted to the role of lieutenant in the island militia. As an officer, Bonny's chief duty was to spy on the men: sniffing out any dissenters in the work gangs, or rebels within the general population, and report them to Turnley. Rogers himself found such a task personally repugnant, but he recognized the need for information and, as Turnley insisted, there was none better to gather such gossip than Bonny.

Bonny was on the fringes of many groups and at the hub of none. He was grudgingly accepted by the pirates-turned-planters as a harmless turtler. Indeed, Bonny's chief claim to fame was that he had been husband to the pirate queen, Anne. Many supposed that he must have some hidden assets to so beguile this amazing woman, though he had been almost invisible for the two years he and Anne had lived on New Providence.

When Anne returned on the arm of Calico Jack Rackham, however, James Bonny's prestige plummeted on the island. He had made a minor kingdom out of browbeaten shopkeepers and novice whores too frightened to charge him for their services. But now he heard the whispers behind his back, and one doxy went so far as to laugh in his face.

"I see yer wife's back in port, Bonny. Has she been to see ye yet?" She grinned. "Or has she found another flip-flop more to her likin'?"

Bonny slapped her and left her bed, but her words—and especially her laugh—burned his mind until he took little pleasure in his other petty triumphs. He recalled with a fierce resentment Anne's promise to make him a gentleman that night in the shadows of her veranda. He knew he could have been, should have been more than a minor officer in this pisspot of a pirate island.

If it weren't for her, he'd have owned half of Charles Town by now. As long as she ran loose, he thought, he would never be free of her taint. No decent woman would have the former husband of a pirate whore. As Anne and Jack settled into domestic life on the island, Bonny's frustration and anger simmered to a boil. One night he followed Anne and Jack home from the House of Lords and stood a long hour out beneath their window, wondering what twisted scenes were being played within.

Bonny was gnawed by his loss of face, and he became obsessed with thoughts of revenge. With Turnley's help, he picked eight men who could be trusted to do his bidding without question. One hot July dawn Bonny and his men collected quietly outside the house where Anne and Calico Jack had lived since they'd arrived four weeks before. Bonny had not seen Anne face to face since her return.

Now he waited outside the window in the scant dawn light, his men behind him. At his signal they silently slipped inside and encircled the bed where Anne and Jack slept.

It was warm, and Anne lay on top of the linen wearing only a light shimmy. Bonny had to gesture to two men three times before he could get their attention. They stood and stared at Anne, her limbs gleaming in the dim light.

Bonny finally shook Anne roughly. She opened her eyes to see six pistols pointed at her. Two men stood at her head holding shackles. She screamed; Jack awoke instantly and reached for his sword, but Bonny kicked it across the room. They were surrounded by weapons in the dark chamber. Finally Anne's eyes adjusted to the lack of light, and she saw James Bonny.

"James!" she said, still dazed from sleep. "What in God's name are you doing?"

"Quiet, whore," he answered viciously. "You're under arrest."

"For what crime?" hollered Jack. "We're pardoned!"

SEA STAR

"Not by me. Put on the shackles." He nodded to his men.

At that, Anne erupted in rage. It took two men to bind her wrists and drag her out of bed, kicking and cursing. As she was yanked out into the darkness with Jack stumbling behind her, she thought she glimpsed Bonny's plan—to haul the two lovers through the town in a humiliation that would, in some twisted way, vindicate his own pride. She instantly quieted and let herself be led to the governor's quarters. So docile was she that few in the little settlement even realized a party of nine officers and two prisoners walked the streets.

Woodes Rogers was awakened by the uproar Anne made the instant she was within his house. All docility slipped away once she was inside, and she bit and clawed at the men who tried to hold her. Jack stood silently behind her, his head down, still numb from his abrupt shock out of sleep. They were pushed into Rogers' office, and Bonny went to hammer on the door to the governor's inside chambers.

"What in the name of heaven is all this!" Rogers demanded, as he stepped out of his room.

"I've arrested two felons, milord," said Bonny. "Their crimes demand immediate trial."

"On what charge?"

"The wench consorted with a man not her husband," answered Bonny stubbornly.

Rogers grimaced. "What *idiot* brought this charge?"

Bonny stepped forward and saluted, the picture of military precision. "I, milord. Her husband. Lieutenant James Bonny."

Rogers scowled and paced to his office angrily, throwing open the door. He stopped when he saw Anne and stared, for the moment shocked into silence. Anne stood before him in wild magnificence. Her hair was tossed as though she'd fought a storm; her eyes blazed. She wore only a scant cloth about her lithe body, and her cheeks flamed with rage.

Rogers recovered himself and asked quietly, "What do you

248

mean by coming to me in such a manner, mistress? Your naked-ness is as brazen as the charge against you."

"This is the manner in which I was pulled from my bed and shackled. They dragged me through the streets thus."

The governor turned and glowered at Bonny. "Is this true, Lieutenant?"

"Ay, milord. But 'twas necessary to take her by surprise, else she'd escape. Jack Rackham, the notorious pirate—"

"Pardoned," interrupted Jack.

"Pardoned, but no less dangerous, milord. He'd have fought to the death. As would she. She's a hellcat. As you yourself know, milord."

Rogers gestured angrily. "I know no such thing, Bonny. Have the good sense to cover her now."

A soldier brought a coat and dropped it over Anne's shoulders, but since her wrists were manacled, pushing her breasts forward, the coat could not be buttoned. She thrust back her head defiantly, disdaining the glances of the men all around her. Her beauty momentarily confused Rogers, who had been celibate for more than a year. He was suddenly exasperated—perhaps with himself—and spoke harshly to Anne.

"Kindly remember that you are in a court of law, mistress, however humble. I'll not have you defame it with conduct unbecoming a gentlewoman."

Anne shot back, "And remember, sir, the debts you yourself said you owed to me and this man. Dismiss this ridiculous charge and arrest that simpleton, James Bonny!"

"I won't be swayed by past favors, mistress! The charge is a valid one." He glanced at Bonny. "No matter how unseemly it may be, Lieutenant Bonny is within his rights. If he can prove what he says."

Anne spat out, "Arrest him on the same charge then! Ask him whose bed he's shared since I left!"

Rogers whirled and shouted back, "No law governs his habits, woman! And since you're the one who voluntarily left the island and his bed, you've no call to question his companions. Now I'm judge here, and I'll not be intimidated by your bold manner. You'll fare far better if you restrain yourself in my presence!"

Anne seethed, but she was silent. She glanced at Jack. He merely rolled his eyes and withdrew into a corner, sullenly pulling away from the guards who held him.

Rogers leafed through a giant lawbook on his desk. He finally looked up at her, and Anne saw a trace of regret on his face.

"The law is clear in black and white. I should like you to understand its seriousness. If I find you guilty of consorting with a male not your husband, you'll receive a public flogging and two years in gaol or four years in bondage as a servant."

Anne's eyes flinched momentarily in shock, but she concealed her panic. Jesus Christ, she thought, how can this be? She glanced again at James Bonny who did not meet her eye but stood stiffly at attention near the office door. If I escape this foul trap, I will surely kill that sneak, she swore to herself.

She collected her emotions with an effort. "If you find us guilty of this charge," she said quietly to Rogers, "the guilt will be as much on your head as our own. It was you who welcomed me and Captain Rackham back to New Providence, knowing full well our history and our relationship. 'Twas you who told him to put me to bed and care for me!"

The governor frowned uncomfortably. "What you say has some truth to it. I'll take that into consideration . . . as well as other matters in your favor." He turned to Bonny sharply. "And you, sir. Have you nothing to say? How is it that you waited so long to bring such a charge against this woman?"

Bonny was caught off guard. He blurted, "I don't know, milord. I was busy in your service. 'Twas only recently I learned of her conduct." He straightened and said loudly, "I felt it my duty to bring this matter to your attention, no matter how personally painful to me, sir."

"Yes, I see," said Rogers dryly. "And it was necessary to do so in this way?"

"Ay, sir! As I told you, this wench is a hellcat! She'd have killed me if she had warning. Or at least escaped!"

Rogers sighed. "Well, since you've brought the charge, I must deal with it."

Jack looked startled, and Anne stiffened.

"Have you proof you're married to this woman?" Rogers asked.

Bonny stepped forward, proffering a paper. "Ay, milord. Here is the certificate of marriage, sir. Signed by the woman herself not three years past."

The governor glanced at it, then showed it to Anne. "Do you refute the truth of this paper?"

Her eyes flashed. "Just the man himself, milord."

Rogers thought for a moment. He turned to Jack in the corner of the room, dressed only in a pair of light cotton breeches. "And you, sir. Do you deny you've consorted illegally with this woman?"

Jack glanced at Anne, uncertain of what to say.

Rogers went on, "I should inform you that under this law, you, sir, are liable only to one sentence—to wield the whip with which your mistress is publicly flogged. If you wield it lightly, then you yourself share her fate. I'll have your answer now."

Jack shrugged helplessly and cursed under his breath. "Milord, all on the island know that this woman and I have lived together as man and wife." He gestured to her. "Can you blame me, sir?" Rogers flushed slightly, and Jack hurried on, "I beg you, sir. Consider one request. Let me purchase this woman from her husband. A divorce by sale. She could then marry me and legalize our union."

There was a shocked silence in the room. Before Rogers could reply, Anne said indignantly, "I will not be bought and sold like a heifer at market, sirs!"

"You'd rather a whipping and gaol then?" Rogers shrugged impatiently.

"I'd rather some justice!" shrieked Anne. She pointed her manacled hands at Bonny. "*There* is the cowardly whelp who should be whipped for even bringing such a charge before you."

Rogers banged his fist on the desk. "It is not he who is on trial here, mistress. And you shall have my harshest sentence at this very moment if you don't keep peace in these chambers—"

Rackham interrupted him, "Please, Anne, please be quiet. You yourself said the governor is a man of honor. He'll see justice done."

"If justice be truly done," grumbled Rogers, "I would send you all to gaol at dawn. Now hear me closely. Rackham, I'm reluctant to let you purchase this woman, since divorce by sale is a practice I personally abhor. Still," he said quietly, "it would seem acceptable under some extreme circumstances. And this may just be one of those cases." He turned to Bonny. "You, sir. Are you prepared to sell your wife?"

Bonny hesitated, wary. "For how much?"

Again the governor's fist banged on the desk, his face mottled red. "I'll have no haggling in these chambers, sir! Will you sell your wife or no!"

"You mean now? Let her go free?" Bonny's face paled. "My lord, she'll kill me!"

"If she did," Rogers replied calmly, "she'd hang for murder." A small smile creeped over his face. "Do you fear her so much, then?"

The answer was obvious. Bonny turned his face away, silent.

Rogers said scornfully, "You may go, Lieutenant. I have no more need of you."

Bonny strode from the room, his back stiff but his hands shaking.

The governor went back to his lawbook and scanned it a second time, still uncertain of his course. After reading for a few long moments, he looked up.

"There's a possibility here. A certain piece of the law that allows me to pass a sentence in suspension. That means I could set your sentence, but it wouldn't be carried out unless you were brought before me on the same charge again."

He motioned Jack and Anne before him, shoulder to shoulder.

"Hark ye, mistress! Hark ye, master! You will henceforth leave off this lewd manner in which you've been consorting. If you can convince Lieutenant Bonny to agree to a divorce by sale, all well and good. Then you can be wed and conduct yourselves as you please. However, should he remain unconvinced, and you try to bed together again, I'll have you arrested within the hour and your sentence will be carried out. Now get hence both of you. This court is done."

Anne opened her mouth to protest, but the soldiers hustled her out the door. Once outside the chamber they removed her manacles.

"That bloody bastard!" Anne choked in rage. "I thought I left all the hypocritical swine back in Charles Town."

Rackham tugged at her hands. "Come, love. We're well away from here afore he changes his mind."

"Let him!" she shouted. "Better hell than a slow purgatory."

Jack moved her quickly out of the governor's quarters and off the streets before the settlement could witness the spectacle she made. He left her at their house and went to sleep at Jennings' hut. Once inside, Anne collapsed on the bed, deeply depressed and humiliated. She slept late that morning, and when she awoke her anger was no more than a dull ache in her head.

James Bonny had betrayed her. Betrayed her just as maliciously, even more shamefully than her father. For James had taken a vow to stand by her for good or ill. Yet, she knew, she'd broken the same vow.

Had they ever cared about each other? Where was the young man whose eyes bored into hers at the Green Gull? For that matter, where was the young girl who'd given up so much for passion? Why had she married him? Because he was everything her father was not . . . as far as possible from the man her father might have chosen for her?

She got up and went to the glass. She touched her breasts softly. She'd borne a babe. She'd held six men in her arms and a few boys. She peered at her skin closely, looking for signs of the sorrow she'd lived through. Beauty creates as many woes as it bestows advantages, she thought. I could have gone unnoticed, unmolested, if I had a face like a suet pudding. Or if I was stupid. Cowlike, dull-witted girls abound, but I was blessed—or burdened—with a brain. Yet now my mind seems more a curse than an asset.

She thought over the women she had known. It seemed to her that the less intelligent women had far more contentment, were more able to be happy in such a world. While she and others like her always fretted against something or someone, exhausting themselves with what they could not do, or fighting against insidious fences over which they were not allowed.

She remembered how free she'd felt when she dressed as a man; left in peace to go wherever she wanted unaccosted, moving freely without the binds of hoops, stays, and petticoats. She even noticed, when she wore a man's garments, that she felt more wanton—even arrogant and domineering just as men often were. She wondered briefly how it was that the mind expanded outward in such a way to the flesh's release.

She turned from the glass then and went to the window, gazing out to sea. She missed Jack already. He had no doubt gone to the House of Lords, his frequent and favorite place of oblivion. Of course the entire settlement knew of her arrest by now. She cringed inwardly as she thought of the taunting she and Jack must suffer at the hands of their friends and sometime friends. Damn James Bonny's eyes! It was a low and scurvy trick to serve her so. And publicly, too. He called me a hellcat, she remembered. And so a hellcat I will be. James Bonny will rue the day he dragged me from my bed and from Jack Rackham.

She dressed and went to the House of Lords to find Jack. A crowd of their friends was there; some laughed but most were sympathetic to her outrage. After several rounds of rum Anne felt like standing on a table, waving a sword, and shouting threats to Bonny for all to hear. But she kept her counsel. She knew that James was smart enough to stay well out of her way. A more immediate problem was her status with Jack.

Clearly, they could not stay on the island and keep away from each other. The thought of passing gold to James Bonny for her release soured in her mouth like an unripe fig. She'd not be bought and sold unless there was no other option. Even if James was willing though, he'd likely not sell her to Jack except for an exorbitant sum—and Anne knew they had but little left of Jack's last plunder.

As Jack walked her back to the house, she leaned heavily on his arm. "Well, what shall we do, Jack? Will you bed me tonight?"

Rackham stared at her. "But Anne, you heard Rogers as well as I. How can we bed together?"

She grabbed his arm. "Out on the seas of course. That's where we belong at any rate, Jack. Not in this hypocrites' paradise. I'll not be told where and with whom I bed."

This was the most fire Jack had seen in Anne since the loss of the child, and he warmed to her spirit. "Ay, but how? The *Seahorse* is beached, and we've no crew."

"We'll take John Haman's sloop, the *Kingston*, the fastest ship in the Caribbean. She'd need but a small crew, and she's ready and waiting out in the harbor, provisioned and eager to sail."

John Haman was a planter from an outlying island who'd brought his common-law wife and children to New Providence, fearful of the impending Spanish attack. He had sailed into the harbor two days before, and all the island knew his sloop could outrace anything on the waters. He and his wife were ashore, leaving the *Kingston* lightly guarded, since he had no fear of local pirates.

"If you round up a crew," she said, "I'll secure the ship."

As Jack went back to the tavern to whisper in a few likely ears, Anne hurried back to the house. She bound her breasts more tightly than ever, tucked her hair securely under an old hat, and darkened her skin with tannin. In the glass she looked like a mulatto man fresh from some outer island. Jack had left a dinghy at the cover; she shoved it into the water and paddled silently towards the *Kingston*, as the moon rose over the slip lying low in the harbor.

She was alongside the sloop before the watch even noticed her arrival. He peered over the rail, saw only a colored man in the boat, and hailed her aboard.

"Cap'n said go an' see, all be well wid' you, good sirs?" She lowered her eyes and slurred her words in the manner of a respectable freed slave.

"Ay, lad," the watch clapped her on the back soundly. "Yer new his service, ain't ye?"

"Yas, sir. De missus took me woman on fer de babies, an' Cap'n be so good as to use dis chile, too." Anne looked over the decks and let her mouth round in wonder. "Lord Jesus, he's big boat, yas?"

"Ay," the watch laughed. "She's a fine vessel, this, an' ye can tell the captain we keep her so."

"Dese eyes kin se dat, good sir." And she followed the man to the deck cabin, carefully noting the placement of weapons and guns. He opened the door, and Anne quickly surveyed the musket rack on the wall and the three seamen lounging about the room. One was reading by the light of a candle; the other two diced at he table. They looked up as she stepped in.

"Yer pardon, good sirs. Cap'n say go see his boat safe an' sound."

One tar muttered, "Ay, for God's sakes, an' how many times

does he need to ask? The man frets like a woman."

The watch hushed him quickly. "Captain has a right, Tom. An' ye wouldn't begrudge him, would ye now?"

"Nay," he shrugged tiredly. "Tell him all's well."

"De pirates, good sirs. Dey keep de Cap'n wakeful an' worryt."

"The bloody scum is reined in tight, lad, an' even if they wasn't, they wouldn't dare touch John Haman's sloop."

The other guard spoke up. "You might ask him to send a mite more rum round, lad. The breeze off the harbor bites a man right through."

Anne chuckled low in her throat. "Di chile tell him, good sirs. I thank ye for yer curtsy," and she bowed her way from the cabin, keeping her back to the sea.

Anne rowed back to rendezvous with Jack. "How many on decks?"

"One," she said as she shucked her hat, wiping her face on a rag. "And three more in the cabin. I was nearly on them before the watch saw me, but they've muskets enough for a crew of twenty."

"Good," he said, gazing out over the water at the sloop. "We'll need that and more."

"Did you find some likely lads?"

"Ay, I said I would. They'll be here at midnight."

"That gives us time."

"To do what?" he asked.

"To row out a keg to those poor lads out there," she grinned. "Send one of the men out with some rum, saying it's from Haman himself. They're moaning that the harbor wind bites."

Jack laughed raucously. "That's not all that'll bite afore the night's through!"

Soon, the moon was high, diffused by rolling dark clouds, and a light rain began. Anne pulled her collar up over her ears and tucked her legs under her. Jack grumbled about the weather, but she welcomed anything that would keep three of the four guards inside the cabin.

A group of men loomed up the beach. Anne knew two of them, John Howells and Richard Corner, both were well-seasoned seamen. For the rest, she'd have to take Jack's word. As they silently rowed out to the sloop, Jack outlined the plan.

They slid alongside, and she pulled herself up the cable, pausing just under the gunwale to listen. Rain flowed around her and off her hat in the darkness; she looked tall and black with her sea coat about her. She heard no sounds on deck, past the steady patter of the rain. She eased up over the rail and crouched tensely in the shadow of the bulkhead. No one was on deck. Even better than she'd hoped. She leaned over the rail and signaled the men up.

Jack, Howells, and Corner shimmied up the ropes, while she watched the door of the cabin, holding her breath. Her heart was beating fast, thudding in her chest, but she took deep breaths until she felt her fingers tingle. She moved stealthily to the side of the door. The men were instantly at her side.

Jack moved quickly and shoved open the door, holding two pistols at ready. Anne looked over his shoulder and saw two guards asleep in their berths. Two more sat at the table swilling rum. "We're taking the sloop, mates," Jack growled. "You can oppose us and die, or you can go over the side quietly and live."

Anne and Corner moved behind the two men at the table. The guard in front of Anne saw she was a woman, and his hand moved for the knife at his waist. She instantly put her pistol to his head. "Make the smallest move, and I send you to hell," she hissed. He froze, his eyes rolling back in fear.

Corner went on deck and signaled the dinghy. The men climbed up the sides of the sloop, and Jack hustled the guards down into the skiff. Anne watched as they rowed away.

They raised the sails quickly, and Jack took the wheel. The sloop was responsive and eager, sliding out towards the sea. The fog had blocked out the moonlight, and they sailed silently in the darkness, past the reef, past the anchored ships, and out into the open water.

Anne shouted with joy as she felt the sloop surge forward and the rhythm of moving sea under her again. She knew she needed the ocean in some elemental way. She became dazed and withered at her core if she was away from it too long. Now, she felt like a parched flower being renewed. She turned to Jack and hugged him with an intensity born of her relief. She would bed whom she pleased, when she pleased! She made a silent vow to herself never to return to the land and its laws again, except as a visitor.

THE *KINGSTON* cruised southward, looking for a safe refuge and fresh water where the feisty crew might explore their new prize more thoroughly.

Anne rifled through the hold and found barrels of provisions, enough to keep them in belly timber for at least a week. But past that time, she knew they would have to take another ship that was well stocked with goods—one week to get the men in fighting trim.

Morning rainfall steamed up from the deck, and bats flitted about between the masts, snatching mosquitoes and swerving round the tangle of riggings and shrouds. The decks of the sloop were hot as beach sand, no matter how often they were doused down. The men were able to practice fast boarding techniques and mock duels in the morning, but by noon most activity ceased as they waited for the wind.

Their immediate need was more hands. They could not take large prizes with only a skeleton crew. As she gazed out over the men, she got an idea for a means to add their roster.

It wasn't long before Anne spied her prey. Off St. Catherine, near Cuba, a huge Dutch ship, well armed, lay quietly at anchor. The *Kingston* sailed idly by. Anne scanned the decks carefully as they rounded the point. Many of the men seemed to be ashore, but six were guarding the decks. The *Kingston* sailed on.

She pulled the *Kingston* around the point and sent two men

ashore to gather fruit. When they returned, she showed half the crew how to darken their skins with tannin and persuaded them to strip their linen.

"Damned if I care for this," Corner grumbled, smearing the dark oil about his skin. "I signed on as pirate, not nigger."

"Ay," she smiled, "But a proper rogue knows when to use his wits rather than his sword."

She and Jack hustled five men into a dugout on the beach, packed their boat with fruit, and waited.

The guard on the Dutch schooner spied the dugout approaching from the beach and called to his mates, "Ahoy! Arawaks off the bow, swappin' fruit!"

The Dutchmen quickly ran below to fetch some cloth and rum to trade with the savages for their produce. It was dusk and difficult to see, but these natives looked much like those who had paddled out before, waving their grass hats and their bananas.

The pirates climbed up the rope ladders dropped by the obliging sailors, carrying baskets of fruit. In the wink of an eye, they whipped out pistols and daggers from under the mangoes, bound the six guards, hoisted sail, and pulled out of the harbor before you could say *jolie rogue*.

They rounded the island and rendezvoused with the *Kingston*, safely anchored in the cove. The captured tars were soon persuaded by Anne and Jack to join their band.

One of the erstwhile Dutchmen piped up, "If ye'd had yon wench in yer canoe, covered only with berry juice, I'd a joined up right then, make no mistake!"

Now Anne and Jack commanded a fleet of two and twenty men, still undermanned, but a vast improvement in terms of their arsenal at sea.

Their next prize was seized by running up a Dutch flag and lulling the suspicions of the master of a Spanish sloop. Before the confused vessel could pull away she was boarded by a horde of savage, yelling, cutlass-swinging freebooters led by a brazen Valkyrie who'd taken the Dutchman's remark to heart. Stripped to the waist for battle, Anne leaped on decks, whisking her cutlass through the air, screaming like a banshee, her breasts bound only by the leather straps that held her weapons. The Spaniards were goggle-eyed. Indeed, she never had to take a blow or give one, so startled were the Spanish sailors.

Rackham refused to take Spaniards as crew so he let them go after relieving the sloop of a large shipment of gold. The coins filled their pockets but could not buy them men, at least not at sea.

The next morning Anne stood at the rail watching the waters change colors. She had not slept well the night before. She and Jack had argued about her conduct in the taking of the last prize— he was incensed by her partial nakedness.

"Are you trying to incite the whole crew to rape, mistress? You looked a common whore! And before the Spanish, too!"

At first Anne tried to joke off his anger. "Oh, Jack. It worked, didn't it? I doubt these breasts blinded any but the stupid papists. To our lads, I'm one of them."

But Jack would not be appeased. "I'll not have my woman bare herself brazenly to any eyes save mine! I'm still captain here, and if you forget it, I'll have you flogged like any other mutineer, so help me Christ!"

"With or without my jerkin?" Anne mused coolly. "I'll doff my blouse no more, Captain. But neither will I take such words from you. Speak to me like that again, and you'll rue it."

Jack sullenly stomped from the cabin then. He had changed, her Jack. But then so perhaps had she. She made a silent promise to herself to smooth the edges between them.

Now, as she watched the waves, never bored with the movement of the sea, the watch called out from the mainmast.

She grabbed her glass from the rack, her mind already at work. The sea was slowly gathering shape and shadow in the gloom, and there was a bit of gray along the horizon, the lighter gray of a sail.

Jack came up behind her and took the glass from her hand.

"What lass?" He saw the distant tell-tale flash of white. "Up, Billy!" he called to the youngest crew member with the sharpest eyes.

"See what you can spot! If you give me a false report, you'll kiss the mate's arse instead of his daughter!"

Billy grinned and scampered up the shrouds. Anne stayed calm with an effort, but she paced along the rail and strained out over the dark sea, willing the ship closer.

Billy's voice came down from the sky. "She's English, sir! Runnin' afore the wind like a gull!"

"Let's take her!" Anne hollered, casting an eye to Jack to see if once more she'd offended his sense of command. He glared at her, but he whipped the lads to action. "All hands! All hands! Show a leg!"

The sleep-dazed men tumbled from their berths. Groggy and protesting, they crowded to the rail and saw the ship. The sea was no longer empty, and the gap between the two sails was narrowing quickly. They tugged at sheets and braces, and the sloop picked up speed.

In no time the *Kingston* caught the heavy frigate and its master, asking the question, though he dreaded the answer called, "What colors? What port?"

Jack bellowed across the sheet of water, *"From the sea!"* hoisted the black flag, and the pirates crowded from their hiding places to the rails, waving cutlasses and shouting threats.

Anne saw with a thrill of horror the frigate's ports open and the concealed guns appear like a row of shark's teeth.

"Clear for firing!" she shouted, backing away from the rail. She heard a single word, "Fire!" from across the water, and the sloop rocked with a staggering broadside. The shot was slightly high, but choking smoke filled the air and decks splintered all around her. She felt a sharp pain in her thigh as a spear of wood lodged in her flesh. Her lungs were rasping and her eyes filled, but she put her shoulder to the twenty-four-pounder at her feet and helped to push it into position. Already loaded, the guns were lethal and ready. Anne fought with the wind and looked to Jack.

He stood on the quarterdeck watching as the men scurried to get the guns into position. "Fire!" he shouted. There was a deafening explosion, and Anne put her hands to her ears.

The gunner shrieked angrily, urging and cuffing the men as they ran forward with fresh shot. Anne peered through the smoke and saw that the *Kingston*'s broadside had done considerable damage to the English frigate. She listed on one side, and half her decks were blown away.

Jack yelled, "Reload there! Ready to fire!"

Rumbling like thunder, the guns were hauled forward again, but before Jack could call for a second broadside, a voice called out, "Ahoy! Be you Jack Rackham of New Providence?"

Jack hesitated a moment. "I be Jack Rackham from the sea! Who's master?"

"Con Kesby! Hold yer fire!"

Jack glanced at Anne who was leaning against the rail holding her thigh. Through the smoke over the listing ship, she tried to make out the voice's owner.

"Do you call for quarter, man!" Jack hollered.

"Damn ye! Hold yer fire, Jack! Con Kesby calls for quarter from no man, Brethren or no!"

As the wind shifted and the smoke cleared, Anne could see the figure on the frigate's decks. It *was* Con Kesby, and she laughed aloud in spite of her pain.

Quickly the *Kingston* swiveled round to tie up to the damaged frigate, and the crew boarded the ship, led by Anne and Jack.

She limped over to Kesby, her thigh wrapped in a kerchief, and hugged him with an enthusiasm that surprised them both.

"Damn me, Kesby," Jack said as he clapped the old pirate on the shoulder, "what are you doing on a king's frigate?"

Kesby glowered at him. "Where else should I be? Hoein'

Rogers' garden? At least I kept the sea under my feet. And what are ye doin' under a *jolie rouge?*"

"We couldn't abide the safe life, Con," Anne grinned. "You remember, you warned me of the thief's disease—you saw the symptoms even then."

He gestured to her leg. "Ay, an' 'twill scuttle ye yet!"

Anne invited the old pirate to their cabin and Kesby's men willingly left their crippled ship. While the two crews shared grog on the decks of the *Kingston*, Kesby, Jack and Anne spoke of old times.

Kesby's frigate carried sugar and rum, and Jack gave orders to have the cargo transferred to the *Kingston*.

"Kesby, I doubt that hulk'll make it back to port. She's half-blown away from stem to stern."

"Ay, you bastard. Well I know it, too. Ye nearly took off me leg in the process."

"Well, what say we take those of your crew that want to join us, and we'll put the rest off in Jamaican waters. You can come or go as you please."

Anne looked quickly at Jack. She couldn't believe he was offering a seaman's berth to the proud former pirate chief.

Kesby smiled thinly. "Rackham, you and I would get on like chalk an' cheese. For one thing, I be the better captain." He let his eyes wander impudently to Anne's body. "For another, there's yer wench here. She'd be mine afore the month was out." He grinned full in Jack's face, his eyes glinting. "And then ye'd be shark bait, Captain."

Anne saw Jack's face flush with anger and his jaw tense. But he forced a smile. "In that case, Captain, choose your port and we'll see you safe ashore. And next time . . . call for quarter first and save us both the trouble." His eyes narrowed. "But call loud, Kesby. Sometimes I don't hear well over the guns."

*T*HE KINGSTON WAS only a day out of Jamaica and anchored just long enough at a small offshore island to put off Kesby and half his men. The rest preferred to stay aboard the pirate sloop. Anne watched sadly as Kesby was rowed ashore. Her past had trickled away to nothing, like sand through a clenched fist. So many old friends were gone. She wondered where she would be a year from now. Her leg would mend, but the past was gone forever.

After a two-week rest at a cove off Antigua for careening, Jack again set sail for the Mona Passage. Anne's leg was healed now. Two unlucky men had died of their injuries suffered in the skirmish with Kesby's frigate, and they were sent to the sea in torn shrouds. The bay quickly filled with small lemon sharks that cut through the water efficiently, and the bodies disappeared. That left a full crew of thirty-one men, counting herself and Jack. She wondered if they were the only pirate vessel left on the water. From Antigua to the passage, they had the sea to themselves.

A high-pressure system squatted over the seas, and for one hundred hours, the sloop drifted aimlessly, pushed here and there by meandering currents. The watch was squint-eyed and testy from staring endlessly at the horizon, watching for a squall, a cloud, for anything that moved. Six long days since they had left Antigua; six days of watching the sky and testing their wet fingers, waiting.

Anne glanced at Billy, leaning against the riggings. For once, he had no smile for her; no grin of mischief creased his face. And the men lay like corpses, trying to stay in the shadows of the masts. Their bodies were darker than ever from the rays of the relentless sun. Even their scalps were mahogany.

Anne sighed. It was hard to imagine life outside this calm. She knew St. Kitts was out there somewhere fifty miles to the south, and the Mona Passage lay before them, lost in a shimmering haze. But she found it hard to care.

Yesterday, the crew had tried some target practice aiming at old rum kegs floating by the sloop. Anne had joined them to break the tedium. But Jack had hollered, "Belay that! You're wasting shot!" and the men had ambled sullenly back to lie about like hounds once more.

Now, Jack came up through the cabin hatch, already frowning. Like her, he wore a light shirt and breeches, and his hair stuck to his head, darkened by sweat. He looked edgy, and Anne felt his restlessness hover about him like an aura.

"Still no wind," she said quietly.

Jack snapped, "Ay. I can see that." He moved to the bow, and Anne saw him flinch as the sun hit his shoulders.

She asked softly, "How're they doing belowdecks?"

"Not good," he said shortly. "And water rations are short besides."

"I know. But we'll have to keep them that way, Jack. We could be stuck like this for days."

"Jesus," he muttered curtly.

"Then again, we could get a squall tonight."

"You better hope we do, Anne. We can't keep at half-water in this heat for long."

Anne looked away, her face clouded with concern, biting off a short reply with an effort. Of course they had to go on half-water. It was her responsibility to manage provisions, and she'd done so. Now, instead of supporting her in a tough decision, he was as petulant as one of the most unseasoned tars.

The watch shouted out, "Squall! Off the bow!"

Anne raced updecks, peering into the haze. Incredibly, she saw the waves rippling gently, a swell moving towards them, the sails fluttering slowly back to life.

She glanced back at Jack, who swaggered boyishly as though he had filled the sails himself, "Get 'em up, lads! Move her out!"

The *Kingston* began to move, slowly at first, then more determinedly, as the sails were hauled to swallow every last breath of air.

Once more, the lookout called incredulously, "Sail, Captain!

Off port!"

Anne raised her glass, straining to see. Finally, she caught the glimpse of white sail, and her mouth twisted in disappointment. It was just a lugger, small and not worth taking. She yelled the information to Jack.

"A lugger?" He grabbed his own glass. "Stand by to take her."

So he was going to chase her, anyway. No matter what the cost in energy and wind. Once more, the sails flapped round, spilling their precious breeze, causing the *Kingston* to buck and bob awkwardly in the sluggish water, as they aimed for the lugger. Anne tried not to think of what would happen if they lost the wind altogether.

She snatched her glass again. The lugger had raised sails, lifting her stubby snout and moving out.

Corner said, "She can best us, Captain. We're too heavy for this pissant breeze."

"Then lay a shot across her bows!" Jack shouted.

"Why, for God's sake?" Anne asked in exasperation.

Jack whirled on her. "Ay, woman, you could start a fight in an empty room! She may have water, that's why."

That stubborn fool, Anne cursed to herself, as she ran to help load the guns. We could use the same wind and less effort to go for fresh water on the island.

Quickly, the four-pounder barked out a challenge. After just one shot, the lugger meekly dropped her sails and rocked resignedly, waiting Jack's pleasure.

Anne's cabin seemed almost cool after the oven ondecks, and she stood quietly by the window, steadying her raging thoughts. She tried to ignore the muffled shouts and thumps as the men launched a boarding party to take the hapless lugger. All for a few casks of water. She heard the boat return and saw Jack returning with a single cask. So they were just as low as we . . . and now, empty. God help them, and us, if the wind dies once more.

She stood and gazed unblinkingly into the mirror. The months at sea had been harsh to her face. She would be twenty in a few months, and she swore she could not tell when those few lines on her brow had etched themselves between her eyes. Her skin was still soft and supple, but when she squinted, as she did now into the mirror, the skin around her eyes fell into creases that left tracks after she opened her eyes wide again. She held out her hands.

Her nails were broken and stubby from the work on deck. The skin on the back of her hands had begun to show small crisscrosses and diamond mosaics, more like a kneecap than a hand. She remembered the last time she'd bedded with Jack, easy to recall since it had been on Antigua almost three weeks before. He'd complained that her feet were rough and scratchy as salt-stiff canvas. She frowned. She loved him, she knew. More than she'd ever loved anyone. But she also deeply resented him at times, deeply feared her own need for him. She knew that she let him get by with murder, let him dominate her at times, because he was handsome and strong. If he were small, squat, and toadlike, she'd have put him off on the nearest island and run the ship herself way before this. But no one had ever made her feel so completely possessed as Jack Rackham. Not Ben Hornigold, certainly not Bonny, nor Stede Bonnet.

There were so many times she wished Jack gone from her life— and many more times she feared she'd dissolve if he ever left. Perhaps each of us is truly alone forever on this small raft out in a great black sea, she thought. Anne found that she bedded with Jack less and less frequently now, and her desire for sexual congress of any sort had certainly cooled from her former heat. Often her days were so full of a sense of movement, adventure, new waters, and plain physical labor that she fell into her berth at night, eager only for a deep dreamless sleep and the lulling rock of the sturdy hull.

Now BEGAN that time in Anne's life when she truly learned the ways of the Brethren. As one of the few pirate vessels on the sea and certainly the most infamous, Calico Jack's *Kingston* took prizes up and down the Caribbean with impunity.

They rarely engaged in a serious or prolonged battle, for they chose their prey carefully and attacked only those vessels that they felt sure would surrender with little resistance. Anne sewed a more imaginative flag for the *Kingston*—a huge black banner with a skull grinning out of the void and two crossed swords beneath where its throat should be. Across the bottom she stitched, "Catch Me Who Can!" She smiled ironically when she thought of how her needlework had served her.

The men gathered around the mast for their midday meal, standing about the common pot spearing bits of turtle. Anne walked the rails, looking out to sea.

The lookout called suddenly, "Deck there! Three sails off starboard bow!"

Startled out of her reverie, Anne snatched a glass from the rack. Three sails were twisting on the horizon, a break in the line between sea and sky barely, visible in the distance.

"Put her on the starboard tack!" Anne hollered to the wheelsman. She glanced about for Jack to take command, but he was belowdecks resting. The men stood at the mast, looking to her for directions. She shrugged mentally. He'd be up in a moment. For now, she'd simply set them to do what she expected he'd command himself.

"Hands to braces and sheets!" she called.

The men dropped their food like well-disciplined hounds, scampering about willingly to their posts.

The *Kingston* swerved as she gathered the breeze; her sails lofted and bellied. Just then Jack came updecks, alerted by the changed motion of the ship. The watch shouted, " 'Tis a convoy, Captain, bearing north! Ten sails or more!"

God's breath, murmured Anne in her throat. A whole slew of ships and we the only Brethren on the sea.

Jack called up to the watch, instantly alert. "What guns? Do you see the guard ships?"

Anne felt a thrill of anticipation run through her. It was late in the season for fleets headed towards the mainland. The late summer hurricanes drove most of them from the seas before June. But perhaps this fleet carried a cargo worth waiting for.

Anne knew that if this was a typical British convoy, they'd have at least two warships. One, the leader or Van ship, would guard the front of the fleet and set its speed and direction. The second warship, the Bulldog, would keep to the rear, watching for ambush.

She peered through her glass once more. Large white topsails edged over the horizon. She picked out the man-of-war by its flags. She caught a wink of light, the flash of a glass, twice repeated. She smiled. They are studying us, she chuckled, just as we watch them.

Suddenly, the warship ran signal flags up her halyards, bright specks against the cobalt sky. She heard the distant thunder of the signal guns. She lowered her glass, pressing it against her thigh to calm herself. It was dangerous, but if the wind stayed with them, they could back away and outrun the warships even at the last minute.

The full fleet numbered twelve. They were moving into a tighter formation, now that they'd seen the pirate sloop. Anne pictured the British seamen milling about the decks. English merchant ships were famously poor sails; most of the men were pressed and resentful, few were well-seasoned sailors. The English seaman was fiercely independent, more so than his French or Spanish counterpart. Like as not, out of twelve ships, she guessed at least three were fermenting a mutiny right at this moment.

Anne knew that the captains of the convoy would not be fooled; the identity of the *Kingston* was obvious to a tar—her full sails, her guns, and her stripped and predatory hull could only be those of a pirate ship.

Now, the guardship was shifting position, coming downwind to
pursue the pirate sloop. They clearly had their orders—to chase
and capture any rogue ships sighted.

Images whirled through Anne's mind. She heard Jack's commands to put on all sails and run as though in a fog.

Suddenly, she saw in her mind's eye a scene from the riverbed at
Bellefield. She and Charley had been hunting quail all morning.
She recalled the way the mother quail shrieked in simulated terror
and ran with a limp wing to draw the hunters away from her
chicks.

Anne moved to Jack's side quickly. "Why not let them see a
crippled ship, Jack? Put up the sails fast, as if we've just seen them
coming. The men to let the boom swing wild, as though they are
too panicked to do it proper. You could draw her out like a hound
on a scent."

A glimpse of understanding widened Jack's grin. "Ay! And leave
their flanks open to the sea." He hollered out the commands, and
the men jumped eagerly to the ruse.

Anne felt the winds shift from her left cheek to her right as the
Kingston rocked with the violent sweep of her sails. To the British
warship, the sloop's motion looked like just the sort of clumsy
maneuvers that only frightened sailors might try. Jack cursed the
men roundly and loudly, waving his fists at them, sending them up
and down the masts to try to pull the sails back in place.

Anne lifted her glass and peered astern. The warship was still
racing towards them, a scant three miles off. The *Kingston* bobbed
sloppily through the water, at an inefficient angle to the wind,
looking for all the world like she was trying to run, frantically but
incorrectly. Of course, even at her worst, the pirate sloop was
faster than the heavy warship, but perhaps they would not realize
that until it was too late. For now, the warship must think she had
them at her mercy.

The warship came on. The afternoon light began to wane, and,
as Anne had planned, the distance between the hunter and the

quarry began to lessen. They had tricked them. The *Kingston* and the warship headed slowly away from the convoy; eleven other topsails dropped from sight over the horizon as the sun began to set.

Still, the Bulldog came closer. At Jack's commands, the crew, acting panic-stricken, started to throw empty barrels overboard as if they wanted to lighten the ship for speed. This last sham was soon hidden by the gathering darkness. When it was completely dark, Jack set the crew at righting the *Kingston*'s movements. Sails were properly set and filled, and the pirate sloop sped forward, as if relieved to be released from such inept blunderings.

Anne grinned quietly. Now, the distance betwen the sloop and the warship would widen—yet the Bulldog could not see it. By the time the moon rose, the *Kingston* would be leagues away and running hard with the wind.

After several hours of speed, the crew dropped all sails. The *Kingston* shuddered as if her stern had slid into a sea of molasses. She came to a halting roll on the waves, bobbing broadside to the current, her movements unruly and undirected.

Anne felt her heart roll with the sloop. Now came the real danger—they were as good as becalmed, with no sails up to declare their presence. The warship would pass right by them and never know the *Kingston* was there.

Supper was cold and silent, for there could be no fires this night. Anne and Jack went to their cabin to pore over figures and charts. They worked it once, then twice again to be sure they had it right.

Corner had kept the man-of-war in sight through the glass; it was still coming right for them. Anne and Jack stood by Corner's side and looked silently into the black seas while the Bulldog approached. The warship grew larger, and they could see its wake gleaming behind it, shining in the moonlight, its sails silhouetted against the clouds, the glimmer of a lantern ondecks, and even a few sparks from the sailors' pipes. Anne closed her eyes, then opened them, holding her breath.

Slowly, the Bulldog pulled nigh them. Less than two hundred yards off their bow, the warship ploughed determinedly onward into empty open sea, chasing a phantom that rocked silently, but briefly, at its side.

Anne let her breath out slowly. They had taken a grave risk for the possibility of heavy rewards. Obviously, God did not only look out for the righteous.

Anne walked to Jack and put an arm about his shoulders.

"A bold move, Captain. And it worked."

"Ay." Jack grinned in the darkness. "And tomorrow, that convoy'll be mine for the taking."

A̶T DAWN, ANNE went out on the decks and took up her glass. There were dark shapes on the horizon before them. The convoy was huddled on the water like a flock of sleeping gulls, unsuspecting, unwary.

The hands were quietly called up and armed themselves with pistols, muskets, and pikes. The guns were loaded and the men readied themselves for action.

The *Kingston* moved silently through the water up to the rear of a brig that had drifted away from the fleet. The pirates quickly slipped over the side into dinghys and swarmed over the brig's rail like insects before the sleeping lookouts could sound the alarm. Jack left six men behind, after tossing those of her crew overboard if they refused to join the pirate band.

The next prize was a huge ship, a merchant marine of three hundred tons, armed with ten long-nosed cannons. Again, overwhelmed by a rush of boarders, the watch never knew what hit them.

They took one final ship, a brig, which rode low in the water. Her captain shouted a warning, but the pirates were unstoppable, capturing his ship and the crew without a casualty.

As the sun rose, the *Kingston* and its three prizes had slipped into a quiet secluded inlet; there the pirates reconnoitered. "We're rich as lords, lads!" shouted Jack as he came up from the hold of the third prize. "She's full of plate and rum!"

It was true. The convoy had been heavily loaded with goods bound for London. There was an immediate call for splitting up the booty, since several of the pirates were leery of Rogers and his threats and wanted to sneak back to land before they could be apprehended. But for every pirate eager to quit the trade, more were anxious to join. Those from the king's convoy had not seen such wealth in five years of sea duty.

Anne took a quick poll and found eighteen new recruits. Strangely enough, they did not seem surprised to find a woman as second in command on a pirate ship. "Ay, mum, we heard o' Calico Jack an' his lady. But we never figured to see you 'gainst the king's ships!"

"Ay!" laughed Jack. "And neither did your Bulldogs! But see us you did and fall to us, too!"

Anne welcomed the new men to their ranks and swore them to the articles on her customary hatchet. As she did, a small warning voice whispered in her mind. *They knew of me then—as Jack's lady.* She was not altogether comfortable with being so well known—and neither did she particularly glory in her role as Jack's moll. But for now the ships were safe, the hold was full to the brim with booty, and the sea was wide and free.

THE PIRATE FLOTILLA now numbered three. Selling one of the heavier brigs in Hispaniola, the pirates kept two merchant traders and the *Kingston*, the fastest getaway sloop in the islands. Anne laughed mirthlessly when she learned that one of her new ships, the *Queen Royal*, had belonged to Chidley Bayard. It was his cargo they'd stolen, his ship they'd captured. Anne and Jack moved aboard the *Queen Royal* to take advantage of its more spacious living quarters.

The spoils of battle included more than rich coffers. Peter Mazer, their new armorer, was a valuable addition to any pirate crew. He had invented a crude explosive, a flask filled with lead, iron, and powder. It was fixed with a short fuse. Anne marveled at his cleverness. Unlike other crude grenades she'd seen before, it could be timed to explode within seconds or minutes with a burst of iron and hot powder in all directions. Peter also made excellent stinkpots—jars filled with sulfur which, when thrown, blew up in a cloud of stinking, eye-burning, lung-choking smoke. Mazer preferred what he called his "murdering piece" to all his other inventions. He had fashioned a swivel gun with a fan-shaped muzzle that fired a widely scattering charge of old spikes and nails, crockery, and glass.

Of the several sea artists captured from the convoy, Mark Read was definitely the most welcome recruit to the crew of the *Queen Royal*. He was a handsome, slight young seaman who said little and kept his eyes lowered from Anne's. He had a positive genius for clapping close by an armed ship and could keep the pirate vessel in the narrow safety lane where a pursuing craft could not defend itself. Read's adroit sail maneuvers kept the *Queen* from damage while allowing her to twist up close enough to a prize to batter the decks with her guns.

One-eyed Cory Dickson was, surprisingly, the best of the new gunners. He kept the cannons slightly high and clustered his shots so that nimble Billy was able to leap from the prow of the *Queen* to the stern of the ship ahead. Billy, protected by musket fire from his comrades and armed with a mallet and a wooden wedge, would climb like a monkey to the aftcastle. Swinging from the rigging, he could drive a wedge between the rudder and the sternpost of the fleeing ship, making the prize all but crippled and unable to steer. Before the ship could come about, the pirates flung out grappling irons, fastened the *Queen Royal* to the hapless vessel like a huge leech, and swarmed into battle with boarding axes, pikes, grenades, pistols, stinkpots, and murdering pieces.

Their own wild cries added to the din, and the drummer rattled off a frightening tattoo. To add to the chaos, fire men, hanging from the masts, hurled torches aloft, setting the sails aflame. Often, surrender came within moments, and Anne rarely even drew her sword. Jack stayed on the foredeck shouting orders. Few men were wounded; the battles were so brief.

Now the most lethal predator on the sea, the *Queen Royal* rarely missed her prey.

One ship thus captured by the pirate crew was the *Tornade*, a French frigate bound from the African coast. She carried a cargo of slaves—a useless commodity since the pirates could not easily take them to market. When Jack wanted to risk port to barter them for coin, Anne complained, "This is not a damned Spanish slaver but a pirate ship!" and suggested that the wretches be turned loose on Hispaniola. Reluctantly, Jack agreed when he found that the *Tornade* carried one other treasure deep in her hold. Jack's face broke into a wide grin. " 'Tis opium, lass," he said to Anne in private. "A fortune in just one sack alone." He sniffed and tasted the brown powder gingerly.

Anne too was gleeful at first. "That's wonderful, Jack! Now the men need fear the surgeon's knife no more! We've pain-killer for a thousand wounds."

But she noticed that Jack gave only half of one sack to the ship's surgeon. He split up a whole sack between the men as part of their booty, and half a sack, against all pirate law, was hidden deep under his berth when he thought no one watched.

Anne was more shocked by his theft from the crew than she was by his avid interest in that strange brown powder. She had never used the drug before. Indeed, it was in short supply in Charles Town when she was a girl and saved only for near-lethal wounds. She had heard that the governor took opium for frequent dysentery and that the powder turned stools hard as brown pebbles, but she could not fathom why Jack would want to hoard such a find. She resolved to say nothing to him until she knew his plan. He had been sensitive to criticism lately and could not abide her questions. So she held her tongue.

Two nights later Anne was surprised when he called her to the cabin early and shut the door. The captain's cabin of the *Queen Royal* was much larger than that of the *Kingston*. In one corner stood an intricately carved French royal chair upholstered in blue velvet, and in the other corner, a small four-postered bed with a damask canopy. Jack pulled her on the bed, and Anne wondered if they were to have one of their infrequent grapplings.

From his pocket he pulled a long narrow pipe and a small packet of brown powder. "I've a new toy for you, my pet." He grinned. "The pearl of the Orient. 'Twill make you a new woman."

Anne wrinkled her nose at the brown powder; she smiled up at Jack warmly. "And what's wrong with the old one, then? I've no pain that needs dulling. Do you?"

But Jack waved aside her questions, filled the pipe, and lit it, taking long slow draws from the narrow bowl. His eyes squinted through the fumes as he extended the pipe to her.

"Try it, lass. It'll relax you."

She frowned slightly, watching him closely. The fumes of the powder made a sweet brackish odor in the close quarters.

"I'd rather share a pot of rum with you, Jack." She grimaced. "That smells like laundry musting in a damp corner."

He would not be put off but placed the pipe firmly in her hand.

"For me, Anne. If you love me, try it. Then I'll show you things you never felt before."

Anne hesitatingly put the pipe to her lips. Her eyes smarted from the fumes, and she felt a quick irritation in her nostrils but she took a small puff on the pipe.

"Again," he said, putting the stem to her lips once more.

Once more she took a draw at the pipe, watching him through the haze. The smoke felt hot in her throat, harsher than any tobacco she'd ever tried. She stifled a short cough, sensing that once she started she'd hack until her lungs were raw.

Jack sat and watched her, beaming.

Anne felt her will grow weaker as she drew another mouthful of smoke. She felt an overwhelming desire to slump back onto the bed and wondered vaguely why she felt so fatigued.

For an instant she was alone in the cabin and conscious only of the softness of the bed beneath her body, the slight rocking of the room, and the warmth of candlelight on her skin. Her head felt light, but her eyes were heavy. She put a hand to her mouth and could smell her own fragrance. The touch of her fingers on her cheeks were like damp feathers. She pulled her hand away and saw that it was wet, indeed, that her palms were both damp.

She wondered briefly who was on watch, if the ship was safe, the seas were calm. But quickly her mind rolled over and she focused instead on the gold edge of a mirror on the wall where the image of a candle flickered.

Jack reached for her urgently and pulled her down to the linen. Somehow her clothes dissolved from her body, and she felt him on her, his hands moving over her skin like warm molasses. Her body felt electric to his touch, and she welcomed him inside her eagerly, arching her back to meet him. But something was wrong. Try as she might, she could not feel him inside her. He seemed to shrivel once he felt her wetness and fell away limply from her body.

Jack seemed unperturbed and merely rolled off her, softly smiling to himself, lost in some private fantasy.

Anne fell back on the linen, inexplicably tired and saddened. She heard a hundred little lapping tongues of water in her head as the waves caressed the ship. Her mind felt as empty as her body. Suddenly she thought of the dead infant who'd lain at her breast. She wondered if it had died trying to find life or if it had been dead inside her for weeks and never even saw the world at all. It was the first time she'd thought of the babe in a while, at least consciously. She tightened her eyes against the visions that swarmed up before her like stinging wasps. She would not weep again. She tried to wrest herself from the past, to force herself to think of something else. But her will seemed to have left her. Jack was somewhere else, perhaps with someone else; she could see it in his blank smile.

She sat up abruptly on the bed and her head whirled as she moved. Her bile rose in her throat at the rocking of the cabin as it had not done since she was a child. Sometime between her sudden lurch out of the cabin and her staggered arrival at the rail where she spewed her misery to the sea, she swore she'd never touch that foul brown powder again. No, not for anyone would she lose that much control.

In the next month Jack took to the pipe more and more frequently. Anne went belowdecks and into the cabin only to be greeted by a scene out of hell; fumes filled the chambers and that sweet stench clung to everything. Jack asked Anne to join him once more; she refused him so shortly that he never pressed the pipe on her again.

" 'Tis a refined joy, lass. The French do it."

"A pox on them *and* their stinking shit. What joy you find in oblivion, Jack, I cannot see. It's a wretched way to foul your brain, and I'll have none of it." She turned on her heel then, leaving him blinking and smiling in the dark room.

On the mornings after he'd filled himself with opium, he held his head in his hands gently as if it ached at the slightest movement. Then only a grog or two of rum could set him straight. He slept later and later, snoring out fumes of opium and rum so that Anne felt she could almost get besotted simply by stepping inside the cabin. He sweated coarsely, too, and his once pristine cotton trousers were damp and sour with rank odors. Yet the men said nothing. As long as the hold was full of booty and their bellies full of food, they did not rush to capture more ships. Few knew that their captain took anything but rum, and Anne felt more and more isolated from the crew, sensing that she could not tell his secret to any man on board.

To fill her hours, Anne did what she could to make the *Queen Royal* more her own ship. With loot from the captured prizes she adorned the vessel as she used to delight in adorning herself. She put heavy tapestries in the cabins and draped the chambers in silks and satins. She burned incense, partly for diversion and partly to cover the odors of the cabin where Jack lounged. She pulled a huge French tub into the corner of the room to bathe and bought a parrot from a native child for the belowdecks passage. The colorful bird quickly learned to screech, "Catch me who can!" when Anne fed it a biscuit. In quiet moments she slipped to the foredecks perch, where she used to sit as a child, and read books plundered from other ships.

Outwardly Anne seemed calm, but she knew that inside she was ripening to a fine resolve. She felt constantly tense, trying to keep the crew from seeing Jack too drugged to command.

The men were content to loll in and out of the islands, slipping from one white beach to another, and so there was little immediate call for an alert captain.

JACK TIPPED HIS hand irreconcilably when the *Queen Royal* took a Spanish treasure ship off Antigua. He staggered into the midst of the fray from his customary spot at the helm. He was drunker than usual, and Anne could see that his confusion was heightened by the din around him. As she leaped to his side to drag him away from the knots of men fighting on deck, Jack snapped back his head in shock. At his feet was a decapitated Spaniard, his limbs still spasmodically flailing in final reflexive jerks. In Jack's stupor, it looked as if the headless torso was reaching out to grab his legs. He screamed horribly, threw away his pistol, and staggered to the rail, white-eyed and hysterical. Anne grabbed him just before he jumped overboard.

"Jack!" she screamed in his ear, and pulled at his shoulders. "Get back updeck!" She looked over her shoulder frantically for help, but the pirates had moved past the rigging now and were clearly overwhelming those few Spaniards left alive. She was torn. She needed aid to wrest Jack from hysteria, yet if any of the crew saw him now in this condition, his position as captain would be impossible to defend. She suddenly yanked out her cutlass and slapped him smartly on the back with the flat of the blade.

"You fool! Get back to your post!"

Jack lurched towards her, trying to jerk the cutlass from her, screaming blindly. "You Spanish dog!" he shouted hoarsely, not recognizing her at all. His eyes were mad as a heat-struck hound.

Anne plucked out her pistol and held it to his head, yanking his collar, bringing his ear close to her lips.

"I'll plug a ball right through your brain. Move!"

Jack's eyes cleared for a moment. He knew her. His drugged panic was wiped clean by the feel of the cold muzzle against his temple.

She snarled low at him, "Now! Or by God, you'll ruin us both."

He thrust her away and with some dignity staggered back to his place at the helm. Anne followed him and saw, over her shoulder, that a few of the crew watched his departure with appraising eyes.

That night Jack was late coming to their quarters, and when he did he tried to brusquely shove Anne over. As usual, he was sullen with an aching head. He reached for her, but she was having no more.

She pulled back her legs and kicked at him viciously, knocking him off the edge of the bed to the plankings.

"Sleep on the floor or in some rumpot in the hold. I'll no more of your feeble fumblings."

He said nothing, glaring at her with a cold anger. How could they ever love again? He stalked from the cabin and came not again that night.

For a week Anne and Jack avoided each other, keeping the depth of their anger from the crew like two parents before a flock of children. But few were fooled. She now knew she'd have to leave Jack. She could not protect him anymore, nor did she even wish to. It had been two months or more since he'd satisfied her as either a lover or a leader.

Her eyes were straying to the other men onboard ship. She noticed taut male bodies now, whereas before, when she was satisfied with Jack, it was as if he were the only man on the sea. Particularly did Mark Read draw her. His eyes were almost black, which made his every expression intense and piercing. He seemed tough and feisty; indeed, he was often the first over the rail and into the teeth of battle. Yet, more than once, Anne caught him leaning against the bulkhead, gazing at the stars. She guessed that he was struggling with an inner turmoil, much like her own. He was a loner, and so Anne was timid about approaching him.

Anne often avoided the cabin she shared with Jack and spent long hours watching the wake, wishing she had the courage to take command of the ship herself. She knew she was marking time. She no longer loved Jack, could barely muster up enough respect for him to be civil, and she knew that much of the crew had noticed his deterioration.

She hardly dared to hope they'd be ready for a mistress rather than a master. And she could not stay on the *Queen* without Jack, would not be allowed, she knew. If she challenged Jack openly, he just might kill her simply to save face. If she waited until another man challenged his command, she would probably be put ashore beached, with nothing before her but whoring. She had a glimpse of herself passing from one man to another, each less palatable than the last, until she was too old to draw an eye. She shuddered and drew her coat around her.

Anne glanced into the darkness and saw Mark Read leaning against the rigging, all alone. In the shadows she sensed a kindred soul, someone she could speak to.

She moved over quietly to his side. For a long moment she said nothing but only gazed out at the same patch of moonlight that he watched. His eyes slid over her briefly, but he did not speak.

Finally he murmured, his voice low, "Have you the watch?"

Anne simply shook her head. Almost against her will she ventured, "I . . . just don't want to share his cabin."

Anne thought she saw a thin smile in the shadows, but the young man said nothing more.

Anne was very aware, there in the moonlight, of his lithe body, warm next to hers. He seemed so quiet and strong. There was an easy decency in him that drew her. She wondered briefly if he could possibly be unblemished, a stranger to a woman's bed. He never shared the raucously crude jokes of the rest of the crew. When Corner had slipped up on Billy while he slept and gently dipped his hand in tepid water, making the boy wet his berth, Mark had turned away in distaste from the laughter of the men.

On an impulse, borne as much of loneliness as of desire, she put her hand under his chin and gently turned his face to hers. She pushed back his cap and moved her mouth to his. And then she stopped, her eyes widening. In the moonlight, suddenly her perspective shifted, and his profile softened. She was aware that he tensed under her hand.

"My God," she whispered. "Who are you?"

He pulled his face back into the shadows and readjusted his cap back down over his brow. He said gruffly, "Mark Read, of course, Mistress Bonny. As you know well."

But Anne saw clearly now, and she grabbed his arm. "You're a woman! Say it. You're a woman as I am."

The shadowed face nodded reluctantly.

Anne laughed, glancing over her shoulder. "I can't believe it. How have you fooled us? And how many others?"

The silent face suddenly smiled shyly at Anne. Anne was instantly flooded with shame to think she could not recognize her own sex; to know that her desire had been so exposed.

"I've been posing as a man for a long while, mistress." Her voice was low, still not as gruff as Anne had imagined. "My name is Mary Read."

Quietly, Mary told Anne her story as the two women sat under the stars.

MARY READ'S MOTHER was married young to a seaman who got her with child and left soon after on a long voyage. The child born was a boy. The husband was lost in a storm and reported drowned, and Mary's mother grieved for several months. Unfortunately, her mother was of an "airy" personality and soon found ample consolation in the arms of another man and became pregnant again. Before her belly grew too large to hide, she left London and her husband's relatives, claiming that she was going to live with her own parents in the country. She went away, carrying her young son, then but a year old. Soon after she left, her son died of the fever, and her second child was born in 1692. She named the infant girl Mary.

Mrs. Read lived three years in the country until what money she had was almost gone. She thought of returning to London to find her lost husband's family, but she knew they'd last seen her with a young son on her hip. She dressed Mary as a boy, took her to London, and presented her to her mother-in-law as her only grandson.

Thus Mary grew up as a boy and learned at an early age that she had to conceal her sex—else she would starve, her mother said. Finally her grandmother died, and all subsistence stopped. Mary was now thirteen and still looked like a young lad. She was turned out to wait on a Frenchwoman as a footboy.

" 'Course, since I'd been naught but a lad, I needed freedom like any man. I ran away and joined a man-o'-war, for I loved the sea."

Anne eyed her figure as she spoke. Her shoulders were broad as those of a slender man, and her breasts were small, easily hidden under a watchcoat. Even her legs seemed more manly than feminine. Her hair was not simply tucked up inside a cap but was shorn; in the dim light Anne could see the stubble on her neck.

"Why did you not marry?" Anne peered at her in the moonlight.

Mary shrugged. "Those who would have me, I didn't want. The few I'd have didn't want me." She lowered her head. "My mother's talk of marriage did little to make me eager for such bonds." She smiled slowly. "But I did marry once. He was a cadet in the cavalry. I joined the Flanders troops as soon as I left the warship, and I couldn't keep my true identity from my bunkmate. We both yearned for commissions. But mostly they were bought and sold rather than earned. Though we both fought bravely, we left the king's army with nothing but the clothes on our backs and a few guineas."

Anne laughed softly. "And no one in the regiment knew you for a woman?"

Mary grinned. "They thought me mad, for I ran after my lover and followed him into battle just to be near him. They called me a sodomite. He let them think him one too rather than betray my secret. After the war we tried to make a go of an ordinary near Breda. We called it the Three Horseshoes for luck. But it brought us no luck at all. He died soon after." She turned and gazed out to sea.

Anne waited silently for her to go on. She wondered at the pain this shadowy soul must have felt. On an impulse she reached out and touched Mary's hand lightly.

Mary turned back to her, drawn from her reverie. "So after that, my story's short. I took my maiden name again, donned my man's clothes, and sailed once more to the West Indies to find work. I shipped onboard a British convoy and here I am, flying under the flag of Calico Jack."

"What an adventuress you are." Anne breathed in admiration.

Mary shrugged. "You can't choose your destiny, but you can pick a way to live. I couldn't feel . . . at ease in a woman's world."

The soft, tropical night sent a light wind to ruffle Anne's curls. She turned again to Mary. "I thought I was the only woman who'd choose such a berth." She spoke, almost to herself. "Have you ever noticed that life doesn't respond the way it's supposed to? You give it a bone, and its bites your leg. You bite its leg and—"

Mary cut in with a grin. "And it bites your balls."

Anne laughed too loud, muffling her chuckle with her palm. "Ay, and comes back for more." She had an impulse to hug the woman, but she felt too shy to do so.

Mary, relaxed now that she had unburdened herself, turned to Anne with open curiosity. "How did you come to share the captain's cabin?"

Before Anne could respond, her attention was diverted by a sudden movement in the corner of her eye. She turned just in time to see Jack sneaking up behind Mary with his dirk drawn. He sprang at her, rolling over the decks, trying to reach for her throat. Anne leaped on his back, pounding his shoulder with all her strength. It was a silent but deadly tussle, and Mary never once cried out.

Anne jerked the knife out of Jack's viselike grip and flung it overboard. "Christ's nails, you fool," she hissed at him. "What are you doing?"

He turned a cold glare on her. "Save your breath, you poxed whore! I'll cut your young lover's throat and feed him to the sharks and you be next."

Anne rolled her eyes in disgust. Before he could make another move, she reached over and ripped Mary's blouse open, exposing her white breasts in the dim light.

Jack's eyes bugged as Mary reached to cover herself. "Jesus Christ, lad." He looked to Anne, then back to Mary, who demurely lowered her eyes. He slipped dejectedly to the decks. "*Two* wenches," he moaned.

"It's damn lucky for you no one saw you jump her. 'Tis against the articles and you know it." Anne glared at him.

She looked at Mary. Jack would never know she was almost false to him. "Keep her secret, Jack." Briefly, she told him Mary's history.

Jack groaned in disgust at the thought of two women on board but quieted when Anne reminded him that Mark Read was the best sea artist they had.

"Besides," Anne added, "you cannot run the ship yourself, and they won't let *me* run it alone. You know the men'll vote you out if there's none to lead in your stead. Between the two of us"—she gestured to Mary, who stood quietly in the shadows—"we can run the ship without seeming to and you need not give up your berth as captain of the *Queen.*"

Jack's mind worked quickly; even in the darkness Anne could see him coming to the same conclusion. She wondered if he'd been looking for just such a loophole. He wanted to be captain, sure enough, but he was not up to leading the ship. Now he could give orders, and Anne and Mark would see them carried out. A captain in name only, but a captain still. Anne wondered just how long they could keep up the pretense. As long as the hold was filled and provisions were ample, the men would care little who led them. But when trouble struck, the crew was capable of turning on them like hungry eels, tossing all three to the sea. They made an unspoken pact, there under the mast with the edges of dawn just creeping over the railing, that they had much to lose and little to gain by revealing Mary's true identity.

And so, Anne and Mary took command of the *Queen Royal.* They often sought out private times and places to talk. For Anne it was a relief to have a close woman friend—her first. She found a great delight in sharing her feelings with another being who seemed to need no preface and few explanations. Anne felt that she could tell Mary anything. Gone was the effort to be smart or beautiful or witty or desirable. When Anne conversed with a man she was always aware of their differences, but when she talked with Mary, all she could see was their similarities. Anne sensed that Mary wanted nothing from her, that it was not necessary to barter a piece of herself to gain Mary's affection. In that sense she felt this union with Mary was more ideal, less subject to trouble than her marriage had been.

Mary had often said that she'd never love again, and Anne teased her that such a pledge was sure to be shortlived. As if to prove Anne's point, Mary soon had to take back her vow.

The next prize taken was a ship bound to England from Jamaica. One of the men pressed into service was Tom Deason, a fine sea artist. Tom was not yet twenty-one, a full six years Mary's junior, yet she was drawn to him in spite of her determination to keep distant from all men. When the pirates attempted to persuade Tom to join the crew of the *Queen Royal,* she pulled him aside and warned him.

"Stay as you are, lad. This is not the life for such as you."

Tom looked askance at this slender pirate who seemed so solicitous of his welfare. The rest of the crew were quick to detail the pleasures and advantages of a pirate career, and Tom was finally caught up in their raucous welcome. Mary watched with mixed emotions as Tom signed the articles and joined the *Queen*.

Later she whispered to Anne, "I swear, I don't know what has dazed me. He's naught but a boy and most likely still wet as an unlicked cub. Yet he stirs me, Anne. I want him near and I want him gone."

Anne smiled. She remembered similar feelings she'd had for James Bonny a lifetime ago. She only hoped that Mary's choice would bring her more happiness than her own had.

Mary was so smitten that she spent almost as much time with Tom as she did with Anne. The boy came to trust this strange silent partner who was so often at his side and to admire his skill and daring. Meanwhile, Mary came to Anne at odd moments, bewailing her enforced disguise.

"How can I get him to know me for a woman and still keep the rest of the crew in ignorance? Oh," she moaned, " 'tis the first time I've missed my locks since I shorn them."

Anne's advice was direct. "Anything is better than the agony of not knowing. Take him to a dark corner, lass, and reveal yourself to him. If he's a man, he'll do the rest." She smiled gently, mindful of Mary's pain. "Just do what I did to you."

Mary grinned impishly as she remembered that night, but her own modesty kept her at bay a while longer. Finally, when she could no longer suppress her feelings, she arranged to be on deck for the same watch that Deason drew. Alone in the shadows, she approached him nervously.

After a few moments of idle conversation, she ventured, "What do you think of Mistress Bonny, Tom?"

Tom shook his head reluctantly. "She don't belong on a pirate ship, mate. She ruined her health and her beauty on this tub. And for what? A berth with that rascal, Rackham?"

Mary went on with some apprehension. "You speak bold for a new hand, Tom. If Jack heard you talk such, he'd—"

"Oh, I'd not say such but to you," Tom reassured her. "But you asked."

That I did, winced Mary to herself, as she cast about for another tack. "You been wed yourself, lad?"

"Nay." He laughed low. "Never found a woman that'd take me on." He gazed out over the silver water. "But did I, mark me, she'd not take to the seas like a common rogue. She'd stay at home, all soft and white, and wait for me."

Mary felt almost desperate with the desire to take him in her arms at this moment. She could think of no graceful way to tell him the truth, however. She feared that their times together in private might be few in the days to come. Already she worried that the crew had noticed her attachment to the young seaman. She moved closer to him.

"Tom," she started with a brave smile and then faltered,

"Tom—I be not what I seem."

He glanced at her casually, not alarmed by her stammer but only curious. "No?" he grinned. "Be you a king's spy?"

Mary flushed, glanced once around the deck and stepped even closer to him. To her relief, he did not flinch, but only regarded her warily.

"I am a woman, Tom," she whispered. And she opened her blouse slightly to expose two white pert breasts.

He recoiled in shock then, and she hastily covered herself. Turning to the rail away from him, she went on hastily, "I knew no other way to show you, Tom. I could not bear to keep the secret anymore. Not from you."

Tom recovered, passed his hand over his face quickly and leaned towards her urgently. "Does anyone else know of this?"

"Ay," nodded Mary sadly. "Mistress Bonny and Rackham. 'Twas she who sent me to you."

"Why?" questioned the young man. But Mary only turned away and lowered her eyes. Tom suddenly grinned. He was not quite as naive as Mary had supposed. Silently, he drew her into the shadow of the rigging, and she told him her story.

In the days that followed, Tom's natural admiration for Mary as a seaman turned to desire and love for her as a woman. They were increasingly careful to keep their feelings from the rest of the crew, but even so, eventually they were challenged.

Will Janner, a common seaman new to the *Queen*, had eyed the sturdy sea artist Mark Read, and had twice tried to press Mary into his own berth. Mary had answered him with a quick insult and a flash of her dirk, and he'd kept off her flanks of late. But now that he saw the obvious bond growing between this Mark Read and a new mate, the fresh young face of Tom Deason drove him sour with jealous anger. He taunted Deason frequently in the hearing of the rest of the crew.

"Ye bugger!" Janner would laugh mirthlessly, glancing about to be sure all listened. "Can 'e poke as good as 'e pulls, eh? Watch 'im, he don't pox ye end to end!"

At first Tom took the ribbing with casual humor, but as the jibes grew more frequent and cutting—and as his love for Mary grew—his pride was rankled and he began to exchange insults with Janner, both of them spoiling for a confrontation.

One day, when Mary was not around to deflect the taunts, Janner rode him dangerously hard, and Tom snapped. He pulled his dirk in a quick motion and shouted, "Stow your tongue or lose it, Janner! I'll take no more o' your bloody crap!"

Janner circled him gleefully, like a cat about a crippled bird, slapping at his cheeks and daring him to fight. Instantly, Tom realized his error. Mary raced on deck just in time to hear her lover challenged to a duel to the death, according to the articles, with half the crew as witness.

She moaned softly, keeping to the edge of the crowd. Rackham came forward and listened as Janner formally requested satisfaction as soon as the ship could put to shore. There was no turning back now. Tom must fight or be branded a coward and marooned. Since he pulled first weapon, he could not decline.

That night Mary crept to Anne's cabin and wept in her arms. "He can't fight!" she cried. "I love him, but he can't hold his own against Janner! He'll be killed right before my eyes!"

Anne held her and rocked her silently while she wept, searching her mind for a plan. "We could put you both off in a dinghy with provisions some time before we get to shore. No one need know until you're well away."

"No!" Mary shook her head frantically. "He'd never agree. He's too proud."

Anne shrugged in exasperation. "Well, then. I suppose you could scuttle Janner before he gets a shot off. But 'tis against the articles."

Mary pulled away. "No, Anne. Tom couldn't live with the shame." She gestured futilely at the cutlass lying on the linen. "He thinks he must defend me."

Anne snorted derisively. "Were it not for pride, they'd be a fine sex, men. Women are more practical by far." She took Mary's hand gently. "What will you do, then?"

Mary's brow cleared as she pondered it. "I could take Janner with ease, I think."

"On what pretense?"

"I'd find one."

"And what of Tom's pride?"

"With luck, he'll not know 'til it's over. Better shamed than dead. And he need only be shamed to me. None else would know."

Anne squeezed her friend's hand urgently. "I'll not try to stop you, lass. Though I wish I could. God knows, I'd rather see Tom shot than you, hard as that sounds."

Mary flared quickly. "Don't say that again, Anne. Not if you're my friend."

Anne shook her head in resignation. "He's not good enough for you."

"And I suppose Rackham is a prize?"

Anne pulled up stiffly. It hurt her to know that she and Mary could spar over anything, much less these two men. "No. He's just as useless. Neither of them is worth our efforts." She grinned. "But who is?"

Mary softened and smiled. "Ay. Well, Tom is honest and good, young though he be. And I could not bear to see him drop under Janner's pistol."

"So you'll take the shot yourself?"

"No. I mean to give it."

WHEN THE *QUEEN ROYAL* put to shore the next day, the pirates clustered on the beach, eager for the diversion. Most were growing discontent with Rackham's slovenly command and were just hostile enough to welcome blood, no matter whose.

Jack leaned over the edge of the ship as she lolled in the shallows, urging the circus on.

"Drummer, beat the long roll!" he hollered, laughing senselessly.

Anne stood at his side, silently watching the pirates splash to the shore. Some rowed, others waded, but all were raucously enjoying the outing.

"Step and growl, growl and go!" shouted Jack, waving his cutlass.

Anne waited. Soon she saw Mary jostle Janner out of the nearest dinghy. Mary had on her largest hat, pulled clear over her collar, and her voice seemed all the more gruff over the waves.

"Get out of my way, you drab-colored son of a bitch, or I'll cleave you myself!"

Janner spun around, amazed to be so accosted by Mark Read, who had kept largely silent and withdrawn through the voyage. "Ha' a prayer, lad. I'm in no mood to trifle with trash," he growled.

Anne could see from where she stood that Mary's brow flashed in anger like a bleached bone. "Trash, is it? Damn your eyes, perhaps you'd like to prove your words afore you bow to yon youngster." She gestured impudently to Deason, who was still back on decks. "I'd like a piece o' you myself afore he splits you ear to arse!"

"Done!" grinned Janner, drunk on action. "I'll take ye both! Jes' get in line!"

"Oh no, you pimp. I take first cut or none!" She stepped right under Janner's jaw and punched him in the belly, spitting up into his eye. "I'll split ye for the cockroach ye are!"

The men surrounding the two set up a small cheer, and the word passed quickly that Mark Read was to duel Janner before Deason. Mary glanced hastily back to Tom who had come to the rail, frantic at the news. As she watched, Anne slipped to his side and whispered urgently in his ear. His cry of protest was stifled.

Mary gazed at him as the dinghy was rowed to shore. Dimly, she heard Janner shouting insults from another boat, but all she saw, all she was conscious of, was Tom's face as the two boats pulled away. His look was ashen, but she felt as free as a wheeling gull and sure of her course.

The two boats reached the sand, and Mary never looked over her shoulder again. She felt Tom's eyes on her, even across the water, but she gave all her attention to the moment.

Corner called the two together and on two barrelheads placed two flintlock pistols, powder, and two swords. He stepped away.

"Are ye ready, men?"

Mary nodded silently, never taking her eyes from Janner.

Janner laughed raucously. "And what do I get if I win this bout, mate? 'Sides a shot at yer pullet? A poke at ye both, eh?" He smiled ferally and patted the front of his breeches. "One 'twill be as good as the other, I 'spect. This'll teach you both who's to be master."

Mary's eyes narrowed to slits. From the decks even Anne could see the stiffening in her body, the concentration in her stare. "Get on with it, Corner," Mary growled in her throat.

Corner called out to the fringes of men about them. "Hark'ee men! There's been challenge issued an' answered! One shot apiece, as to the articles. He who misses, dies. If they both miss, then to swords. Step back, lads, for I seen 'em shoot wild as women!" The men ringed the two adversaries, and all grew quiet.

Mary felt her mind leave her body for an instant and float above her head, watching the scene. Just for a moment she felt only the breeze, heard only the soft lapping of the waves on the beach. She dared not gaze back at Tom, his face was as white as the wake. She wrenched herself back to the moment, wondering briefly if what she'd felt was a prelude to death.

Corner was watching her. She grimaced tightly, and her facial muscles trembled. Swiftly, Corner's hand dropped, his sword slashing through the air.

She reached for the pistol, watching Janner all the while. She loaded, primed, and brought the weapon up pointed towards his chest. In an instant she saw a brief flash of wonder in his eyes as he realized he was too late. Almost unconsciously, she pulled the trigger. A single shot burst loudly, and the pistol recoiled back as her trembling arms could not hold the full force. Janner dropped to his knees, one hand dangled to his pistol, the other fluttered in the air as if he'd hoped to stop the bullet. A bright blossom of red splayed over his chest. He wavered for an instant, then Mary saw his eyes go dull, and he fell forward heavily, dead.

There was a long silence in the crowd. Only now did she turn and stare at the *Queen Royal,* still bobbing in the water like an unconcerned tern. It had happened so quickly she had no time to plan what she would do or say next. A few of the crew straggled to her side and clapped her roundly on the back, while two men dragged Janner by the heels into the brush. The only evidence of their confrontation was a brown stain and two long furrows in the sand leading up to the beach where he'd been dumped. When the tide came in, there would be no sign at all.

Anne released a long sigh as she watched Mary walk steadily back to the dinghy and step inside. Only when she saw it was over did Anne let go of Tom's arm. When she did, he went quickly across the decks to the rail away from the beach and vomited quietly over the side.

*T*HE *QUEEN ROYAL* set sail for Trinidad to provision, and there Anne and Jack met up with their old comrade, Captain Charles Vane. Incredibly, Vane bore neither hard feelings, and the two pirate crews all but ransacked the village in a riotous celebration.

At the Red Cock Tavern, Anne sat at Vane's table and heard of his exploits since he'd left the *Seahorse* to their command. It had been two years since she'd seen him, and she knew she owed him much. Under his command, Anne had learned the ways of the sea, signed her first articles, gone into her first battle, and been accepted as a pirate in her own right. To Anne, Vane was like a long-lost uncle. Perhaps one reason he bore no grudge for his ouster was because he had done so well.

"After ye put us off"—he glared at Anne—"we sailed for Honduras and took seven prizes on the way."

Anne lightly patted his leg and grinned full into his scowl. "I never doubted that you would, Captain."

He slowly smiled back at her then and downed his ale with relish. "Ay, no thanks to you, mistress, and yon scut ye've got on yer arm"—he gestured to Jack—"but we done better than most."

While the pirates were celebrating, word reached Trinidad that the Spanish armada had sailed for New Providence. Anne was sobered by the news.

"Poor Rogers." Anne shook her head. "That scum'll never fight for him. The island will be in papist hands in a week." She looked up at Jack sadly. "And those of our friends who're left alive won't be for long."

Woodes Rogers had known of the impending attack and had begged London for troops and warships, but no reinforcements arrived. Left to his own devices, he labored feverishly to fortify the island, stirring the population to fretful efforts by playing on their fears of the papists. Since even the most demure woman could recall tales of gruesome horror that the Spanish had wrought on hapless captives, Rogers was able to spur some of the inhabitants to action.

Rogers managed to collect enough excess food and liquor to bribe the pirates into a state of almost continuous labor.

For nearly a year the Spaniards had been building an attack force at Havana. Naturally, all of the Caribbean knew of its intended target—the pirate republic of New Providence. Reports had regularly reached Rogers that betrayed the Spanish plans and preparations, yet the governor was largely unready. Thanks to the deaf ears in London, even after emptying the jails and arming old men and children, Rogers had a land force of less than four hundred.

His navy consisted of three partly armed ships and half a dozen sloops, one manned by Captain Ben Hornigold and the others commanded by reluctant ex-pirates who were more inclined to flight than fight. With this small brigade, Rogers intended to repel a Spanish fleet of five heavily armed warships, three massive brigantines, and eleven sloops carrying a total of two thousand troops.

"Damned if I care for that!" shouted Vane. "I hate Rogers like the devil, but I'm blowed if I'll stand by an' see the pirates' republic turned papist! After all, we be Brethren ourselves."

There was a low murmur of approval that ran through the tavern.

"We've not near enough guns to run off such a fleet," Jack said flatly. "We'd be sailing into our coffins."

Vane's eyes narrowed to slits, and he leaned across the table to face Jack squarely. "Seems to me I was run off the *Seahorse* for just such reluctance in battle, Captain Rackham. Be you turned soft in two years?" He glanced at Anne, who stiffened at the implied insult to both of them.

"God bless, I say we go home, lads!" Vane pounded the table. "What do you say to that, mistress?" He peered at Anne.

Anne glanced quickly at Jack and then away. "God certainly doesn't love that place, so I guess we must." She smiled. "I say, we keep the pirate republic under England's flag!"

There was a roaring chorus of yelled salutes, and the die was cast. The next dawn six pirate ships were under sail for New Providence. The mighty *Queen Royal* was the flagship, followed by Vane's schooner and four swift pirate sloops.

In spite of the quick decision, however, the Spanish fleet had a substantial lead and was the first to reach the vulnerable island of New Providence. The force of nineteen ships and near two thousand troops under the command of Don Francisco Cornejo had sailed from Cuba through the Florida channel and approached the pirate republic from the north.

As the Spaniards anchored off the eastern extreme of Walker's Point in New Providence harbor, Rogers sat waiting with his ragtag navy and about four hundred ex-pirates. From their vantage point in the harbor the Spanish saw no fortifications, and they assumed the island was unprepared for their assault. They planned to launch a few boats for a beachhead, then attack the town by land while their warships battered the settlement from the sea.

But they were surprised by a small cavalry force which sped down the beach towards the helpless boats rolling in on the tide. Before the Spanish could beach their craft, ex-pirates on horseback led by Rogers, whirling a sword over his head, attacked and drove them back towards the large mother ships. The landing Spaniards frantically signaled for support from the guns out in the harbor. It came.

The warships lumbered in as close as they could come and pounded the beach with heavy fire. The cavalry, now greatly outgunned, fell back, leaving about a fourth of their number dead or dying on the littered beach.

The Spanish longboats tried again for the surge ashore. They were met by brave but feeble fire from Rogers' militia hidden in the thickets at the top of the sand. Instead of fleeing again, the Spanish dug in. One hundred and fifty soldiers gained a foothold on the beach, firing into the bushes. Instead of advancing on the pirates, the Spanish held fast, hoping for more troops to move ashore and bolster their members. This proved a fatal mistake.

Suddenly, from around the bend in the harbor, six fast pirate sloops appeared and daringly sliced in between the Spanish warships and isolated the force onshore.

Anne stood on the deck of the *Queen Royal,* her glass trained on first the beach and then the Spanish warships at the mouth of the harbor.

"Stand fast, mates, we're coming," she muttered to herself as she watched the Spanish ships flounder in confusion at the new attack.

Anne gave the commands and a signal flag was hoisted high for all to see. In an instant, the pirate ships responded, and their guns blasted the beach, blowing apart the landing party.

There was a brief moment of shocked silence from Rogers' troops. Then, without hesitation, their gunfire joined the barrage from the sloops. The Spanish longboats were swiftly cut to pieces, and debris flew high into the air. The screams of the landed Spanish could be heard above the gunfire, and sharp Latin curses cut through the smoke.

Anne felt her mouth fill with sour bile as she watched through her glass and saw one Spaniard dismembered sloppily before her eyes. She walked swiftly to the rail, spat out to sea, and then went back to her place again, her glass once more to her eye.

From her post, Anne could see all of the battle, could signal commands to the rest of the pirate fleet and effectively cut off any attempted flight by the Spanish force. This part of the fight was hers, and she almost relished it.

She gave another quick command, and a second signal flag flew up the mast. The pirate fleet turned towards the sea, catching the armada in a lethal pincer movement. They opened fire as one ship, and there was a sudden deafening blast as a powder magazine was hit. Flames and smoke sprang up high from one of the Spanish warships. Anne yanked her glass from her eye and saw the enemy launching longboats—this time to find refuge on undamaged ships.

"Move in! Move in!" she shouted and ran to the closest deck, watching as the sloops buzzed about the huge warships like biting insects, harassing first one flank and then the other. The Spanish fleet had the greater firepower, but the deft maneuverability of the pirate sloops was more important in these shallow waters. One Spanish warship stood its ground and flung mighty cannonballs at each pirate sloop that crossed its bow, but it was like trying to smack flies with a shovel. The pirates literally sailed circles about the huge brigs, peppering them with shot.

Anne turned her glass to the sand then and saw that all firing had stopped. From their hiding place behind Hog's Island, the small navy that Rogers had assembled now sailed into the fray. Although this action stripped the town and harbor of all sea protection, the concerted force worked. Anne saw Rogers himself sail by, leaning far over the rail, exhorting his crew to speed. As she watched, the little sloop bombarded a second Spanish warship, crippling its guns and adding to the chaos.

Suddenly two of the Spanish brigs turned and headed out of the harbor in retreat—right towards the *Queen Royal*. Anne hesitated for an instant. If they stood and fought, there was a good chance they'd sink one, maybe both of the ships. And just as likely a chance that they too would be crippled or lost. She looked across to Jack at the foredeck, but could not read his expression. She glanced to the men and saw that half of them looked to her, half to Jack. In another moment the decision would be made for them, as the Spanish ship wore fast upon their bow. Still Jack said nothing, as if daring her to alter the plan, daring her to break order, to breach the line and run. She silently cursed to herself.

"Wheel about!" she shouted, leaping to the mast line and tugging hard. "Let them pass!"

The *Queen* turned slowly, eased sideways with the wind, and the Spanish ship sailed past in retreat. Two of Rogers' ships swooped after the warship as if in defiance of the *Queen Royal*'s quarter. The Spanish proved more effective in fighting a rearguard action. Anne saw now that most of their guns were still trained back on the harbor, and they blew hot lead at Rogers' sloops.

One was hit badly and began to sink; Rogers' own ship had to wheel to come to the aid of its floundering sister. The two remaining Spanish ships pulled off into the sea, and the rest of the fleet followed, those that could.

Several of the pirate sloops were still doughty and full of life, though some had taken shots to the flanks. They sailed close past Rogers' flagship and out to sea, waving to him as much in derision as in triumph.

Anne hesitated. She faced Rogers from the decks of the *Queen*, with only a small watery passage between them. Rogers stood on his deck, overseeing the rescue of one of his fleet. Anne knew that if they sailed into the harbor Rogers would have to capture them, no matter how they'd helped rescue his island. He would be obliged to take them back to New Providence to hang. He had no choice.

She grinned widely at him across the water as he turned and stared at her. As she watched he lifted one hand, waved a salute, and then turned back to his own crew.

She ran to the mast and hoisted the *Queen Royal*'s colors to flap gracefully in the wind. CATCH ME WHO CAN the flag read, and Rogers could not have missed the message therein.

To Jack's commands, then, the great *Queen* turned slowly about and made her way out of New Providence waters into open sea and back to Trinidad.

ANNE WALKED out on the beach one afternoon and surprised a cluster of the crew under a palm tree in secluded shade. Anne stiffened, for she knew instantly what was afoot.

She walked to the fringe of the group and merely stood quietly, watching and listening. Several of the men looked up, but then returned, almost defiantly, to their discussion. The meeting was to decide whether or not Rackham would stay on as captain.

Fenwick said sullenly, without looking up at her, "Ye know yerself he ain't been sober for near a month."

Anne saw that she was going to have to own up to the truth, and quickly, too, or lose all credibility for them both. "You're wrong, lads. We all know he's not been himself . . . but no one else does. Certainly not the prizes we take under his flag. A flag that still makes them heave to without a fight. If you keep him captain, at least in name, we continue to rule these seas. If not, then half the crew'll go with him and the other half'll be without a groat."

Fenwick said quietly, "Likely ye'd say such, mistress, an' we all know why. Ye run Rackham an' the *Queen*, an' nobody can buck ye both. But articles is articles, an' I say he don't belong in the captain's cabin, nor do ye."

Anne put her hand to her pistol that jutted out from her waist. She turned steely eyes to Fenwick, a man she'd never really liked. "And *I* say nay." She slowly pivoted about the circle, pinning each man's eyes with her own. "Has any cause to grumble of his share of booty? Has any lacked for rum or belly timber? Has any been shamed in battle?"

Most eyes were lowered.

"No. I thought not. Those who wish to, can leave aboard the *Kingston.* Choose who you like for a captain on any ship save the *Queen.* The *Queen Royal* is Calico Jack's—and mine—and shall stay so. And there's those—like Mark and Corner and Billy and Tom— who'll stand by me and say so as well." Anne pushed out her jaw and waited.

Most of the men looked at ease, even relieved, that a stronger voice had prevailed. Only Fenwick continued to glare at her defiantly.

"Fenwick," she said abruptly, "take what men care to join you and sail tonight. The *Kingston* is yours. If I catch you on the *Queen* past dark, I'll feed you to the sharks. I'll have no caballing in corners on our ship. And Fenwick"—she leaned lower and whispered in his ear so all could hear—"if I catch your wake in these seas, I'll sink you for the scurvy lot you are."

Fenwick glanced around the circle and saw little support in the eyes averted from his. He got to his feet and went for his sword, as liquid a movement as Anne had seen in any battle, but she put her pistol to his neck before he could wrench himself away.

"Go!" she hissed softly.

He whirled on his heel and strode down the beach. Anne watched him as he disappeared and then turned back to the crew.

"Thank you, lads. I'll not betray your trust. Nor will Jack. The *Queen* is yours as well as ours."

As she walked from the thicket, she felt the tension slip from her, leaving her wrung out and exhausted. She would not tell Jack of this narrow escape. But Mary—ay, Mary she would tell.

A<small>NNE HAD REACHED</small> the height of her career as a pirate queen. The *Queen Royal* was a floating castle with a full crew of forty men and a sumptuous quarterdeck.

Mary had long since put off her disguise as a man, and most of the crew slipped easily into a grudging tolerance of her skill, since she had proved herself long before as sea artist and swordsman. Unlike Anne, however, Mary did not flaunt her femininity. She retained her somber seaman's dress and close-cropped hair, running barefoot up and down the riggings with the rest of the crew. She took no pleasure, as Anne did, in dressing up in brilliant buccaneer plumage. But Anne spent her leisure hours fashioning silken blouses and velvet breeches.

The *Queen*'s master, George Featherston, ran the ship smoothly now, consulting with Anne over daily decisions. Rackham, still the nominal captain of the ship, was happy so long as he had ample rum and opium. Twice a day he hauled on his frock coat and walked the decks, speaking heartily to the crew, praising this rigging or that sail set, then sat down to dice with a few favorites or pored endlessly over maps, muttering to himself of old conquests and remembered haunts. Jack and Anne were no longer lovers, but they were still friends. Siblings, almost, bound together by their past memories and their mutual support of the *Queen Royal*.

On those rare occasions when they shared a berth, Anne and Jack were infinitely tender, as if they held the pieces of each other's dead dream in their hands. Anne knew that their present circumstances could not last forever, yet for now she was happy to live day to day, glorying in the ship, her freedom, and the sea.

Once, in the privacy of their chambers, she asked Jack why he drank. He said, glancing over a full tankard dreamily, "Rum loosens the ropes that tie down the god within."

Anne was immediately overwhelmed by a sharp sorrow and an irritation at his lost potential. "You mean the beast," she grimaced.

He smiled sadly. "Whatever."

The first ship taken in the next month was the *Queen*'s richest prize to date. It was a tall ship, a New England merchant, deep-laden in the water and sailing heavily. But as Anne looked through the glass she counted an ominous number of gunports along its sides. They were not painted, but the real thing, with grim nine-pounders all in a row. The ship was gliding slowly, seemingly unaware of their stalk. Featherston came to her side.

" 'Tis right, mistress. Ye needs show the men ye won't shirk a scuffle."

Anne thought of Vane and how he was ousted for veering off from a fight. However, this prey was well alerted. Anne's gut instinct told her that this was too high game for them to fly at. Yet retreat, now that all the men were looking to her for a cry to battle, was out of the question.

She signaled the crew down to the rails and watched the merchant through the glass. They seemed unaware of their peril. Featherston took the helm, and Mary conned the ship so as to gain the weather gauge. The crew huddled below the level of the gunwales out of sight, nursing their weapons. To all external appearances, the New Englander saw only a large sloop, apparently in ballast for it was high in the water and sailed fast.

Jack came on the foredeck, and Anne handed him the glass. "Sail, Captain," she said distractedly, "a New Englander full laden."

He snatched the glass from her hand and took his time scanning the ship on the horizon. Then he glanced at the men already hidden below the rails.

"We shall take her!" he snapped, whacking the glass against his hip. Not a man smiled, for each had a part to play now.

They were within hailing distance before colors were shown or identity given as nautical courtesy required.

"*Prudent Hannah* of Boston, Israel Bemis, master!" shouted the New England skipper. "What ship from what port!" he added, as he sent his blood-red Union Jack up and fluttering from the masthead.

"*From the sea!*" roared Jack, and climbed to his position on the foredeck. Anne saw Featherston give the signal almost simultaneously, and the huge four-pounder on the fo'c'sle boomed a round of shot that sprayed a geyser of water over the New Englander's bow.

"Boarders!" Jack bellowed. "*Boaarders!*"

Anne saw Mary hoist the jet-black flag up the masthead and signal the crew. At once they sprang to their feet, yelling like demons and brandishing their weapons. Anne rushed with them to crowd the gunwales. With a quick maneuver, Featherston brought the *Queen* downwind and ran squarely alongside. The grapnels arched through the air like arrows into the riggings of the New Englander, drawing the two sloops close alongside.

There was a swift, savage brawl. It was over in moments. The air thwacked with a lethal slice, and Billy staggered back, his skull split by a sword. The weapon came up, arching through the air for another blow, but in that instant Anne drew her knife and thrust it under the British seaman's raised arm. She felt it go through him like a spoon through pudding, but she was in so close, she feared the downward swing of his sword. Rather than pull back, she leaped in closer and crushed herself to his heaving chest. Fortunately, he was a small man, and Anne held the crumpling tar until his lungs bubbled with blood and his eyes turned white. Surprised by her own daring, she pulled her knife from the corpse, wiped it swiftly, and turned to meet the next enemy. But the call for quarter stopped her.

Israel Bemis, his bloodied cheek opened to the bone, was thrown whimpering from the *Hannah*'s deck into a longboat along with most of his crew. Anne looked at Billy lying at her feet. His eyes stared back into hers, opaque and sightless but somehow wondrously calm. Anne felt a sob rise in her throat, but she fought it down. She raised her head and saw Jack still standing on the foredeck, taking off his captain's coat now, shouting lusty praise to the men. She felt instantly old and haggard, her own hand next to Billy's looked withered and calloused. His was curled softly like a child's.

Later she cleaned her pike before returning it to the rack. The rich blood running down the shiny edge reminded her of the way gravy ran down her jackknife at supper, and she tasted keen metal in her mouth. She felt a sharp disgust, sickened at her participation in death.

The next day Billy and two other men were sent to sea. Jack, following the immortal custom of the sea, auctioned off the dead men's belongings. Anne bought everything of Billy's—which was pathetically little. His blouses barely fit her, for her shoulders were broader than his. But his ivory flute she carefully stowed away in her personal cache so as to remember his blue eyes and wide grin.

That night Anne sat in her cabin sewing as Mary carefully cleaned her pistols. She had quite a collection, six all told, and she oiled them as carefully as any fine lady might groom and brush her hair. Tom and Mary were content as two long-married spouses now, retiring early to a separate cabin, working side by side during the day, watching out for each other in battle. Mary never flinched from either chores or fighting, and Tom never relieved her. Anne thought it a strange gallantry, but she said nothing.

Now Anne noticed Mary's content expression and idly remarked, "You know, lass, in a way, I envy you."

Mary looked up with some surprise. "For mercy sakes, why?"

Anne kept her head down over her sewing, her voice low. "Twice in your life you've had love. Once in Flanders and once at sea." She looked up, biting off a thread. "Some women never know love in their whole lives."

Mary smiled. "I would hardly number you among those unfortunates. You've surely never lacked for love."

"I've never lacked for men," Anne corrected her. "But love's something else altogether. I've never known a man yet who really knew me and loved me, in any way that lasted. Jack has come the closest." She put her head down again. "And now even he's gone."

Mary shrugged. "I'd not waste my tears over such as he. I've often wondered why you set yourself on him at all. He's a born sot."

Anne stiffened, but then she said sadly, "He was not always as you see him, Mary. I don't know why he changed. 'Tis more than just the smoke and the rum. It's as if he embraced both, feeding an emptiness that was already within him." She picked up her sewing again. "Maybe I drove him to it in some way. He was never as strong as he seemed."

Mary scoffed lightly, in no mood to be drawn into Anne's deepening gloom. "You mean, as strong as you." She checked an empty pistol. "Do you regret your life?" She looked about, gesturing to the fine linens on the bed, the spaciousness of the cabin. "Isn't this what you always wanted?"

"Ay," Anne nodded slowly. "No, I don't regret my life. But"— her eyes flickered, dark with a secret sorrow—"for the first time, I feel . . . fear." She looked up at Mary piercingly. "Ay, I feel afraid. Of what, I don't know."

Mary smiled at her knowingly. "We all do. But I always pressed myself to do the things I feared the most. To take fear by the scruff of the neck and proclaim myself its master. That's when I feel most alive."

Anne continued to sew, her thoughts confused. There must be other ways to feel alive than by mastering fear and risking one's life each day. Was she always doomed to love a man who was less than herself? Would her emotions always rage and then become so tepid that they left her passive and lifeless? Was she as addicted to danger and drama as Jack was to rum? She glanced at Mary. She seemed so sure of herself. Would she ever know the same contentment, the serene confidence in love that shone from Mary? Restlessly, she laid her sewing by her side and rose to walk on the decks.

Watching the sea stars, the stars the mariners used to guide them through the tropical waters, she felt calmed. Star headings were easier to use in the tropics than in northern latitudes, for there were fewer clouds, and their bearings remained more steady. There was no polestar, but Anne was so familiar with the rest of the constellations that they seemed shining fingers pointing the way of her destiny. The largeness of the sea and the sky made her feel so small, made her realize again that the whole earth was simply a tiny raft in the blackness, and that her ship was a small speck on the whole earth, and she only one of its crew. And the haunting isolation she felt just one thought in the universe of her mind.

THE QUEEN ROYAL headed north. The crew was now down to thirty. Anne was not concerned, since the number of hands fluctuated, depending on the prizes taken and the men pressed. Nonetheless, she knew they could not attack a well-armed vessel with such numbers, and each hand had to pull duty until they were back to full strength.

Just north of Hispaniola the Queen came within sight of a taut-looking ship flying the Union Jack. Anne watched the ship cautiously through the glass. She knew that at least three men-of-war—the *Diamond*, the *Ludlow Castle*, and the *Winchelsea*—were operating out of Jamaica now, searching for the *Queen* and her pirate crew. They could ill afford to meet with one of His Majesty's warships with only thirty men on decks. As soon as she saw that the ship was not a man-of-war, she called Mary to her side.

Mary silently took the glass and peered across the sea for a time, then clapped it closed and nodded to Anne. "I'd take it. We need provisions and hands."

The women began to move the ship to attack position and George Featherston put on full sail; within three hours they closed with the vessel which, strangely, did not attempt to flee.

Anne wondered briefly if she should wake Jack, who was sleeping off an exceptionally hard binge. She decided against it. She sensed no real danger.

"What ship!" she shouted across to a uniformed officer on deck, as the *Queen Royal* approached.

"His Majesty's prison ship *Jewel!* I am Captain Scarett, and I warn you to keep clear!"

The two vessels were so close now that they were almost touching, and Anne ran to another perch on the deck to get a better view. Mary came once more to her side.

"Did you see that rack?" She pointed to a strange contraption at midship. Anne gasped when she realized what it was. On the decks of the *Jewel* was a huge torture device with room for four men at once. At its edges were leather shackles to stretch its victims into gasping oblivion. Across the deck were three whipping posts, splashed dark with stains. Anne looked again and realized that some poor semblance of a man was strapped, hanging limp and unconscious from the farthest post. Chains, shackles, and other intricate hardware lay strewn about deck.

"My God, we've interrupted a whipping! That bastard's running a floating hell." She called to Featherston, "Drummer, beat the long roll!"

The drummer boy took up a long, murderous rhythm, and Anne shouted again to the scowling captain across the short expanse of water. "We be from the sea!" The black flag fluttered up the mast. "This is Calico Jack Rackham's ship, and we mean to board you!" She glanced to the men who were gathered and waiting on the decks. "We kill any who oppose us!"

Anne gave out a strident war cry and unsheathed her sword, leaping into the riggings. The two ships closed instantly, but there was no battle.

Captain Scarett exhorted his men to fight, but none lifted a sword. When Anne and the crew boarded the *Jewel,* they found a line of seamen standing respectfully at attention, swords sheathed and eyes down, well back from the advancing pirates.

Anne gestured to Mary, and she went immediately to the whipping post and cut the ragged victim down. "He's gone," she called across the decks.

Anne turned then to the captain, a cold fury kindling her eyes to green fire. The captain faced her, drawn up with stiff dignity, glaring at his men. He was short, paunched, and had a brutal, livid face. He spat at her feet and sneered, "So you're the infamous Bonny bitch, eh? Terror of the seas?" He deliberately turned his back to her, swaggering before his men.

Anne swiftly drew her sword. The captain whirled at the hiss of steel from scabbard, just in time to catch the full flat of Anne's weapon sharply across his cheek. The blow dropped him to his knees; a thin line of blood oozed down his jaw.

He slowly rose before her, his face twisted malevolently. "Get off my ship! I'll have you all flogged!"

Anne glanced to his men, who stood as quiet as tree trunks, their eyes averted as if they did not wish to witness such a disgrace. Her own crew muttered behind her restlessly. "Indeed," she said. "It looks to me as if you've had quite enough flogging for one day."

"This is His Majesty's ship! I'm His Majesty's officer! I demand that you leave these decks at once!"

Anne put the point of her sword to the sputtering man's throat and said calmly, "I don't like your manner, sir." She called to Corner, never taking her eyes from Scarett's sweating neck, "Dick, tie this scurvy excuse for a captain to his own whipping post."

As Corner hustled the man away, Anne heard a noise from under the planks, a ragged scuttling sound like a dozen huge vermin. "What was that?" she whirled, sword in hand. "Who's there! Come forth and show yourself!"

There was a strange clumping followed by a rattle of chains. Then a ragged figure appeared out in the sunlight, blinking furtively. He was bearded, but his hair could not hide the scars that wreathed his face. The old wounds on his cheeks left white trails through his filthy mane. The clothes that hung on his hips were encrusted rags. A chain ran from an iron collar around his neck and was linked to the ankle of his left foot. Like an old stork, he hopped on one palsied bare foot, with the other leg drawn up behind him. He tripped precariously out on the deck, leaning heavily on a gnarled stick.

Anne was appalled. "Good Lord, man. Who are you?"

The fellow said weakly, "Boyd, mum. Newgate felon."

"And where are you bound?"

"To the West Indies, they say, mum. To work the cane."

"Well, Holy Jesus, man. What did you ever do to deserve being hobbled in such a manner?"

The gaunt old man pulled back with some remnant of injured dignity. "Why, I be captain's right-hand man! Luckier than most."

Anne's eyes widened and she strode to the hatch covers and heaved on the heavy iron ring. It was stuck fast.

"George! Corner!" she called, and several of the men yanked on the hold guards until they were off. A cloud of noxious air billowed up out of the hold, forcing Anne and Mary back from the hatch.

Corner came from the deckhouse. "Anne, there's a pack more like 'em," he said, gesturing to Boyd. "All chained like hounds in there."

Anne walked to the quarterdeck and looked in the deckhouse. A dozen feeble men huddled, chained together and to themselves. Trusted deck workers, they evidently were the elite of the transported convicts.

The bowels of the ship held the rest of the prisoners like a black hell writhing with victims. The stench was overpowering in the darkness, but Anne, Mary, Tom, and several of the men managed to climb down with flares and survey the lot. There were murderers, rapists, and robbers packed in with panderers, whores, and petty thieves. Men and women, young and old, were all chained together like beasts, cowering in their own filth. Many appeared subhuman. Some had an *F* for felon branded on their foreheads. All were weak and nearly helpless with deprivation. They sprawled in the hold, barely looking up as Anne and Mary stepped cautiously down the ladder.

"Mother of God," Mary whispered. "Look at that." She pointed with her flare to the dimmest corner of the hold. Two men were shackled together, both dead, each half-rotted, half-eaten by vermin.

Anne dragged herself up the ladder, her shock slowly giving way to outrage. When she reached the top, she was livid with anger.

"We must bring them up, lads," she said tightly. "Those who can walk, shall. Those who can't will be carried to the light."

Surprisingly, not a man balked. In time those prisoners still alive were laid gently on the decks, their limbs unbound, their faces to the sun. When the pirate crew saw the full extent of the misery on this king's ship, they began to call for justice.

"String up the captain!" shouted Featherston. "Tow him behind an' let the sharks feed on his miserable carcass!"

"Ay!" came a chorus of agreement. "And the officers, too!"

Anne looked at the ship's crew, a dejected-looking line of men now slumped in the shade of the gunwales, eyeing her warily. They had made no move to help or to hinder her efforts to save those wretches in the hold. But the captain could not have done this all alone, she knew.

"No," Anne restrained her men. "Let the prisoners have them. They'll mete out their own justice."

Most of the convicts were blinded by the unaccustomed light, but they gradually grew stronger as Anne and her crew parceled out fresh water and broth. Several of the prisoners were unconscious, their misshapen limbs stretched out of joint from the rack. One was in an incoherent delirium.

"That's the ship's surgeon," Boyd whispered to Anne. "He tried to take our part, but the captain racked him as well. He banded together a mutiny, but they was too many for us."

The surgeon moaned and rolled on the deck, and Anne could see fresh and livid scars on his back where he'd been brutally whipped. Despite the torture he'd undergone, he looked less ruined than most.

"Who is he?" she asked Boyd.

"Dr. Michael Radcliffe, mum. We took him on in Bristol. Hope 'e lives."

Anne set her chin grimly. "He shall, Boyd."

She looked to the captain, still bound to the whipping post. "Though I shan't vouch for the rest."

After several hours of what care the *Queen Royal*'s provisions could provide, those prisoners left alive finally realized that they were free.

Before Anne could even direct their fury, they descended on the bound captain like frenzied wolves, tearing at him with their bare hands. One pulled out a whip, another convict grabbed a pike; within moments, the captain was a bloody, lifeless mass, his uniform in ribbons, his eyes protruding from bulging sockets in his final contortions of fear.

The men then turned to the officers, their vengeance scarcely slaked. Several crewmen jumped the gunwales into the sea rather than face the awesome torture they'd seen inflicted on the captain.

Anne knew she could not stop the senseless tide of violence, for her own crew had been infected with it as well. She gave orders for the *Jewel* to be provisioned and sent on its way, and then she and Mary gathered up the surgeon who was barely able to stumble between them and left the king's ship to its fate.

As she reached the decks of the *Queen Royal,* she looked back and saw that the mate of His Majesty's ship had been flogged nearly unconscious, then forced to squat with his head in front of the cannon mouth. As she watched, a convict touched the gun that fired and burst the man's head like a pumpkin, spattering blood, bone, and brains over the plankings.

She looked at Mary, who had not been able to tear her eyes from the scene, either. "When the pickings are few, rats turn on each other," Anne muttered. Mary grimaced, and they lowered the semiconscious surgeon belowdecks.

Unbelievably, Jack had slept through much of the afternoon's helter skelter violence and was now sitting up in bed, bleary-eyed, trying to clear his head.

Anne and Mary carried the surgeon down the passageway into Featherston's quarters and put him to bed. As the doctor fell into the bunk, he instinctively lashed out at Anne, forcing her back with his fists. He tried to rise up on one elbow; his eyes were open, dark, and haunted. But just as suddenly he fell back again and was still once more.

Anne stood and gazed at him a moment. *Even as he faces death, he refuses to give up,* she thought. *He is a warrior.*

*T*HAT NIGHT, Anne paced the decks restlessly, her thoughts roaming wide as the sea. She felt a great divide within her, an expanse of gray loneliness. There was no one to share her turbulent feelings with. Now Mary, her sister in most ways, had turned her heart to Tom's, and rightfully so.

Her thoughts were like a flighty wind blowing over barren soil. She couldn't get Jack out of her mind. How had their love turned into a lack of respect and trust? They were having a hard time just being friends. Who could tell which hand slapped first when two took up a quarrel?

Her thoughts were interrupted by the sound of whispering and mutterings close at hand. It was the sound of caballing in the night. She knew the men had gathered under the mast to air grievances, but she could not approach them. She turned resolutely away and walked to the stern.

Just as she had feared, the morning brought with it the inevitable confrontation. Gunner Harwood came forward, bearing the blackball before him like a white death notice. He held it aloft for all to see, then silently handed it to Anne. A rush of resentment swept through her. He had handed it to *her*—not to Jack. Anne glanced quickly at Jack, who kept his hands firmly on the wheel, his face turned forward. Only the clenching and unclenching of his jaw gave him away.

She nervously unfolded the letter and read: "We accuse Jack Rackham," it said, "of drunkenness and swerving from prizes. We take the ship back into our own hands and out of those of wenches unfit to man the tiller. Provisions is short, and the hold is empty."

She shook her head slightly in confusion, for the moment, unable to speak. Jack set the wheel and strode among them, snatching the paper from her hands. As far as she could tell, he was stone sober. He barely glanced at the petition, then flung it away contemptuously, turning his back to her.

He faced the crew now, and Anne could see the set of his shoulders, could sense his will rise like a banner. For an instant, she wanted to rush and hold him as she had in the dim past—for a moment, he was her old Jack. He glanced at her with a cold look, silvery with a grim strength.

"Do you think I don't know what you want, lads?" he asked grimly. "A proper ship sailed right enough, and a hold full of booty besides." He looked about at the circle of faces, never once turning to Anne. "And do you think I don't know how we got to this pretty pass, eh?"

There was a grumble from the edge of the crew, and Jack whirled on the man, ready to fight. "Ay, man! Speak up—your captain listens."

Carty mumbled sullenly, his eyes cast down. " 'Tis the wenches, Jack. Ye know as much. They's bad luck onboard. None 'as signed on no hospital ship, an' now we got bleedin' below an' our pannikins near empty from givin' it all away."

"Ay," another voice shouted, braver now. "Either lead us or leave us, Calico! An' take yer piece with ye!"

Jack grinned now, amiable as an old uncle. Anne felt her pulse quicken with rising anger, but she said nothing. "Ay, lads," Jack chuckled. "I know as much. 'Tis true, I let the wench and the rum get the best of me for a spell. As who hasn't?" He clapped the nearest man on the shoulder. "You, Corner, I seen you sotted by both in your time. And you, Earl, and you Featherston besides!" He laughed forcefully, an edge to his bray. "And who amongst ye blames me, eh?" He leered openly at Anne, almost inviting the others to do so as well.

Anne felt shocked and humiliated. They are all united now, she thought, and he'll climb out of this trough on my back!

He went on in a comradely fashion, "But I be pistol-proof yet, lads, an' I call each of you to test me. Indeed," he glowered, suddenly ominous again, "you'd have to take the ship from me, one by one. I'll lock the wench in the hold if I must, but I'll not be deposed."

" 'Tis too late for that, Jack," Corner spoke up firmly. "The lads want you out."

"And you in, Corner?" Jack whirled on him angrily. "You figure to ride the *Queen* in my stead?" He grinned evilly. "I say you don't have the spine to face my steel, lad."

Corner said quietly, "I take your challenge, Jack. 'Cause the lads will have it so."

Jack contemplated him for an instant, and Anne could not read his eyes. "Ay, then. I'll take you all, one by one, according to articles. 'Til I best you or blood your sword to the hilt."

Now that it was decided, there was a deathly hush ondecks, as each man saw a piece of what was to come. In the silence, Jack turned on Anne, and his eyes narrowed. "And you, bitch, go below. After I've shown this lot who's captain of the *Queen,* I'll show *you* as well."

Anne stifled her sharp reply, sensing that she'd find no quarter from Jack before the crew now. She held his gaze for an instant, keeping her chin steady with an effort. Then she turned on her heel, and Mary followed her below, stiff with indignation.

THEY ANCHORED IN a nearby cove, and Jack and Corner were rowed ashore in separate dinghys, each surrounded by comrades who shouted encouragement over the sounds of the surf. At the last moment, Anne leaped into one of the other boats, ignoring Jack's command to stay onboard.

She recalled their angry words of the night before. "How dare you blame me before the men for your own weakness!" she had spat. "I should've told them about your evil habits. You're even worse than they suspect—no good ondecks or in bed, for your damned pipe and grog!"

But he turned from her calmly, refusing to be ruffled. "And what would you have had me say? If they put me off without a fight, they put you off as well—both of us on some bloody barren bar to starve or worse. Now, when I best Corner, I best you as well, and you can keep your place." He grinned. "Just see that you know it."

She had whirled angrily from the cabin and gone to tend the

surgeon. He was beginning to have longer periods of consciousness, but he'd still not spoken nor recognized his surroundings. She wondered what would happen to him if she and Jack were driven from the ship.

Now, the landing party had reached the shore, and the two men strode up the beach. All hands pulled far enough back so that no one could stop the battle before it reached its final deadly conclusion.

Jack primed his pistol casually. Corner checked his sights. Harwood counted off twenty paces as the men walked away from each other, back to back. Suddenly, they turned and fired, and there was an answering screech of startled birds as a flock burst from the palms.

Anne blinked through the smoke and saw, incredibly, that both still stood unwaveringly. Each had missed. It occurred to her suddenly with a sort of blind wonder that Mary had dueled to the death for her man, yet here Anne stood, watching almost calmly, as Jack, once her lover, fought against what looked to be impossible odds.

Harwood gave a second signal, and both men yanked swords from their belts and went for each other relentlessly. They twisted and clashed, the edges of steel catching the light. Anne counted the clangs of the swords, trying to concentrate on the battle, but soon, all seemed a blur before her as sweat seeped down her forehead and into her eyes.

Corner leaped agilely about, darting away from Jack's lethal edge. Anne could see Jack's thrusts become more labored—he was making short jabs at Corner.

She closed her eyes painfully. It was high noon and the sun beat down with fierce intensity. She could not bear to watch. Both men were wounded slightly now, both seemed indifferent to their own blood, seeking only the other's. She dared not move suddenly lest she draw Jack's eye from Corner's sword.

Anne could see that Corner was weary too. He stumbled once,

twice, and in an instant, Jack had him on his back, sprawled beneath his sword. The men roared in excitement, for the moment forgetting loyalties in their lust for a bloody end.

Jack whispered something to Corner no one could hear. As Corner lay beneath him, Jack turned and walked back to the line of men on shore. He glanced once towards Anne. She could not read his look. The mood was still taut, and she did not feel the surge of relief she'd expected. The crew let out a sigh and the murmurs began. She felt her knees tremble. She yearned to sink into the sand, but stood firmly, swaying in the sun.

Jack turned to the men, hands on his hips. "Pick up your weapon, Featherston. See if you're a better man than Corner, here."

Featherston ignored Jack's taunt and turned to the men. "It's over, lads. I'd not be captain, even if I bested him."

The men murmured again, and one voice from the group called out, "One fight don't make a captain!"

Featherston growled, "Come an' take him then, if you've a mind!"

No one stirred. Finally, Harper jostled to the front of the crowd. "I will. And when I do, there be no wenches on the *Queen* save whores!" He turned to the men, expecting a cheer of approval, but they were still.

Jack barely gave Harper a glance. He was a weaselly little man who had never found his niche ondecks. Jack walked off and stood with his back to him. Harper clambered after Jack and stood behind him, grinning, his hand on his pistol.

Harwood gave the signal once more, the two men whirled on their heels, and there was a sharp crack. Anne winced at the look on Harper's face as he lurched through the smoke. He saw the moment of his death clearly, and put his hand up as if to stop its coming, his eyes white with terror. He died in bleating, bubbling shock, his hands fluttering over his chest desperately, trying to staunch the flow of his own blood.

Jack grinned and swaggered once more to the line of men. "Who's next, lads?" he asked calmly.

"It's over," Featherston said quietly. "Captain he is; captain he stays."

Anne knew that there would be muttering, but the mutiny was quelled. Jack was still pistolproof and had stemmed the rebellion. For now.

When she got back aboard the *Queen*, she embraced Mary quickly, then went below. She was relieved Jack had saved himself and her own position in the bargain. Surprised and glad that he'd shown some of his old spirit, she still did not feel the passionate gratitude she thought she might.

Anne could not forget that he had thrown her to them to save himself, however he might defend his words. She wondered, would this triumph keep him sober? How long, before he betrayed her once more? But she had little time to brood. She heard Dr. Radcliffe stirring across the passageway.

MICHAEL RADCLIFFE had spent four years in the British army; then, after achieving the rank of captain, left to become a doctor. He was skillful but unorthodox, preferring to found a clinic in Whitechapel, one of the worst slum areas of London, rather than tend to those who could best pay his bills. Tall and roughly handsome, he shunned the attention of aristocratic women who might have encouraged him and, instead, married his assistant, Barbara Teasley.

Radcliffe was tormented by his morality. On the one hand, he wanted to heal man. On the other, he was outraged by the poverty and despair he saw around him and his outrage drove him to battle those very elements in society that might have been persuaded to help his cause financially. He often insulted rich matrons who came to him for help; drawn by his reputation, they were quickly repulsed by his obvious scorn for their minor ailments.

So Radcliffe never felt quite at peace within himself, no matter how he tried to reconcile his conflict. He realized that he preferred treating those who most needed him and was aware that he suffered from the sin of pride. His wife finally convinced him that he would have to cater to those very clients he'd snubbed if he wanted to provide adequately for his future.

But, before he could set up a new practice, a pestilence ran through Whitechapel, slaying thousands. The Black Plague, carried by fleas on rats, spread like smoke through the city, felling rich and poor alike. His wife soon succumbed; Radcliffe tried in vain to save his beloved infant son, but the child died in his arms. Exhausted and ill himself, Radcliffe set fire to the house and lay for days on a cot above the clinic, not caring whether he lived or died.

Somehow, he survived. He sold what few possessions he had left, invested the proceeds in Jamaican shares, and, unable to bear the memories of London, sought passage to the West Indies.

The only carrier he could find that would take passengers from the plague-infested port was the prison ship *Jewel*, which needed a surgeon. Michael signed on.

After the ship left port, Dr. Radcliffe went about his duties mechanically, scarcely aware of his surroundings. Gradually, however, the horrors of the ship penetrated his own sorrow. Some of his old anger returned to him, and he complained to Captain Scarett about the inhuman conditions of the prisoners in the hold.

The captain smiled sourly. "I'm sorry you find our methods distasteful, Doctor. I should like to remind you, however, that we're dealing with common criminals here. If we treat them as animals, it's because they've forfeited their rights to be men."

"Only God can take away the rights of men," snapped Radcliffe.

"On this ship," Scarett replied stonily, "*I* am God."

As though to prove it, he had several of the noisier felons brought on deck. As each was shackled and roughly held by two of the officers, Scarett himself branded an *F* on the screaming convict's forehead. The smell of searing human flesh slapped Radcliffe out of his detachment, and he was vividly reminded of the pestilence in London. Infuriated, he knocked Scarett down, ripped the branding iron from his hand, and beat the two officers with it. Three of the chained deck workers attempted to join the doctor in the impromptu mutiny, but they were too small a force. Hard as they fought, they were quickly overpowered by the crew and beaten insensible.

For days Radcliffe fluctuated between oblivion and a dim, painful consciousness. Once he found himself tied to the whipping post. He could hear the swish and feel the slash of the cat o' nine. He could see Scarett bearing over him with a sneer of hatred. Then he was in the hold again, finding himself next to a corpse, the man's wretched rotting foot against his own cheek. On the rack he was hurtled back into the nightmare of reality when his arms and legs were stretched nearly out of their sockets, and his whole body quivered with pain. His mind, unable to bear such torture, retreated into darkness again.

And now, as he awoke, he was lying in a small berth in a dim passageway. He heard the creak of timbers about him and thought he was back on the *Jewel*. Yet a woman was looking anxiously down at him.

*T*HE BED, THE QUIET, and the woman seemed too improbable to Radcliffe. He closed his eyes, hoping that his mind would sort itself out. When he opened them again, she was still there. Against the dark background, she had the vivid intensity of a figure seen in a dream. Her hair was red and gold, her eyes as clear and green as the sea. She was beautiful.

Michael tried his voice. He scarcely recognized its husky whisper. "Who are you?"

"I am Anne Bonny."

Michael frowned skeptically. "The pirate?"

"Ay. You've heard of me?"

"Of course. But I expected a Medusa." He looked about the room. "Where am I?"

"The aftcastle of the *Queen Royal,* our ship."

"How did I get here?"

"We carried you. Off the decks of the *Jewel.*"

Michael nodded slowly as pieces of memory slipped into place. "And the *Jewel.* What's become of those men?"

"We turned the ship over to the prisoners. I expect they've turned to pirates by now. Or made land. At any rate, Scarett is dead as are most of his officers, I guess. And you're alive."

Michael was suddenly aware of his clean shirt, shaven cheeks, and trimmed hair. "And you've been caring for me?"

Anne smiled.

"You're an odd pirate."

"I'm a woman first and a pirate second." She wondered what prompted her to blurt out such a thing, something she'd never have confessed to in the past.

In the days that followed, Radcliffe healed quickly. He was out of bed and walking gingerly over the decks, then carefully exercising his stressed body, then doing mild chores about the ship. Anne found herself drawn to him often, to his tall leanness, to his jet hair and stubborn jaw, to his piercing blue eyes. He was not overly strong or muscled like Jack, yet he had a quiet inner strength, a sturdiness of character that attracted her attention. His voice seemed to have an authority that sounded familiar, and the keenness of his intellect made her remember, light-years before, her own love of learning. For the first time in years she felt inadequate and wished she could remember all she'd read and thought about when she was in Charles Town.

He quickly formed the habit of standing at the rail, gazing out to sea. At first she watched him from a distance, wondering what he thought, whom he remembered. Then she moved closer and asked him. He told her his story briefly, almost briskly, as though he had swept that part of himself from his mind. But she knew the pain was still raw.

"I know," Anne said quietly. "I've lost a child, too. I know the pain and anguish—" She broke off and hurried away, surprised to find herself fighting off tears for the first time in a year. It had been that long since she'd allowed herself to speak of—to think of—her babe.

Later she drew Mary to the privacy of the cabin. She thought she wanted to talk about Rackham and various problems with the crew, but instead she found herself mentioning Radcliffe repeatedly, as though he was firm in her mind's eye.

"Do you want him?" Mary suddenly asked.

Anne had not even asked herself such a question, but she knew instantly the answer. "Ay. And I want him to want me."

Mary smiled. "At last I'm able to turn your advice back in your lap, mistress. If you *want* him, have him."

Anne smiled with embarrassment. It had been a long while since she'd had a man, and she felt nervous at the prospect. More than nervous, confused and trembling. But she knew he thought her beautiful; he had said as much.

She waited, watching for the right moment. When they were next alone on deck with a full moon over the water, she went to him. She was wearing her silken red blouse, and her golden hair streamed over her shoulders. He turned to her, surprised, and before she could lose her courage, she pressed herself against him, twining her arms about his neck, gazing into his eyes. To her surprise, he chuckled low in his throat and pulled slightly away. There were nailheads of light in his dark eyes.

"You're damned intimidating, Mistress Bonny. Do you make all men feel so inept?"

She grinned, but she felt her mouth tremble. "Nearly all. To date."

He looked at her then, piercingly. "Is this a sport with you?"

She merely smiled, unsure of his meaning.

He moved away to the rail, distinctly putting some small distance between them. "It's been a good while since I've been with a woman, Anne."

"What an interesting confession." *Why* did she say that? She all but bit her lip in confusion.

He frowned slightly. "I gather this game is rather important to you."

"What do you mean?"

"Sex, Anne. Let us say the word clearly. Is that what you want from me? To tease Rackham perhaps?"

"I want from you what you wish to give."

He smiled for the first time. "I doubt that. I imagine you want what you wish to take. But you are mocking me. You have no right—no call—to do that."

"Mocking you?" Somehow this was going all wrong, not at all as she'd planned. She opened her blouse slowly, letting the roundness of her breasts show gleaming in the moonlight. Thank God it was a warm night and they were alone. "Lift your eyes and look at me, Michael. Would you not like to hold me?"

He looked at her breasts briefly, then to her face. He smiled sadly at her. "I may not be as roaring a lover as your pirate, Anne, but I'll not be your fool. When the times comes, *if* the time comes, we shall both know it. In the meantime, I'll not be toyed with like a clumsy pup. If and when I want you, it'll be in my own manner, and not at your command." He bowed shortly to her, turned from the rail, and was gone.

For a week Anne ignored him. She went from deep rage to quiet humiliation whenever she thought of his last words to her. She threw herself into her responsibilities and tried to put him from her mind. Yet in spite of the tension she felt, some small piece of her heart felt almost serene, peaceful. As if some large question had been answered forever. Somehow, she had lost. But she had won as well. One day they found themselves tugging on the same rigging, and she ventured to break her silence.

"We could use a surgeon, Michael." She glanced at him. He was listening attentively as if the silence of the past week had never been.

"Ay, even a leader. Rackham's only a figurehead, you know." She kept her eyes from his, not trusting herself to look at him directly. "In time you could be captain of the *Queen Royal*, Michael."

The idea seemed to amuse Radcliffe. "I can't think of anything with less purpose than piracy. When I fight, it's for something with meaning. When I destroy, I would hope it's to rebuild something better. Not just to lay waste."

Anne tightened and her temper flamed her face, making her eyes flash. "You think *I* have no purpose in life? That I'm a wanton destroyer?"

He took her arms, sensing that only by touching her could he calm her, and said quietly, "I think you must be yourself, Anne, and I must be as I am. We both have storms in us which blow in different directions."

"Then the sooner they blow us apart, the better!" She jerked free of his hands and strode off the deck.

Suddenly Rackham lurched into view. He'd been lounging in the shade of the rigging and had overheard their conversation. He was not drunk, but his hands shook and his eyes were bleary, as if the rum lived in him still.

"Beware of that one," he muttered to Michael as he came unsteadily forward, grasping for the rail. Anne turned, her anger still hot, in time to hear him add, "She'll destroy you. And you'll not be the first man she's done for."

"Yours would seem to be self-destruction, Rackham," Michael replied firmly and turned to hurry after Anne, who had fled to the cabin.

He found her in the aftcastle, still seething.

"You can rage all you like, Anne. I'll not be blown away by

your temper. And I'll not let you win an argument by striking and running."

She tried to twist away, but he held her fast by the shoulders. "Your temper leaps too quickly, Anne. It blinds you to the truth."

"Your truth, you mean."

He smiled. "Yes, my truth. It's important to me that you see it."

She stopped at the tone in his voice, hearing something unsaid beneath his words. She waited.

"You *can* change your mind, Anne. You can change your life. Always, until the last breath, you have that choice. You *must* choose, or you'll destroy yourself."

She frowned prettily. "I don't understand."

He pulled her closer to him. "You've overplayed your luck in this life. Choose another."

"And what other life would you suggest?"

"One with purpose."

"How? Where? I'm hunted over every sea."

"There's no such thing as a problem, Anne, that doesn't reveal its own solution. In fact, some would say that each snare in life brings a gift of sorts—hidden in its hands. And you seek that problem because you need those gifts. But you don't need this anymore. Do you? The how will reveal itself. As to the where, you've the whole New World to choose from. Why, I was on my way to Jamaica—"

She broke in with a bitter laugh. "They'd hang me as high as the moon in Jamaica."

"Well, then, choose another place. Some other island, if you're so set on the sea. Or if not, there's all of America waiting, virgin as a new dream. We could find a safe place where no one's heard of Anne Bonny, pirate."

Again, Anne was struck silent by his words. "We," he had said. Her mind grasped for assurance, not daring to risk another rejection.

He reached up slowly, brushed an errant lock of hair from her cheek, and then traced the line of her chin to her lips. She felt a quick thrill run through her. Her skin seemed to glow from within, and she flushed and lowered her eyes, suddenly, inexplicably shy.

"I know now what it is with you and Rackham. You're old lovers. Sometime friends."

"Who told you?" She found her voice.

"I have eyes, Anne. I see you sleep alone."

"I have for some time—"

He stopped her with a finger on her lips. "I don't need to know."

She stood still, waiting. Slowly, he drew her to him until his lips were a few inches from hers. I want you, said his eyes, but his lips were still.

She could feel the warmth of his breath, sense the tidal current that ran between them. Still she waited, her eyes half-closed. An inch now, barely an inch apart. Finally she murmured softly, "Is it time?"

He smiled slightly, his eyes warm, his lips almost on her own. "Only if you wish it as well."

Her lips hovered under his, still not touching, her body braced against his own. "Tell me," she whispered throatily.

His voice was husky but sure. "I want you."

At that, she felt her body go liquid and she kissed him, pressed against him until she could feel no difference between his heartbeat, his pulse, and her own.

They were interrupted in their embrace by Mary, who rounded the corner to the aftcastle and nearly stumbled into them in the gloom.

She grinned. "So here you are."

"Ay," Anne said, pulling gently from Michael's arms. She smiled at Mary's obvious pleasure.

"I hate to plague you, but it looks like bad weather blowing up. We'd best put into St. Catherine."

Anne agreed quickly and went on deck. She felt like leaping into the rigging and trumpeting her joy to the world, but she contented herself with a quiet smile and the measured activity it took to maneuver the *Queen Royal* into the harbor of St. Catherine.

While the crew caroused in the tavern ashore, Anne and Michael explored the tropical island hand in hand. They walked the palm-lined beaches, climbed the green slopes into the interior, and pushed through tangles of thorn bush and seagrape, searching for secret hidden beauty, imagining themselves the first to see it. Laughing, like children in a new world, they crawled through a maze of mangroves and emerged on a grassy bank overlooking the sea.

The sun was out, hot and strong, and the water was brilliant with color.

"The storm has passed us, I suppose. The sky's clear," Anne said.

Michael took her hand, playing gently with her fingers. "In a way, I'm sorry. Storms can be exciting."

Anne laughed, grasping his hands firmly. "Not at sea, Doctor. The *Queen*'s been lucky. She's never been taken by hard winds. We've always run for land in time."

"Perhaps that's the problem. For all their fine talk of bravery, I wager piracy is one of the least courageous trades I know."

"What?" She pulled away her hand but still grinned at him. "Don't let *those* louts hear you, Michael. They'll cut your throat to prove their courage."

He laughed. "Takes no courage to cut throats, Anne. Takes courage to stand on a piece of land and make it produce a living, day after day. Takes courage to pit yourself against the rest of the world and win by cunning and superior skills. But to lie in wait and steal it from those who've earned it, that takes no courage at all. Daring, maybe, but not real courage."

Her smile was fading now. "You sound mighty smug, Michael. You must not think highly of me, then, to speak so."

"I guess I do sound arrogant. That's my failing, and I know it." He looked at her intently. "What do you think of yourself?"

She answered quickly, "The world takes me for a pirate. And a bold one at that."

"The world can't judge men fairly, much less women. Men'll judge women on less evidence than they'd used to hang a dog. So your reputation means naught, Anne. What's *your* opinion of yourself?"

She turned her eyes away, briefly, thinking. When she finally answered, it was with a tinge of bewilderment, even sadness. "I remember at home . . . at Bellefield"—she turned back to him—"when Gillah wanted a chicken for the pot, she never just grabbed one and chopped off his head on a block. When I asked her why, she said it gave him too much time to think. Instead, she poured a teaspoon of rum down his beak, 'til he was besotted and unsuspecting, and then twisted off his head. But by then, he didn't give a damn about his fate. She said he died happy, and that was more than happened to most people." Suddenly her eyes filled with tears, and she reached blindly for his hand again. "I have felt, often, like that chicken. Rushing to die happy. Yet often, I feel I haven't even lived. As if my life's been one of waiting. Waiting for something to begin." She straightened and brushed invisible tears from her eyes, her face calm again. "But I've always believed I was a match for life. I still do."

He smiled gently at her. "As do I. I've never known a woman of such heart. Why you've gone dashing madly after death, I'll never know. You were made for life."

He drew her to her feet, and she noticed the horizon. Dark clouds had rolled towards the sun as they spoke, and rain was imminent. She went into his arms and suddenly rain began to pelt down. Laughing, they ran for cover. Higher up a small slope, they found a cave. They had to crouch to get inside, but it had a comfortable moss floor and was shelter from the storm.

"I'm wet clear through!" Anne laughed, shaking the rain from her hair. Then she stared at him, suddenly serious.

He reached for her urgently, pulling her into his arms. He pressed the small of her back, then lowered his hands to her buttocks, cupping them gently, fitting himself to her body.

"Anne, you are so lovely." He lowered his mouth to her throat, murmuring against her skin. "You know how I've wanted you."

"Yes," she whispered, "yes, and I you."

He put his hands under her rib cage and lifted her until her arms dangled about his neck, her eyes level with his own. He kissed her deeply then, his mouth gently probing hers, his hands strong and urgent on her body. He put his lips to her hair, whispering.

"But I wanted to give us time. I didn't know you...well enough to love you."

"And now?" she breathed.

"And now, I know you're more beautiful within than without." He kissed her again, kissed her insistently until she felt her stomach roll under her heart convulsively and her loins tremble. "I love you, Anne. Can you love me?"

For answer, she pulled his head again to hers, pulled his lips to hers, her voice sobbing deep in her throat. "I have. Oh, Michael, I do."

Her mind briefly tugged at her. So much time had passed since she'd allowed herself to be touched and possessed. Or had she ever, really? She had often imagined herself in his arms, naked beneath him, then atop him, and these sweet thoughts were pale ghosts to the reality of him holding her now.

She came back to the moment when she realized that Michael's eyes were wet with emotion, and she was moved to a tenderness she'd never known. She kissed his eyes, his cheeks, his throat. He slowly untied her blouse, and she shrugged it off.

"Your breasts are like warm moons," he said softly and lowered his mouth to her erect nipples, tugging at them gently. "So soft," he murmured. She sighed, and he slipped off her breeches and knelt before her. He saw a welt of scar tissue along her leg and it hurt him to think of the pain she'd endured. He tenderly kissed the line of puckered skin, and he felt her stiffen. He wanted to tell her that she was beautiful, perfect, and did so with his hands, his lips. He moved his fingers up her legs, over the curves of her calves, the taut muscles of her thighs, until he reached the glossy red pubic brush and the hairs tendriled against his face. He stood and cupped her buttocks in his hands, gently kneading her taut flesh, and she moved against him. Anne felt his kiss deeply in her belly and when it ended she said, "Please hurry. Now."

He quickly stripped off his clothes and laid her down naked next to him on the mossy cave floor. He took her in his arms, murmuring her name, and she knew for the first time the exquisite pleasure of his whole body next to hers with nothing between them.

After a while, but long before he actually entered her, she felt her mind melting into his, felt him moving inside her heart, her soul, as if they were one creation, blending in some secret understanding that needed no more words than sighs, no more signals than indecipherable whispers, whispers that moved her body in a private dance only for him.

Only after did she realize that he had whispered, murmured, moaned to her throughout their pleasure, urging her, never once letting his mind drift from the fact of her, indeed, loving only her each instant, feeling only her with each touch. She felt a tremendous tide of tenderness and affection and need achingly sweep through her, and she knew that she would never be able to let him go.

LATER THEY LAY side by side in the moss, holding hands, heartbeats gradually easing. Anne was physically and emotionally wrung by her feelings. Michael had given her much more than sexual pleasure; she had felt something else, something new to her, something splendid and powerful that was beyond any words she knew to describe it. There was a tenderness about him, a quality of mercy that made her feel entirely safe—and yet completely free to be herself. And with his tenderness, there was no weakness. Unlike any man she'd ever known, Michael felt like the one man who might be worth the risk of letting go completely. Of trusting.

He rolled on his side, facing her. He kissed her throat, her cheek.

"What are you thinking?" he asked.

"Of you. Of me," she answered truthfully. She tried to ease herself up, but he pulled her knees out from under her and, giggling, she fell back into his arms.

"I'm not at all sure I can walk," she gasped.

He grinned. "Then I'll carry you. Isn't that what love is?"

Her heart paused infinitesimally at his mention of love, but she laughed low in her throat. "I no longer know what love is. But I do know it's got nothing to do with carrying each other." She looked about the cave, feeling with one hand while the other held him tightly.

"Do you see my breeches?"

"They melted."

She laughed gleefully and pulled herself over on top of him, climbing him, molding to him like a wet, warm glove. She wriggled until she could feel his skin stick to hers.

He moaned as he laughed. "You are absolutely disgusting."

"I know," she chortled. "Isn't it wonderful? Do you think it will stop?"

"Not for a few days at least."

"Rutting cad," she murmured, and kissed him deeply, wetly, and he was in her once more.

Later she lay in his arms, once again quiet.

"How wonderful it is to laugh. With you." She stretched, content and comfortable.

He leaned up on one elbow and gazed into her eyes. "It's the most intimate thing I know, and I'd forgotten that. You made me remember."

"I?"

"Ay," he grinned. "I'm always trying to change the world. You know how to live in it." He hesitated just an instant. "Anne, I cannot let you go. Not back to the sea. Not away from me."

"Does one necessarily have to mean the other?" She smiled and rolled over him once more, her chin on his chest. "I'm so happy, it's hard to be serious."

He chuckled. "Then I shall simply plague you with my question morning and night until you answer."

"What question?"

"Will you be my wife?"

She stopped, suddenly startled into silence. Sadness creased her forehead as she remembered, against her will. "I already have a husband," she said, her voice low.

"It doesn't matter. He is husband in name only. We will find a way, if you're willing. If you want it. Do you want me, Anne?"

"Oh, Michael." She turned back to him again. "With my life. Would you actually marry a pirate?"

"No." He smiled. "But I will a woman." He took her chin in his hands and looked into her eyes. "Could you give it up, Anne? Could you choose a new life? With me?"

She saw, in a brief eye of calm, what she wanted. This man offered a merging, a partnership of mutual respect, a willingness to lead and be led, to adore, to magnify and drink in each other's strength instead of resenting or attacking it. There would be no testing this man, no games. And she felt a flood of white relief fill her eyes and her heart. She was ready to leave the pirate life . . . but not without one final understanding.

"My love, I'm ready to choose a new life. But not a new me. I will always be an outlaw."

He pulled away slightly and frowned. "Do you mean a criminal?"

"No. I mean an outlaw. Like a dolphin is an outlaw of the sea. A shark is a criminal. I mean someone who lives outside the law, who goes over walls, who's free. Who chooses uncertainty over security, who takes disorder and surprise and magic over righteousness."

"And if you're captured?"

"I won't go quietly. Besides, I won't be captured if I give up the trade. I can only be punished by attitudes—just as your attitudes are punishing me now."

"Mine?"

"Ay. I will and can give it up, but only once you understand that I do so because it no longer pleasures me...."

He reached for her and held her tightly for an instant.

She pulled away and looked at him seriously. "You talk of my luck running out, Michael. It will only when I stop stirring the stew of my life and settle into someone else's view of what I should be. The world loves a cage, I've found. And I can't live in one."

He kissed her softly. "And I'll not ask you to. I'd be a fool to try to smother that fire of joy in you." He grinned. "Especially when I need to warm my own soul at its flame." He tilted her chin up to him. "I ask you again, Anne. Will you marry me?"

She hesitated barely a jot. "Ay, Michael. I will. Somehow."

*T*HE NEXT MORNING Anne reluctantly walked with Michael back to the settlement. The pirates were taking a small boat over to Cuba for a cache of turtles and other provisions. Michael agreed to go, since he needed medicinal supplies.

"You and Mary get the *Queen* ready for sail," he said to Anne gently, kissing her.

"To where?" Anne was ready to leave, but she knew of no place where they could retire safely.

"When I'm in Cuba I'll scout out a likely spot." He held her face in his hands. "I take you with me, Anne. Everywhere I go."

It was agreed that Tom Deason should stay with Anne and Mary to help bring clothing ashore to air and to help organize the rest of the crew for sail. Rackham and five other pirates were holed up in St. Catherine's only tavern, too drunk to move. Michael and ten of the crew set off across the isthmus for Cuba, and Anne stood on shore waving until she could no longer see the dinghy.

As Anne and Mary then worked to ready the *Queen Royal*, the blue sky was beginning to be mottled by leprous, altocumulus clouds. Anne paused on the beach, watching the sky blacken.

"My God!" she called to Mary. "The storm is on us!"

An ominous stillness hovered over the island. Mary came to her side and began to pull her towards the settlement.

Suddenly there was a great rushing wind that quickly swelled to hurricane savagery. Palm trees bent about Anne as she struggled to the bushes for protection. The sea was whipped to a seething frenzy before her eyes, and torrents of rain lashed down. The whole world seemed suddenly to have become the belly of a gray-black, heaving, striking monster.

"Michael will be lost!" Anne shrieked over the roar of the wind. She, Mary, and Tom fought their way to the trees. "We must help him!" she called frantically, looking out over the towering waves.

"Don't be insane!" shouted Mary, her face contorted by the pressure of the wind. "You can't even walk on land, let alone sail out to sea!"

To add to the force of her words, a sudden gust of wind shoved Anne to the sand. Mary clung to a tree trunk, and Tom snatched her arm, pulling her towards shelter. "Get to the tavern!" he yelled. "To the cellar!"

It was all Tom and Mary could do to drag Anne from the beach. Her hair whipped about her face like wild vines, and she moaned low in her throat, fighting first the wind, then her own fear. They half-carried, half-dragged her to the settlement, then pulled her down into the tavern cellar, where everyone else on the island had taken shelter against the sudden hurricane.

Rackham looked up at her as she staggered in, her eyes wild and her face white with pain and shock. Anne scarcely recognized him, so intent was she on Michael's fate. She wailed, half to herself, half aloud, "He'll be drowned. Oh, Jesus, Michael! Michael!"

Rackham turned his back to her, curled into a dark corner, and waited out the storm. And the wind moaned as if it too had lost a mate.

After countless hours, the gale subsided. Anne had quieted herself by sheer force of will, refusing to lose hope. She sensed without knowing that Michael was probably lost. But there was a slim chance that the pirates had seen the storm in time to row the small dinghy to the protection of some island or sheltered cove. She twisted her memories this way and that, trying to think of any possible shelter in their path, but could picture only sea. It was open water between St. Catherine and Cuba, and unless they'd had phenomenal luck or foresight, the dinghy was destroyed and all hands lost. She slept fitfully that night, tormented by blurred images of Michael and the sea, of his caresses, of his hand waving slowly to her from the boat, of the shriek of the storm, and the toss of the black waves.

By morning she was exhausted but determined to find him. It had all happened so quickly. In a matter of hours, she'd found love, consummated it, committed herself to it, and lost it. Even as she tended to the physical realities of seeing to the *Queen Royal* and readying a small rescue boat, her mind seemed vague and numbed as if coming from a deep sleep. At one instant she stopped and stared at her hand, pricked by the rope splinters of the line that lowered a second dinghy to the water. It was as if her body were separated completely from her head and moved by the will of some mechanical force within her, unconscious of the delirium of her mind.

Featherston and Corner readied the ship for sail, while Anne went off with Tom, Mary, and John Davies, the mate, to find any survivors. As they rowed vigorously, Anne watched the sea and the sky for some possible clues to Michael's fate. The air was sullen and gray, and the waves still had not calmed completely. The sea seemed fitful and angry, slapping at the sides of the dinghy in restless provocation, as if still looking for a fight. As if it hadn't had enough, Anne thought.

As they rounded the back of the island, they saw bits of wreckage on shore and rowed quickly to examine it. Anne raced out of the waves and to the sand, gathering up bits of wood and oar.

Trembling, she called out, "Michael! Jeff! Harris!" She could not think of the names of the other crew members who had gone along. "Michael!" She cast wildly up and down the beach, peering under foliage, expecting at any instant to find his body. But she found nothing but more wreckage, mute testimony that the dinghy from the *Queen Royal* had been battered on the reef and thrown mercilessly on shore. Perhaps on several shores, for there was scarcely enough wood on the sand to make a third of a skiff. Mary came to her and embraced her, murmuring words of comfort that Anne scarcely understood.

Tom called from the beach. Anne unconsciously pushed Mary aside and ran down the sand and saw, there in a tidepool, the body of Harris Simon, the gunner taken from the *Prudent Hannah*. He was dredged with sand and seaweed; his face was calm and still. If there had been any room for hope, it was gone now. Michael could not have survived such a storm. He had not been plucked by some provident hand from the sea and somehow saved. He was lost.

As the realization hit Anne completely like a fist to her chest, she sank to the sand on her knees, still holding the pieces of wood she'd picked from the beach. Silently at first, and then with shrieks to rival the storm winds, she wept for the second time in her life until her throat was as seared as her heart.

For two days Anne and her companions scoured the coast of Cuba, hunting for Michael. She felt she must find him, must see for herself that he was dead before she could begin to rebuild her life. But she was denied even that small ending. He was nowhere to be found. There were other bodies and wreckage flung on the beaches, but no sign of life. No footprints, no discarded clothing, no smoke or signal fires. And no body. Nothing. Michael had disappeared into the sea as completely as rain, leaving not a trace.

Mary finally pulled her gently away.

Anne sat in the dinghy as they rowed, staring out over the waves. She was dry-eyed now but still in shock. The sea, her refuge, her favorite haven, had stolen the only person in the world she loved. She did not believe in ghosts or fate, but she could not help cursing the water's placid green depths and cursing too the life that had led her to such desolation. As she had once before, she felt a terrible void, a lifelessness in her heart. A dull, aching apathy possessed her, and she barely responded to Mary's gentle proddings.

"Don't despair, Anne. Michael would not have wanted you to forsake life for him."

"What Michael wanted was for me to give up this life. To leave the sea and be his wife." Mary looked at her, surprised and silent. "And I would have too, Mary. But now I don't give a damn. It doesn't matter how I die."

Back on St. Catherine, she withdrew into herself. The other pirates, lacking a real leader, were undecided about which course to plot. Of the original crew, only nine were left. Featherston, Corner, and Rackham were the only real possibilities for captain, yet no man seemed able or interested to mount the effort it would take to get the *Queen* out to sea once more.

Rackham was still ostensibly the pirate chief, but he was so inconsistent that few seriously suggested that he return to full command. Finally, Mary pulled Anne aside.

"We must get off the island," she urged. "There's no real provisions left, and the men must be led. There's murmurings already, against you and Rackham and Corner and all. If they leave, we may be stuck here until we're captured."

Anne stared at her silently. "So?" she finally said. "What would you have me do?"

Mary snapped at her. "I'd have you care whether you lived or died!" She took her by the shoulders. "You must go on, Anne. I too lost a love, but it comes again. As it will for you."

Anne turned away, disgusted. "Do as you wish. You lead the men. I've no more taste for it."

"Lead them aboard what? The *Queen* is too heavy for a crew of nine."

Anne's pain turned to rage. "I don't care! Don't you understand? Stay or go, it matters not to me! Steal a turtler if you wish and leave me!"

Mary turned from her in silence. Two nights later she led a secret raid to the settlement and stole a small sloop. Ignoring Anne's alternating lassitude and anger, she shoved her aboard, and Mary and Tom took over command of the little vessel, aided by Featherston and Corner.

That night, as Anne lay languishing in a tiny berth belowdecks, sullenly picking at a meager meal, Rackham lurched below and confronted her.

"So you've lost your gentleman then," he muttered, ignoring her glare. "What'll you do now?"

She had a moment, an instinctive jolt of fear moving through her like cold honey, when she wanted to run to Jack and hide inside his arms. But they were not the arms she remembered. And neither was he the man. He seemed so cold, so shielded from her now. As she hesitated, he prodded her.

"Eh? Speak up, lass. You've lost your usual fire. What's it to be? A new ship? A new life?" He almost sneered. "A new man?"

The rage surged back in her mind and made her stronger. "I'll not be sharing your berth again, if that's what you mean."

He flashed her a tight smile, a ghost of the grin she'd known from that brown robust face a lifetime ago. "Who asked you?"

He turned on his heel and stumbled down the hatchway, rolling with the movement of the ship in a practiced gait. He was not drunk this night. And still they had nothing to say to each other. Whatever they had once had been poisoned by jealousy, suspicion, and contempt. Whatever physical charms drew him to her before had no lure for him now, she knew. And she wasn't even sorry. She only regretted that they must fret against each other always, even now, when she most needed a friend.

For the month of August the pirate sloop, new-christened the *Providence*, moved erratically about the Caribbean without purpose. Because of the sloop's small size, there were few prizes they could take comfortably. Finally, later in the month, the once formidable Rackham crew was reduced to taking a small fishing boat off Jamaica simply for food. The pirates stole a load of fish, turtles and rum, but those provisions did not last long.

In early September they raided a fishing village on Harbour Island, again seeking food. After herding a half-dozen fishermen and their families into one of the huts, Corner and Featherston plundered the squalid settlement. While Mary and Tom and the rest of the crew stripped several boats in the harbor of any spare coin, Anne kept watch on the *Providence*.

She joined them later, at Mary's insistence, and they surprised Dorothy Thomas, a village woman, rowing home in a canoe full of fresh provisions she'd bought from a nearby plantation. She too lost her cargo to the crew. Their total booty was four pigs, six chickens, several large fish, a barrel of yams, a can of salt, and a few loaves of bread.

With at least enough food to fill their bellies for a few days, the sloop crossed to Hispaniola, seeking more lucrative prey. After a week of hunting, they were once more forced ashore to kill wild cattle for food. That evening they were hauling the carcasses to the beach for a feast when they spied a battered ship limping into the cove.

The ship was a trading sloop carrying no cargo, as they soon discovered, and the pirates magnanimously offered to share half their beef for half the visitors' rum.

Around the campfire, one of the traders addressed Mary Read as "Mistress Bonny."

Mary laughed and said, "You've made an error, man. That's Mistress Bonny." She pointed to Anne, who had withdrawn from the circle and sat alone at the fringe of light.

The trader scoffed. "That silent one? I would have expected more sound and fury from such a pirate!"

"She's changed much of late," answered Mary.

The trader lowered his voice. "Because of the death of her husband, James Bonny?"

Mary was startled. "No! She doesn't know! Where? When?"

"In the Bahamas. His turtling boat was lost to the hurricane, and his body washed up at New Providence."

Mary quickly went to Anne and told her the news, hoping it might stir Anne to some emotion, either good or bad. But Anne merely shrugged.

"It scarcely matters. If such news had come while Michael had lived...Now..."

The traders brought other news from New Providence. Governor Rogers was all but bankrupt, had used up all his own funds, and the lords proprietors in England had ignored his urgent requests for aid. The colony was dissolving quickly, and there was talk of another pardon.

"He'll never do it," said Mary. "But if he did, I'd consider the offer."

Tom laughed. "Cheer up, lads. Perhaps our luck will change with the tide. Lord knows, it can't get worse."

Some of the crew of the trading vessel opted for joining the pirates with little persuasion, and so with larger numbers the rovers were able to sail again with renewed determination. They again crossed the Caribbean and pulled a series of raids on a schooner, two trading sloops, and several fishing settlements off Jamaica. Only the schooner taken near Porto Maria bay turned out to contain anything of value. The master, Thomas Spenlow, was relieved of a gold watch and a bag of coins.

"You'll rue this day!" Spenlow raged at the pirates. "I'll live to see you hanged!"

Anne watched from the deck as they sailed off, a cold shiver coursing up her spine. The time had come to leave the crew. She resolved to watch for a likely port and slip off as soon as she could. She did not relish her farewell, for she would miss Mary, Tom, Jack, and the others. But there was little for her now. Little for any of them.

THOMAS SPENLOW complained directly to Governor Lawes in Jamaica of this latest harassment and demanded the capture of Rackham's gang. Lawes was tired of having his pride pricked by the Bonny female and doubly incensed that she had the temerity to cruise his waters. He recruited a young navy captain, Charles Barnet, and outfitted him with a sleek, heavily armed sloop flying no official flags or other government markings. Hidden in the bow of the sloop were two four-pounders and a well-armed crew.

Barnet's sloop wound its way along the coast, searching every cove and inlet for the *Providence*, which happened to be anchored off Negril Point. The pirates had just taken a turtling boat which carried four barrels of rum.

The crew immediately broke open the barrels and invited the fishermen to share in their own liquor. The party went on all night and into the next day, October 21. By then all of the pirates except Anne, Mary, and Tom Deason were either sprawled on deck or huddled in the hold below, insensible with rum.

The fishermen managed to totter back to their boat, hoist anchor, and sail. As they rounded the point, they were stopped by Barnet's sloop.

"You're too late!" the skipper called out. "Some other pirates already took us!" He laughed ironically at his own poor luck.

Captain Barnet leaned over the rail and shouted, "What pirates?"

The master gestured vaguely back up the coast. "Offshore there, drunk as lords on my rum!"

Cautiously, Barnet sailed his sloop around the point. When he sighted the pirate craft, he quickly marked the strength and the direction of the wind, which was brisk and blowing offshore. He then swung about in closer to the coast and moved up toward the *Providence*.

Mary was the first to notice the strange ship's approach.

"What's that?" she asked Anne, pointing.

Tom picked up a glass and surveyed the moving ship. "It's just a sloop. Looks harmless enough. What do you think, Anne?"

Anne shaded her eyes and looked out across the bay. "I guess Tom's right," she said with a marked lack of interest. "It looks harmless enough."

But Mary was not appeased. She checked her pistols, glanced at the pirates sprawled on the deck, and said, "We'd better rouse these drunken dogs." She kicked Rackham, who was slumped near an empty barrel. "Get up, Jack! There's a sail heading for us!"

Rackham merely grunted. Mary kicked him again. "Get up, I say!"

Jack blearily opened one eye. "Why are you tormenting me, wench?"

Mary wasted no time with arguments but began to kick the other pirates awake. "Get up, you rum-soaked sots! Get up!"

Two of the four pirates lying on deck stirred only feebly. The others angrily protested, and Mary, arguing with them, did not notice Barnet's sloop as it suddenly swung about, caught the direct force of the breeze, packed on full sail, and came swooping towards them.

"It's an attack!" Tom shouted.

The battle cry snapped Anne out of her lethargy. For just a moment she was her old self. "Everyone to the rails!" she ordered. "Repel boarders! Break out swords!"

She dashed across the deck and snatched up a cutlass for herself. At the same time, Barnet's sloop let fly with its two cannons. The solid shot hit the mast, which fell, striking Anne a glancing blow on her shoulder, knocking her down, and tangling her in the rigging. The crash brought the pirates to their feet, but most were panicked and confused and scuttled for the hold.

At the rail, Tom was the only pirate in position to repel the boarders, now only a few yards away. One of the navy sharp-shooters took careful aim and shot a musket ball whistling into Tom's chest. He was dead before he even slumped to the deck.

Mary ran to him, screaming. She stood up abruptly, staring at Barnet's sloop in disbelief. Then she raced over the deck in a wide-eyed fury.

"You cowards!" she shrieked, running to the open hatch where most of the crew had stumbled.

Anne meanwhile called to Mary, kicking her way from the rigging, slashing the cords with her cutlass. Mary fired both her pistols into the hatch shouting, "You yellow dogs! You bastards! You've killed him!" Anne heard Jack scream from inside the hold, "My leg! You bitch!"

Anne sprang to Mary and yanked her to her senses. They each turned to face the boarders, cutlasses in their hands. But they were too late. Barnet's men were already over the gunwales. Anne fought bravely, glancing once over to Mary who battled for her life, her face contorted in grim rage. In moments they were overpowered.

With her cheek bleeding and her shoulder burning with pain, Anne was brusquely shackled, her arms twisted behind her. As she and Mary were led off the ship, she looked back to see the rest of the crew, Rackham among them, meekly climbing out of the hold, their hands on their heads in surrender.

PART FIVE

~~~~~~

Port Royal, Jamaica, 1720

Where there is great love, there are always miracles.

ANONYMOUS

PORT ROYAL SIMMERED in the sun like a vat of rancid oil, and the stench of the clogged harbor reminded Anne of her early days at New Providence. Infamous as the "most wicked city in the world," Port Royal boasted more brothels than Paris and more ragged, malformed urchins than the seamiest slums of London.

The merciless tropical sun glared down on Anne as she was roughly shoved from His Majesty's sloop to the dock. She stumbled against Mary, who stood sullen and silent and bound in chains at the edge of the water. Anne moved her wrists cautiously, easing her own shackles past chafed flesh to a spot of less-raw skin.

The short passage from Negril Point to Port Royal on this side of the island had been brutal but mercifully quick. She and Mary were kept in the deckhouse, guarded by six of His Majesty's tars, bound hand and foot in the stifling darkness. There was dried blood on Mary's arm where she had taken a cutlass swipe, and Anne's head throbbed with the blow she'd caught from the mast. The last time she saw Jack, he was being hustled belowdecks on Barnet's sloop, his hands at his head, his mouth twisted in grim fear.

So they were taken at last. She was still shocked by the sudden capriciousness of their capture. Just as she'd resolved to leave the trade and go honest, that's when fate, laughter up its sleeve, delivered her into the hands of her enemies. She grimaced, silently cursing her luck. Anne glanced around, as she had twenty times in the past two hours, for any possible means of escape.

The rest of the crew was being shoved off the sloop now, and Rackham, Featherston, Corner, Davies, and the rest stumbled to the dock. Anne glanced once more at Mary, but she seemed oblivious to her condition. She only stood and gazed at the sea behind Barnet's sails. The guards smartly cracked those of the crew who attempted to speak to one another; together, they were brusquely herded to waiting tumbrels on the shore. Anne felt Jack look at her once, twice, but she did not return his glance.

Anne and Mary were pushed into one cart with wooden stakes set all about as bars. The rest of the crew were loaded into the back tumbrel. Armed seamen, king's men all, walked on both sides of the slowly moving carts and Anne stared out at the city.

The sun grew stronger as they made their way down the rutted dirt road away from the harbor. Port Royal looked surprisingly cramped, drab, and colorless, given its reputation, Anne thought. The buildings were squat, ugly huts of limestone and mud. Only three were in any sense imposing: Near the waterfront was a church with a gilded spire, and across town, where Anne knew the aristocracy, government officials, and wealthy planters made their homes, a three-story building made of imported brick shone pinkly in the sun. That must be King's House, she guessed, the official residence of Sir Nicholas Lawes when he's in port. But most imposing of all was the Citadel, a grim fortress erected on a promontory overlooking the harbor. Twelve cannons placed at intervals in a thick stone wall literally hung out over the water, and sentinels in scarlet uniforms marched stiff-legged on the catwalks, their muskets gleaming.

Above the city and its fortress, Anne could see the Blue Mountains and green patches of the Liguanea Plain, a grassy rising plateau where busy cane workers dotted the fields. She turned and gazed back at the harbor as the tumbrels creaked up to the center of the town, wondering if she would ever feel the roll of sea beneath her feet again.

There was more traffic than usual on High Street, and Anne guessed their arrival had been anticipated. A handful of trollops stopped to stare as the two carts lurched slowly by, shouting taunts and catcalls. A few blacks lounged in the shade of a banyan tree, and a family of goats, led by a scraggly male with a gnarled goatee, pranced sedately in single file down the dusty road. A little girl of perhaps ten or eleven, showing blends of Negro and Arawak blood in her face, was crouched beside a wicker basket that held a few withered bananas and pineapples. As the carts approached, she smiled and held up the basket, exposing two painfully thin arms beneath her rags. One of the lead guards growled at her to get out of the way and slapped at her basket, knocking the fruit to the ground. She stared malevolently at the cart, then picked up a banana in each hand, hurled them violently at Anne and Mary, and ran off, her bare feet flashing pink in the sun.

The fruit spatted dully against the bars of the cart and fell to the hay, startling Mary briefly out of her daze. Anne reached for her hand, squeezed it tightly, and searched her face for some recognition, some semblance of her old defiance.

"Mary, he never felt a thing. At least he died fast."

Mary pulled out of her blank fixed stare long enough to look penetratingly at Anne. "Ay." She glanced over her shoulder to the cart behind her, the pirates all shackled together, their heads sunk on their chests in a dismal cluster. "I wager *we* won't." And then she pulled back into herself, closing her eyes in a tight line.

Anne could feel Mary willing everything away from her—the heat, the dust, the entrapment, the degradation, the fear, even Anne herself. Anne thought briefly of Michael, grateful at least that he was not alive to witness her so humbled.

THE GAOL AT Port Royal was built into the side of the cliff, a subterranean labyrinth of dank rat holes and cold stone. Each cell was cramped and sour, furnished only with a clay pot or two for waste, two stark wooden benches, and a few vermin-infested rags for blankets. There was no window and the only light through the thick bars came from smoky, flickering lanterns in the corridors.

Anne and Mary were hauled down the dirt passageways to a small cell, stripped roughly of their shackles, and prodded inside. Mary leaned against the stone wall and rubbed her wrists absently. Anne paced back and forth before the bars.

"Goddamn them to hell!" Anne finally spat, enraged all over again when she thought of the cowardice, the almost abject surrender of the crew.

She stopped and listened, her ears already more attuned in the dim light. Someone was approaching. Suddenly the door opened and a burly guard threw in two bowls and a flask of water, sloshing the liquid over the dirt floor, making rivulets of mud at their feet.

" 'Ere's dinner, ladies!" He laughed viciously as he sauntered back to the corridor.

Anne waited until his footsteps died away and then leaned down to inspect their food. "They must be planning to hang us soon, for they're sure not wasting good victuals on us."

The water was cool and fresh, but the bowls held nothing but a few hunks of brown bread and two overripe bananas.

"You can have my portion." Mary turned away in disgust.

Anne sat at her side and methodically began to eat the bread, tearing off small chunks, mashing banana over them, and pressing the food on Mary. They sat like that as the day waned.

For a while Anne talked of little but the past—adventures, jokes, secrets they'd shared—in an attempt to comfort Mary. But finally she turned to the silent figure next to her, needing to feel her presence, to know she was there as more than a blank ear.

"When Michael was lost," she started, her voice low, "I thought I would die. I *wanted* to die. At least for a while. You know how I was. You helped me, Mary. You made me keep going until my body and heart could take over again." She looked to see if Mary was listening.

Mary turned slowly towards her and smiled, ever so tentatively, briefly. Anne thought with a quick gulp of relief, that her smile at that moment was the most beautiful thing she'd ever seen, perhaps would ever see again. She went on, encouraged.

"You told me love would come again, remember?"

After a long while, Mary spoke, with only a trace of bitterness. "Now, nothing will come, ever again. They mean to hang us, Anne. No time for excuses, no time for apologies. We'll be dead inside a week, mark me."

Anne clasped her hand again. "I can't believe it, Mary. I won't! Until the rope actually drops around my neck, I'll not believe it. And neither will you." She gripped Mary's hand tightly, trying to squeeze some pain into her flesh, anything to nudge her out of her lethargy.

"Tom's dead, Mary, but you're *alive*. You're alive! And we may get out of this yet!"

Mary's face crumpled suddenly, as if her whole body was wrenched by a huge angry fist. "Ay, I'm alive! I'm more than alive! I'm with child!"

Anne pulled back in shock, her eyes wide. "Oh, Jesus, Mary," she whispered. "Are you sure?"

Mary nodded dismally, her eyes knotted shut, fighting back the sobs. "Near three months now." She turned and fell into Anne's arms. "And Tom was so glad! He wanted a son!" Mary let out her grief then, muffling her sobs as best she could.

As she held Mary, murmuring what words of comfort she could manage, Anne was distracted by a spell of uncluttered fear. She had not thought of it, had not even noticed its absence, but she had been without her flux herself. Two months—or was it only one month? She'd noticed, but attributed its pause to her grief and the shock of Michael's death. Perhaps, oh God, perhaps she too was pregnant. She cast her eyes about the cell wildly. To be in gaol was anguish enough, but to be pregnant besides? A double entrapment!

She tried to think back to her symptoms when she was with child before, but she was too confused and panicked to keep her thoughts straight. All she could remember was a still gray bundle by her breast. She firmly pushed that memory from her mind. She would *not* let Mary see her despair. A small voice of reason spoke in her heart—only time would tell her the truth. She would say nothing for now, Anne promised herself grimly. One pregnant woman in this cell was enough.

That night she lay on the hard bench, trying to sleep. Mary had been able, mercifully, to fall asleep easily, exhausted by their ordeal and her sorrow. Anne lay in the darkness, listening to the scratch of vermin, grateful that at least the bench was a foot or more off the dirt floor. She had thought she'd known darkness before but nothing could compare with the blackness of this wretched hole. She could see nothing, but her sense of hearing was intensified so that she could make out the scurrying noises of a cockroach at her feet.

She lay for what seemed like hours until she heard soft footsteps approaching. Whoever, whatever it was stopped outside the cell door, and Anne saw a flicker of light as a taper flashed over the stone wall. Suddenly the door creaked open, the sound like a gunshot in the black silence, and she was near blinded by the single light of a candle.

The burly guard was back. Without a word he glanced at the two women, a feral shark's grin on his creased face. Anne knew at once his mission. Her mind flashed to the babe inside Mary. Perhaps inside herself. She would die before this creature would touch either of them.

She growled low in her throat, her voice shockingly loud and threatening in the tiny cell. "Get the hell out of here!" she cursed, balling up both fists and leaping to her feet.

The guard hesitated for a moment, licking his lips nervously, looking from Mary, who was awake now and meeting his stare, and then to Anne, poised as a coiled snake. In a flash he reached for Anne's arm; just as quickly she arced the other arm, swung full circle with all her strength, and boxed his ear with her closed fist. The glint went out of his eyes like a blown candle, and he yelped in pain and surprise.

"Out!" shrieked Anne at the top of her voice, and her shout echoed down the corridor. She heard approaching noises, other sentries, and the guard swiveled on his heel, slamming the huge door behind him. He stood for an instant, glaring through the cell at her with a menacing sneer. Then he was gone.

"Quick!" whispered Mary. "The candle!"

Anne snatched the candle stub from the floor, extinguished it, and hid the remnant in her blouse. Mary was right. Even the meanest possession might have value in this hell.

ANNE AND MARY huddled in the cell, sweating in the daylight hours and shivering in the night. Since there was no light and no window, the only way they could tell the passage of time was by the change in temperature. The guards, there were two who tended them, continued to throw them scanty food. They ate, not because they were hungry but because they realized that they must sustain their strength to escape. And escape was all they talked of, all they planned.

They guessed there was no hope of exit from the cell by force. The walls were thick, and the door never opened long enough to allow them to overpower the guards even if they had weapons. They also knew, however, that they would be taken from the cell at some point and transported to trial. Their chief hope was that they would not be confined so long in this pit that they would be unable to move swiftly once they had the opportunity. They waited, and together, they managed to keep up their hope.

After a week several curious visitors began to appear, carrying welcome light and offering some small diversion. Finely dressed women, wives of planters and the island aristocracy, ladies carrying silk parasols and placing dainty slippers hesitatingly from stone to stone, traipsed down the dark passageway, in clusters or on their husbands' arms, to view the captured pirates.

Anne and Mary were unique, not because they were "women gone bad," for indeed, specimens of that type were rife all over the islands, but because they had infiltrated a male bastion and had dominated the seas for nearly two years.

The ladies pressed their delicate noses to the open panel in the massive cell door one by one. Their eyes widened in surprise as they stared the captives up and down, blinking as if they spied on some new and vulgar breed of spider. They turned abruptly to each other, whispering in tones of shocked horror as though Anne and Mary were incapable of understanding their speech. Finally they withdrew, renewed in their sense of smug righteousness and secure in their superior station.

At first Anne deeply resented providing such a show, but soon she welcomed any entertainment, no matter how tedious. After each visitor left, she and Mary spent as long as possible dissecting each woman's clothes, her manner, and the varied expressions that contorted her features.

But one day a new face appeared at the gaol door. A man's voice whispered, "Anne! Anne Cormac! Is it you?"

Anne was jerked to attention by the sound of her maiden name. She hurried to the cell door and peered through the hole. "Ay! 'Tis Anne Cormac. Who's there?"

A vaguely familiar face moved up closer. The candle flickered about the planes of a rough visage with a great gray beard, wreathed in smiles. Anne felt the warmth of that face even through the door, but she couldn't place the features. Familiar... yet not known.

Then came the voice again, and this time it clanged in her head, shaking down memories from childhood.

" 'Tis I, lass! Robin! Yer ol' mate from the *Profit!*"

"Robin!" Anne laughed, her eyes filling with hot tears. "Robin, my old friend!" She tried to reach up and touch his face, but the hole was too small and the bars too tight to allow her hand passage. "How ever did you find me?" she called, her voice trembling.

"All the Caribbean knows yer here, lass, an' half the world besides. I been hearin' o' yer scapes fer two years o' more."

"Oh, Robin. My God, but it's good to see a friendly face in this hellhole. How good of you to come."

"I could do naught else, mouse. Remember when I called ye 'mouse'? Ye were but a sea scamp then, an' full o' mischief." His face dropped. "But I never thought to see ye end this way."

"Nor did I, Robin. But here I am. Do you have any news? What do they plan for us?"

"Yer the biggest thing to hit the island in a year, an' Sir Nicholas means to hang ye all. But there's plenty who shout against it, an' I be one o' them! There's them who say 'tis not fittin' to hang a woman, no matter what her crime. So ye still got a chance, lass. A chance at least."

Anne hastily asked Robin more questions, knowing that at any moment the guard could order him off the door. He'd been a merchant sailor in and out of Charles Town for the last ten years, he said, sailing to New York, Newfoundland, Bristol, and the African coast.

"Ay, an' I heard o' the infamous Bonny wench in most southern seas. I knew t'was you for I heard you'd wed that rascal James Bonny an' fled your father's wrath."

Anne said nothing but only lowered her eyes at the mention of her father.

"Can't he help you, lass? He's still a strong voice in the Carolinas, an' perhaps he could—"

"He'll never help me, Robin," Anne interrupted him shortly.

"He gave me up as lost years ago and will not own me now. No"— she smiled gently—"I must look to myself to get out of this scrape."

He leaned as close as the bars would allow. "Ye know I'll do all I can fer ye, lass. I'd not stand by quiet an' see ye hang."

Her throat tightened, and she reached once more for his face, only to be stopped by the wide bars. "Ay, Robin. It's so good to see you."

Robin turned at the sound of the guards coming to move him off. "Don't lose heart, mouse. I be just an old tar, but I'll do what I can fer ye." He grinned. "Old mates must stick together, eh?" And he was gone.

Anne felt like crying out to him, calling him back, but she held herself composed. She turned to Mary, who had listened quietly from the bench.

"Can he help, do you think?"

Anne shrugged sadly. "If he can, he will."

AFTER TWO LONG weeks of deprivation and despair, the women were taken out into the light and loaded into yet another tumbrel for the journey to St. Iago de la Vega, or Spanish Town, the government seat of Jamaica.

Anne stumbled out into the road, her hands bound before her, her eyes squinting painfully in the sudden glare. She knew Jack, Featherston, Corner, and the rest of the crew had been inside the bowels of the same labyrinth for Robin had told her, but she was still shocked when she saw them herded out, shackled together, and loaded into another waiting tumbrel.

Do we look as wretched as they? she wondered. She was appalled at how quickly the human spirit deteriorated when something so simple as sunlight was taken away. The men looked like creatures of the earth, filthy vermin who scuttled from one corner to another, blinking like bats and mutely gaping all about them. She pushed the thought from her mind and concentrated on the long ride ahead. Perhaps the cell at Spanish Town would be better. God knows, it could be no worse, she knew.

In fact, the gaol at Spanish Town was more habitable, not because of any benevolence from the government but because of the haphazard violence of nature. The same hurricane that had ravaged St. Catherine and swept Michael to his death also savagely buffeted Jamaica. Because the gaol at Port Royal was built into the earth, it was relatively unscathed. But the gaol of Spanish Town was severely racked by the winds, and though the cells were secure, there were slight chinks in the walls and small windows that let in some light and air. With these favors, however, came another punishment. Because the cells were more open, the guards left the prisoners in shackles.

Anne and Mary were shoved into a cell with stone along one side and hardwood walls on the other. Both women's ankles were quickly rubbed raw by the heavy metal chains with which they were hobbled, and they knew that infection was just a matter of time.

Down the corridor they could see part of the cell that held the rest of the crew. Trial was set for the next day, November 16.

But the next day no one came to take Anne and Mary to trial. Jack and the men were rousted from their cell, and the women shuffled to their small window to watch them escorted across the courtyard to a government building. In spite of their chains, the men were still under heavy guard.

"Though how they could run off, God knows," Anne said bitterly, "if their chains are as tight as ours."

The plaza was filled with spectators, far more than Anne had seen from either tumbrel. Fine ladies and gentlemen, cane workers, merchants, seamen, and natives swarmed before her window, separated from them by only a tall wooden fence and a ring of armed guards.

"Look there," Mary pointed. Across the plaza was a hawker

selling tiny replicas of the gallows, calling out his wares.

All day Anne and Mary waited to be taken, and all day no one came. Anne racked her mind for ideas, searched the cell up and down for escape clues. She hoped, against all reason, that perhaps the crew had devised a plan for their deliverance; perhaps Jack had thought of a way to set them free.

"I won't go quietly, damn them," Anne said. "When they do come to get me, I'll take at least one with me."

Mary grimaced. "That'll be a mean trick with both hands tied and your legs bound like a trussed calf."

"They have to take them off sometime."

"I've seen men hanged in shackles."

Both women grew silent, picturing other hangings they'd witnessed. Anne simply could not believe herself in such a plight. These were things that happened to others, not to her. Somehow she could not accept that she was actually in gaol, much less that she was about to be tried and hanged. And with child. She knew now, though she would not speak of it, could not think of it, that she carried Michael's child.

The spectators came and went from the courtyard all day; those who could not get into the building milled about outside, exchanging gossip. Now and then Anne caught snatches of conversation from a guard or a gawker, but for the most part, she and Mary simply waited and wondered.

Finally, late in the afternoon, the men were once more escorted back to their cell. Howells and Davies moved like sleepwalkers, their eyes to the ground, their faces impassive. Anne felt a strange lethargy blanket her as she realized what the sentence must have been, an awful leaden calm that cleansed her of any hysteria.

Later, a guard came to the women's cell and called them to the door.

"They're to hang, you know," he said, and a gentleness in his voice softened the harsh words.

"Ay," Anne said, wary of his kindness. "We guessed as much."

"If I can," he whispered, "I'll let Rackham come to you for a spell."

"Why should you do such a thing?"

He shrugged. "I got a wife myself, mistress. Were I to die tomorrow, I'd sure as hell like to see her tonight."

Anne smiled then, but she moved no closer to the door.

THAT NIGHT ANNE heard a rhythmic clanging and a shuffle of feet, and a candle flickered at the edge of the cell. The door was opened and Jack shambled in. Anne went to him without a word and held him briefly. Whatever rancor she had had for him—for his craven betrayal, for his weakness—was gone from her now. Before her was a man who had once loved her, one whom she had loved and fought alongside. A man about to hang.

She released him and stepped back to look into his face. He was cold sober now and calm. Whatever demons had plagued him were not evident in his unperturbed gaze.

"Tell us, Jack," Mary spoke up from her corner.

"They got us fast, ladies," he shrugged, a ghost of his old grin on his lips.

"Witnesses?" Anne asked.

"Ay, enough to hang half the Brethren on the seas. And no quarter given." He ran his hand through his hair in a familiar gesture that wrenched Anne's heart. "Did you hear the sentence?"

"Nay," said Anne, her eyes shining with unshed tears. "The crier called out the news from the window of the courthouse, but the mob cheered so and laughed that we couldn't hear the details."

Jack's grin twisted wryly. "But you know."

"Ay," Anne said, her eyes down. "Guilty."

"As sin. Lawes is foaming at the mouth to hang us. He brought in Spenlow and—"

"Spenlow!" Anne had almost forgotten that measly prize.

"Ay. For all the ships we took, to hang for that scow is the real sin. Spenlow told of how we took him and seven other fishing boats and two merchants. Then that bastard Dillon came up and told the judges how we took the *Mary*. You remember, off Dry-Harbor Bay a year back?"

Anne nodded.

"Well, they got it all down in that damned little black book, and they say we hang in two days." He laughed mirthlessly. "Two days they give us 'stead of one 'cause they want to try ol' Fenwick tomorrow and hang us all at once. So as not to waste the crowds, I wager."

"Fenwick!" Anne gasped. "He's caught, too?"

"Ay. And Tom Brown. They took them off Kingston four days ago. The fools robbed Spenlow last June."

So Fenwick had turned pirate captain after all and unluckily stumbled into Barnet's clutches as well. The irony of it twisted her mouth like a sour mango. She was silent. She could think of nothing to say to Jack to comfort him.

"We should have taken the pardon," he said.

"Ay." Anne shrugged. "Well, hell is paved with might-have-beens."

Then he said tiredly, "If you'd 'a been content to stay on Rogers' island, we'd be free today. But no. You had to drag me off to bed you at sea."

Suddenly Anne realized that Jack blamed her for his downfall, his deterioration, and his eventual capture. Instead of anger, she felt only a weary pity. Yes, it was true, she'd been the real force that moved him off the island that second time. But it was he who had turned her pirate in the first place. He who took to rum and opium, and he who, finally, had cowered in the hold, thus delivering them to Barnet. He had probably blamed her all along. But she would not argue the past at this late date. It was clear they had nothing left to give each other—not even comfort.

"Have you nothing to say to me, Anne?"

"What would you have me say?"

"That you're sorry for wrecking my life, for putting me in the shadows of the gallows. For everything."

She sighed and turned away. "Jack, I'm sorry for everything. Everything and anything I may have done to bring us *both* here today. But if you'd fought like a man, you'd not have to die like a dog."

He sneered, suddenly coldly hostile. "Ay, always the last word. And always sharp as a spar. I hope to God you find a man worthy of you in the next life, for 'tis sure there's none to match you in this one."

He turned and pounded loudly on the door. "Guard! Guard, I'll go to my cell now!" As he went out, he threw back over his shoulder, "A man should be able to get some small bit of peace in his last hours. I'll get none here."

The cell door clanged shut, leaving an ominous stillness behind. Anne threw herself in the corner on the bench, angry, saddened, and exhausted all at once. She felt like shrieking on and on like some mad thing, but there was no one to help and none but Mary to hear.

The next day Tom Brown and John Fenwick were hauled to trial past Anne's window, scarcely recognizable from when she had seen them last. Governor Lawes' court took even less time with these prisoners than it had with Rackham and his crew. Within four hours the two were herded back to their cells, sentenced to hang.

The next morning guards came down the corridor towards the men's cell with a priest and a minister in tow. Anne watched, numbed, as the black-frocked clergy solemnly swayed down the passageway, their hands folded in prayer.

It was actually happening, her mind was racing. My God, there will *be* no escape. She realized how much her hopes had been pinned on some miraculous effort, some amazing plan that would somehow hatch itself and free them all.

After what seemed like only moments, the men clanked out of

their cell, one by one in a single file, their chains still on their bare ankles, the clergy behind them. Mary came to her side; together they watched as their comrades filed past, flanked by armed guards—on to their death.

Anne felt a curious tingling run through her body as if she herself were in that line, as if she could feel the rope tickling her ear. She knew she would never see any of these men again. Not in this life and not in any other, for she did not believe any other existed. She calmed herself with a will. She knew that if she herself were on her way to die, she would not appreciate any hysterics from onlookers. She vowed to be as strong as she could, to be a source of unconquered courage to any who might need it. God, here they come.

George Featherston was first in line. He walked swiftly, his head down, his face grim. Briefly he shifted his eyes, and she felt her attempted farewell smile tremble with the weight of her facial muscles. He barely met her eyes, a scowl heavy on his face, and strode past as if eager to get it done.

Richard Corner was next, shuffling close behind George as if he hoped to draw some support from his stride. His face was blank as chalk, his eyes wide and unseeing. Anne sensed that he was in another world already, and she breathed a prayer that nothing would jostle him from his self-imposed oblivion.

Then came John Davies and Dobbins. Poor Davies, he'd never even been able to spend much plunder and now it was gone and so was he. And Dobbins looked too simple to even realize his impending fate.

John Howells and Pat Carty passed her together, clinging to each other. With lips twisted in rictus grins, they rolled their eyes at Anne as if to say, "Did you ever see the like?"

Thomas Earl passed her weeping silently, his hands working themselves like wrung laundry.

Noah Harwood, the old gunner who had had a penchant for slapping around new recruits, glared ferociously at Anne as he went by. He stopped, spat venomously at the women's feet, and walked off.

Finally, Jack pulled up the rear, walking before both clergy. Strange that he should be the last, Anne thought. The first to lead them into battle and the last to walk to his death. He looked more alive now, here in the bowels of the prison, than he had in the cabin of the *Queen,* bleary-eyed with opium. Her heart was wrenched when she remembered how they'd parted. She wanted to reach out to him, to touch him one last time as she would a brother in pain. That's what they were to each other now, brother and sister—with all the assorted bickerings and jealousy that went with such a relationship. He stopped for just a moment, so abruptly that the clergy all but jostled his bound hands. "Good-bye, Anne." His voice was strong and unwavering. "Let's forgive each other all. I intend to die with honor."

She smiled at him gratefully. "I, too, Jack. You captained them in life. You captain them in death as well."

"Ay," he grinned wryly. "At the gates of hell I'll be crying 'Boarders! Boaarrders!!' "

His shout died away as he was hustled off.

Anne slipped to the floor, Mary beside her. Neither spoke a word, for there was nothing to say. Mary took her hand and gently held it, each lost in her own memories. Anne was suddenly, fervently grateful that the bastard Lawes had not thought of forcing them to witness the hanging. There would be enough gawkers at Gallows Point this day. Anne hoped that all of the men, but especially Jack, would be brave to the end. That none of them would give any of the hypocrites a chance to say, "You see, those pirates were cowards after all."

That night the guard who had allowed Jack to visit her came to them.

"What news?" Anne asked, as soon as he entered with their food.

"They died well, they say. Rackham made a speech afore he

swung."

"What did he say?"

"He asked for mercy for you women and said you were forced against your will." He looked at them skeptically. "Of course he was hooted to silence at that, but he went out without a whimper."

The image left by the guard was sobering, and Anne and Mary vowed to die with dignity. Then they both realized what they were saying and retreated into silence. They were no longer plotting their escape but planning their death.

*T*WO DAYS LATER Governor Lawes himself came to their cell. Escorted by three guards, he sauntered in, grimacing disdainfully.

Anne did not get up from her bench, but only glanced at Mary, lying in the corner, then sat up as straight as possible, her spine stiff with wariness.

Lawes wasted no time with pleasantries. "So, mistress. We meet again. And this time you've no Chidley Bayard to protect you."

"Or to bribe you," Anne said silkily.

Lawes laughed caustically. "I don't expect anything else from the great Bonny bitch. I come only to tell you that your own trial is set for November twenty-eighth. A mere nine days away. Since I wish no pious widows plucking at my sleeves in horror for your souls, I came to ask you if you need anything to prepare yourselves. Clergy? The Good Book, perhaps? Even pirates have souls, I hear."

Mary only shrugged and turned from him, refusing to be taunted from her composure. Anne knew she should do the same, but she could not resist the opportunity to vie with him.

"Pirates have need of souls, for they spar with death every day. Governors don't, for they already belong to the devil. For you, I'd wager a soul'd be like a fifth wheel to a wagon."

Lawes grinned tightly but there was little joy in his face. "No attempt to win me, I see. Or to soften your fate."

"Would there be any chance of that?"

He laughed, this time with real pleasure. "Not a whit, mistress. Not one damned jot."

She turned away, her face hard. "I think we have some rights even on *your* island. And one of them is not to be kenneled with dogs." She deliberately stood and turned her back to him.

In a flash he was at her side, yanking her about, his hand grasping her chin viciously. "A dog is a dog until he faces you. Then he is *Mister* Dog. *Sir,* to you, mistress!"

She slapped away his hand, her eyes fiery even in the gloom of the cell. "Get out." She spat in contempt.

He glared once more and left, slamming the door behind him.

"Why did he come, do you suppose?" Mary asked in the silence. "Not just to tell us the date of our trial, surely. Do you think he's worried?"

Anne thought for an instant, forcing her heart to beat more slowly, her rage to soften. "Could it be that he's getting protests about hanging us? Let me think." She paused. "Robin said something about it, didn't he? That some citizens had objected to hanging women?" She clapped her hands. "Ay, Mary! That must be it! That son of a bitch came here himself so he could say he had looked out for our welfare, so he could say we turned down bibles and spiritual comfort!" Then her face fell. "Which I did." But she brightened. "Perhaps we can turn that to our own use."

She sat down, mulling it again, picturing herself in the courtroom, wondering what weapons had just been handed her. Michael had said each problem brought its own solution in its hands. If she could only find it.

The next day a candle again flickered down the corridor and footsteps approached their cell. Anne reared herself for combat again, feeling sure that Lawes was returning to ride them once more.

But this time when the cell door opened, Anne was struck

dumb, unable to move. Mary cried out, "Jesus God in heaven!" but Anne could say nothing and only blinked, her mouth open and working but issuing no sound.

Finally, she breathed, "Michael!" and hobbled frantically to his arms.

She wept then, clutching to him, patting him all over his face, squeezing him as if to reassure herself that it was, in fact, really he.

"Anne," he murmured, his voice cracking. He held her close, calming her, burying his face in her hair. "Hush, it's me. Yes"—he laughed as she kept pulling away and feeling his face—"it's really me!"

"But what . . . How?"

"I'm here, Anne. And God be praised I found you in time, before it's too late!" His words tumbled out, and in between kisses and sobs as they clung to each other, he told her his story.

"You were right, the hurricane hit us, lass. Hit us hard and left us for dead. The dinghy was blown to a hundred bits of planking, and I was lucky enough to cling to a spar."

"My God," she wept, and squeezed his hands.

"I was swept by the wind and the waves, huge dreadful canyons of water, to a reef where I clung until the storm abated. I washed to shore, half-dead, and was never so happy to feel dry sand under my face in my life."

Mary wept quietly in the corner as he went on.

"Then I made my way to a village, not knowing for sure where I was. When I was able to, I persuaded a fisherman to take me to St. Catherine. When I got there, you'd gone."

"Oh, Michael! We hunted and hunted for you!"

"Ay, I guessed as much. But of course I had no idea where you'd gone, for the *Queen* was still sitting there, big as life." He took her head in his hands. "Oh, Anne, it broke my heart to see it there and you gone, I knew not where."

"And I . . . I was looking for traces of you in every clump of seaweed!"

He smiled. "Well, I got a trading sloop to Jamaica, finally, after nearly a month of waiting on that cursed island." He ducked his head and lowered his voice. "I even went back to our cave once to feel you closer to me."

She hugged him convulsively, her eyes wet with joy.

"Finally," he continued, "I made it to Kingston. When I arrived, I heard you were taken prisoner and so I came at once." He took her hands. "Oh, Anne, I won't let them hang you. I swear it." He looked to Mary. "No, nor you, either, lass. I've already been to see Lawes. He's a hard-headed bastard, and he's determined to see you swing, but we've got some pull on our side. And we'll use that and more!"

"Michael!" Anne cried, collapsing in his arms, "I'm so grateful you're alive, I can't think past that. How is it he let you see me?"

"I told him I was Mary's long-lost brother. The guards patted me down so thoroughly they all but split the seams of my breeches."

Anne laughed then, so delighted at his presence that for the moment she was oblivious to her surroundings.

"Anne, I saw the men." His face was sobered now. "They've hung Rackham, Featherston, Corner, Davies, and Howells at Gallows Point. They left the rest at Kingston—Harwood, Dobbins, Carty, and Earl."

Not even together, Anne thought, even at the end. "And Fenwick and Brown?"

"They hanged them on the Monday next at Gallows Point."

Right next to Jack. Her mind twisted at the irony of it. Fenwick, the one man who tried the hardest to take Jack's command in life, ended up next to him in death. And they wouldn't hang them on Sunday.

But Anne's sadness was shortlived, for the presence of Michael kept curving her mouth up with joy, no matter how solemn she felt she should be.

"Michael," she whispered finally, "I too have a remembrance

from our cave." She smiled and laughed low in her throat, a sound filled with delight. "I'm with child."

At first Michael's face registered only shock, then in rapid succession, a broad smile then harsh dismay crumpled his features, and he clung to Anne urgently. He whispered to her hoarsely, over and over, "Oh, my love. My dear. My God, what will we do?"

For long moments she simply held him, was held by him, remembering with a bitter twinge how different this was from the first time she had revealed a coming babe. But finally he put her from him, the better to look into her eyes.

"Anne, we shall have our child. And our life together. I swear it."

She clung to him then, and they put their heads close together, murmuring, supposing, scheming. Finally they began to see exactly what they must do, and a plan took form. That night, for the first time in weeks, Anne slid into sleep on a vast tide of lightness and peace.

*T*HE DAYS BEFORE the trial went quickly. Michael was allowed only one more visit, and when he came he brought a small wrapped bundle from his pocket. As he placed it in Anne's hand, he said, "I wanted to bring you something from the sea. But everything dies when you take it up. Except this. This endures. If you take its arm, it grows another, even stronger, even more beautiful than before. It is like you, Anne."

Anne unwound his handkerchief from a small object. A starfish. A bright orange creature that pointed with all five of its fingers to different corners of the cell. It was alive, and it smelled of the sea. One of its arms had been lost in some ancient battle with its own kind or while escaping from a predator, but in its stead was a small nubbin growing quickly, fatter than the rest of its arms and even brighter in color. She gently fingered the million tiny questing pads.

"In Charles Town, they called this a sea star."

"That's even more fitting, then. The Africans say that the stars are the children of the moon, and the starfish are those children come to earth."

She wrapped the creature up again and gave it back to him. "Thank you for the memory, Michael. Take it back so it may live." She grinned. "When I was a child, I always thought the moon followed me."

He laughed and held her. "It probably still does."

N OVEMBER 28 DAWNED clear and hot. Anne and Mary had prepared for their roles as methodically as they had for any battle, inspecting and priming their words and gestures as they once had their pistols. They'd been given clean shifts the night before, so as not to shame the decency of the spectators. Bound at the wrists, their ankles were left unshackled and Anne felt exhilarated at being able to walk again.

As they crossed the courtyard, Anne looked to the crowd. Hundreds of gawkers circled the plaza, doxies and ladies, merchants and planters, blacks, whites, and Arawaks. It seemed the whole populace of Jamaica and half the outer islands was clustered in this small pathway, craning their necks to see, hollering catcalls and jeers. Several bold propositions were tossed at the two women as they traipsed silently, their heads down. They had decided that brazen bravado at this stage would only hurt their cause, and so Anne and Mary portrayed the injured, silent victims with dignity. On the fringe of the crowd, Anne spied Michael, smiling at her, waving encouragement. It was all she could do not to grin openly at him, so eager was she for this test of wits.

The courtroom seemed almost as crammed as the courtyard outside. Anne and Mary were taken to the dock, facing a long, low table. Twelve men in red frock coats faced them grimly; their powdered wigs and black buckled shoes seemed out of place in the island dust and heat. The registrar called the court to order.

"His excellency Sir Nicholas Lawes, knight, governor of Jamaica, here present at the High Court of Admiralty, St. Iago de la Vega, the twenty-eighth of November in the seventh year of the reign of our sovereign lord George the First, by the grace of God, of Great Britain, France, and Ireland, king of Jamaica, lord, and defender of the faith, calls the prisoners to the bar. Mary Read and Anne Bonny, harken to the charge."

The audience leaned forward, and all whispering stopped.

"That you, Mary Read, and you, Anne Bonny, on the first of September, upon the high seas, in a certain sloop of an unknown name, did feloniously and wickedly consult and agree to go with John Rackham, George Featherston, Richard Corner, John Davies, John Howells, Patrick Carty, Thomas Earl, James Dobbins, and Noah Harwood, to rob and plunder all such persons and ships which you should meet with on high seas; and in execution of your said evil designs did, with force and arms, from Harbour Island, within the jurisdiction of this court, piratically, feloniously, and in a hostile manner, attack, engage, and take seven fishing boats and certain fisherman."

Anne sat quite still, her head down, although she yearned to look about the room and at her judges. She caught a movement and saw Lawes gesture impatiently to the clerk. The registrar took a deep breath and went on.

"That you, Mary Read and Anne Bonny, did afterwards on the first day of October take by force and arms upon the high seas, from the island of Hispaniola, within the jurisdiction of this court, piratically and feloniously set upon, shoot at, and take two merchant sloops to the value of one thousand pounds of current money of Jamaica."

A gasp went through the courthouse then, and Lawes had to call for silence.

"That you, Mary Read and Anne Bonny, afterwards on the

nineteenth day of October, did with force and arms upon the high seas, from Port Maria Bay in the island of Jamaica and within the jurisdiction of this court did piratically, feloniously, and in a hostile manner shoot at, set upon, and take a certain schooner of an unknown name, whereof one Thomas Spenlow was master, and did steal, take, and carry away the value of twenty pounds of current money of Jamaica."

Another gasp, call for order, and another deep breath by the harassed registrar.

"And finally, that you Mary Read and Anne Bonny, did afterwards on the twentieth day of October, with force and arms upon the high seas about one league from Dry-Harbor Bay, in the island of Jamaica and within jurisdiction of this court, did piratically, feloniously, and in a hostile manner set upon, board, and enter a certain merchant sloop called the *Mary*, whereof Thomas Dillon was master, and did put said Master Dillon and all the other mariners of the same merchant sloop in corporeal fear of their lives and then did steal, take, and carry away the said sloop to the value of three hundred pounds of current money of Jamaica."

After the registrar finished the muttering again broke out; once more, Lawes shouted for order.

"Mistress Anne Bonny and Mary Read, are ye then guilty or not guilty?" Lawes hollered through the room.

Anne spoke up clearly before Mary could even shift her weight in her seat. "Milords, we are not guilty."

Lawes rolled his eyes and called out in a bored tone, "Registrar, call witnesses for the king."

At his call, six men and a woman passed the bench and took seats between Anne and Mary and their judges. The registrar swore them in as a group and then called, "Dorothy Thomas, step forward and make your witness!"

A stout woman popped out of her seat and strode vigorously to the center of the room. Unabashed, she faced Anne and Mary, pointing her finger at them in remembered fury.

"That's the one we took in the canoe," Mary whispered. Anne said nothing but only stared straight ahead.

"I seen them two bawds afore, yer lordships! I was in me canoe on the north side o' the island, makin' me way back from Orchards with a full stock for a week, when they swept upon me like thunder an' stole every last victual I had about me and coin besides!"

"Do you recall any coin?" Anne whispered to Mary, loud enough to be heard.

"Not a farthing," Mary replied audibly.

The woman glared at the two and went on, swinging her arms wide in showy gestures for the crowd. "An' these two were aboard, 'longside Calico Jack an' his pirates, a' cursin' an' be-foulin' the air with threats o' murder!"

"How were they dressed, mistress?" asked the registrar.

"They wore men's coats an' long trousers, an' had red kerchiefs about their heads. An' each had a pistol an' a musket in their belts. But I knew they was wenches for all that!"

"How did you know them to be females?"

She looked about disdainfully. "By the largeness o' their breasts, o' course," and the audience erupted in glee, craning their necks to get a better look at the prisoners.

"An' they told the men to murder me, your lordships!" she shouted above the din. "So's I couldn't come against them later!" She smiled in triumph. "But here I be!"

Then Thomas Spenlow was called and swore that both women were aboard Rackham's sloop and "seemed to be willing to do most anything." That admission delighted the spectators.

John Besnick and Peter Cornelian, two Frenchmen, were produced and sworn, and Mr. Clarke acted as their interpreter. Among the three of them, they declared that Anne and Mary were not only present when Rackham took their sloop, but that they were "very active" and that Anne herself handed gunpowder to the men, wore both men's and women's clothes, and did all the men did "of her own free will and consent."

And, finally, Thomas Dillon took the stand and told his tale. When Rackham's crew took his sloop, the *Mary*, he said, "I seen both women, leaning over the rail, urgin' on their comrades.

"That one there," he said, pointing to Mary, "had a pistol in her hand an' swore she'd beat them all aboard and take first choice o' swords lest they jumped to best her—!"

"Which woman was that?" interrupted the governor.

Damn him, Anne breathed quickly. He's enjoying this.

"That one, milord," he said, clearly indicating Mary Read.

The registrar then chanted, "Ye've heard the witnesses against ye. Do you wish to question them?"

Both women shook their heads quietly.

"Do you have any witnesses of your own to produce or any questions to ask?"

Anne glanced quickly about the courtroom, hoping to God she was on the right course. She nudged Mary, who spoke up and said, "No, milord. No questions."

"Take them away!" called the governor.

Quickly two guards came behind them and hustled them off. In less than an hour they were escorted back to hear their sentences.

"You, Mary Read and Anne Bonny, have been found guilty of the piracies and robberies and felonies charged against you in this court," intoned the governor. "You are to go to the place from whence you came and from there to a place of execution, where you shall be hanged by the neck until you are dead. And God in His infinite mercy be merciful to both of your souls." He looked piercingly at them. "Have you anything to say or to offer against this sentence of death?" He smiled a quick flickering grin. "If you have a plea, best voice it now."

At that Anne stood suddenly and her voice rang out clearly through the courtroom. "Milord, we plead our bellies!"

A raucous clamor of hoots rippled through the crowd, together with the gasps of outraged matrons.

Lawes, with a ferocious scowl, said slowly, "The Court does not understand the plea. Do you mean you took up piracy because you were hungry?"

Anne said with stiff dignity, "No, milord. We are both quick with child. As you yourself know as a minister of His Majesty's law, you cannot hang us in this condition."

Then the crowd erupted.

"Order! Order!" called the governor, but to no avail. It was long moments before he could speak above the laughter and speculations of the crowd, who shoved each other aside to get a better view of the pregnant pirates.

Lawes was enraged. "Order!" he thundered into the gradual silence. "You shall both be examined by at least two, no *three* doctors, madam! And if you're plaguing this court with more lies, or you come up empty, I'll see you both hang *slow!*"

Anne barely had time to flash Michael a quick victory grin before she and Mary were jerked back to their cell.

That afternoon three separate doctors examined them individually, and all of them reluctantly agreed that the women were, indeed, with child. Mary was about four months pregnant and Anne was three. Governor Lawes and his registrar visited the cell soon after, unable to wait for the doctors' published verdict. When he heard their findings, he shouted at the women through the bars.

"So, then, we shall stay the execution! But that only prolongs it! The minute you both give up your babes, you're off to the gallows!" He smiled as a thought struck him. "You can die wondering how well your pirate bastards will be received in Christian homes."

In the next days Anne and Mary became the chief diversion on the island of Jamaica, indeed, Anne often thought, in the whole Caribbean.

Troops of well-intentioned matrons trudged to their cell to offer them Christian consolation for their souls and fresh fruit for their growing bellies. As much as Anne resented the intrusions, she welcomed the fruit, for prison fare was dismal, and Mary was already complaining of a fever and a troublesome cough.

One afternoon Anne looked up to the door of her cell to see an old wizened face peering at her curiously. Unlike most of the visitors, this woman was not particularly well dressed, and it was clear she had known hardships in her past. Anne watched her warily, but said nothing.

Finally the woman spoke. "So 'tis you, Anne Cormac. Just as they said."

Anne jumped up then and went to the door, examining the old face carefully. Try as she might, she could not put a name on the distant memory that tugged at her. She knew the face, but not the woman.

The old woman smiled softly. "I wouldn't have recognized you either, lass. Time has trounced us both. I'm Mistress Darcy. I was a friend of your sainted mother. My daughters and I sat in your parlor one afternoon a lifetime ago. Do you recall?"

Anne felt as if a fist had jammed her belly, suddenly deflating her of air. She remembered how she had tried so hard to be gracious that day to Rachel Darcy and her sister and—two visiting cousins, wasn't it?—and Fully sat in the corner and braced her through the long tedious hours. She grinned to herself. She could be just as gracious now.

"Well, of course, I remember you, Mistress Darcy. This light is so dim. Whatever are you doing here in Jamaica?" The fatuousness of her own smile almost made her laugh aloud.

Mistress Darcy answered her as serenely as though they sat across the Cormac tea table once more. "Oh, when Mr. Darcy passed, we sold the house on Broad Street, and Rachel moved to Kingston. Did you hear? A fine man, well fixed, with a plantation just north of Free Town. They call it Conrad Groves. You must have heard of her good fortune?"

Anne smiled. "Ay, I did, madam. I'm sure I recall hearing of

Rachel's happiness." Though, of course, Anne had not given Rachel Darcy a thought for over five years. She must have had ample heartache to age her so, Anne thought, as she peered at the old woman.

"Well, of course," the matron went on, "Rachel pressed me to join her, and since her sister was wed as well, I could hardly refuse. And I've been enjoying country life ever since."

Anne smiled, waiting for the inevitable question. And so it came.

"But what of you, poor dear? Is it true what they say?"

Anne was suddenly, briskly, eager for her to be gone. "Ay, mistress, it's true."

The Widow Darcy clucked sympathetically as if Anne had just told her that her best gown had been ruined. She produced a small package and pushed it through the bars. "Here, lass, I brought you this." She smiled vaguely. "For you and your babe. It's the least I could do for your poor mother, God rest her soul."

Anne looked at the parcel in her hand, dumbfounded. The old woman had brought her, all the way from Kingston, a skein of soft wool and knitting needles. How she ever got them past the guards, Anne would never guess. Perhaps the Widow Darcy was not quite as sunstruck as she seemed. Yet as she handed Anne the bundle, her face was guileless and childlike, never indicating by a change of expression that she had just handed Anne a potential weapon for escape.

"Thank you." Anne grinned. "This will help to pass the time."

"Of course it will, lass. And I'll add you to my prayers each night until you're safe in the bosom of the Lord." She started to turn away. "Oh, have you any message for Rachel?"

Anne almost laughed aloud. "Yes, of course. Please tell her I'm overjoyed at her good fortune, and I wish her a long and prosperous life."

The widow beamed. Now the trip was clearly worthwhile. "Just like your mother, ever a gracious lady. I shall give Rachel your dear regards, my child." And she shuffled down the corridor.

The next day when Michael was allowed his weekly visit, she showed him the widow's gift.

"Anne, you mustn't think of such means yet," he cautioned her.

"Oh, Michael," she moaned, "I can't help but think of escape every waking moment! Given a pistol, I'd kill each guard without blinking and ravage half the town besides."

"I know," he soothed, "and I'm not blaming you. But we've got six months to get you a pardon. Much can happen in such a time, Anne. And a pardon would mean freedom—not just for you but for our child. Can you trust me a while more? Can you let me work for your release, at least until we see it's a useless venture?"

Her heart twisted painfully in her. He could not know what an agony it was for her to be so confined, she who had never known anything but freedom for years.

At night she dreamed of the sea and the wind and then awoke to find herself still locked in a fetid, sour hole, her only companion silent Mary who coughed half the night and sat gazing placidly like a nun out a tiny window. She could not make him feel her hopelessness, her belly growing daily, her deep fear that the child within her would die, thereby hastening her own death—or that it would live, and she would hang in anguish, never knowing its future. But for now she had only herself and Michael as hope. She would trust Michael as long as she could, she decided. In the end, if she had to, she would save herself or die trying.

"Yes, Michael. I can wait a while longer." He kissed her gently as best he could through the bars and then left for another week.

The next morning Anne was startled out of her self by the realization that Mary was truly ill. She did not get up from her bench at all, and when Anne kneeled at her side and felt her brow, she was shocked to feel the fever rise off Mary's flesh as off a brick in the sun.

"Guard!" Anne screamed, pounding on the heavy door. "Water!

Bring a doctor at once!"

It was a full hour before she got a response, and then a guard brought fresh water and the news that a doctor could not come before dark. Anne paced the cell, watching Mary, splitting herself with guilt for not recognizing Mary's illness sooner. She knew she'd often complained of an aching head in the last week, and she shivered in the night. The day before, Mary had refused most food, but Anne was so used to her silence that she scarcely noticed or asked her why. Mary was now deathly pale, and sweat beaded her upper lip, which was twisted in a grimace of pain.

All afternoon Anne hovered over Mary, wiping her brow, kneading her hands, and raging over her own uselessness. She called continuously for water, sponging Mary often, hoping to bring the fever down. She cursed herself for not paying more mind to Fully when she talked of the fever, for she had no idea how else to ease her friend. Once Mary's eyes fluttered open, and she smiled weakly up at Anne.

"Don't look so scared, Anne. 'Tis just my babe looking for the exit."

"Do you mean you're in labor, Mary?" Anne's eyes widened for she knew it was much too soon.

"Ay, since dawn."

"But Mary, there's no—" She stopped, not wanting to alert her to trouble. Mary's stomach had barely moved, and there was no indication that labor had begun. No water, no heaving, seemingly no life.

"Well, I'll help you, lass," she said as confidently as she could. "The doctor'll be here soon, and 'til he comes, you and I can manage."

Mary closed her eyes peacefully.

Anne cast her mind about in a panic. When she was in labor, a delivery that resulted in a stillborn child, she'd had more movement, more energy than Mary. And she never remembered being so fevered. She tried to recall the details of her own labor, but the edges of her mind were fuzzy with confusion.

A few hours later Mary awoke again, this time in a delirium; she called Anne "Tom" and cried for more powder for phantom battles. One moment she was struggling, her hands fighting off Anne's damp cloth, the next instant she was still, her mouth curved in an almost bewildered smile.

Anne leaned over her, closer and closer, horrified at her sudden stillness. She reached out and touched Mary's cheek, still hot with the fever, and saw that a single tear had crept out from under her clenched lids as if in some final unconscious exertion.

Anne leaped back then, spun around with clenched fist and pounded on the cell wall, pounded again and again in incoherent rage and despair, until she slumped spent, slowly, to the cold floor, sobbing quietly.

She was allowed to accompany Mary's body outside the gaol, escorted by six armed guards. On the morning of December 4, Mary Read was buried in unconsecrated ground outside St. Catherine's Church. There were no bells, no services, and no mourners save Anne. One clergyman offered to stand by her side, but since he had already warned her that he could not say a Christian prayer over Mary's grave, she dismissed him with weary contempt. She stood by the side of the open hole, alone except for the guards and a single black crow who soared on the air currents, dipping so low Anne could see his yellow beak. The wind in the trees sounded like surf, and she whispered a few words of farewell. Death had been swimming behind them for months, and Mary had faced his cold gray eyes and scaly skin and was gone. Whatever my fate is to be, Anne thought, I must face it alone now. And as she walked back to the cell she felt her babe roll in her belly for the first time, as if with blind eyes it turned to look over its shoulder at the yawning grave.

MICHAEL WAS ALLOWED his weekly visit the next day. He had

long ago given up the pretense of coming only to see Mary, and
the governor had heard endless, impassioned petitions from him
for Anne's life as well. He consoled Anne as best he could.

"She was the truest friend I ever had," Anne said, her voice
throbbing with sadness. "And yet I scarcely paid her any mind the
last two weeks. So full of my own pain, my own plans, I never
even tried to draw her out of her despair."

Michael did not try to tell her that Mary's death was for the
best, for both of them knew that was a lie. But he did say, "She's
out of it now, Anne. In fact, from what you say, she was out of it
since she was captured."

"Ay, that's true. She wasn't herself at all. Not since Tom's
death."

He reached out and grazed her face, and she felt her whole body
respond by leaning into him.

"I won't let you die, Anne. I swear it."

In spite of her sorrow, she felt a small smile warm her lips at the
fierce determination in his voice. She sighed and turned from the
bars. "Oh, who's to know, Michael. Mary had a faith I never
shared. Perhaps she's found a better berth than any she's known
so far."

"There are more who believe so than don't, lass. What the
caterpillar calls the end of the world, life calls a butterfly."

"I'm glad you didn't mention God to me, Michael. Right now,
I don't need to hear that word—not while I'm in this hole."

He smiled. "And that's exactly where you'll hear His name
most often. In the deepest man-made hells." He shrugged. "But I
won't profane your solitude with unwelcome thoughts. For now,
put your mind from Mary's fate. It won't be yours. Mary did you
one last great favor."

Anne looked at him quizzically.

"Because of her death I've been able to persuade the governor
to grant you some small freedoms. You'll now be allowed a daily
exercise outdoors and a better diet, so you and the babe can stay

strong."

"Ay." Anne's lip curled in disgust. "Strong for the gallows. He doesn't want to lose his prime spectacle."

"Perhaps," Michael said. "But whatever the reason, we can turn it to our advantage. This is just a step, Anne, but it's one step closer to the door."

She shrugged her contempt.

"Don't you see?" he went on. "There must be some other reason that Lawes doesn't want to lose you—not just for the hanging but something else. Perhaps he's getting pressure from other voices besides mine!"

She leaned heavily against the bars, suddenly weary of all false hopes and disappointments. Michael left and she remained standing, staring out at that tiny square of light, wondering if she would ever be free again.

For two weeks Anne paced the cell, glancing a thousand times a day to the bench where Mary last laid her head. She was grateful for her new daily outings and used them to exercise her legs. The better to run, should she have to.

*I*T WAS CLOSE to Christmas now, and Anne felt the infant move in her often. At night, when she could not sleep, she would hold her belly and talk to the unseen child, stroking her skin, telling the babe within her all she wanted it to know, in case she was not there to relate her story.

She thought a great deal during those hours of her past, since her future seemed so blank. Often she heard her mother's voice, talking of vice and virtue. She had always thought them such bothersome divisions, such worthless concerns. Instead she had tried to rise above what others called morality and simply live life to its fullest. The word "sin" had never been part of her vocabulary. But now she pondered the question again.

She could never, would never, no matter how anguished her

mind, be able to ask forgiveness of God—for she felt she was addressing herself to a sepulcher, a phantom, a void. But in her heart, now in the darkness of the cell with her hands on her belly, she saw that sin was not what it was thought to be. Sin was not stealing and lying and fornicating. Sin was certainly not the infant inside her, though she was unwed. Sin was, instead, when one person walked carelessly over the life of another, oblivious to the wounds he left behind. And of that sin she knew she was guilty. In her heart, then, she did repent—not to a god—but to lost comrades, forsaken lovers, and parents whom she had not forgiven. In her mind she forgave them now, and she asked for their forgiveness, wherever they might be.

The day before Christmas in the late afternoon Anne was resting, her mind far away, when suddenly she heard footsteps approach. Before she could prepare herself, three guards entered her cell, bound her wrists, and pulled her out the door.

As she was walked out the gaol, she looked about anxiously. "What is it?" she asked, but received no answer. "Where are you taking me?" she demanded, but the guards said nothing.

They walked her past her exercise area, and Anne felt a chill of panic flood her limbs. Jesus God, she thought, they're going to hang me now, right now with no witnesses, no more waiting, while Michael is absent and I'm helpless! Her mind all but shrieked her fear. But she was hustled to the King's House, led up the steps, and, before she could calm herself, thrust into a room before a huge desk.

Behind the desk sat Governor Nicholas Lawes. Michael stood in the corner and came to her instantly.

"Anne, say nothing," he whispered. "Nothing to rouse him."

She stifled her questions and her angry indignation at being so briskly transported, and stood, waiting.

"Mistress, it's Christmas eve," the governor said.

Anne glanced at Michael. He nodded imperceptibly.

"I know, milord," she answered with quiet dignity.

He picked up two packets of papers and held them out to her as if in offering. Since her hands were bound, she did not move. "Do you have any idea what these are?" he asked.

"No, milord." She wet her lips nervously.

He leaned back expansively. "Well, one is a pretty little missive from Captain Woodes Rogers. I believe you know the man?" Lawes glanced down at the open sheet before him. "He writes,

'I feel the Bonny woman should be allowed a pardon. Regardless of her past, there is much of worth in her. She once helped rout the Spanish from New Providence at some risk to herself and her freedom. I myself in the role of governor and chief justice of the Bahamas did once misjudge her on a minor charge, one which may have led to her return to her outlaw status. I, of course, have no wish to infringe upon your jurisdiction, but I would urge you to consider a pardon for her past crimes.'"

He looked up. "What do you think of that, mistress?"

Again she glanced at Michael and said, "I'm most grateful to Captain Rogers for his plea on my behalf, sir."

Lawes smiled wryly. "As well you should be, mistress. As well you should be." He leaned forward. "But I have still another letter. Can you guess its contents?"

She remained stolidly silent, for her own patience was wearing thin.

"No, I suppose not," he went on. "Well, this particular message is from one William Cormac." He glanced up at Anne's involuntary gasp, rattled the paper, and read.

"'I beg you, sir, to pardon my daughter's past. She was ever headstrong and willful, but she has had much excuse. She has a fine mind and a loving heart and could be an excellent woman in a new life, if you would but give her that chance. I would humbly remind you of Swift's wisdom:

"It is in men as in souls, where sometimes there is a vein
of gold, which the owner knows not of."

The same can be said of women, of course, and certainly of
my daughter, Anne.'"

Anne stood as marble, her face white, tears coursing silently
down her cheeks. She could not speak.

"You have had some good men plead gracefully on your behalf,
mistress." The governor went on. "And it is the season of charity
and good will." He leaned forward. "If I give you your freedom,
will you promise to leave these islands and never return?"

Anne cleared her throat, her mind in confusion. "Ay, milord."

"And never take up arms against another vessel?"

"Ay, milord."

He leaned back in his chair, rocking slowly, tapping his fingers
together and appraising her. In the silence, Michael stepped
forward.

"Sir, if you'll grant her freedom, we will be wed. Now, if you
will officiate. I vow to you I will take Mistress Bonny from these
seas and we will never return."

The governor pointed a finger at her. "Mistress, I will give you
your pardon. And your child a name. And God help you if I ever
see your face again."

As she stood before that desk, her hand in Michael's, repeating
wedding vows for the second time in her life, Anne's mind
whirled. Her heart was too full to contain her joy, her relief, and
she wept silently, not caring who saw her tears.

THE NEXT NIGHT Anne and Michael stood on the dock at Port
Royal, watching a schooner made ready to take the tide out to sea.
They were sailing to Norfolk within the hour.

The night before had been one she would remember all of her
life. She felt she was home, finally, in Michael's arms. He had

saved her life and perhaps her soul for her in countless ways, and
not only from the certain death at the end of a noose. She knew
he would do so for all of their life together. That was the core of
what they were, she and he. And when he could no longer do so,
he would die with her. Her eyes had flooded with sudden salt
then, and she rolled into his shoulder and buried her face in the
hollow of his neck. He pulled her closer and stroked her hair, still
damp with the heat of their loving. Even in that simple act she felt
her whole body respond as though it were tugged by invisible
thrumming strings. She had pulled him over her, locking her arms
and legs about him, arching her feet to curve around his, pulling
him into every curve, losing herself to the fierce, hot joy that
started in her belly, flooded upwards, curled her fingers, and
slammed her eyes closed with its power. She had felt nothing like
it before.

After they had exhausted each other with love, she asked again,
"But why did he release me, do you think?"

Michael laughed softly, teasing her with his fingertips. "Not out
of conscience, you can be sure." He stroked her hair, winding it
slowly around his wrist. "Rumors are rife on the subject, but
there's one I'd like to believe. Have you ever heard of a Captain
Roberts?"

She frowned in thought and then shook her head, nestling
closer to him.

"Well," he said with a grin, "that's good for me, I'm sure. But
this Captain Roberts has heard of you, my dear. And gossip has it
that he sent a letter to our friend Lawes telling him to let Anne
Bonny go or feel the thunder of his pirate guns from Port Royal to
Kingston and back again."

"God's breath!" gasped Anne. "Bartholomew Roberts? I never
even met the man. But I heard he had a fleet of four or more."
She glanced slyly at Michael, arching her neck in a gesture that
caused him to reach out suddenly and squeeze her. She giggled. "I
swear, I never even saw him. Besides, I hear he's a psalm-singing

blusterer who's death on women on board ship."

Michael sighed in mock relief and lowered his hands from her hair to her belly, turning her giggles to low moans of pleasure.

Now, waiting on the shore, he playfully took her arm and led her to the water, leaning down and removing her shoes. They strolled together in the frothy surf, watching the moon.

"And will you teach our child to swim, lass?" He grinned. "Or will you fence him even from the smell of seawater?"

She smiled pensively. "To warn a child from water is to warn him from life. He'll love the sea as I. But he won't need it to be happy."

He bent his head then to hers and held her close, kissing her deeply while the warm water lapped at their ankles.

"You are an amazing woman," he murmured over her lips. "And you love me. Say you love me."

She moved her lips an inch from his, a smile flickering over her mouth, and said, "My flag reads, 'Catch Me Who Can.'"

He grinned, his eyes fastening on hers, holding her gaze. "And you'd follow me anywhere, no matter where I go."

She murmured, moving her lips ever closer, brushing over his mouth deliciously, "Only if I want to."

He kissed her, softly, persuasively. "Even if I am arrogant, prideful, and a bore?"

She pursed her lips then, her breath warm on his mouth. "I would leave you in an instant." But her body leaned into his.

"Say it, say it," he whispered.

"I love you," she answered, and she kissed him, her mouth open and promising, her heart set free.

Postscript

IN MAY OF 1721 a young wife wrote a letter to her mother in
New York. She and her husband were joining a wagon train
heading west from Virginia. She told of meeting another young
couple bound for new frontiers over the Appalachians, a man and
a woman who joined their wagon train and were well accepted by
the pioneers. The man was a surgeon, and his wife had a beautiful
infant at her breast.

The young wife wrote:

> Mother, I feel our companions most suitable for our arduous
> journey west. She is lovely and laughs a good deal. And unlike
> the rest of us who clasp our bonnets tight against the wind
> and heat, her long red hair flows free.

Acknowledgments

THIS IS NOT, strictly speaking, a work of fiction, nor can it entirely be claimed a work of truth. Much of Anne Bonny's life is a matter of record, and I pursued those records from the depths of the Library of Congress to the small back rooms of Charlestown historical societies with vigor. But, after all, her story must be a blend of fact, legend, and imagination. Frankly, I believe she would have wanted it that way. There are occasional departures from the fact, for example, in the history of her lovers, but there is no doubt that she loved them all. Any changes or alterations add truth to history and history to fiction, and will, I hope, be overlooked by a reader who seeks to feel the gist of Anne's world.

I am especially indebted to John Carlova whose excellent biography of Anne Bonny, *Mistress of the Seas*, was my principle source of research.

Naturally, this book would not exist without the help of a great many people—most of whom were as enthusiastic about Anne's history as I was. Special thanks are due to Allen H. Stokes of the South Carolinian Library of the University of South Carolina; to A. Osborn of the South Carolina Historical Society and Mrs. Isabella Leland of the same institution; to Wylma A. Wates, reference archivist of the South Carolina Department of Archives; and to Patrick Frazier and Mr. Coker of the U.S. Library of Congress. In addition, I'd like to thank the many local librarians who helped corral the hundreds of books about pirates and eighteenth-century life required for this research. In fact, without those earlier texts, those many authors as fascinated by pirate lore and Anne Bonny as I was, this book could not have been written. In a large sense, history belongs to those who write it, and their own imaginations and accounts of Anne are now indelibly part of the facts of her life.

On a personal note, I would like to thank my parents who supported this idea from the start with their usual enthusiasm, faith, and great good humor; my mother-in-law, Juanita E. Koons, who traveled with me to unearth the truth about Anne Bonny as far afield as our imaginations and her car would take us; and the rest of a whole cadre of family and friends who know who they are and know the various parts they played in Anne's creation.

And finally, I'd like to extend my gratitude and love to a special friend and agent, Roslyn Targ, who believed in Anne and my ability to tell her story, right from the start.